"Scream," Vassily said.

Lorna attempted to move, and he forced her back, and knelt above her.

"Scream, as you screamed in passion for the Tsar."

She sucked air into her lungs and expelled it as loudly as she could. The wailing cry hurtled up to the ceiling, drifted round and round, died slowly.

His face twisted. "Aye," he said. "That is the sound of passion."

Lorna stared at him in awful understanding. He had gone nowhere last night. He had spent the entire night outside, watching. And he had heard her cry out in ecstasy.

The fingers were relaxing on her hair, leaving her arm. And she wanted to weep for him. She sat up. "Vassily. Now. Please. Go." She bit her lip.

He walked to the door. "You are the Tsar's whore. For the present. I will send your maids to you."

# THE POWER
## *and the*
# PASSION

## *Christina Nicholson*

A FAWCETT CREST BOOK

Fawcett Books, Greenwich, Connecticut

*THE POWER AND THE PASSION*

THIS BOOK CONTAINS THE COMPLETE TEXT OF THE
ORIGINAL HARDCOVER EDITION.

Published by Fawcett Crest Books, CBS Publications, CBS Consumer Publishing, a Division of CBS Inc., by arrangement with Coward, McCann & Geoghegan, Inc.

ISBN: 0-449-23411-8

Main Selection of the Doubleday Book Club, April 1977

Printed in the United States of America

10  9  8  7  6  5  4  3  2  1

# THE POWER
### *and the*
# PASSION

# Chapter 1

The crisp thud of the axes echoed in the still morning air and was suddenly overtaken by a tearing sound, as of the entire universe being wrenched from its place. Sean MacMahon gave a hasty upwards glance and shouted, "Timber!"

His sons threw down their tools, stood to one side, watched the huge cedar commence to sway, while the tearing sound grew in intensity, and was joined by a long whoooosh as the branches scythed through their neighbours, and the trunk came hurtling to the ground with a crash which made the earth tremble, left the men dazed.

While Sean MacMahon smiled. He was a big man, better than six feet tall, with shoulders to match and a mop of thick red hair, a boisterous giant on whom the surprisingly delicate features, the small nose and pointed chin, the warm blue eyes, seemed almost incongruous. He wore a threadbare smock over equally well-worn breeches, and a flat hat, and sweated with his labour, as did the three younger men. But he owned this land. With this tree down he could see the river once again. It was called the Patuxent, an Indian name, and it marked the eastern boundary of his homestead. Twenty miles to the west his boundary was marked by another river, called by the Indians the Potomac. Southabout he could travel another ten miles to his house and still be on his property. Northabout there was no telling where it might end. He had never had the time to explore; the Indians spoke of high land and deep valleys. Time then, to call a halt. Flat country was best for farming.

He watched his three sons, grown men now, gathering the axes, preparing to move on to the next cedar. Autumn was a season for clearing, with the harvest already in and before the icy grip of winter descended on the Chesapeake. Then they would have wood for their Christmas logs, and they would have additional pasture lying fallow, to be sown come the spring. It was possible to look that far ahead, here. There was no fear of the morrow, of the year 1691 to come, in Maryland. Not with all the land a man could clear, not with a healthy wife and three strong sons. And not with Lorna to make him smile.

It was noon, and there she was, punctual as ever, legs braced unladylike against the dashboard of the cart, strong fingers tight on the reins, although she guided the horse by word alone, halting as she saw her brothers. At a distance, she looked like a boy herself, save that she wore an utterly shapeless grey gown; her hat was a flat straw, like theirs, and her red-gold hair was drawn back with a ribbon.

Sean dropped his axe beside the others, made his way down the slope to the cart track. Seamus was already there, dragging out the meat pies and the jugs of home-brewed beer, while the white head of Snowdrop, the cat, appeared from inside the cart, hoping for scraps. Lorna got down, stretched, and rubbed her bottom to restore feeling after better than an hour on the unsprung seat; grace and strength rippled beneath the slow, easy scratching. She knew better; her mother had seen to that. She could sing, beautifully, in that high clear voice of hers; she could carry on a conversation in French—as if that would ever be of any help here in America—she could sew and she knew which fork was intended for what course. But she had been born on this farm, had been no farther afield than St. Mary's, had grown almost to womanhood under the aegis of her three brothers, and was, indeed, as uninhibited and confident as the cat who was her constant companion.

Almost to womanhood. There was a looming problem. She would have suitors enough; her visits to the little town were more in the nature of a parade. But was any of those louts good enough for a MacMahon of Morne?

"Papa." She kissed him on the cheek without effort; she already stood to his shoulder.

Or was the real problem that he would never be able to bring himself to let her go? Senseless to say she reminded him of her mother. At almost sixteen, Lorna was beautiful where Kathleen had been no more than pretty. She had the exquisitely delicate MacMahon features, to which had been added the wide O'Neill mouth to temper the MacMahon austerity with bubbling pleasure. And she had the O'Neill eyes, the greenness of a forest thicket, concealing recesses no man could judge, but shot through with morning sunlight to make him want to dream of what might be hidden. Perhaps there was a shade too much strength in the shoulders his hands now gripped, but there was a woman's softness in the bodice pressed against his chest. And when she went wading, skirts lifted above her knees, even her brothers stopped to gaze at her legs, at the little ridges of muscle rippling beneath the slender white flesh.

"Papa," she said again, and frowned at him. "You have a pain."

Because he did, from time to time, have a pain, high on his right side.

He smiled and gave her another squeeze, then held her hand to walk toward where her brothers were already eating. "Not today, sweetheart. I was thinking, no man has a right to so much happiness. Promise me you'll never be unhappy, Lorna. Whatever must be done, do it. But stay happy."

She gave him another kiss, released him to climb back on to her seat. "I promise. Shall I tell Mama dusk?"

"Dusk," said Ryan MacMahon, her second brother. "By then we'll have this entire hillside clear."

She blew him a kiss, flicked the reins, started the horse walking back down the slight slope to the track. She was in no hurry. She knew this plantation like the interior of her own bedchamber, loved every inch of it, felt secure in every inch of it. And today she was happy, because Papa was happy, and she thought that Papa spent a lot of his time endeavouring to reassure himself that he was indeed happy to be here. He was a MacMahon of Morne for all that he had been born on this very farm. His cousin was an earl. And his father had been younger son to an earl. Grandpa had died before Lorna's birth in December 1674, but his painting stared at his descendants from the place of honour over the fireplace in the farmhouse, willing them to accept his choice of happiness.

When in 1642 King Charles I had raised his standard

in Oxford, the Earl of Morne and his eldest son had crossed the Irish Sea to pledge their support. They had had the preservation of their lands and their titles and their wealth as much in mind as any loyalty to the Stuarts, or so Papa claimed. Grandpapa had been more honest. He regarded Charles and his crew as tyrants, and had said so, on more than one occasion, thereby coming close to imprisonment. But he would not fight against his King, especially when it involved opposing his own family, and certainly when it meant siding with Puritan rebels. Instead he had taken his young wife and crossed the Atlantic, seeking the freedom of Lord Baltimore's Catholic colony in the Virginias. He had started the clearance of this land, and his son had continued it, and more, founded a new MacMahon clan in this magnificent wilderness.

But did Papa never have regrets? Temporarily exiled by Cromwell, Seamus MacMahon, Grandpapa's brother, had returned with King Charles II to regain his earldom and his wealth. But even Seamus MacMahon, timeserver as he was, had been unable to work with or for James Stuart, and three years ago he had finally retired to his Morne castle, or so it was said; Papa no longer corresponded with his family. He declared, with perfect honesty and good sense, that *he* was neither a Tory nor a Whig, but a Marylander; when last winter the legislature in St. Mary's had voted to recognize the Dutch usurper, William, and his Stuart wife, Mary, Papa had voted along with them.

The cart topped the last rise, leaving the small herd of milch cows behind, and the farmhouse lay beneath her, a foursquare log fortress, loopholed for defence for all that it was ten years since a shot had been fired in anger on MacMahons, surrounded by its outbuildings like a mother by her children, with a wisp of smoke rising from the chimney. Lorna smiled and frowned at the same time. Then what of her? Had Papa stayed close to his family, instead of deserting them altogether, she might live in a castle instead of what was really nothing more than a large cabin. She would have a maid to brush her hair, instead of having to spend half an hour each evening attending to her own toilet. She would have a choice of gowns, instead of just one, to wear on special occasions; indeed, every day would be a special occasion, instead of having to wait for the monthly visit to St. Mary's.

And her suitors would be of noble blood, arriving before her gate in crested coaches. Because undoubtedly there was the reason for Papa's strange advice. His name was Patrick Burke, and his father farmed the land next to the MacMahons. Patrick was a pleasant boy, so far as she could gather; when in her company he did no more than smile and blush and twist his hat in his hands. He had quite ruined the brim while she had watched him. He was a good Catholic, and his father's farm was not a great deal smaller than hers. But the fact was that the Burkes were ordinary country gentlemen, nothing more. Then what was Papa now, but an ordinary country gentleman? It occurred to Lorna that he worried less about the level at which she might marry than at the fact of her marrying at all.

Marrying at all. There was a remarkable consideration. She had no idea what it would entail. It was a subject on which Mama never touched; she kept saying, "Time enough for that when a young man comes courting," and Patrick had not yet done that. But why should the subject not be discussed? Marriage, as exemplified by Mama and Papa, seemed to be a distinctly pleasant state of affairs. Young men, as typified by her three brothers, were delightful companions. So marriage would involve leaving home, but not to travel very far. It would also involve having children.

She shifted her seat on the hard wooden board, her frown deepening; Snowdrop made a plaintive mew and fell into the back of the cart. This was another subject Mama would not discuss, although she had suggested it was to do with the monthly passing of blood. Which involved pain. On the other hand, as it also involved love, in a physical sense, she had come to the conclusion that it must be a very interesting experience. Love, between Mama and Papa, meant a great deal of physical pleasure, so far as she could decide. In the privacy of her own bedchamber, which Papa had added four years before—when indeed she had first begun to menstruate —tearing off part of the roof to make an additional floor, she delighted in examining herself, pretending she was someone else, her lover, discovering her beauty for the first time. Because she was beautiful. Even had she not been told this by everyone who met her, a simple look in the glass would have confirmed it. It was, indeed, her dearest wish to posses a full-length looking glass so that she could see herself in her entirety, instead of having to make do with the small mirror which was all she owned. Perhaps when she was married. Although perhaps then it would no longer be necessary, for then her true beauty, the long slender legs, the tight drawn flesh on her flat belly, the silky pale hair which slipped down her groin, and more than any of those, the entrancing swell of white breast which rose away from her ribs—all of this would belong to her husband.

She confessed her thoughts to Father Derwent whenever he came to the house. And received a pat on the head. "You are a conceited child, Lorna," he would say. "But at least it cannot be described as a false conceit. Now, away with you and a dozen Hail Marys every day."

But what would he think, what would he say, what would he prescribe as a penance, indeed, if he knew her thoughts, knew how eager she was to have the reality instead of the dream? Presumably she was committing a considerable sin in not confessing that. But Father Derwent was too close a friend of Papa's. He was almost like an uncle. And in any event, if Patrick Burke was really going to come courting, the time for dreaming would soon be over.

Except . . . She chewed her lower lip as she guided the horse down the final slope towards the farmhouse. Patrick gawked at her in any event. What on earth would he do when confronted with the wonder that lay beneath her gown?

She frowned and tightened the rein, and the horse obediently stopped. Dust clouded on the road which led up to the gate, and then down the peninsula towards St. Mary's. Her heartbeat quickened. Visitors were always welcome at MacMahons. They brought news of the outside world. She turned the cart and directed it at the gate, to be the first to greet them, and then checked again, as the breeze carried the worst of the dust away, and she saw the glint of a steel cuirass.

Instinctively Lorna took off her hat, and a quick tug released the ribbon holding her hair, allowing the red-streaked gold to flutter around her ears and over her shoulders. She had never seen soldiers wearing breastplates before, and now that the three men approached, she realised that she had never seen uniforms like these in any form. For they wore buff jackets, breeches, cross-belts, and gauntlets. Black thigh boots and a flat black hat composed a distinctly sombre picture.

They drew their horses to a halt, and the leader raised his hat. "We seek MacMahon." His accent was foreign, and he was a red-faced, pale-haired fellow, so that she immediately supposed him to be Dutch. They had been warned that now William was ruling England they might expect to find Dutchmen everywhere.

"This is MacMahons," she said.

"Are there no savage Indians in these parts?" asked the second man, darker than the first, and heavily moustached.

"Indeed there are, sir," she said. "I am surprised you have not seen them."

"And you sit here, alone and unarmed, at this distance from your house?"

She frowned at him. "I am Lorna MacMahon, sir."

The two lead horsemen exchanged glances, but their companion, who rose behind them, smiled. "And there is your answer, gentlemen. Lorna MacMahon has no cause to fear any man."

Lorna turned her frown on him, suspecting mockery. He was younger than his two companions, not indeed many years older than herself, she estimated. Tall, that could be decided even as he sat on a horse, well shouldered, with a long face and serious grey eyes, but these were clearly ruled by his mouth, which was wide and had a splendid generous lilt to its corner. His whole expression suggested a man who found life a continual pleasure, but who also, when given a responsibility would carry it through no matter what the cost.

He raised his hat in turn; his hair was light brown and straight. "Lieutenant Lennart Munro, Miss Mac-Mahon. May I introduce Colonel Gustav Stahl and Captain Axel Nielson, of the army of His Majesty King Charles the Eleventh of Sweden."

"Sweden?" she cried in surprise.

"We are touring your province, Miss MacMahon," the colonel said. "And were informed that Sean Mac-Mahon's homestead forms one of the bastions of the Maryland settlement. We would much appreciate a word with your father."

"Oh, I . . ." She discovered the young man was still gazing at her and felt suddenly breathless. "You are welcome, I am sure, Colonel. And your officers. I will fetch Father; if you will attend the house, I am sure my mother will be pleased to see you."

She turned the cart, heard their hooves behind her, felt her cheeks glowing. She had never been looked at like that before. Certainly not by Patrick Burke. And this man was a Swede? That meant he had to be a Protestant, and not even an ordinary Protestant, but a Lutheran. Papa always said there was a world of difference between the various sects of the protesting Christians. But he would make them welcome, no doubt about that; she could not ever remember anyone being turned away from the MacMahon house.

The cart rattled into the yard and was immediately surrounded by the barking mastiffs. Behind her a horse whinnied nervously.

"Quiet, Brutus. Quiet, Caesar," she commanded. "These gentlemen are friends." She picked up her hat to climb down, saw her mother in the doorway.

"Mama," she shouted. "Mama. Three gentlemen to see Papa. From Sweden, Mama."

Colonel Stahl had dismounted and was raising his hat. The dogs sniffed his boots, but were silent. "Well, not all the way from Sweden, Mistress MacMahon."

"None the less, sir, welcome." Kathleen MacMahon was a suggestion that Lorna would retain her beauty well into middle age. "Lorna, you'll seek your father."

"I'll take the mare." She ran for the stable, clapping

her hands; from the security of the cart Snowdrop peered at her in disapproval. "Fred Blamey. Put a harness on Paleface for me."

The old man obeyed, led the mare from its stall. " 'Tis careful you'll be, Miss Lorna. There's thunder about. You can feel it in the air. And so will Paleface."

"She'll not throw me." She swung herself over the mare's back, riding astride, checked in dismay as she saw the shadow of a man, and knew who it was before he entered.

"No saddle, Miss MacMahon?"

" 'Tis my own horse, sir." She tightened her knees, and Paleface walked forward. Her skirt was riding up past her calves in the front, and she had no idea what might be happening behind, but she did not dare attempt to straighten herself.

"And you'll ride out to your father, alone and unarmed?" Munro inquired. "We cannot permit that, with your permission."

"You are obsessed with danger, sir," she remarked. "We have no enemies. The Susquehannocks are our friends." She urged the mare into the yard, kicked its ribs. Paleface raised her head inquiringly at this unusual treatment, but broke into a trot. Which quickened as Munro's stallion drew alongside. Lorna smiled. Now *he* was breathless.

"Then are you the unusual ones, Miss MacMahon," he said. "Most of your neighbours fear the Indians, even while admitting there has been no trouble with them these last few years."

"They need only to be treated as friends, to be friends," she retorted. "Now perhaps, sir, as you find my habits so confounding, would you answer *me* a question, as to how a man with a Scot's name finds himself in a buff uniform?"

"Why, because my grandfather commanded a regiment in the army of Gustavus Adolphus. Perhaps you have heard of him?"

"The founder of Sweden's greatness, it is said."

"Quite true. And that regiment, Miss MacMahon, consisted entirely of Scots, discontented with conditions in their native highlands, and seeking a new life as mercenaries. Without them, Gustavus would not have won his victories."

"And they found their new home?"

"Oh, aye, Miss MacMahon." Munro permitted himself a smile. "Although, lest you confound me with a barbarian Swede, let me hasten to assure you that my father returned to Perth for his bride, so that although I swear allegiance to a Swedish King, I am as good a Highlander as any."

"Why, sir," she said. "The fact of it had not entered my head." She pointed at the trees. "There we shall find Papa."

Lorna added rosewater to her bath, a luxury she permitted herself almost every day, as it was she who filled the buckets from the pump outside the door and carried them upstairs to the tin tub. She never heated the water; if it was too cold to bear she simply did not bathe until the weather warmed up. For the rest she settled her mouth in a hard line which no one had ever seen—as she never displayed such an unladylike firmness of will in public—tensed her muscles, and sat herself in the tub at the count of three. Her flesh glowed, her heart pounded, her nipples stood away from her chest, and for several hours afterwards she was dramatically *aware* of herself. The secret itself, of course, she shared with Mama, but with no one else; they both adored to hear people whisper, "The MacMahon girl, how *healthy* she looks."

A patted towelling in front of the fire was followed by a heavy application of powder, for tonight she would wear her best gown. She had, in fact, never worn it before, as Mama had bought it at the summer fair in St. Mary's and had not since then discovered an occasion important enough for its display. But three Swedish officers, now—Papa was fetching up a barrel of his precious apple brandy from the cellar. So Mama, having smoothed Lorna's stockings, was prepared to settle the six petticoats, in lilac taffeta, one on top of the other, standing back to purse her lips and frown.

"I wonder we should not have purchased some corsets while we were about it."

"Corsets, Mama?" Lorna gave a twirl in front of the little mirror, bending this way and that the better to see herself, and also to listen to the delightful rustle of the material. "I need no corsets."

"Every woman needs a corset," Kathleen MacMahon insisted. "Your belly is flat enough, but it could be tighter. And more important, stays would gather you here." She put her hands under Lorna's arms to push the breasts together, compressing the valley between. "There is a woman's true beauty."

Lorna's mouth dropped open in surprise. Mama had never done that before. But there was no doubt that it made her breasts seem much larger than they were.

"On the other hand," Kathleen said, half to herself, "there is time enough. And these are only Swedes."

She turned to the bed, where the gown had been laid. "Careful now." She picked it up, held it for Lorna to step in. It was pale blue satin, intended more for summer than winter wear; the lining was silk, in a darker shade of blue, as were the undersleeves. The bodice was very low, edged with white lace. Lorna was disappointed to discover, as the material settled into place and Mama busied herself with the ties at the back, that it was far more modest than she had supposed and hoped.

"Now then." Kathleen MacMahon came round in front. "Remember to walk with your left hand tucked into your skirt, so . . ." She demonstrated on her own gown. "Make sure you hold only the gown itself, now, so that the gentlemen can see your petticoats. Oh, do it naturally, girl. 'Tis supposed to help you walk, not display yourself."

Lorna paraded the room. "Did I really wish to help myself walk," she said, "I'd lift all six."

"Then would you reveal your legs and prove yourself no lady at all," Kathleen said. "Now, the fan. Take it in your right hand. Oh, the entire hand, girl, for pity's sake. Close your hand on it, leaving the thumb free. Control it, with your thumb. There." She pursed her lips, while Lorna turned back to the mirror once again.

"Do I look beautiful, Mama? Do I?"

"You are a conceited wretch, Lorna MacMahon. No woman looks beautiful without jewellery."

"Jewellery? Oh." She stared at herself.

Kathleen was smiling. "So I'm to make you a present." She extended a small, velvet-covered box. Lorna opened it slowly, heart pounding. The thin gold chain glinted at her, but faded as she lifted it out and gazed at the emerald solitaire.

"Mama," Lorna shouted. "Oh, it is magnificent."

"Hush. Or the men will be in here to discover what you are screaming about. Aye, it is that. I wore it when I was your age," Kathleen said, and hung the chain round Lorna's neck, settling the pendant in the valley between the breasts. Lorna gave a little shudder at the cold touch, but it was sheer delight.

"Now . . ." Kathleen frowned once more. "You'd do better with rings on these ears. But as you're not pierced, you must manage without. There we are. You'll keep that young man entertained, to be sure. "

She sat next to him at dinner, with her youngest brother, Terence, on her left, toward the foot of the table. She knew her cheeks were too pink, and kept taking sips of her brandy, which only made them grow hotter. She was aware of almost nothing that was said, remembered merely to smile and incline her head whenever he did speak. But for the most part the loud voice of Colonel Stahl dominated the table.

"Indeed, Mr. MacMahon," he explained. "The Swedish colony was on the Delaware, why not a hundred miles north of here. But our interest lies in Eastern Europe, not over here in the Americas. The days of the Vikings are gone, eh?" He gave a bellow of laughter, for he too was a fairly regular drinker of the brandy. "So we ceded the place to your new King. But, he now . . . he has one object in life, and one only. I tell no secrets, Nielsen," he insisted, as his second in command frowned at him. "Dutch William means to beat Louis. And to do that he needs all the help he can get. And where will he get better help than from Stockholm. Our army, Mr. MacMahon, is the finest in Europe. Not the largest, mind. But the best." Stahl brooded at his empty goblet, and Seamus MacMahon hastily refilled it. "And so, King William, knowing that when it comes to war with the French part of it must be fought here, sought the assistance of our experience. We are on a tour of inspection, Mr. MacMahon, of the colonies."

"And what do you find, sir?" Mama asked quietly.

"Ah, Mistress MacMahon, that is confidential and

will be in our report. But look to yourselves, I beg of you. We leave from St. Mary's in a matter of weeks, but of all our travels, our visit at MacMahons will rank amongst the most pleasant. Mistress, Miss, gentlemen, my officers and I drink your healths." He rose to his feet, a trifle unsteadily. "The MacMahons. Look to yourselves, I beg of you."

At last it was over. Lorna would have waited to help Mary Blamey clear away and assist her with the washing up, but Mama caught her eye and shook her head, and she found herself on the porch, still accompanied at once by Terence and Lieutenant Munro. But almost immediately a bellow from inside fetched Terence to bring up some more wine.

"Your family is most remarkably generous, Miss MacMahon," Munro said.

Lorna sat on the bench seat by the door. Her fan lay forgotten in her hand. "We seldom have visitors, sir," she explained. "It is always a reason for celebration."

Munro sat beside her, carefully arranging his sword belt. "I meant in permitting me the pleasure of sitting out here with you, alone."

"Why, Mr. Munro," she said. "The door is open. My brothers are not twelve feet away."

And at that moment a gust of noise and laughter came out of the house.

"Nonetheless, it is an honour and a privilege." He hesitated, then lifted her left hand from her lap. "There is a quality about you, Miss MacMahon . . . I am unpardonably bold, I know, but yet, it is unique. You are of a famous house, you yourself are a lady in every way, and yet, you have a physical . . ." He seemed to be groping for words. "Strength? That is but part of it."

She smiled at him because she could think of nothing to say. No man or no woman, either, had ever said anything like that to her before.

"You are not angry," he said with relief.

"Should I be? I had considered you were paying me a compliment, Mr. Munro. Are you finished with my hand?"

"I but wanted to feel its strength," Munro said, giving it a faint squeeze. "And yes, you may be sure, I intended a compliment. Miss MacMahon, I want you to know . . ."

"Mr. Munro," she said. "I beg of you."

His turn to give a quick smile. "We are separated by birth, by nationality, by religion, and soon by four thousand miles of water, Miss MacMahon. I but wished you to know, that should I live to be a hundred, my visit to MacMahons, my meeting with you, will prove one of my very happiest memories." He raised the hand to his lips.

"And then he released your hand," suggested Father Derwent.

"Oh, yes," Lorna said.

Father Derwent waited for some seconds. He was a small, dark man with more patience than his animated face suggested. "But you wished him to do more."

"Father?"

"I am trying to obtain a confession, my dear child. And this far you have confessed nothing."

"Oh. Well, I . . . I'm not sure. I was so surprised."

"That a young man should wish to kiss your hand?"

"Well . . . that he should hold it. For so long."

"But you enjoyed having your hand held."

"Oh, yes." She gave a start. "Is that wrong?"

"*Did* you wish him to do more?"

"Well . . . no. Not like that. I . . ." Her tongue made a quick circle of her lips. "I thought that it might be very pleasant if he *could* do something more. I . . . if we were betrothed, or married, or . . . or something. It was of no importance," she hastily added. "He was departing the next day." She sighed. "I shall not see him again."

"Ah. In other words, this young man fitted rather neatly into these terrible daydreams you suffer." But Father Derment was smiling as he spoke.

Colour flamed into Lorna's cheeks. "Well, I . . ."

Father Derwent stood up slowly. He was growing old. "You are a very wicked child," he pointed out, continuing to smile. "Daydreams, God knows, and He does, you know, are innocent enough, providing they are not accompanied by self-abuse." He forced a frown. "You have never confessed anything of that nature to me."

Lorna had no idea what he meant.

"And soon enough," Father Derwent continued, "they will be overtaken by reality. There is their danger, of course; the reality never actually measures up to the dream. This man is a Lutheran, I am told."

"Is that so very important, Father? Here?"

"It is very important everywhere, my dear. I understand that you will never see him again, for which we must all be thankful. Imagine, were he to be a neighbour and seek your hand. Marriage would be impossible, saving of course your lieutenant consented to become a member of the Church."

"Oh, I . . ."

Father Derwent smiled and rested his hand on her head. "And think of this, Lorna. As he happened to be here and found himself next to a pretty girl, he indulged a flirtation. After an hour's acquaintance. Does that not suggest to you that he makes a habit of it, has by now kissed the hands of another half dozen young women? So keep him for your dreams, and as he fades, let him be replaced by young Patrick Burke. There is a good stout lad. Not a MacMahon, to be sure. But here, as you have just said, family does not matter so much as the possession of health, and strength, and a determination to make our land a rich and happy one. You and Patrick, why, you could create your own aristocracy. Twelve Hail Marys." He released her and wagged his finger. "And no more Lutheran Swedes."

He was a dear old soul and so understanding. She *could* tell him things she would never dare discuss with Mama or Papa. While as for Terence and his brothers . . . in many ways she felt a total stranger to them, and not only because she was the youngest of the four. They enjoyed doing everything together. It was fast becoming a proverb in Maryland, that where you found one Mac-Mahon, you'd very rapidly discover another. She preferred solitude.

Next day, having escaped the house after dinner, she climbed the shallow slope south of the house, a protesting Snowdrop under her arm, to her favorite copse, a rough circle of trees surrounding a nest of fern, damp in the morning but dry and warm by midafternoon. Not far away was the little cemetery, where Grandfather and Grandmother were buried, their gravestones overlooking the land they had first cleared. Here she could sit and think, watching the clouds drifting by through the foliage. Or, if she preferred, she could lean against the trees and look at the river. The river debouched into Chesapeake Bay, some distance away. And Chesapeake Bay stretched all the way down to St. Mary's, where it joined the ocean. And where, no doubt, the Swedes were completing their travels and preparing to return home.

There she was, already breaking her penance. And suffering for it, as Snowdrop sank a claw into her forearm.

"Wretch." She set the cat on the ground, and Snowdrop darted into the bushes in search of an interesting rustle. Lorna allowed her back to slide down the tree trunk until her bottom reached the ground. Supposing they had been Frenchmen, or Great Britain and Sweden had been at war. She would have known none of it, would have ridden confidently down to meet them, and they would have seized her as a prisoner. And then what? She had no idea, save that her heart pounded most pleasantly at the thought. But she could just remember one horrifying occasion, ten years ago, when there had been a band of Indians on the warpath, when her brothers had all been small and there had been only Papa and Mr. Blamey to defend the farm, and the shutters had been up and everyone had been priming muskets and whispering, and Papa had said to Mama, "Two pistols, over there, Kath. One for you and one for the lass. No redskin must take either of you, alive."

And Mama had nodded, her face suitably grim.

But that had suggested murder, and then suicide. Which broke every law in the Bible. So capitivity, by an enemy . . . because of the torture, of course. They would burn them. Yes, she had heard that. The pain would be excruciating. Better to die, than to be burnt alive.

But she really could not imagine Lennart Munro burning anybody, even his most desperate enemy. He had held her hand so firmly and yet so gently, and his flesh had been dry. Patrick had only once ever held her hand, last May when they had danced together, and his flesh had been wet and clammy, and he had seemed positively anxious to let her go at the end of it.

She sat up as the heat left the afternoon, peered

through the trees at the heavy dark clouds which had come sweeping out of the bay. And with the clouds a breeze, setting the branches rattling to and fro, whipping her hair into strands across her face.

She dropped to her knees, parted the bushes. "Snowdrop," she shouted. "Snowdrop. Come on here, you silly cat."

She listened, but could hear nothing over the breeze. And then a drop of water, big as her fingernail, slanted through the leaves and hit her on the back of the hand. To be followed immediately by a dozen others.

She got up. "Snowdrop," she called, angry now. Although in any event it was too late; they were both going to be soaked by the time they regained the house. "Snowdrop."

The rain brought the cat back. She scurried through the bushes, leapt into Lorna's arms, thick white fur already damply drooping. "It's all your fault," Lorna grumbled. She braced herself—it was, after all, no more difficult a decision than lowering herself into her cold tub—and left the shelter of the trees. Instantly the wind plucked at her; it was so strong walking was difficult, even downhill, and the rain seemed to be traveling horizontally, slashing at her face and eyes.

She bowed her head. So long as she kept going downhill she knew she had to arrive at the farm. Snowdrop purred and wagged her tail at the same time, nestled her head into the crook of Lorna's arm. She stumbled forward, tripping and staggering, feeling her gown begin to plaster itself on her shoulders and to her back as it became soaked, fell to her hands and knees at the foot of the slope.

She scrambled back to her feet, raised her head to find the farmhouse, discovered that the entire afternoon had closed in, the teeming rain limiting visibility to only a few yards, while now there came the rumble of thunder. Oh, bed was going to be good, this night. She identified where she was from the rail fence in front of her, enclosing the flower garden, turned to her right, and stopped in surprise. For not thirty yards away, looming out of the rain mist, there was a horseman.

"Whoa there," the man shouted. It was difficult to decide whether he was shouting at her, his horse, or his companions, for now that Lorna dragged wet hair from her eyes she discovered that the stranger was accompanied by a half dozen other men, all mounted, wearing cloaks and flat hats, and all armed, with swords and pistols.

"I assure you, sir," she said. "There is no need for alarm. Would you be lost?"

The horse was close now, and the rider peered at her. "By all that's holy," he remarked. "You'll be Lorna MacMahon."

"I am, sir, although you take me at a disadvantage. But *you* have to be Irish." For his brogue was unmistakable.

"Oh, aye, that I am, Miss Lorna. James Butler, at your service." His teeth showed in a grin. "My mother was English. As for catching you at a disadvantage, why, that would not be possible. They told us you were the most beautiful creature in all the Americas, and they were understating the truth at that."

"They, sir?" she demanded. It was not that she resented the compliment, but she resented it from him, now that he was dismounting, for although he was a fine figure of a man and big, with heavy shoulders and a ruddy complexion, she found it hard to meet his eyes, which were dark brown, and darted from her face to her sodden bodice to her no less sodden thighs, while the lower half of his face was entirely obscured by his black beard, which was not trimmed in any way, but descended from his cheeks and his chin like a mat.

He raised his hat, careless of the rain pounding on his head. "The good people of St. Mary's, to be sure, Miss Lorna." He pointed with his hat. "You're wet through."

"It is raining, Mr. Butler," she reminded him. "You're seeking my father? The house is over there." She opened the gate, waiting for them to follow.

"'Tis a tidy place you have here," Butler said, leading his horse, and signalling his companions to dismount. "You must require a deal of people."

"Papa and my three brothers are sufficient."

"With help from you, I'll wager," Butler said. "And no one else at all?"

"Well, there's Mr. and Mrs. Blamey. Blamey is too old for heavy work, but he cleans up the yard, and Mary helps Mama about the house."

"And dogs " Butler checked as the whine came through the dusk.

"Mastiffs," she agreed. "But they'll have been locked away. The thunder upsets them." Her bare feet squelched in the mud.

"Well, let's see," Butler said, half to himself. "I make that five men, and three women."

"Are you on a military mission?"

"Eh?" He seemed surprised.

"We had some soldiers by, oh, but a week gone, considering our defences against the French. Are you soldiers?"

Butler considered. "We have been soldiers, to be sure, Miss Lorna, but now we are on a mission of peace. Eh, Ned?"

"Oh, aye, Captain Butler. Oh, aye," said Ned.

"On the other hand," Butler went on. "We cannot help but consider places we visit from a military point of view. Five men and three women, with all this talk of marauding Susquehannocks, 'tis not sufficient."

"Oh, away with you," she cried. "Why, the Indians are our friends."

" 'Tis not what they're saying in St. Mary's," Butler insisted. "Oh, no, not at all." He paused before the door, his hat in his hand, water dripping from the end of his beard, while Lorna banged on the wood.

"Lorna?" Kathleen MacMahon peered at her in total horror. "Holy Mother, but you're a drowned cat."

"Not quite," Lorna said, setting Snowball on the floor. The cat gave a squawk and headed for the warmth. "We've company." She stepped inside. "Captain James Butler."

"An honour, Mistress MacMahon," Butler said. "And all the way from Ireland."

"From Ireland you say? Well, for goodness sake. Come in, man, come in out of the rain. Lorna, run and change your clothes, do, or you'll catch your death."

"You'll have to introduce your people, Mr. Butler." Lorna dripped her way across the floor.

"She'll have rheumatism, she will," Kathleen grumbled. "Butler, did you say? You're not related to Ormonde?"

"A cousin, ma'am, distant, to be sure, but a cousin. You're alone at home?"

Kathleen smiled. "My husband has just come in, Mr. Butler, along with my sons. All as wet as Lorna. Oh, I've a family, I have, not one with a thought for his or her health. Now come in, man, and introduce me to your men, and I'll get something hot for you to drink."

Lorna reached the top of the steps and looked down. Butler was looking up, and she had hoisted her wet skirt above her knees to get up the steps. Hastily she let them go again. And again wondered at her anger. He looked at her exactly as Lennart Munro had done, and no doubt beneath the beard was just as handsome a man. And he was Irish, into the bargain, and well related. Yet she was offended because he looked at her.

She stepped out of her gown, dropped the wet shift on top of it; left the pair lying on the ground. She toweled herself, standing by the window to look at the rain. She adored rain. It isolated the farmhouse, left it even more lonely than it really was. And the noise isolated her inside the farmhouse.

But this night she did not wish to be isolated. From Ireland. The thought had not truly registered before, except that it was a vast distance. But he had come from Ireland. She had never even been there.

Someone banged on the door. She turned, holding the towel in front of her. "Who is it?"

"Terry," her brother called. "Papa says you're to make haste. Mr. Butler has important news."

"I'll be quick as I can." She toweled her hair, then seized her brush to drag it through the tousled strands, straightening them into their normal silky smoothness, even more exaggerated tonight as they were still wet. She watched the muscles rippling up and down her belly, her breasts quivered as she worked, and she suddenly knew why she had instinctively disliked Butler. He had looked at her in the same way as Lennart had done, but he had *seen* more. He had seemed to be able to see through the sodden gown and know what lay beneath. He had stripped her, with his eyes.

And yet, having thought that, she felt curiously excited, as well. It was not something she could ever remember happening to her before.

Her decision was made; there was not time to confer

with Mama and obtain permission, in any event. Already she was opening the drawer containing her petticoats, dropping the crisp taffeta over her head. She was dressed in minutes, walking round the room while she fumbled behind herself to tie the silk cords for the gown.

Then the necklace; she kept the box on her table. She had put it on and taken it off every day this last week, so she was an expert.

She found herself panting and suddenly terrified. Whatever would Mama say? But the man claimed to be a cousin of the Duke of Ormonde. She had to dress for him.

She opened the door, descended the stairs, into a buzz of conversation. But the voices slowly died as all heads turned toward her. The clink of glasses ceased.

"Why, Lorna," Kathleen remarked.

"Well." She paused, one step from the floor, and felt her tongue circling her lips. "As there is company . . ."

"Company which is honoured by your courtesy, Mistress Lorna," Butler said, coming across the room.

"Do you know my daughter, then?" Sean Mac-Mahon asked.

" 'Twas she guided us here, Mr. MacMahon," said one of the other men.

"Soaked she was, but not caring," said another.

"I . . . I got caught up at the copse," Lorna explained. "The rain was that sudden."

"Sudden?" Sean demanded. "You could see the clouds gathering all afternoon. You were daydreaming. You'll not credit this, Butler, but there's naught between those pretty ears but wool."

Butler offered her his hand, and after a moment's hesitation she took it. "You'll not quarrel with her, I beg of you. Not tonight. 'Tis a special occasion."

"Mr. Butler and his friends have tremendous news, Lorna," Seamus said. "There has been a great battle."

"In Ireland it was," Ryan said.

"At the Boyne," Butler said. "The river by Drogheda." He felt Lorna, having reached the circle of men, give a gentle tug, and squeezed her fingers before releasing them.

"It seems King James determined to regain his throne," Sean explained. "And so invaded Ireland, where he could be sure of support, with money and French soldiers, too."

"Oh, aye," Butler said. "And got licked." He chuckled. "They say 'tis the only battle Dutch William ever won."

"Poor man," Kathleen said. "Oh, poor, poor man."

"Dutch William?" Terence cried in amazement.

"Of course not, you daft boy. I meant the King."

"But Dutch William *is* the King," Sean said.

"To them that it suits," Kathleen grumbled.

"The Stuarts have brought us, the entire nation, nothing but disaster," Sean said. "So William is a foreigner and a Protestant. He fights against the French, and there is an Englishman's duty, and an Irishman's, by God."

"And the Queen is still a Stuart," Seamus pointed out.

"You'll not have considered Mr. Butler's feelings," Kathleen remarked. "Or those of his companions."

Sean frowned at his guests. "You're not fugitives?"

Butler laughed, while his men exchanged amused glances. "Fugitives? Not us, Mr. MacMahon. Although I'll tell you this, we were at the Boyne ourselves."

"With your cousin, Mr. MacMahon," Ned said. "The Earl himself."

"And his two sons," Butler said. "Oh, fine lads they were, and all he had in the world."

"Were?" Sean asked.

"Well, you see, there were no daughters, and the Countess, may God rest her soul, she passed away a long time ago."

"And you're telling us that Morne fought for the Dutchman, against his own people?" Kathleen asked.

"Aye, well . . ."

"Renegade," she declared.

"Ah, well, now," Butler said. "It was a matter of understanding who was going to win. And the Earl had already declared for the King. William, I mean. Oh, the point can be argued, Mistress MacMahon, until kingdom come, I have no doubt. But you've cause to be grateful for his action. Like I said, he went to war, his two sons at his side, and right gallantly they fought. But not one survived. The last died of his wounds, in these very arms of mine, inquiring only if the battle had been won, which it had."

"What?" Sean asked, plainly bemused.

"What indeed, sir?" Ned said. "Why do you think we took ship in haste across the Atlantic? 'Twas a mission given us by Edward MacMahon himself, just before he died."

"Find my cousin, he said," Butler said. "Find him. And we have done that. Lads, down on your knees. My lord, we crave your indulgence. But to be sure, why, we had no idea how to go about telling you."

"Telling me?" Sean cried. "Telling me?"

Butler got up again. "That to the best of my knowledge, my lord, you are now the Earl of Morne."

Sean MacMahon sat down.

"Lorna," Kathleen snapped. "Pour a glass for your father." Then sat down herself. "And I'll have one too."

"But what does it mean, Papa?" Seamus asked.

"Mean, boy?" Butler shouted. "It means that your father is an earl. And so will you be, in the course of time."

An earl. They'll call me my lady, Lorna thought, as the jug clattered against the goblets.

"One for these gentlemen as well, Lorna," Sean MacMahon said. "You'll forgive me, Captain Butler, but the news was a little sudden. And more than a little unbelievable."

"You've no knowledge of any other claimant?" Butler asked, suddenly anxious.

"Claimant?" Sean protested. He took his glass from Lorna, drank deeply. "I'd not go to law over such a matter. I never wanted the earldom, anyway."

" 'Tis one of the richest in all Ireland," Butler said. "Why, they say Edward MacMahon's personal wealth is equal to that of the King, all but."

"It'll mean returning to Ireland." Sean gazed at his wife.

"What I meant was," Butler explained, "you've no knowledge of any member of the family with a closer relationship than yourself, my lord."

"Why, no. There was no one else. If both boys were killed as well . . . I find that all but incredible."

"Watched it happen," said the man called Ned. Lorna had by now reached him with her tray, and he winked at her.

She frowned at him. Presumably it made some sense that these men should have come all the way across the Atlantic to bring news of such importance. They could hope for a rich reward, and they could expect to remain in Sean MacMahon's gratitude for all of their lives. And yet she felt uneasy . . . about them? Or was it just the suddenness of what had happened, the importance of Papa's words. Leave MacMahons, for

Ireland. But, then, leave this simple life to be a great lady? Her knees felt weak. She wanted to sit down, and think about what had happened.

"Well, then," Butler declared. "If you're positive, my lord, that there's no one with a better claim to the title, I think we can allow ourselves a toast."

Sean looked up. "Oh, aye, Captain Butler. A toast, by all means. Forgive me, indeed. I am overwhelmed. You'll think I a total fool. But you'll understand that my father turned his back on Ireland, and his family . . ."

"All of that wealth? All of that power?"

"All of that responsibility, too," Sean pointed out. "Ireland is not a happy place."

"And old Seamus turned his coat, in any event," Kathleen said fiercely.

"As I said, my lady, 'tis all a point of view," Butler pointed out. "And now the matter is settled, my lord, why, Ireland can be happy again. But only if you and men like you take the lead. A toast, aye, a toast. But wait . . ." His glass was poised. "You've servants?"

"Blamey and his wife. They'll be at their supper."

"On such an occasion, my lord? Should they not be amongst the first to drink the health of their new earl?"

"They will certainly want to hear the news," Kathleen said. "Terence, fetch Mr. and Mrs. Blamey. And not a word, mind, until they're here."

Butler smiled at them all, his teeth gleaming through his beard. "So you'll just have to be patient a little while longer, boys," he said. "Oh, they've waited a long time to bring you this news, my lord."

"Good heavens." Sean got up again, held out his hand. "You've traveled better than four thousand miles, and here I am worrying only about myself. Captain

Butler, I am forever in your debt. There's my word and my hand on it."

"I never doubted it, my lord. But it was our plain duty, told us by the late earl, may God rest his soul. You'll draw your swords, lads."

For the Blameys had just come inside, accompanied by Terence.

"And close that door, lad," Ned said. " 'Tis a blustery night, and we've had enough of those."

"Swords?" Sean inquired as the steel rasped out of the seven scabbards.

"Custom, my lord, custom," Butler explained. "Swords must be bared when the health of the new earl is drunk."

"New earl?" Blamey asked. "What's this, Mr. Sean?"

"Aye, well, it seems, old friend, that in some utterly remarkable fashion I have inherited. These gentlemen have come a long way to bring the news."

"Swords?" Seamus MacMahon inquired. "We have none."

"Then do not worry with it," Butler explained. "The custom applies only to those wearing weapons at the time, to be sure. It will be sufficient for you to raise your glasses."

"Lorna," Kathleen said. "Wine for Mr. and Mrs. Blamey."

Lorna poured, her back to the Irishmen.

"Now then," Butler shouted. "Ladies and gentlemen, I give you, the earldom of Morne. Fetch her, Ned, and the rest, set to."

Lorna turned, her tray still held in front of her, to see the man Ned springing at her but in that same instant the entire night seemed to explode, into cries and grunts and panting fury.

She brought up her tray, and he struck it with his fist,

sending it sailing across the room, sending her bumping into Mary Blamey. Mary gave a shriek of alarm and fell over, and Lorna tripped too, landing on her hands and knees close by the fire. She glimpsed the man Ned rearing above her, looked past him to her brother Terence, slowly falling, a sword thrust clear through his chest. Her brain seemed to freeze. She was unable to believe what she was seeing, what she was hearing, for in that moment Kathleen MacMahon screamed, a long wailing sound which echoed around the rafters of the old farmhouse.

Ned gripped her shoulders, sliding her sleeves aside to dig his fingers into the bare flesh and raise her to her feet. She kicked at him, but was hampered by the gown, so she struck at his face, and he grunted in pain as her nails tore down his cheek. His fingers relaxed and she turned away, only to feel his hands closing on her skirt, to bring the gown ripping around her waist and once again throw her off balance.

She crawled away from him, and was again paralysed by horror as she saw blood splattering on the wall, oozing across the floor towards her, as she heard a moan of pain from close by and saw Blamey, his neck nearly severed by a savage cut, his eyes staring sightlessly at the ceiling. Then Ned was back again, this time ducking under her arms to drive his shoulder into her waist and rise to his feet. Her head fell down behind, and she felt his hands closing on her thighs, biting through her skirts to dig into the flesh. She drummed her fists on his back and found the hilt of his sword, which he had thrust through his belt before assaulting her. She seized it and attempted to draw it, but then her head banged against the door as he got outside, and they were immediately soaked in the teeming rain. And at that moment he released her, so that she rolled off his shoulder and struck the muddy earth with a force that drove all the breath from her body.

Ned gasped for breath. "A regular hellion," he snarled, wiping water and blood from his scratched face. "A regular . . ." He stooped to tear the last of her gown, and was brought upright again by a hand seizing his shoulder and jerking him away.

"Now then, Ned," Butler said. "You'd not be thinking of harming the Countess of Morne, would you?"

He grinned at her, and blood dripped from the point of his sword on to her shoulder.

# Chapter 2

Slowly Lorna straightened the remnants of her skirt, rose to her knees. It was desperately important to concentrate on little things. To attempt to understand what had really happened would bring madness, she was sure.

"Easy, now." Butler offered her his hand, and she shrank away from it.

Another man joined them. " 'Tis done, Jamie."

"Set it alight."

"I doubt it'll burn, in this downpour."

"It'll burn, if you do it right. Spread the liquor about," Butler instructed. "Make a good job of it."

The dogs whined from their pen. They could sense something was wrong. Lorna reached her feet. Should she run? But they would catch her easily enough.

Butler peered at her. "Fetch a jug of that brandy," he commanded. Ned went inside. "You're soaking again," he said. "A drink will warm you up, my lady."

She watched the water dribbling down his cheeks and

dripping from his chin. This man has just murdered my family, she thought. After we had welcomed him, given him food and drink, he has just murdered my family.

She swung her hand, reaching for his cheeks with her nails, and he caught her wrist. She struck at him with her other hand, and he caught that as well.

"Paddy," he roared.

Lorna raised her leg and stabbed at his calf, and he gave a grunt of pain, but then she was seized round the waist from behind and dragged away. Butler came forward, still holding her wrists, and now he bent her arms together.

"Cord," he said. "We need cord. Ned."

She hissed in her fury, and scythed her legs sideways, and found herself thrown to the ground to lose her breath once more, and have her face thrust into a puddle of water.

"Easy," Butler roared. "You'll drown the girl. I'll not have her hurt." He was kneeling across her, and she felt her wrists being drawn together and secured, then he held her shoulder and pulled her up to sit. "You've the jug?"

She twisted her head to and fro, but he dug his fingers into her hair to hold her head straight, and with his other hand gripped her mouth, hand wrapped round her chin, squeezing to force the lips apart.

"Pour it in," he commanded. "Easy now."

The man's face was very near. *I'll bite it,* she thought, but could not close her mouth. Water dripped in and she saw the jug, and a moment later the rain was washed away in the burning liquid. She coughed and choked, and tried to close her throat, but it still trickled down.

"Easy," Butler repeated. "We'll not have her vomit."

Other feet stood around them, squelching in the mud. "It's burning," someone said. "For the time."

"That'll do," Butler said. "Fire the outbuildings as well, then ride behind us." He thrust his fingers into Lorna's armpits, pulled her upright. Her knees gave way, and he held her against him. She looked past him at the smoke issuing from the shattered windows, the flames already leaping up the stairs to attack her bedchamber. She found her mouth open, and knew what she had to do. She screamed, and a man caught her shoulder, but Butler thrust him away.

"Leave her be," he grunted.

Her breath was gone, and she sagged against him. A white ball appeared in the window for a moment, then scattered down the sloping roof to disappear.

"What the hell . . ." demanded a man.

" 'Tis only a cat," Ned said.

Snowdrop. The only survivor. Except for her. But why had *she* been saved? What had she been daydreaming, only that afternoon? Of being taken a prisoner? But by Lennart Munro. Not by James Butler. Oh, God, Lennart Munro. He was probably on his way back to Sweden.

And now the dogs began to howl, and the horses to stamp and neigh, as the stables were set alight, while a tremendous squawking rose from the coop.

"Oh, God," she screamed. "Not the animals as well."

Ned grinned at her. "And here was I thinking you'd gone dumb with shock."

"They'll get out," Butler said. "The flames will not survive this rain. But they had to be fired, Lorna. The Indians would have fired it."

"The Indians?" She gaped at him.

He held her arms, half pushed, half carried her across the yard to where the Irishmen's horses had been assembled. "Why, who else do you suppose would commit so dastardly a crime?"

"The Indians are our friends," she repeated senselessly.

Butler grinned at her. "So you keep saying. They don't hold with that in St. Mary's. No, sir. They'll not find it hard to believe. Up you get." He swung her across, pulling her tattered skirt up her legs to make her sit astride, then mounted behind her, urged his horse into the rain. At the gate they heard the rumbling crash of the upper story of the farmhouse collapsing. Lorna wanted to look away, but stared at her home in fascinated horror. Flames leapt through the suddenly opened roof, sizzling as they encountered the teeming rain. No doubt in time the pouring water would put out the fire, but the building would be destroyed. The bodies inside would be charred skeletons.

The tears came without warning, seeming to rip their way up from the very pit of her belly, hurting her chest and burning her eyes.

"Aye," Butler said. "There's naught like a good cry."

Her shoulders shook against his chest. "You'll hang, James Butler. So help me God," she sobbed. "If you'd not, you'd best kill me now."

He smiled into her hair, urged the horse into a trot. "Now, do you know, it's a fact me grandfather was hanged. By your dear departed dad's uncle, to be sure. Oh, they're a cruel lot, the MacMahons of Morne. You're the best of the lot, Lorna, girl."

She twisted against him even as she sobbed, but he kept one hand round her waist.

"Countess of Morne," he said. "There's a title to conjure with. And all that money. That'll bring a smile to your cheeks, even if your husband don't manage it first."

"My . . . husband?" She cursed her curiosity, wished she could just lie here and cry herself to death.

"It will be an honour, my lady."

Another desperate striving against him. "Marry you? I'll watch you hang."

"You'll marry me, Lorna. 'Tis arranged. Came to me like a flash, it did. There was poor old Ned MacMahon, lying in his blood, his dad and his brother dead beside him. He thought he was dying too, poor fellow. 'Find my cousin,' he said to me. 'Find my cousin. The line must not die.' "

Lorna's head jerked, despite herself. "Thought he was dying? *Thought?*"

"Aye, well it was a shame to disappoint the lad. There was a career for you. Earl of Morne at five in the afternoon, dead at half past. Pure shortage of breath it was; someone left a pillow on the boy's face. Tragic."

"You . . ." She searched her mind and hated her own innocence. She knew no words sufficient to sum him up.

"Well, it made sense. The only heirs a pack of farmers in Maryland?" Butler asked. "But Ned was a mine of information. 'They'll make good,' he muttered at me. 'There's three sons there, and a daughter. They'll make good.' That's when I had me a flash of light, you might say."

"You're mad," she shouted. "Mad. I'll not inherit."

"Ah, well, now, there's no saying whether or not you will ever be Countess of Morne, to be sure. I looked into that; 'tis a matter for the King, God bless the man. But you'll inherit all the old boy's personal wealth, and that'll make us the richest couple in all Ireland. All England as well, if all I heard tell was true."

"Marry *you*? Never."

"Lorna Butler," he mused. "It has a ring to it. Wives

can't testify against their husbands, you'll know. Aye. Lorna Butler. It has a ring to it.

It continued to rain all night, and the little cavalcade continued to ride all night; soon they were joined by those who had remained behind to complete the destruction. But by then the glow of the flames had died, and there was nothing but the pouring rain, and the occasional distant growl of thunder, carried on the wind and whipped away again by the wind, for it was now blowing very nearly a gale.

And by then Lorna was a torment of discomfort, her bottom aching from sitting astride the heaving animal, while her torn clothes clung to her half-naked body in sodden misery, causing her to shiver, and her mind to become exhausted with fear and horror, so that she dozed, leaning against Butler's cloak, and then rearing awake again as memory returned to assail her. Papa was dead. Mama was dead. Seamus and Ryan and Terence were dead, the farmhouse destroyed, the dogs and the horses and Snowdrop driven into the woods. The MacMahons were no more, saving only her, and for her the future did not bear contemplation.

She must live for the present, live for the moment Butler lowered his guard, the moment when they were again in company, and she could shriek his infamy to the world, and see him taken and hanged.

Ned rode his horse alongside. " 'Tis a gale, and from the southeast," he shouted. "We'll not get to sea this night."

"Nor should we," Butler agreed. "I'm all for a smooth passage."

"But the girl . . ."

"Can do us no harm, out in the stream," Butler said.

"Anyway, we'll be wed by morning. You've no cause to worry."

"By morning," she whispered. "You'll be waiting the gallows."

He chuckled, and squeezed her round the waist. "Still awake, love? Now, why should I wait for the gallows? By morning I'll have a bride to see to."

"And do you suppose no one will know what you've done?" she asked. "Your man said the truth. You'll remain in St. Mary's the next week."

"Enjoying you, Lorna, sweet," he promised. His hand slipped up from her waist to caress her half-exposed breast, inducing a most peculiar sensation which descended to meet the revulsion rising from her belly. No one, save herself, had ever touched her there before, and now he was moving his hand, gently, the fingers extended, her frozen nipple caressing his palm. "Oh, I'll do that."

"They'll find out what's happened," she promised.

"Not they," he said. "I've done a deal of thinking about this one, Lorna. The priest called but yesterday, and your family are not due to visit St. Mary's for two weeks. No one will go near MacMahons for several days. And supposing they did, why, they'd think the obvious, those murdering Susquehannocks again. No one will even know you've survived."

"And do you not suppose I will tell them?" she shouted. "Or am I to be kept prisoner for the rest of my life?"

"You'll remain prisoner until I say so, Lorna," Butler promised. "The ship is on charter to me, and we've the whole wide Atlantic to cross. I'll have you licked, or loved, into shape by the time we see Ireland again, if we have to sail up and down for a year. And when they say, why didn't you alarm the settlement, having driven off the Indians, why, I'll go down on my knees, Lorna, sweet, and tell them I was that upset, at having rescued only you, the sole surviving MacMahon of Morne, that it never crossed my mind. But by then . . ." His hand slipped down from her breast to give her belly a gentle squeeze. "I won't have to be on my knees. By then I'll be the husband of Lorna MacMahon. Why, I doubt not you'll be carrying my child, by then."

*Carrying his child.* But thought would take her no further than that. She had no idea what to expect. His child. Why had she not realized from the start that that had to be what he intended?

The horses stopped. " 'Tis the settlement," Ned said.

"Aye." Butler squinted at the sky; the rain had dwindled to a drizzle, but was still driven by the gusting wind. "We'd best not take a risk on it; 'tis too near to dawn. Give me your scarf." Before Lorna could decide what was about to happen her hair had been seized to pull back her head, her mouth was again forced open, and the scarf, an evil tasting rag of wool, was secured on the nape of her neck, under her hair, pressing on her tongue and keeping her mouth wide, leaving her unable to make a sound. Then they rode down the slope and into the cluster of houses which surrounded the little fort.

Desperately Lorna struggled. All around her were her friends. Why, but a month ago she had taken tea with Lord Calvert and his family, and there was the governor's house, a two-storied building which could almost be described as a mansion. But it was in darkness. It was four in the morning, and there was a gale blowing. The good folk of St. Mary's were in their beds. And it was not a large town; already the waters of the Potomac were gleaming in front of them, whipped into whitecaps by the wind howling up from the narrows. There were several ships riding to two and three anchors, and they all had lights. They would have lookouts, too. But she could not cry out.

Butler dismounted, pulling her after him. "You'll stay with the horses, Paddy," he said. "Take them back to the stable at first light."

"What'll I tell him?" Paddy asked.

"Tell him we saw no game and we got wet for our pains. So we're away up the coast."

"Shall I mention Indians?"

Butler considered, holding Lorna against him. "No," he decided.

Lorna got her foot free of her wind-trapped gown and kicked him on the ankle. He laughed and swept her legs from the ground, his left arm under her shoulders, then carried her down the dock, where the rest of his men were already untying a dinghy. Butler got into the stern, still carrying Lorna, causing the whole boat to sway uneasily.

"You'll have us in the water," Ned grumbled.

"Holy Mother," Butler remarked. "You've risked so much and won, and now you're afraid of getting your feet wet? Cast off, lads. Give way. Father Tod will be waiting."

Ned sat beside them on the transom; Lorna was seated on Butler's knee—she felt as if she was being impaled.

"The whole thing is too risky by far," Ned grumbled. "I'd not considered it properly before."

"Or you'd not have come," Butler agreed. " 'Tis a right coward you are, Ned, to be sure. All life is a risky business, and if you'd gain more than most you must risk more than most. And wouldn't you say this one is worth taking a risk for?" He kissed Lorna on the neck.

"For you," Ned said.

"But there's the money. It'll be shared all round when she comes to her senses and claims her inheritance. Mind your way," he bawled, as a wave broke on the bow of the dinghy and sent spray flying into their faces.

"Sinking, that's what we are," Ned wailed.

"So bail her out," Butler told him. "By Christ, Lorna me love, but I'm surrounded by fools and cowards."

A dark shape loomed above them.

"Is that you, Captain Butler?" called the watch.

"It is me, and I've a lady. Send down a basket."

The dinghy came into the side of the brigantine and was made fast. Already the basket was hanging beside them, occasionally dipping into the water as the boats surged against each other.

"You'll get a wet backside," Butler said. "Can't be helped."

"And you'll be drying it for her soon enough, Captain," said one of the crew. The rest laughed, and Lorna found herself being gripped by several hands and deposited into the swaying rope cradle, which immediately commenced rising. *Now,* she thought. *Make an effort and throw yourself out. Remember what Papa said, better to drown than to be a prisoner.*

But she did not want to die. She wanted to live, and not only to avenge her family. She realised with a strange self-horror that she *wanted* to experience whatever was going to happen to her, that she would rather experience anything than actually die.

A moment later she bumped on wood, and there were eager hands reaching for her as the ropes were pulled apart.

"Avast there," Butler shouted. "She's my bride." He had come up by way of the accommodation ladder, and now took her arm to raise her to her feet. "Time enough," he shouted. "You're invited to a wedding, lads."

Lorna was gathered in the rush of men to the companionway. The door was pulled open, and she gained a moment's relief from the wind and the rain, before being bundled down the ladder and into the cabin; the deck beams were so low she bumped her head, causing her mind to swing in time to the lantern guttering an uncertain light into the corners. The place stank of tar and cordage and bilge water, and, above all, of unwashed human bodies. She thought she might well vomit at any moment; she had never been on a ship before.

"You're back, then." The voice was quiet, but it trembled, and the words were slurred.

Lorna focused with difficulty, discovered a man seated on the berth in front of the stern windows. He wore a priest's cassock and a cross around his neck, but he had not shaved in several days, and his breath rushed rum at her.

"In triumph." Butler pushed Lorna to her knees. "We'll do better there, me darling," he said, and joined her. "Settle down, lads, settle down," he bawled at his crew.

Men knelt about them. *Oh, God,* Lorna thought. *This cannot be happening. I must be having a nightmare.*

Father Tod peered at her. "She's wet," he said.

"We're all wet, Father," Butler said. "The sooner you make us man and wife the sooner we'll be able to take off our clothes and get dry."

"And she's not decent," Father Tod pronounced. "No woman can be wed with her breast uncovered."

Lorna looked down for the first time, discovered that she was, indeed, naked from the waist up. Not only had her dress been reduced to nothing more than a skirt, she had also burst the straps of her shift.

"Holy Mother," Butler remarked. "I'll be uncovering the rest of her in a moment." But he took off his jacket and placed it around her shoulders.

Lorna got her head up again and gaped at the priest. He had not, apparently, noticed the scarf tied around her mouth.

Father Tod looked happier. "Now, brethren, let us begin. Dearly beloved . . ." He paused, as if realising even in his befuddled mind just how much of a mockery were those words alone. But then he was proceeding, bringing out a well-thumbed book to read from in solemn tones, while the wind howled and the ship rolled to its moorings, and Lorna's knees began to ache from the hardness of the deck.

"Do you, James Peter Patrick, take this woman to be your lawful wedded wife?" Father Tod was asking.

"I do," Butler said.

"And do you . . . ?" Father Tod hesitated.

"Lorna will do, man."

"Lorna, take this man to be your lawful wedded husband?"

"Mmmmmm," she gasped, and shook her head to and fro.

"I cannot hear a word the poor child is saying," Father Tod remarked.

"Well, I can," Butler said. "She says yes. Doesn't she say yes, lads?"

"Oh, aye, Captain," they shouted. "She says yes."

Lorna attempted to rise and was forced back to her knees.

"Then I pronounce you man and wife," Father Tod said. "You've a ring?"

"Aye." Butler reached behind Lorna's back, where her hands were secured, and she felt something being pushed on to her finger. "And it's a fit."

Father Tod sighed. "Those whom God has joined together, let no man break asunder." He peered at Lorna. "And may the Lord have mercy on your soul, my child."

"That's not part of the service," Butler objected.

"No more it is," Tod agreed. "There'll be papers to sign."

"In a day or so," Butler said. "We've the whole voyage ahead of us. Away with you," he yelled in a sudden bellow. "Leave a man with his bride."

The sailors scurried up the ladder. Father Tod followed more slowly, and at the top he turned to look back. "I doubt not you'll pay for this crime, Jamie," he said.

Butler merely grinned at him. "So long as God waits until I've consummated the matter," he said, "I'll die laughing."

The hatch slammed shut. Lorna once again attempted to rise and was once again restrained. But this time his hand went round the back of her head, under her sodden hair, and released the gag. The cloth fell away from her mouth, and she sucked evil-tasting saliva, but it was like nectar to her. A moment later her hands dropped at her side. Had she not seen them she'd not have known; they had lost all feeling.

"It'll come back," Butler said, and sat on one of the bunks which lined the bulkhead.

"That was no marriage," Lorna muttered.

"It'll be legal when you sign the paper," Butler said. "Feeling yet?"

Her blood was starting to prickle as it made its way down her arms. She thrust her hands together, twisted the fingers against each other, determined not to give him the satisfaction of seeing her weep any more, although the pain was intense. And gazed at the gold band, the symbol of her imprisonment. She felt his coat slip down her back to the deck.

"Take off your clothes," he commanded. "Do you want to catch cold?"

"I've already caught cold." She got up, and fell over as the boat lurched. She landed on the bunk away from him, and he leapt across the cabin, holding her there, running his hands into her hair, fondling her breasts, kissing her cheeks and her neck and eyes while he was doing so.

"Christ, but you are a charmer," he said. "Your mouth, girl, your mouth." He twined his fingers in her hair, forced her head back, gazed into her eyes as he slowly lowered his head. She snapped her teeth, but he had jerked away and was smiling. "You and me have got to understand each other, Lorna. I ain't gained nothing yet, but I ain't lost nothing yet, either. If no one was ever to find you, they'd just suppose you'd been taken by the redskins. Oh, aye, that'll be a source of gossip around many a campfire." He gave her hair a tug. "So mark my words. Bite me, and so help me God I'll give you to the crew."

His breath rippled on her face; it still stank of her father's brandy. And his head was coming closer again. She felt paralysed, unable to make up her mind what to do, save to submit, and wait for some opportunity to avenge both herself and her family.

His lips clamped down on hers, and instantly his tongue darted into her opened mouth, scouring her gums, seeking to thrust its way down her throat. Instinctively she started to bite, and only just managed to stop herself in time. Instead she pushed against him, used her own tongue to drive him back, but this seemed to delight him.

When he released her she could only sink against the wooden back of the bunk, exhausted with even that brief struggle. She lacked the strength to raise her arm as he dug his fingers into her disarranged petticoats, and tore them down the front.

"I'll dry you myself," he said.

She closed her eyes. *Lie still,* she told herself, *and he will not hurt you. Lie still, and in time he will be sated, and leave you alone. Lie still, and he will be weak when you are strong.*

She felt hands on her thighs, on the inside. She wanted to scream, and kept her mouth closed with an immense effort of will. Only a few minutes longer, surely. But then she felt his beard, stroking across her legs, across the inside of her thighs. He was going to kiss her. *Oh, God,* she thought. He cannot. Her knees started to come up, and encountered his body; he grunted, and she forced them down again. Lie still, lie still.

And then she felt his hands on her knees, and they were being parted, and now on a sudden his body descended on her with a force which made her eyes open as her mouth opened as well, and she was aware of an immense fullness in her groin, accompanied by a sudden stab of pain which seemed to race through her, and was followed immediately by a succession of others as his weight thudded on her belly, before suddenly he collapsed, sweat dribbling from his hair, lips breathing saliva into her ear, breath rasping. And she realized that in her agony she had closed her hands on his back, had actually grasped him against her. The marriage had been consummated.

He lay so still she thought he might have fallen asleep, and his weight grew increasingly intolerable. Cautiously she attempted to slide herself to one side, so that she could get up, and to her horror watched his head raise.

"Well, then," he smiled at her. "That wasn't so bad, eh?" He frowned at her expression. "Say it."

"I hate you," she whispered.

"Bitch." He rose above her, straddling her with his knees, and she could not help but look at him. And away again. She had grown up with three brothers, and knew what a naked man looked like. Or she had thought she did. But never had she seen an aroused member.

"You were just afraid, that's all," he said. "A girl is always afraid, the first time. And maybe I was a little rough, eh? I'll tell you this, I was impatient. Christ, I've never seen a body like yours, Lorna. There can't be too many in the world." He began to knead her breasts gently, so that she was almost surprised, gathering them and pulling them, allowing his fingers to slide over the flesh and then to close on the nipples, again very gently, elongating them, and then stroking them across the palm of his hand, as he had done while they had been riding. And once again she discovered a remarkable, and at the moment hateful feeling, for her blood seemed to tingle, and she had a tremendous desire to spread her legs, and then remembered what would happen if she did and hastily clamped her knees together. But the feeling remained.

And Butler was sliding his hands down her rib cage,

still with amazing gentleness, moving himself backward down the bunk, as he did so, his buttocks also sliding over her thighs, his member rearing above her like a predatory bird, about to strike.

She watched his face change as his passion rose; his high colour deepened, and he fell at her, mouth wide. She turned her head and he kissed her cheek, before he gripped her chin with his hand and turned it back again, to seek out her tongue. But by then her attention was caught with what was happening between her thighs, with that overwhelming feeling that she wanted to stretch her legs, wider and wider and wider, and yet with another thrill of pain as well, although not so severe as the first.

Butler smiled at her, his face close. "I thought you might be difficult, Lorna love. But you've been dying to get a man inside you, for years."

She stared at him in sheer horror. Because she had almost enjoyed it. Almost. She would never enjoy it. Not from Butler. But just for a moment there she had understood what it might be like, with a man she could love, a man she need not hate, need not determine to destroy. But she was more than ever determined now, to destroy Butler. It was more than the necessity to avenge her family. It was to take back what he had stolen, not her virginity, not her pride, but that secret something which had hovered between them, for just a moment. Because now she knew at least one of the reasons for his hitherto unbelievable confidence, that she would not always oppose him, that she might even be brought, in time, to support his story and be his wife in more than law.

"Dawn." He pushed himself up, picked up her clothes and looked at them. "Rags," he muttered, and opened a locker on the far side of the cabin. She gazed at his back. He was a big, strong man. She needed a weapon. But now? That would leave her at the mercy of his crew. Unless she jumped through the stern window.

She sat up, swinging her legs to the deck, and thought of her necklace. She put up her hands, but it was gone, torn away at some time during the night. There was nothing left of Lorna MacMahon, save the physical shell, and that would soon be lost as well, if she did not escape. She gazed at the window. The small glass panes were filthy, but she could see out. The wind still blew, and the ship still heaved to its mooring, and the land was better than half a mile distant. To jump through the window would be to risk drowning. But would she not be better off, drowned? Especially if she had killed Butler first. She would have completed her vengeance. She would have no reasonable cause to continue living in torment.

The brigantine swung to her anchors slowly, and another ship came into view, also moored, but not two hundred yards away. The wind was still high, and the flags and pennants were streaming almost flat. Blue, with a yellow cross. The flag of Sweden. Her heart gave such a lurch she almost felt sick.

Butler straightened, holding out a white shirt which seemed, unbelievably, to be made of cambric, with lace at the collar and cuffs. "That should come down to your ankles," he said. "And I'll not have Ned and the lads looking at those tits any more."

"I should like a bath," she said.

"A bath? There's no bathing on this ship."

"A bucket of water," she begged. "I could have it on deck." Oh God, just let her get on deck. The Swedes were there. Lennart was there.

He gaped at her, then he went to the door, pulled it

open. "Ned. Fetch a bucket of water in here. And a bottle and some grub. The wife's starving. On deck," he snorted. "Wanting to make an exhibition of yourself, eh?" He jerked his head. "Lie down."

She lay down again, and for the first time realised how exhausted she was. Her body seemed strangely relaxed, and for that reason had developed every ache and pain she could imagine. But part of the exhaustion was despair. They were so close. So very close.

Butler spread a blanket over her. "Now lie still," he said, and pulled on his breeches. A moment later Ned came in, followed by another of the crew. Between them they carried a full bucket, and a bottle of red wine, and some bread and cheese.

"And how was she, Captain?"

"She's a beauty," Butler said. "You'll never know her like. How's the weather?"

"Aye, well, it's starting to veer."

"And no hubbub from the shore? No firing of cannon?"

"Not a sound, Captain. Not a sound." Ned backed to the door, grinning at Lorna.

"You'll want to make sure naught ever happens to me," Butler said, closing the door behind them. "Think of having those scum crawling up your crotch."

"Can there be a difference?" she asked, and sat up in consternation at her own boldness.

He continued to smile. "You'll find out, if you're unlucky. There's your water. Sit there." He opened one of the panes on the sloping stern.

"And will you not do me the courtesy of privacy?"

He shook his head. "You don't want to have no secrets from your husband."

There was no help for it, as she was extremely uncomfortable. She wedged herself into the window, while he sat on the bunk and watched her. She tested the panes with the palm of her hand, but the glass was stout, and, anyway, she realised as her heart slipped all the way down to the pit of her stomach, not one of the apertures was big enough for her to fit through; which made sense—the stern window was no more than a glass-filled grating, so that should a big sea overtake the vessel and break there, it would not do serious damage.

She washed herself, while Butler continued to gaze at her. Lacking soap or scent it was difficult to accomplish much, but at least she could rinse herself with water scooped in her hands, wash some of the tears and the sweat from her face, some of the mud which still clung to her legs, the scent of him from her body.

"Oh, you're a clean one," Butler agreed. "That's good. I've never known a clean woman before."

She dried herself with a blanket, dropped his shirt over her shoulders, tied the ties, adjusted the lace at her neck. Surprisingly, the garment seemed almost clean. She fluffed out her hair, combed it with her fingers, smoothing it down on her shoulders.

"There's a glass." Butler held out a broken sliver of what had once been a mirror, spotted with damp. But she could see herself, and was amazed at the sight of her face. Because it was the same that she had looked at yesterday morning, and yesterday morning she had been a virgin, a happy girl who had been secure in her home, her mother and her father, her brothers and her pets, her every way of life. Whereas now . . . but what had she expected? Her hair to turn white with distress? Lines suddenly to appear on those smooth cheeks? Bruises? There were bruises on her body, but he had carefully avoided harming her face.

"Ah, you're a beauty, Lorna," Butler said. "I'd not

known a woman could be so lovely. And you're not even a woman, yet. How old did you say you were?"

"I didn't." She sat at the table, discovering that she was really very hungry. "I'm fifteen."

"Fifteen," he said. "Christ, I'd not have believed it possible. Take off the shirt, girl. I'm hard as a bone all over again."

It was noon before he allowed her to sit at the table and have something to eat. By then she needed her bath all over again, but by then it no longer seemed important. Her breasts were at once aching and sensitive from his continuous fondling; between her legs no longer felt as if was part of her own body; and she was so exhausted she could hardly keep her eyes open. And she was terrified the Swedish ship would no longer be there.

He gave her a glass of wine, and she drank it greedily. As his own peak had passed he had lost interest in arousing her and had concentrated only on arousing himself; she felt as if she had been turned inside out. She was too exhausted even to hate.

Butler crammed bread and cheese into his mouth, washed it down with a mug of wine, belched. "Eat up," he spluttered at her, spitting half-masticated cheese. "We'll not have you dwindling away."

She nibbled cheese. Would he ever leave her alone? He had to let her sleep, sometime. He had to sleep himself. She yawned, and he grinned at her. "Sleepy, eh? That's how it should be, after a good tumble."

"May I lie down?" she asked.

"Aye," he said. "I'll just tie your hands, eh, to stop you having any dreams about getting over the side or something. Not that it would do you much good." He looked up as there came a rap on the door. "Yes?"

"The wind's dropping, Captain," Ned said. "And veering all the time."

Butler got up. "Fetch a length of rope."

"Aye, aye." Ned climbed the ladder.

"Please," Lorna said. "May I come up? I may not ever see America again."

He chuckled. "You won't, and there's a fact. 'Tis a barbarous country. I'll not be sorry to see the back of it. That's the stuff, Ned, lad." He took the length of thin rope, jerked his head. "Come on, now."

She wanted to say no, she wanted to hit at them, kick at them, force her way past them and up the ladder to the deck. But she knew she would not succeed. It would just give them another excuse for touching her.

She lay on the bunk, turned her face against the bulkhead. He pulled her arms behind her, made them fast, lifted the shirt and gave her a pat on the bottom. "There now," he said. "Christ, but I feel the urge coming over me again. You ever seen legs like those, Ned, lad?"

"Nor a backside neither," Ned agreed.

"Aye, well, stop your gawking. She's not for you, lad."

The door banged, and the cabin was quiet save for the whistle of the wind—it might have dropped from the gale of last night but was still strong—the creaking of the timbers as the boat rolled, and the slap of the waves against the hull. But now she would be putting to sea. Leaving America behind, forever. Leaving Mac-Mahons, and its smouldering corpses. Leaving Snowdrop, deserted with winter coming on. Leaving the Swedish ship, only feet away.

The tears came with terrifying violence, bursting from her chest as they had first done last night, leaving her gasping for breath.

And equally, suddenly, she was angry. Before, when she had fought, it had been like a frightened, trapped animal. She had struck out blindly in every direction, not properly understanding what she was about. Now, even as she wept, clarity seemed to enter her mind and sweep away the exhaustion, the shock waves, leaving memory and determination clear and cold. Butler had killed Mama. He had killed Papa. He had killed Seamus and Ryan and Terry. He had probably killed Caesar and Brutus and her mare. He would be the cause of the death of Snowdrop.

And undoubtedly he would kill her as well. He enjoyed her at the moment, but he would soon tire of her, and once he had got his hands on her inheritance he would have no more reason to keep her alive. So she accomplished nothing by lying here, hoping for something to happen to her advantage. She must *make* it happen, and she would never be better placed than now, with Lennart Munro only a few yards away, St. Mary's only a few yards beyond that.

She sat up, panting, looked around the cabin. They had taken the bottle, and the edges of the table were rounded. A heave against the rope convinced her that it would not easily be broken. Yet there was no rope could not be broken. What had Lennart said? How much he admired her obvious strength, of will as much as of body.

She gazed at the sill beneath the stern window. This had a brass rim, and in places the metal had been scuffed and even torn. She sucked air into her lungs, and rolled herself off the bunk. The ship lurched as she did so, and she fell to her knees, but now she was driven by the sound of feet on the deck above her. It would not take them very long to prepare the vessel for sea.

She regained her feet, staggered across the cabin, turned her back on the window, and felt for the sill with her fingers. She found the place she wanted, rested her wrists on it, and tried sawing them back and forth. Almost immediately another lurch of the ship threw her off balance and the broken brass edge cut into her flesh. The pain was excruciating, and she could feel blood running down her fingers, but she gritted her teeth and resumed sawing to and fro, missing time and again and cutting herself time and again, but refusing to give up. She could not give up, now, because Butler would certainly realise what she had been attempting, from a single glance at her wrists.

Voices shouted, and she heard the rasp of ropes running through blocks as the first sail was set. She resumed her desperate scraping, pulling her wrists as far apart as she could, sawing her back up and down now as well. Sweat stood out on her forehead ·and trickled from her hair, and she licked it from her lips.

Another stream of commands, and once again the thrumming of the ropes. Another sail. She had forgotten to discover how many sails there were. But they would hardly set more than two before leaving. And now she heard the groan of the anchor chain and the chant of the seamen as they worked the capstan, round and round, raising the first of the bowers.

Her hands came free before she properly realised she had succeeded. The sudden movement sent her slipping down the bulkhead, banging her head, and for a moment she was dazed.

She settled her breathing with an effort, ran to the door, pulled it in, and gazed at the ladder leading to the quarterdeck. The hatch at the top was open, and as she watched, the legs of a seaman, pants tucked into his stockings, passed before her eyes. He did not trouble to look down.

Yet someone would, soon enough. And she could hear the shouts as the first anchor broke the surface.

Her heart commenced to pound so loudly it drummed in her ears. How tired she was. Her legs seemed filled with lead. Yet it had to be done. Now, now, now.

She hurled herself forward, reaching for the handrail with her fingers while her bare toes scrambled at the rungs of the ladder. She swarmed up, shirt fluttering and hair flying, burst on to the quarterdeck, looked around, and gazed at Butler.

He gave a roar and reached for her. She turned, and he grasped the flying tail of the shirt, pulling her back. She lashed out with her foot and her nails, and heard a ripping sound. She fell to the deck, so violently had he torn the shirt from her shoulders, and now there were shouts from other men, running aft to assist their captain.

But Butler had also lost his balance and fallen against the far rail. Lorna was first to her feet. She ran away from him, leapt on to the gunwale, one hand holding the shroud which descended from the mizzen mast, paused there a moment, reaching for breath, feeling the cold wind lashing at her naked body, gazing down into the surging slate grey water, listened to a roar from close behind, and launched herself into space.

with vigorous overarm strokes, as she had been taught

# Chapter 3

*L*orna seemed to be falling forever, but at least she had time to reach up and grasp her nose between thumb and forefinger before she plunged, feet first, into the river. The water was far colder than she had suspected and drove the breath from her lungs. Desperately she kicked, seeing stars darting to and fro before her eyes, then her head broke the surface, and she tossed hair and water backward.

To her horror she realized she was immediately beside Butler's brigantine, and indeed men were leaning over the side and looking down at her, mostly laughing, although Butler himself was cursing. "Lower the basket," he bawled.

Lorna turned on to her stomach, stroked the water with vigorous overarm strokes, as she had been taught by her brothers when swimming in the Patuxent. But her arms seemed filled with lead and she moved with terrible slowness.

"A boat," Butler bawled. "Lower the boat. Fetch her back, you scum, or we are undone."

Lorna emerged into sunlight, and saw the Swedish vessel. Men clustered on the foredeck, wondering what had happened. She stopped swimming. "Help," she screamed. "Help me."

They stared at her, and she started swimming again. Behind her she heard the splash of the brigantine's jolly boat being lowered.

Lorna stopped again, gasping for breath. "Help me, for God's sake," she screamed, fear making her voice crack. "Lennart Munro, I'm Lorna MacMahon."

There was a flurry of activity on the Swedish vessel, but now she heard the sound of the oars, and the voice of Butler urging his men on. Once again she dug her arms into the waves, forced herself onward even as all feeling left her body, as the cold seemed to envelop her.

A boat splashed into the sea beside the Swedish vessel. It was not fifty yards away, now. But Butler's voice was so close. Desperately she tried to duck her head, to force herself to dive, but she was too cold and the sea water too buoyant. Hands seized her hair, and then her shoulders. She attempted to turn, to roll and to kick, and their fingers slipped on her sodden flesh. She splashed into the sea again, was brought up by the agonizing tug on her hair.

"Get her on board," Butler shouted. "Hit the bitch on the head. That'll quieten her."

Someone swung at her with his oar, but missed and only struck her shoulder; she was so cold she hardly felt the blow. Then they had her far enough out of the sea to grasp her legs, and a moment later she tumbled into the bottom of the boat, shaking and shivering, while they grinned at her.

"Help me," she screamed, having got back her breath.

"Shut your trap," Butler bawled and swung his fist, but she jerked her head away and ducked under his arm, sitting up to look over the side of the boat at the Swedes, now coming close, and at Lennart, standing in the bow.

"Stay away," shouted one of the Irish. "You'll break an oar. Stay away."

"Release that girl, sir," Lennart shouted, and a moment later there was indeed the crackle of a snapping oar, and the Swedes came alongside with a crash.

"Fools," Butler shrieked. "You'll have us in the water."

"Lorna?" Lennart demanded, staring at her naked body. "Is that really you?"

She attempted to get up again, and was thrust down by Butler's arm. "She is my wife, boy," he shouted. "You'd best be careful I don't remove your ears."

"Your wife?" Lennart asked in bewilderment.

"Help me, for God's sake," Lorna begged. "He's murdered Mama and Papa. He's destroyed the farm. Lennart, please."

"Push them off," Butler commanded. "Push them away."

"Not so fast, sir," Munro said, and levelled a pistol.

"You . . . you . . ." Butler temporarily seemed unable to speak, while the cheeks above the beard went purple.

"You'll release that young lady, sir," Munro said. "Take off my cloak, Johann," he told one of the seamen.

"You . . . by God," Butler said, "had I a sword . . ."

"You will have one, sir," Munro assured him. "And

face me with it, as soon as I have attended to Miss MacMahon."

"Avast there," shouted a new voice, and one which Lorna recognized. The hullaballoo had been observed from the shore, and another boat had come out. She twisted in Butler's arms.

"Mr. Brownsea," she shouted. "Oh, thank God. Save me from this man, Mr. Brownsea, I beg of you."

The sheriff also carried a pistol and was supported by several armed townsmen.

"You'll release that young lady, sir," he commanded.

"She is my wife," Butler shouted. "You have no right."

"Your wife, sir?" Brownsea asked.

"Your wife?" Lennart demanded.

" 'Tis all a fraud," Lorna cried in desperation. "He is a murderer and a rapist. Take me to the Governor, Mr. Brownsea, please."

Brownsea hesitated but a moment. "Aye," he decided. "That will be best. You'll appear before Lord Calvert. Lorna, you cannot remain so."

"There is my cloak." Lennart had holstered his pistol.

"My wife," Butler shouted. "You have no right." But his fingers had relaxed, and Lorna slipped away from them, clambering over the rocking gunwale into the Swedish boat, where Lennart wrapped his cloak around her.

"My wife," Butler roared, reaching behind her, to be brought up short by an oar thrust into his chest.

"Stop that brawling," Brownsea commanded. "Lorna, you'd best return with us. Give her here, Master Swede."

Lennart looked down at Lorna. Her face was pressed

against his buff coat, her arms were tight around his waist.

"You'd best do as he says, Lorna," he suggested.

"You'll come too?" she whispered.

"I'll come." He looked over her head at the still fuming Butler. "I have a date to keep, with your husband."

"Lorna," cried Alison Calvert, throwing her arms around Lorna's bedraggled cloak. "My *dear*, whatever has happened?"

Lorna sank into the armchair by the fire, allowed water to drain down her shoulders and legs, dampen the rug.

"It's an outrage," Butler bawled. He had followed her into the house, but his men had been stopped at the door.

"Indeed, sir, so it appears," Lennart agreed. He had been joined by Colonel Stahl, and all were accompanied by Mr. Brownsea.

To whom the Governor was looking for an explanation. "A disturbance in the harbour, my lord. Miss MacMahon was swimming in the water, and . . ."

"Miss MacMahon?" Butler shouted. "Her name is Mistress Butler."

"Mistress Butler?" Calvert questioned. "Who are you, sir?"

"James Butler, of County Morne, your honour."

"And you claim Lorna, Miss MacMahon, is your wife?"

"It is a foul lie, sir," Lennart declared.

"You are Lieutenant Munro," Calvert said, happy to be able to identify one of the protagonists. "Colonel Stahl? Can you explain this business?"

"No, my lord, I cannot," Stahl confessed. "I have met the young lady, of course, and know her as Miss MacMahon."

"Surely," Alison Calvert said quietly, "it is Lorna to whom we must look for an explanation?" She was a small, grey-haired woman, quiet in her voice as she was quiet in her habits. But all the men stopped to listen.

"Lorna?" Calvert peered from beneath bushy eyebrows.

Lorna shivered and felt the warmth from the fire begin to scorch her skin. Now the endeavour was over, and she had gained land and safety, she did not wish to look at any of them. She wanted only a bed and a blanket, and sleep. But they had to be faced. Or she would be lost all over again.

"You are all right now, Lorna, safe and sure, here at Government House," Alison said, and snapped her fingers. "The poor child needs a glass."

Brownsea poured from the decanter, and she sipped the brandy, and shivered again. "My wife," Butler began.

"Hold your tongue, sir," Calvert interrupted. "Lorna, will you not tell us what happened?"

Lorna recounted the events of the past twenty-four hours. Because it was, she realised with mounting horror, only twenty-four hours since she had stumbled down the hill from the copse and encountered Butler and his men.

"My God," Alison said at last. "Oh, my God, you poor, poor child. But Kathleen, Sean, the boys. Oh, my God." She glared at Butler. "You will hang, sir."

"You'd believe those . . . those ravings?" Butler shouted. "Oh, the poor girl is out of her mind."

"Indeed, sir?" Calvert asked, his voice cold. "How do you account for what happened, then?"

"Well, my lord," Butler spoke in a lower tone. "Of course the substance is correct. As you know, we dropped anchor in the harbour here three days ago, straight from Ireland, sir. We had the most momentous news for Sean MacMahon. Old friends we were. Knew each other as boys, we did. Well, as I said, I had the news of his inheritance, so I hurried out to MacMahons. And was he glad to see us? Why, it was eat and drink and be merry. And Lorna, why she was overjoyed to see me. Betrothed we were . . ."

"Never," she shouted.

Alison squeezed her tight.

"Betrothed," Butler insisted. "From her birth, almost. Because we were friends, Sean and I. So there we were, enjoying our meal, toasting the new Earl, when there was this whoop and next moment the Susquehannocks burst in. I thought our last moment had come. And Sean shouted, 'Take the girl, Jamie, save my daughter. She's your affianced wife.' Well, it was cut and thrust and fight and die, but we fought clear, me and my lads, and I had Lorna with me. We got her to safety, as Sean had told us, and then went back, but by then, why, the house was already burning and the Indians were whooping and we could see there was no one left alive. So maybe you'll say I should have ridden in here and given the alarm, and I meant to do that. But Lorna had to be thought of first. Distraught, she was, at seeing her folks killed. And I could think of nothing but that here was this poor girl, suddenly an orphan, crying her heart out, with not a relative left in the world. Well, I've a priest on board my ship. I figured the best thing was to make sure she had a legal protector. So we were married last night. I was going to come ashore this morning, and alert the settlement. I was just lowering my boat to do so, but I made the mistake of telling Lorna what I was doing. The word 'Indian' seemed to snap her brain. She went wild, ran out of the cabin, threw herself over the side. And that's the truth, as God is my witness."

They stared at him, Lorna aghast at the sheer effrontery of the man.

"A sad tale," Lord Calvert said mildly. "You've been to the Americas before, Captain Butler?"

"Not I, my lord. Ireland is my home."

"Ah. And Sean MacMahon has never left Maryland, to my certain knowledge. Friends as boys, you say."

Colour flared in Butler's cheeks as he realised how he had been trapped.

"Wretch," Alison said. "You'll hang."

"On what evidence?"

"Evidence, sir?" Calvert demanded. "Why, Miss MacMahon's tale will be sufficient evidence. Brownsea, you'll take this man into custody. And send riders out to MacMahons to discover what happened there. Lorna, my dear child . . ."

"Lorna Butler," Butler declared. "My wife. There's no evidence. She cannot testify."

"Your wife, sir? You cannot prove that."

"Can I not?" Butler growled. "There's a priest on board my ship will swear to it. There's my crew, who were witnesses."

"Your men, sir."

"There's Lorna." Butler pointed. "She wears my ring."

Lorna looked at her hand in dismay; she had forgotten the ring.

"Say it wasn't, girl. Say it wasn't," Alison begged.

"Say the truth, Lorna," Calvert said.

Lorna dared not look at Lennart. "There . . . there was a ceremony."

"What did I say?" Butler boomed.

"Lorna?" Lennart's voice was stricken.

"But I was forced," she shouted. "I refused to say yes, and they said it for me."

"Lies," Butler declared. "We are married. The priest will say so. You'll not find a priest lying." He grinned at them. "And it has been consummated. She is my wife."

"Lennart," she begged, looking at him for the first time. "I was forced. There too. For God's sake, help me."

He hesitated, glancing at his superior, then he pulled off his glove and slashed it across Butler's face.

"Why, you . . ." Butler started forward, was checked by Mr. Brownsea.

"I have challenged you, sir," Lennart said. "You may name time, place, and weapons, but let it be soon."

"Soon?" Butler roared. "Why, you young whipper-snapper, I'll carve your liver, by God I will."

"Duelling is forbidden," Calvert snapped.

"Geoffrey," Alison said, still speaking quietly. "The marriage was consummated."

He hesitated, flushing.

His wife lowered her head. "You are sure of what you do, Lorna?" she whispered. "Sure? He may kill your young man."

Lorna gazed at Lennart. "I cannot permit you," she said.

He smiled at her. "You cannot stop me, now, providing his lordship will but give his permission."

Calvert chewed his lip, glanced from one to the other. He could see the dilemma as well as any. To rid Lorna of her husband legally would take a term at law, and if she was indeed heiress to the earldom of Morne it would be a matter for the House of Lords in London.

Months, perhaps years of litigation, during which time Butler would go free, as she was the only witness against him, and would indeed retain his conjugal rights as a husband.

"He says she is demented," he said weakly.

"And I say she is as sane as myself," Alison declared.

"Yet . . . she could be too shocked for truth."

"Brownsea," Lady Calvert snapped. "Fetch Father Derwent."

The officer hurried off, returned in seconds, accompanied by the priest; indeed by now there was a considerable crowd outside Government House.

"You've a Bible, Father?" Alison asked.

"That will not be necessary, my lady." Father Derwent took Lorna's hands. "You've something to swear, child?"

Lorna hesitated.

"Say it," Father Derwent commanded. "You have naught to fear, providing 'tis the truth."

Lorna felt his fingers tight on hers, giving strength. She gazed at Lennart for a moment, then turned to look at Butler. "I swear," she said. "By Almighty God, that James Butler did murder my parents and my brothers and Mr. and Mrs. Blamey, that he did abduct me to his ship in the harbour and there forced me to undergo a mock ceremony of marriage, and that afterward he did take possession of my body, illegally and violently. I swear it, so help me God."

The room was so quiet they might all have been turned to stone.

"She is my wife," Butler said. "She can swear what she likes. She can say nothing against me, in law."

Calvert gazed at him, then at his wife, and then at Lorna. "Arrest that man, Mr. Brownsea."

"On what charge?" Butler demanded.

"There is no charge as yet. I have sent men to discover what happened at MacMahons. You are under arrest until their return. And, Mr. Brownsea, have the cannon trained on his vessel, and fire into it should it attempt to put to sea."

"Tyranny," Butler shouted. "That is not legal. I demand a writ of habeas corpus."

"Twenty-four hours, Mr. Butler. Habeas corpus requires twenty-four hours. My people will have returned in six."

"And what of my challenge, sir?" Lennart Munro asked.

"Duelling is forbidden, sir, by the laws of England."

"And supposing there is no proof, my lord?" Colonel Stahl inquired. "From that man's confidence I doubt there will be. You cannot let him escape, and with this poor girl."

"You cannot," Alison said.

"I will do my duty," Calvert said enigmatically. "Take Captain Butler out, Mr. Brownsea."

Alison Calvert gave Lorna a hot bath, and while she was soaking managed to discover some clothes which would fit her. She considered it necessary to keep active, and to keep Lorna active as well.

She chattered about nothing. Lorna answered in monosyllables. Because she could not prevent thought, could not prevent memory, overtaking her with frightful clarity. She still had not slept, and the nervous energy which had carried her over the side of the brigantine had abated but not died.

"Your wrists," Alison cried, noticing the cuts for the first time. "You poor child. Did you attempt suicide?"

"I was cutting my bonds," Lorna said.

"My God. He kept you tied up? My God."

"I won't be forced to go with him, Aunt Alison?" Lorna asked, putting into words the one thing they both dreaded.

"I . . . no, child. No, I promise you. No matter what happens, you will not be forced."

Lorna sighed and gazed at herself in the mirror. No change. She had thought that on board the ship and been surprised then. Now it seemed even more remarkable. She had bathed and was clean. Her hair was dry. Her bruises were once again concealed beneath clothes. And her face was unmarked, its expression unchanged. Save for a tightness at the lips. Would she ever smile again?

But she had been raped. How many times? She could not remember, exactly. It was odd, how some things were very clear, and others were misty. But she could remember Butler, naked . . . she wanted to shut her eyes and shake her head to drive the memory away. And she could remember him inside her. Oh, God, she had almost felt pleasure then. Would she ever be able to look at another man, would she ever feel pleasure with another man? Or would those memories always hang before her like a curtain?

And after that she could remember dropping through space, into the sea. She had been naked, before the crew of the brigantine, before the crew of the Swedish boat, before Brownsea and his men. Before Lennart. How could she ever face any of them again?

She turned from the mirror, her mouth dropping open, the tears starting to her eyes.

"Lorna," Alison cried, and took her in her arms. "Oh, Lorna, sweetheart. It will be all right. I promise you. It will be all right." Her head jerked at the rap on the door. "Who is it?"

"Geoffrey." He stepped inside. "The men have returned. MacMahons has been burned to the ground."

Lorna's knees gave way, and she sat on the bed.

"The horses were driven off. So were the dogs and cattle."

"Butler did that," Lorna muttered.

"I've no doubt he did. But it is what the Indians would have done." He looked at his wife, his face the picture of dismay. "I've no right to hold him."

"Lorna swore on oath."

"She is his wife."

"I'm not," Lorna shouted. "I can't be."

"Aye, well . . . it is an odd situation, to be sure. But you'll not go with him, Lorna. Not now, anyway. The case will have to go to Court, I have no doubt. Especially if you *are* Countess of Morne. My word, 'tis us should be on our knees to you." He glanced at his wife, cleared his throat. "I'll strike a bargain with the fellow. Oh, yes. We'll release him, but you'll travel to England on separate ships. And we'll let the King decide."

"That Dutchman?" Alison said scornfully.

"It is best," Calvert said.

"Best?" his wife shouted. "Have you no wits, man? Best? Do you think King William will care of the rights or wrongs of a case like this? Morne was a turncoat. 'Tis well known Sean was a good Catholic. Butler claims to have fought with the Orange at the Boyne; Butler was a faithful man, by the Dutchman's rights."

"I would rather die, Uncle Geoffrey," Lorna whispered. "I would rather die."

"Now, now, my dear."

"It will come to that choice," Alison insisted.

Calvert licked his lips, glanced at them, and then,

strangely, at himself in the mirror. Then he turned and left the room, closing the door behind him.

"Aunt Alison," Lorna wailed, clutching her arm.

"Hush, child. All will be well." She smiled. "We have been married these seventeen years. So I will say again, all will be well." She got up, went to the window, stood there, half hidden by the drapes.

"What do you look for?"

"A man."

Lorna was at her side in a moment, and Alison seized her arm to draw her aside. "Stay out of sight."

Because, Lorna realised, the crowd remained, gathered in the square before Government House. And there were not only Marylanders. She made out the buff tunics of the Swedes. Alison's fingers tightened on her arm, as she would have spoken.

The people were beginning to shout. The two women could not see the front door of the house itself, as they were over the porch, but definitely something was happening.

"Ladies," Lord Calvert shouted. "Gentlemen."

The noise slowly subsided.

"This man, Captain James Butler, is free to go," Calvert shouted. "I would have you all understand that. There are no charges made against him." He paused and seemed to be taking breath. "Unless there are some of a private nature."

No doubt he was looking at the Swedish officers, and no doubt it had been arranged, for Lennart stepped forward.

"I have charges, Your Excellency."

"You?" Butler bellowed. He certainly did not lack courage, Lorna realised. "Whippersnapper. We have still an affair to settle."

"Indeed we have, sir," Lennart agreed.

"You spoke of charges," Lord Calvert said.

Lennart extended a gauntleted hand, forefinger pointing. "I charge that man with being a blackguard. I charge him with being a liar. I charge him with being an abductor. I charge him with being a rapist. And, most of all, I charge him with being a murderer."

The crowd was shocked into silence.

"Oh, my God," Lorna whispered.

"Must I stand here and listen to that?" Butler demanded.

Lord Calvert appeared to hesitate. "There can be no duelling, by the laws of Maryland," he pronounced.

"Justice," howled the crowd. "There must be justice."

"But," the Governor shouted, "as I understand it, the colony of Maryland, and therefore the jurisdiction of its laws, ends at the highwater mark." The crowd turned as he pointed, to gaze at the three feet of wet sand separating the still boisterous waves from the line of seaweed pushed up by the tide. "So," Calvert said, "if you gentlemen will wait just a few hours, there will be a fine platform for a settlement of your grievances."

"Wait?" Butler shouted. "That beach is wide enough. And there is all the ocean at the end of it. I'll teach that lad a lesson, by God. Unless he is too frightened to meet me."

"Frightened to meet you, sir?" Lennart inquired. "Why, sir, 'tis all I desire."

"Then let us to it," Butler bawled.

"Hooray," shouted the crowd. "To the beach." They flooded across the road and over the low wall separating them from the sand, carrying the would-be contestants with them.

"No," Lorna shouted. "Lennart will be killed. He

can be no match for a man like Butler." She pulled at the sash.

Alison caught her arm. "You will not stop them now, Lorna. And it is your only chance."

She glanced at the older woman. "And he is a Lutheran, so you care naught what happens to him."

"Not true, Lorna." But Alison's eyes were gleaming. She had been bred at the Court of Charles II and grown to womanhood where bear baiting and cock fighting, disembowelling for treason and public whippings were the principal entertainments. She was a dear, sweet woman, Lorna knew; but at this moment she was recapturing her youth. "Besides," she said, "it will be splendid. A duel, over you. My God. It is like a joust, in the Middle Ages." She crossed herself.

Lorna pressed against the glass. But it was, in any event, too late. The two men were stripped to their shirts, and already the blades gleamed in the evening light. The next wave came rippling up the beach to surround their ankles with swirling water, and as if it had been a signal Butler gave a great shout and a lunge, and when Lennart jumped backwards, made a sweep, left and right, scything the air.

"Oh, my God," Lorna whispered and closed her eyes. Alison clapped her hands with delight, and she could bear to look again. Lennart had parried and thrust in turn, and now the swords were clashing and slithering all the way up to the hafts, so that the two men stared at each other from a distance of not more than inches and the crowd cheered. Then Butler thrust his antagonist away, with such force that the young Scot stumbled and fell to one knee and then on his side as a wave broke against his back.

"Hold," Lord Calvert shouted. "I declare you the victor."

"Bah," Butler shouted. "You have admitted you have no jurisdiction here." He thrust down, and Lennart rolled farther into the water, disappearing completely, to emerge a moment later, spluttering and gasping. Butler gave another shout and turned, to meet Lennart's blade in another clash, and to be forced back in turn, a look of alarm crossing his face as he found the arm opposed to his stronger than he suspected. He reached dry sand, gave another shout, and lunged. Lennart hardly seemed to move, and Lorna gave a moan. But this time she kept her eyes open. Butler had thrust clear beyond his enemy, and kept on going, falling to his knees in the shallow water. Lennart stepped aside, his hands empty. His blade protruded from Butler's back, having passed right through the body. And the foaming white sea was turning pink.

Lorna's knees gave way and she sank to the ground. And yet could still hear.

"That man is guilty of murder," Calvert was saying. "He'll not set foot in Maryland again, Colonel, or there will be a warrant."

"We sail the day after tomorrow, Your Excellency," Stahl said. "Lieutenant Munro will remain on board until then."

Lorna raised her head. "He's gone," she said. "He cannot have gone, without saying good-bye."

" 'Tis best," Alison said. "And he kissed his sword, at this window, before leaving."

Lorna looked down at her left hand. She had not been able to make herself touch it before. Now she drew off her ring and dropped it on the table.

The sound of the earth landing on the coffins echoed in the afternoon air. Lorna sighed. There were no tears. She did not suppose there were any tears left.

She raised her head, looked past the circle of people and down the slope at the blackened timbers of the farmhouse, and beyond, at the less damaged outbuildings. Everything she possessed, everything she had known, was hidden under that rubble. It would be rebuilt. And it would be avenged. Butler was already dead, and the other members of his party would surely hang; she had spent the morning writing out her deposition and placing it under seal in the Governor's House.

But would she ever be happy here again, where she had been happy all of her life up to two days ago? Would she ever be happy anywhere, ever again? Butler was dead. But with every day the memory of him came back with more clarity, the gleam of his teeth, the caress of his fingers, the tickle of his beard on her thighs, the sudden thrust which had hurt and sent her spirit soaring at the same time. She wondered, had he managed to get away from St. Mary's, if he would not perhaps have succeeded in turning her hate into at the least a physical necessity for his love, his manhood.

And shuddered. Was she, then, so frail a creature? What of the girl who had looked at the Swedish soldiers and said simply, "I am Lorna MacMahon."

Alison Calvert touched her arm, and she turned. The men and women, wearing black coats and black gowns and black cloth covering their bonnets, stepped aside to let her through. She could not bear to look at any of them.

"Lorna. Miss MacMahon. My lady." Patrick Burke twisted his hat in his hands.

How long ago he seemed. How long ago was the girl with whom he had danced.

"Away with you, lad," Calvert muttered. "This is not the time."

"I but wanted her to know . . ."

"She knows and is grateful," Alison said, and urged her onward.

The Governor's carriage waited on the track by the white paling where she had first met Butler. Calvert walked at one elbow, Alison at the other. They were proving the true friends of her parents she had always known them to be. But she realised they were also paying her the deference due to a possible countess. There was a remarkable thought. A countess, living in a tiny colonial settlement like Maryland.

They passed the garden fence, and a streak of white shot out, mewing. "Hold there," Calvert shouted in alarm.

"Snowdrop," Lorna shrieked in delight, and the cat leapt from the ground, straight into her arms. Snowdrop's fur was stained with smoke and matted with ash; she must have been prowling around the ruins the moment it had cooled sufficiently, looking for food, looking for her mistress. Now she gave a rusty purr, and buried her head in the crook of Lorna's elbow.

"She must be starving," Lorna said. "Oh, Snowdrop." The tears began again, not loudly or painfully, just dribbling down her cheeks.

"We'll see to its food." Alison held the door of the carriage, Calvert gave her a hand up, and she sank into the cushioned seat, Snowdrop nestling on her lap.

Alison sat beside her, Calvert sat opposite. The coachman flicked his whip, and the equipage moved over the rough track, lurching in the ruts, each jar causing the inmates to jerk upright.

Calvert peered out of the window. "Sad," he said. "Sad. But it will rise again."

"I had already determined that," Lorna said. "With your help, my lord."

"My help? Why, it will be a pleasure. But . . ." He glanced at his wife, frowning.

"No one could have expected you to give any thought to the future, Lorna," Alison said gently, "during these past two days. Yet it must be done."

"I . . ." Lorna bit her lip. "Rebuilding MacMahons is all the future I wish to consider at this moment."

"Of course, my dear. And it shall be done. His lordship has promised that. But you could not live there. The land is yours, the property is yours, but you are not yet sixteen years of age."

"Besides," said her husband, gaining confidence now that he saw he could count on his wife. "There are more important things afoot, eh? Your inheritance."

"Oh, bah, my lord. If you will forgive me. Was that not all merely part of Butler's masquerade?"

"On the contrary, my dear. It must have been the reason *behind* Butler's masquerade. Why go to the expense of chartering a vessel, the dangers of a long sea voyage, the even more serious dangers of carrying out a dastardly assault upon your family, if he did not know the rewards would exceed the risk? Oh, no, no, I think there can be no doubt about it. On the other hand . . ." Calvert leaned forward. "Who knows what garbled tales will be making their way back across the Atlantic with the next ship, and not merely from St. Mary's? This story will very soon reach Jamestown. The MacMahons murdered. The earldom and the inheritance gone abegging."

"But I don't want the inheritance," Lorna explained. "I don't want to be a countess. I want to be Lorna MacMahon."

Calvert rocked back in his seat in horror. "Not *want* to be a countess?"

"I'd have no idea how to set about it."

"They will teach you." He gazed at his wife in despair.

"Lorna." Alison stroked Snowdrop's head. "You cannot refuse an inheritance, when it consists of rank as well as property. You have a duty, to your family, to your tenants, of whom there must be thousands, to your country, to yourself, and most of all, to your unborn descendants."

"But I am not going to have any descendants," Lorna cried. "How can I, now?"

"My dear child, you are but fifteen years of age."

"And I've been raped," she said fiercely. "Not just once. Who'd want to marry me?"

"Who? Why, the whole world," Alison declared. "You are a lovely girl, and a wealthy one, and an important one. . . ."

"And anyway," Calvert said, "raped? What stuff and nonsense. You are a widow. Your name is Lorna Butler."

"It was no marriage."

"I think it should be considered a marriage," Calvert said. "I have questioned Butler's accomplices; he has no near relatives who could complicate matters for you. And as you say, if you were not married, then you were . . . ah, raped. But if you *were* married, now, then you are a most attractive and desirable widow. Why, suitors will come flocking to your door, especially when there is an earldom attached. But there is the point, Lorna. We'll not have Dutch William bestowing Morne upon some upstart favourite because it has been let go by default, or even by false rumour. No, no, I have arranged a ship, and I have arranged a woman, a very good woman, the widow Mountfield, you know her, Lorna, to travel with you, and I have prepared letters for the Chancellor and, indeed, for His Majesty himself, or rather, Her Majesty, for I had the privilege of knowing her when she was a girl, and I am sure she will read me with interest. You must take the news of your catastrophe yourself, my dear, and be sure that you obtain your inheritance. There. It is all settled."

He leaned back with the air of a man who has done well, while Lorna continued to gaze at him in consternation.

"Of course MacMahons here will still be yours," Alison said. "We shall find some good tenants for it, who will farm it and clear the land and rebuild the house. Who knows, one day in the future you may be able to revisit it, us. We should adore that."

Lorna sighed. But she knew she would have to go. On the other hand . . . "I am sure you know best, my lord, my lady," she said. "But surely there is no need to arrange a vessel especially for me. Are not the Swedish gentlemen returning to Europe tomorrow? I am sure they will find room for Mistress Mountfield as well."

"Good heavens," Alison said. "But you are a wayward child. Travel with the Lutherans?"

"And with a man who may even suppose he has some claim upon your affection?" Calvert inquired.

"And has he not, my lord? He risked his life to save my honour. My life, indeed."

"Bah, he is a soldier. Anyway, the thing is quite unthinkable. He is no more *than* a soldier, and a foreigner, and a Lutheran to boot. You are, or soon will be, I have no doubt, Countess of Morne, peeress of England. You must raise your sights, my dear. Not that you will have trouble over that, once you regain England."

*Regain* England? Lorna wanted to shout, I have never been to England. I do not wish to go now.

Alison Calvert smiled and gave her fingers a gentle squeeze. "But you may take Snowdrop," she said.

"Ah, the Court," said Alice Mountfield loudly. "The glory of it, my dear. Oh, dear . . ." She gave a high-pitched giggle. "I should say, Your Grace."

"No, no," Alison Calvert corrected. "My lady, or Countess."

"I am sure Lorna will do, Mistress Mountfield," Lorna said. "As we are to be shipmates."

"Oh, my dear, you are so sweet," cried Mistress Mountfield. "My poor dear husband, may God rest his soul, always said you were the sweetest child in all the world. Why, it will be a pleasure, my dear Lorna, and to deliver you to Court. . . ."

"Will be most exciting, for both of us. Will you excuse me, Aunt Alison?" Lorna pushed back her chair and stood up. "I am very tired, my lord."

"Of course, Lorna, of course," Lord Calvert said. "A good night's sleep will do wonders for you."

Father Derwent also got up, walked with her to the door. "Will you sleep, my child?"

"I think so, Father. I slept last night."

He peered at her. "And no dreams?"

"No daydreams, at any rate."

"Ah." He did not return her smile. "But perhaps now is the time to put your daydreams to a proper use, my dear. Look to the future, Lorna. Only the future. Promise me."

"Then would I have to be a monster, or a half wit."

"Lorna . . ." he sighed. "A night's rest. There is what you need. I will come to see you tomorrow."

"To hear my confession, Father? To hear how I prayed for a man to die. To hear my thoughts about God?"

"Lorna . . ." He was clearly perplexed, having never known her in such a mood. But then, she had never known herself in such a mood. "You'll not rail against God."

"Should I not?"

"He moves in a mysterious way, His . . ."

"You'll not quote the Bible to me, Father. As you say, His ways are mysterious. Incomprehensible. You'll not expect me to pray to something incomprehensible."

"You need faith, Lorna. Only faith. Whatever was done was for the best."

"The best?" she shouted, her anger surging. "The best, that Mama and Papa and my brothers should be killed, my home destroyed, me subjected to every imaginable indignity?"

"Aye, well, 'tis a difficult matter, I know . . . no doubt your people were too good. Aye, maybe that was it."

"And I am a criminal?"

"Lorna . . ." Father Derwent's face brightened. "You prayed to Him, Lorna, and your prayer was answered. You escaped Butler."

"*I* escaped Butler," she said. "There was no help. Look at my wrists, Father, and see how I managed it."

"You are indeed distraught. We'll talk tomorrow."

"Aye," she said. "We'll talk tomorrow, Father."

She climbed the stairs slowly, holding the skirt of her borrowed gown free of her shoes. It was black, with a white apron, hastily tucked in at the waist and shoulder to make a better fit. And it was old. Not only did it smell of the cupboard in which it had lain the past ten years, but the style was that of the Commonwealth, with full sleeves and a high neck; she wondered they had not given her a Puritan's cap to go with it.

It symbolised the past. Which was so hateful. Even the happiness she had known was hateful, because of the way it had ended. Did she mean what she had said to Father Derwent? She did not know. But she felt no remorse, no fear at having uttered those blasphemous words. If she must be alone, then would she be alone, in every way. She dismissed Lady Calvert's maid, locked her bedroom door, undressed, overseen by Snowdrop, curled in a ball on her pillow. The maid had laid out a nightdress, again a very plain, white garment, but she ignored it.

She stood before the mirror. Lorna Butler was her name. Lord Calvert had decided that was best, and there the matter rested. Lorna Butler, until she could change it for a better. But that could not be done for months, perhaps years, perhaps never. So she must become used to Lorna Butler. Did that hopeless old fool not realise the memories that name must bring back, day in and day out?

She lay down, on top of the coverlet. The fire still blazed in the grate, and the room was warm. And was immediately asleep. To awake suddenly, in a room smelling of burnt wax, for the candle had dwindled and then extinguished itself; the fire was low, the room was beginning to chill, and the house was utterly quiet.

Then what had awakened her? The chill? No doubt. She rose to her knees, pulled back the coverlet, sending Snowdrop scurrying down to the foot of the bed, and heard a gentle tap on her windowpane, which brought her heart leaping into her mouth and then begin a furious pounding which had blood flooding every part of her body.

She got out of bed, remembered she was naked, hastily seized the undressing robe Alison Calvert had lent her; it was far too small and came only to her calves, while it would not fasten properly in front. But the room was dark.

She stood at the window, attempted to peer through, and saw the man on the balcony. One of Butler's men, come to murder her? But they were all in gaol. Gently she eased the casement. "Who is it?" She was surprised at the evenness of her voice.

"Lennart Munro."

"Oh, my God," she said. "They will charge you with murder."

"If they catch me, Lorna. We sail in the morning. I could not leave without saying good-bye."

She pushed the casement the whole way, and he held her hand. For a moment she hesitated, but her mind was already made up, as it had a habit of doing before she truly understood it. She stepped back, still holding his arm, and he came into the room. He had removed his boots and his weapons to climb up the wall, and wore only shirt and breeches.

"Close the window," she whispered.

He released her to obey, while she waited, in the centre of the room. She trembled, but had no doubts now. Save that he might not, after all, be able to obliterate memory.

He stood in front of the window waiting, uncertain what to do, what she wanted of him, now that he was actually in her presence. "You are not angry?" he whispered.

She stretched out her hand, touched his face. "You saved my life," she said.

"To think of you, belonging to that scoundrel. . . ."

"I did belong to him, Lennart," she said.

"I . . ." He took a step forward, and so did she. His hands caught hers, and then hers went around his neck. His slid on to her waist, checked in dismay at discovering flesh where he had pushed away the robe. But her mouth was on his, now. And now she knew what a man wanted. And what a woman wanted, too. She licked his lips, and as they parted, his teeth, and then his tongue, and his arms closed on her shoulders to hug her against him. And then to push her away. "Lorna, I am a scoundrel."

"No," she said. "Had you *not* come, then would you have been a scoundrel."

"You are bereaved, you are . . ."

"Tormented," she said. "By memory. By fear. I belonged to Butler, Lennart. Do you not like me a little?"

"I love you, Lorna. Oh, God, how I love you." His hands were on her shoulders again. "I loved you the moment I saw you. I have dreamed of nothing but you, ever since."

"Then make me yours, Lennart. Please. Do you not understand, I am Butler's, now."

He hesitated. "I cannot," he whispered. "It would be criminal."

"Criminal not to." She slipped her hand down his chest, found the buckle of his belt, released it, and thrust her hands inside.

"Lorna . . ."

"I must," she said fiercely. "I must. God, I cannot see only Butler for the rest of my life. I must."

She stroked and felt him rise beneath her fingers, and was vaguely surprised to discover that he had not been fully aroused merely by being near her.

"Lorna," he whispered. "Oh, Lorna . . ." He thrust the robe aside, found her flesh, touched her ribs and then came up, slowly, to lift her breasts from underneath. She wanted to shout for joy. Butler had not done that. This was different. This was a special memory, between him and her. Then he had slipped from her fingers, for a moment, as he completed his undressing, while she in turn threw the robe on the floor, lay down, and felt his face on her thigh. Instinctively her knees started to come up, and then relaxed again. Lennart wore no beard, and these were his lips only caressing her flesh. And quickly moving upwards, almost shyly. Then his head was between her breasts, and she was hugging him, because these too were new experiences, memories to be shared, only with Lennart. Then must she also create a memory, unique to them. She moved her legs, spreading them to allow him between, and then wrapping them around his thighs to hold him close from groin to neck, as his mouth came up to regain hers.

"Now," she whispered. "Please, now, Lennart." *And, please,* she thought, *let it be good.*

There was no pain. There was no violent thrust. Instead there was a slow, caressing entry, a spreading of desire away and away and away, like waves receding from a stone thrown into a pool of still water. She felt a lightness in her loins, in her womb, combined with a building excitement, a growing feeling of flying up and up and up, a flight which would culminate in a convulsion of pleasure, she had no doubt at that.

But his movements were quickening, and then he was still. No, she wanted to shout. Don't stop. Not now, please don't stop.

He kissed her ear, her cheek, her forehead, her eyes. He found her mouth again, but this was a soft kiss. The passion was gone. He frowned at her, from a distance of inches. "Lorna? Lorna, my love?"

She realised her fingers were still tight on his shoulders, her nails eating into his flesh. It required a conscious act of will to make them relax, make her body relax, make her legs relax. "Lorna? Did I hurt you?"

"No," she said. "No, you did not hurt me, dearest."

She returned his kiss gently. Because if he had come so close, then the next time . . . but so close to what? She did not know.

"I still feel I have committed a crime." He rolled off her, lay beside her, his head on her arm.

"You have saved my reason," she said.

"Lorna . . ." He raised himself on his elbow. His face was a blur in the semidarkness.

She put her finger on his lips. "We are separated by nationality, by religion, and soon by distance. That is nonsense, Lennart. You are a Scot, I am Irish. Besides, why should one nationality not marry another? Religion is more difficult, perhaps. Father Derwent has explained it to me. But yet will it succeed, if we wish it to."

"And distance?" he asked.

"Can be overcome. It seems I must go to England. But it will bring me closer to you. There I will claim my inheritance. They say I will be the wealthiest woman in the kingdom. Who then will say me nay?"

"You would marry a soldier?"

"Can you not cease to be a soldier? And become an earl instead?"

"What dizzy heights we climb," he said, smiling.

"If you love me, it were no more than a gentle slope."

"And I love you, Lorna. Oh, how I love you. I will obtain a release from my allegiance. I swear it. King Charles is a hearty fellow, much given to understanding love. He is in and out of it continuously himself. But I must return to Sweden, Lorna, both for that purpose, and to acquaint my parents with my decision."

"It will be but a short separation," she said. "I will be busy enough, by all accounts, making good my claim. A few months, and then . . ."

"Then I will come to you, I swear it."

She rolled over to lie on top of him, shook her head

to stroke her hair to and fro across his face. "If not, I will come to you. I swear that. And until then, I swear that no man shall touch my lips. It shall be our secret, for be sure that should my so-called friends learn of it, they would do their best to separate us. But we are betrothed, as of this moment."

He kissed her mouth. "As of this moment. And now, my dearest, dearest love . . ."

"I feel a stirring beneath me," she said. "You cannot be in such haste to regain your ship, Lennart. It is several hours yet to dawn."

But no doubt his passion had indeed been spent. Or perhaps the enormity of the pledge they had agreed had clouded his desire. As he had taken her again, she loved to remember it, moment by moment, recall every thrust, every moan of passion, every sigh of exhaustion. But it had not regained the fervour of their first embrace. So then, she must possess her soul in patience, for only a short time, surely. Unless she dared . . . for Father Derwent's words spoken in that nebulous, unbelievable, before-Butler world, came back to her, time and again. She had an idea of what he had meant, now, was even determined to risk an exploration, when she had at once the time, and the courage, and the solitude. Certainly it was not a practical proposition on board the *Centaur*. The ship was not very large, and the weather was unfailingly bad. And although they had left St. Mary's two weeks after the Swedes, she had hoped, at the beginning, that the two ships might somehow sight each other. Surely, for lovers, all things were possible.

But as the winds and the seas had buffeted them, day after day, it had become not only impossible, but undesirable. She had never vomited in her life before.

Now she spent a week in her narrow bunk, to the amazement of Snowdrop, who seemed not the slightest bit upset by the heaving deck and the howling elements. Her only relief was that Alice Mountfield, in the other bunk, was equally distressed.

But that was the least of her worries. There seemed even less privacy on board this vessel than there had been on board Butler's brigantine, and now she was overanxious to achieve that solitude she had always valued. She was terrified to think what would happen when her period was due, but for the first time she missed it—a fact she put down to the unnatural movement to which she was constantly subjected.

And having survived that possible misery, she immediately began to feel better, although the weather remained atrocious. But now she could venture on deck, wrapped up in the cloak Alison Calvert had given her, and hang on to the shrouds to watch the tumbling whitecaps surging by, to feel the occasional rattle of spray slapping her face.

"Ah, 'tis all a matter of the legs," Captain Crowther told her. "Sea legs, there is what a lass needs. I beg your pardon, my lady. I should have said, a lady."

"Please, think nothing of it, Captain." He had, no doubt, been told of her inheritance; her passage money had been laid at the charge of her estate, whenever she achieved it. "How empty the ocean looks. Do we ever sight another vessel?"

"God forbid, my lady. Other ships are as like as not to be either French privateers or common pirates."

"Up here?"

"Ah, well, those scum like to lurk around the Florida passage and rush out on lonely merchantmen. They've no stomach for the North Atlantic. But this wind now, it does no good to your ladyship's complexion."

Yet she preferred to remain on deck as much as possible. Below there was only Alice, who refused to leave her berth, and declared that if she had truly remembered what life at sea was like, she would never have come. But apart from Alice, there was that temptation, when she was below and part undressed—she had not actually removed all of her clothes since leaving St. Mary's, and stank like a fisherwoman. The deck was safest. She even took to bringing Snowdrop up with her, much to the cat's displeasure; she enjoyed the noisome recesses of the cabin, and would find her way through the galley and into the hold, for down there was an army of the largest rats Lorna had ever seen. At the beginning of the voyage one had even ventured into her cabin, to bring her upright with a gasp of horror. But the beast had been no match for Snowdrop, who had snapped its neck in seconds, and who had then investigated the hold with increasing pleasure and increasing success, judging by the picked carcasses which kept appearing in the great cabin. But the cabin itself, with its endless army of cockroaches, was sufficiently attractive.

Lorna supposed Alice was in many ways right, and this was the longest and most tiresome penance any human being could inflict upon her. The dirt and the smell and the discomfort and the increasingly inedible food, as the voyage dragged on, made her feel quite honest again, and she had been troubled by her very brief and inaccurate confession to Father Derwent before she had left. But even he could not have prescribed this. She dreamed of being on the same ship as Lennart, not a difficult matter, as surely, wherever he was, he was holding on to a similar shroud, feeling the same spray slap his face, the same wind tug at his hair. The deck he was standing on would have the same movement, his stomach would be doing the same gyrations. But why, she wondered in sudden alarm, was her stomach doing gyrations now, when she had, according to Captain Crowther, her sea legs?

He approached her, clutching his sextant, having just taken his noon sight. "Seven weeks," he said. " 'Tis the longest voyage I have ever made, out of sight of land, and there's a fact. You'll think me incompetent, my lady."

"I do not think you in the least incompetent, Captain," she protested, but could not stop herself frowning at the sudden bile which rose into her throat. "If you could but promise me we shall soon be there."

"Ah, there is the good news," he said. "I will have to work it out exactly, but I would say that Ireland is but seventy miles away." He waved at the bow. "We shall see it at sunup tomorrow, and England the day after, I wager. And I'll be thankful for that. Do you know we're down to our last half-dozen bottles? And not a cheese left after dinner."

"Cheese," she groaned. She had cut mould off hers last night. She dropped Snowdrop to the deck, turned to the rail, and vomited.

"My lady," the captain shouted in alarm.

"I had thought to have done with it," she moaned.

"And so you were," he said. "You are ill. To bed, my lady, to bed." He put his arm round her shoulders, escorted her down the companion ladder, sat her on the bunk.

"Whatever is the matter?" Alice inquired.

"Snowdrop," Lorna gasped. "Fetch her down, Captain, before she is washed overboard."

"I'll see to it." The captain straightened. "The poor lady is ill."

"God knows," Alice declared, "if He had intended human beings to go to sea He'd have given them fins."

"Ill," the captain said again. "Not seasick."

He closed the door, and Alice crossed the cabin to sit beside Lorna.

"Ill? Are you truly ill, Lorna?"

Lorna shook her head. The dreadful giddiness was already passing. "It was just nausea. He would talk of his cheese."

"Nausea?" Alice flushed, her entire face flaming. "Lorna . . . I'd not known how to mention it before, but . . . are you not a woman grown?"

"Of course I am."

"Yet, never on this voyage have you passed blood."

"Neither have you."

"Ah, bah, I am past it, child. But you . . . seven weeks, and not a period?"

"Well . . . the motion, and . . ."

"You were used to the motion, a few days ago. And now, on a sudden, nausea . . ." She pointed. "Lorna, sweetheart, you're pregnant."

# Chapter 4

The major-domo struck the floor with his staff. "Mistress Lorna Butler," he announced. "The heiress of Morne."

The form of address had been decided by Lord Calvert before she left Maryland, and Lorna had doubted its propriety then. Now she wished the floor would open up and allow her to fall through. But it was not only the turning of heads. The whole day had been calculated to dwindle her courage. It had come at the end of a nerve-wracking week, during which she had remained on board the *Centaur,* moored in the pool of London, looking at the metropolis of which she had only previously heard, listening to the sounds and inhaling the smells, gazing at the clouds of black smoke which rose into the December air; she had never realised there were so many houses, so many people in the entire world.

The letters to the Chancellor and to the Queen herself had been sent ashore, but Captain Crowther had deemed it best for Lorna and Alice to remain on board until it was discovered exactly how they were going to be received.

Lorna wondered what he would do were the Queen to reject them. What could he do, save take them back to Maryland again? What could she do? It seemed to her that her entire future was circumscribed by what was happening inside her belly. She was terrified that this news would put Her Majesty against her, and Alice's cheerful cuddle and remark, "But you're a widow, Lorna. You're entitled to be pregnant," only brought her near to tears. She did not want the child to be Butler's. Oh, how she prayed it could be Lennart's. Then would their betrothal be sealed, without fear of interruption.

But as the days had passed she had begun to wonder, along with Captain Crowther, whether she would be staying at all. Until this morning a coach, crested and decorated in gilt, and drawn by four of the finest horses she had ever seen, had come rattling down the road beside the dock, and my lady had arrived, to march up the gangplank and gaze at the ship with an expression of the most incredible contempt, which only increased when she had looked at Lorna.

"Lorna Butler?" she had demanded. "Of Morne."

Lorna had instinctively curtsied before so resplendent a personage, and been rewarded with a brief laugh.

"Up, girl. If you *are* a countess, we share the rank."

Lorna gaped at her. A real, live countess? Certainly she was resplendent enough. Her face was a trifle long, but the features were fine and controlled by that tremendous expression of superiority; her hair was fair and worn to the shoulder, straight on the crown and in the centre, but dressed in ringlets to either side, one or two of which were carefully allowed to hang in front of her shoulder itself, for, most remarkably, she wore no hat, but instead a red velvet hood, tied under the chin with a ribbon bow, which she now threw back to leave her head exposed. Her cloak, which all but brushed the deck, was also red velvet, and her gloves were green kid.

"Indeed," she remarked. "It may well be that you will take precedence, as my lord is but a recent creation. His name is Churchill. You have heard of him?"

Lorna shook her head. "You are the Countess Churchill?"

"I am the Countess of Marlborough. My husband is a soldier of some repute, although possibly not yet in the Americas." Then her expression had softened, into a most winning smile. "But we shall be friends, you and I. You may call me Sarah, and I shall call you Lorna." The smile disappeared as quickly as it had come. "You could at least have dressed."

"But . . . I am dressed, Sarah."

Sarah Churchill frowned at her. "That sack?"

Lorna felt her cheeks burning. " 'Tis all I possess."

"Stab my womb with a dagger," Sarah remarked. "And Her Majesty waiting." She sighed. "We will have to go." She stretched out a gloved finger, to rest under Lorna's chin and turn her head this way and that. "But you are a quite beautiful child. You will cause a sensation, one way or the other. Yes, indeed. It will be best. A combination of beauty and rags, and Morne at the end of it. No one will overlook you, you may be sure. Let us be off."

"Mistress Mountfield . . ."

The Countess turned her most arrogant gaze on the little old woman. "Will remain here, to be sure."

Alice gave a reassuring smile. "I am sure the Countess is right, Lorna," she said. "You are a great lady, now. Perhaps you will think of me, when you have a moment."

"Think of you?" Lorna cried, seizing her hands. "I shall send for you in an hour. I swear it. Keep Snowdrop for me."

Sarah had already walked to the gangway. Lorna freed herself, blew a kiss to the captain, and hurried across the deck; to her surprise, her new friend stepped back to allow her first down the plank, while the coachman, clad in a silver cloth coat which came down to his knees, white stockings, and shoes with enormous gilt buckles, was raising his hat and opening the door for her.

She sat down, gazing through the window at the ship, at Alice and Captain Crowther, standing together on the poop to wave at her, and felt the tears starting.

Sarah sat beside her. "You've courage to cross the ocean in that craft. But then, you must have courage, to have survived your experiences."

Lorna turned her head in surprise.

"Oh, aye," Sarah said. "Her Majesty read the letter to us. Your adventure is the talk of the Court." She smiled and patted Lorna on the knee. "They will all wish to know how your husband forced you. Oh, to compare with their own first time. They all claim it was rape." She gave another of her brief laughs. "Courage? You'll need all of it today."

Which had been sufficiently discouraging. But for the moment Lorna's attention had been taken by the huge Tower Bridge across which the carriage had rumbled, by the walls of the Tower itself, the biggest building she had ever seen—the entire fortress at St. Mary's could have been lost inside one of those turrets—and then by the streets, wide and airy in the beginning, with one or two new buildings of some distinction in architecture, if of a style unlike any Lorna had seen before, but for the most part presenting a picture of burnt-out desolation—" 'Twas here was the fire, so it is being rebuilt, mainly after designs by Wren," Sarah explained —but soon becoming narrow and filthy, with winter rain and winter grit and winter filth clustering the paving stones. And everywhere was the stench of humanity, of their bodies and their coal fires, of their bread and their sausages, of their perfumes and their excreta. Lorna had thought the *Centaur* must be unique in its stench, but she realised with some dismay that it had no more than reflected civilisation, beside which the pure air of MacMahons seemed like another world.

Of the people themselves she had seen little, for the cold air kept the streets empty, and those who were abroad were well wrapped up, although occasionally, when the carriage wheels squirted dirty water over a passerby, the hood of a cloak was thrown back and a round-cheeked, red-faced man or woman bellowed curses after them.

"Do they not see the crest?" she whispered to Sarah, who merely gave her little laugh.

"They'd scarce curse us, otherwise."

The carriage had followed the river, as close as possible, and soon debouched from the houses. In the distance she saw the spires of a huge church—"Westminster Abbey," Sarah told her, smiling at her wonder —but before reaching it they turned away to leave the river behind them, and soon to cross a vast open area, dotted with lakes and shaded by gaunt leafless trees— "Hyde Park," Sarah said—before rumbling through the gates of quite the most remarkable house Lorna had ever seen, only two stories high, but with huge sash windows, and wings extending in every direction, while in the grounds, separated from the park by a fence, there was a variety of deer, seeking what food they could discover, and so tame they did no more than raise their heads to look at the intruders. Red-coated guardsmen stood to attention at every door, with throngs of grooms and servants clustering the carriages which waited around the wide marble steps, horses stamping and breathing steam into the cold air.

But everyone had parted for the Countess of Marlborough's coach, and Lorna's nervousness had begun to build. The coachman had helped them down, Lorna again first, no doubt on instructions from his mistress, and they had mounted the stairs together, while the crowd had gazed at them, and a buzz of comment had risen around them.

Once inside the building, maids had been waiting to assist them out of their cloaks, and Lorna could only gaze at Sarah in a mixture of admiration and dismay. In contrast to her own simple black, her escort wore a dark green satin gown, the skirt split at the waist and pulled back to be secured behind her thighs with enormous red velvet bows, thus leaving a magnificent cream silk underskirt exposed, this in turn held away from her hips by no doubt a considerable number of petticoats. Her sleeves, her hem, and her bodice were decorated with white silk ruffles which were in turn edged with white lace frills; now that she removed her gloves Lorna discovered that her fingers were a mass of rings, while diamond pendants hung from her ears and a diamond from the chain around her neck, but this almost disappeared between her breasts, which were gathered together and then thrust forward until they formed the most striking part of her, while the lace frill did no more than show where the nipples were.

Sarah smiled at her. "Remember, now, courage."

But the sound of the staff striking the floor seemed to take away her power of movement, for now the enormous doors swung inward to reveal a long, high, and magnificently decorated room, from the great drapes on the walls, depicting hunting or battle scenes, to the ceiling, which was painted in a variety of figures apparently representing Venus or some other goddess surrounded by cupids and cherubs, a matching display to the exposed torsos in the room below, for if it seemed rather empty of furniture, it was absolutely full of people, men in long coats like the coachman, but of much richer materials, and much more splendid colours, dark blues and bottle greens and deep reds and maroons, every man with a silk baldric supporting a jewelled sword, every one with cambric or lace ruffles protruding from his sleeves, and every one with the most splendid head of hair drooping down from his hat, curled like a woman's and longer than a woman's, too. Lorna stopped just inside the door to stare at them, and Sarah had to pinch her arm and whisper, "They are wigs, goose. Walk, for God's sake."

The women were but less glowing replicas of Sarah herself; Lorna had never seen such an exposure of feminine flesh. But now she was being propelled forward, while the crowd parted before her, and a fresh host of whispers rose around her.

"Gad," a man said, very close. "What a lovely child."

"And there's money to it, as well," said another.

"But she's wearing a sack," cried a woman.

"A sack," said another loudly. "A sack."

The cry was taken up and was accompanied by a burst of laughter, which was soon further accompanied by a rhythmical clapping of hands. Lorna's knees went again, and she wanted to turn and run, but Sarah's hand remained firm on her elbow. "Ignore them," she whispered. "Let them crush you, and you will not face them again. Treat them as dirt. Say to yourself, dirt, dirt, dirt. You are the MacMahon of Morne. There is not one here with the wealth to purchase your castoffs."

The soft whisper filtered through her whirling brain, gave her strength, kept her moving forward, to safety. Of that she was sure. For at the end of the room the space was less crowded, and there were a series of shallow steps, leading up to a dais on which there were two chairs—and what chairs, upholstered in gold cloth—and here there were seated two women, behind whom stood three more ladies and a solitary gentleman.

"Now kneel," Sarah whispered, and Lorna sank to her knees at the foot of the dais, while behind her the buzz slowly died. She stared at the rich carpet over which she had been walking—she had not noticed it until now—and felt her heart pounding, and waited, while a quiet voice said, "Lorna Butler. Rise, my dear, and come here."

She lifted her head and stood at the same moment, and for the first time properly looked at the seated women. There could be no question that they were sisters; they each possessed long chestnut hair, a full face with a straight nose and wide lips to give a most attractive cast; they each wore a décolletage similar to every other lady present, and their gowns appeared no richer, one in deep blue, and the other in rose madder. And they both were obviously and surprisingly young; certainly neither was more than thirty.

Yet there were differences. The lady on the right, in the blue gown, wore a carcanet of pearls around her neck, and pearl earrings to match, while there was a rope of pearls secured to each shoulder of her gown. She was also a trifle overweight; her chin was beginning to sag. The Princess in the pink wore no jewellery at all, and her weight remained under control, suggesting that she was the younger of the two.

"Your Majesty," Lorna said, to the Princess in blue.

The Queen smiled. "Come here, child. This is my sister, the Princess Anne."

Lorna curtsied. "Your Highness."

"How lovely you are," Anne said dreamily.

"Indeed. And how tragic," Queen Mary agreed. She looked past her at the assembly. "No doubt my friends are unaware that you are in mourning," she said loudly. Silence overtook the room, save for the occasional scuffed shoe.

Queen Mary extended her hands, and Lorna took them. "I have studied Calvert's letter. You are the most tragic, most unfortunate of women. But we shall make you happy. It will be my charge. We shall find a husband for you, who will extinguish the memory of the blackguard who so ill used you."

"Your Majesty . . ." Lorna began, but she was silenced by the Queen suddenly standing up.

"I would have you meet His Majesty," she said, and smiled. "He has too little relief from the affairs of state." Still holding Lorna's hand she walked down the steps, while everyone in the room either bowed or sank into a deep curtsey if they were women. The Queen smiled at them. "They will be jealous of you, my dear. Bear with them. Jealousy is no more than the finest of compliments."

She swept towards the doors, her ladies following behind her, Lorna carried along at the end of her fingers. Her head spun. She was holding hands with a queen. And she was on her way to meet the King.

The procession marched through a succession of corridors, each guarded by the soldiers in red coats and flat black hats, armed with pikes with which they snapped to attention as their Queen passed them, while behind them the hubbub once again rose from the reception room they had just left. Lorna scraped her brain for something to say, some method of expressing her gratitude for the favour being shown to her, but she was quite unable to think of suitable words, and she was left breathless by the speed at which they traveled; her legs in any event were trembling after her long weeks at sea without proper exercise.

They halted before a single door, guarded by two men and a major-domo.

"Announce me," Queen Mary commanded.

"But Your Majesty, His Majesty is . . ."

"Announce me," she said.

The major-domo sighed and opened the door. "Her Majesty the Queen."

There was a hasty scraping of chairs within as men scrambled to their feet with incredulous expressions on their faces, while the ladies virtually pushed Lorna and the Queen into the room as they continued to press forward.

"Madam?" inquired the man at the head of the table, frowning. "What means this intrusion?"

"Kneel, girl," Queen Mary commanded. "I have the honor to present Mistress Lorna Butler, my lord."

Lorna sank to the floor, staring at the King. He was, in fact, a fine figure of a man, dressed as were the other gentlemen present, in a dark coat and a full wig, for nearly all of them wore the ribbon of the garter across their chests, but with much better features, thin and almost pale, where theirs were jowled and bloated. There was intelligence in the dark eyes, strength in the firm mouth and determined chin; but there were also deep grooves of worry and impatience carved into his forehead; the powerful mouth turned down, although she realized this might be mere disapproval of their unceremonious entry—more important was the complete absence of humour anywhere to be found, were it eyes or mouth or manner. And his frown was deepening. "Madam, your levity does you no credit." He gave a brief cough. "This is a council of state."

"Get up, Lorna," Mary commanded. "Lorna Butler," she said again. "The MacMahon girl. The heiress of Morne."

The King looked at Lorna again, and some of his expression lightened. He came round the table, extended his hand, and she hastily kissed it. "We have heard of your misfortune, my dear," he said, his accent strangely reminiscent of the Swedes, although not Lennart's. "And will redress it, to be sure." Another cough. "Your uncle was a loyal supporter, and I have no doubt that your father would have been equally so." His mouth widened, without amusement. "And you are such a pretty girl. I will see you, soon."

Lorna opened her mouth but could utter not a sound.

"She is Countess of Morne," Queen Mary said.

The King frowned at her. "Madam, I have already . . ."

"You have not, sir," Mary said. "You are but considering the matter. Now you have seen the girl . . ."

"She is but a girl," William said.

"Who will soon be a woman. A woman of incomparable beauty, or I am no judge."

"Her manners . . ."

"Are entrancingly simple. We shall soon corrupt them, you may rely on that."

William's frown was back. Clearly he found his wife's tendency to humour irritating.

"So, will you make an end of it?" the Queen asked.

William gazed at her, then at the women behind her, then at his councillors. Then he extended his hand once more. Lorna hesitated, uncertain as to his meaning, and he reached out and took hers, walking with her into the centre of the room, coughed. "Gentlemen, may I present the Countess of Morne. My lady, may I present to you His Royal Highness, George, Prince of Denmark; His Grace, the Duke of Norfolk; my lord, the Earl of Danby; my lord, the Earl of Devonshire; my lord, the Viscount of Falconberg; my lord, the Viscount Lumley; my lord, the Earl of Marlborough; His Grace, the Bishop of London; Mr. Sydney; Sir Henry Capel."

Their faces were a blur, although Lorna did gather that she was being introduced to the husbands of both the Princess Anne and Sarah. Each man in turn kissed her hand and made some remark, but she heard none of them.

"We must have a talk," King William said, and delivered her back to his wife, with another humourless smile.

"I wish to thank Your Majesty," Lorna managed to speak for the first time.

"It is my pleasure, my lady," he said. "To perform an act of justice." He looked at Queen Mary. "Now, you will excuse us, madam; there are affairs of state to be considered."

Mary made a deep bow and escorted Lorna outside, into the midst of the chattering women.

"There was never any doubt, of course," Sarah declared.

"None at all," Princess Anne remarked. "George would have supported us had Willie been awkward."

"And he did not even say, *est-il possible*," Sarah remarked.

Mary gave a shriek of laughter. "It is his habit, you

know, my dear," she explained to Lorna. "Why, when news was brought to poor dear Papa that Willie had landed at Torbay, and he turned to George, all he said was, *est-il possible?* He has been saying that, and nothing more, all his life."

Princess Anne sniffed. "Had you such a husband, at least in bed my *dears*," she glared at Sarah, " you would yourselves say, *est-il possible*? Papa never understood George, there's the trouble. 'Tis why he left him."

Lorna felt the room swaying about her. She had not supposed the two Princesses could possibly refer to their father, who was, after all, still legitimate King of this country, with such carelessness, or that they would refer to their domestic life with such immodesty, or that a mere countess should so bandy words with them.

Queen Mary peered at her. "You are looking quite pale, my dear. It has been exhausting, has it not? My lady Wharton, dismiss that reception. I must see to this poor child. Willie was right of course, your manners are too simple. Not fit for a Court. We must commence your education and with haste. And then there is the matter of a husband. We cannot have a widow hanging about the palace like a black shadow." She seized Lorna's arm, paraded her down the hall. "But firstly, there is your list. You'll write it out immediately. You do write?"

"Oh, yes, Your Majesty. But . . . list?"

"People for whom you wish places, my dear," the Queen said. "Try not to make it too long. The Whigs, having brought us over, think they should each be rewarded with at least the chancellorship, while the Tories, having kicked poor Papa out, are now convinced they have done the wrong thing. Oh, I hope he won't come back again. It would be so *annoying*."

"I . . . I have no one. Oh, save Mistress Mountfield."

"Mistress Mountfield? I don't think I know her."

"She came from Maryland with me, Your Majesty."

"Ah. Where is she now?"

"Well, still on board the ship. With my cat. I must have Snowdrop."

The Queen ceased her perambulation, and the ladies behind her immediately gathered round.

"Your cat? Oh, you must have your cat."

"Oh, yes," they chorused, "you must have your cat."

"And your Mistress Mountfield," Mary said. "Oh, indeed, she shall be your maid."

"My maid?" Lorna asked, flushing. "But . . ."

"Your maid," Sarah said firmly.

"And clothes," the Queen decided, tapping her chin. "Your dressmaker, Sarah. Have her here in an hour. Clothes will do wonders. Some jewellery, too."

"I have very little money, Your Majesty," Lorna said. "And that is borrowed from Lord Calvert. And then there is Captain Crowther, who has not yet been paid. . . ."

"God above," the Queen shouted. "You have but to sign your notes, where you choose. Do not be common, I beg of you, Lorna. I will not have commonness in this palace. Jewellery, Sarah. You will see to it."

"Of course, Your Majesty," Sarah said.

"You had best see to everything. Yes. And discover some suitable apartments. Close to mine. You will be my special care," the Queen said. "Yes, indeed. A face as lovely as yours may well bring a gleam to His Majesty's eye. You will be my constant companion."

"But, Your Majesty . . ."

Mary gave a peal of laughter. "Oh, do not be a goose. Willie has not sought *my* bed for three years. Affairs of state, forsooth. Well, it is not such a lie at that. Women were ever a low source of amusement to him. Meanwhile, your husband. Sarah, you'll make up a list."

"Your Majesty," Lorna begged.

"Do not *worry*," Princess Anne said. "He shall be a handsome fellow, and well disciplined. Oh, he'll cause you no trouble at all."

"But . . ." Lorna inhaled slowly. "I am pregnant."

There was a moment of total silence.

"My God," Princess Anne said, at last.

"By the Butler man?" Sarah inquired.

"I . . ." Lorna felt her cheeks burning. "I do not know."

The Queen was frowning at her. "You're not promiscuous, Lorna, I hope?"

"No, no, Your Majesty," Lorna protested.

"Well, it matters naught," the Queen said. "The child, if a boy, will be the Earl of Morne, of course. But you will possess the income until his majority. You will remain a good prospect for anyone. And we shall have only the best. Only the best." She rested her hand on Lorna's arm. "Always providing you survive, dear child."

*Survive?* Lorna wanted to shout. But the Queen was already hurrying down the corridor, followed by all her ladies saving only the Princess and Sarah. "Survive?" she whispered.

"Well, 'tis a serious matter, childbirth," Anne pointed out. "Mary, now, has never managed a live one. I have lost three already; poor little Willie is my only comfort. Ah, men, at least *we* are still alive. I'll leave you with Sarah, my dear. But do not keep her long."

She departed in the opposite direction to her sister.

Sarah smiled at her charge. "They are Stuarts," she said, as if explaining everything.

"But such . . ."

"Levity?" Sarah made a moue. "I doubt either really feels it. 'Tis all an act, an essential piece of dissembling. Think of it, child; between them they deposed their own father. There's no light matter. People do not understand. When Mary first came home she ran about this palace like a child, laughing and shouting that she was Queen, that her days of trial and tribulation were over. She was taken much to task, and was surprised. 'Would you have me weep?' she asked. As indeed she might. Life has not been good to her."

"But the King . . ."

"Is a serious man, as you have no doubt observed. Nor was he ever a rich one, compared with kings; in Holland he was no more than Statholder. His life, his fortune are dedicated to opposing Roman Catholicism in any form, and Louis of France in particular." Her eyes narrowed as she spoke.

"I am a Catholic," Lorna said.

"I suspected as much. It will not be held against you, providing you go about it in a privy manner, and are enough of a hypocrite to attend the Queen into an Anglican church."

"Never," Lorna declared. "I was also brought up by my mother to believe that King James was cruelly wronged, that while he lives no one else can be more than a usurper."

"Kiss my right toe," Sarah shouted, looking left and right. "For God's sake, girl, keep thoughts like that to yourself." She seized Lorna's wrist, dragged her along the corridor. "We will talk about it. But as you are here, as you have been confirmed in your lands and your title, humour the Court as you find it, for the love of mercy. Certainly for the sake of your child. And your husband, whoever he may be."

Lorna pulled them both to a halt. "Now there is another matter that must be corrected. I cannot marry."

Sarah frowned at her. "Butler *is* dead?"

"Oh, Butler is dead," Lorna said. "But I am betrothed."

Sarah's eyebrows arched, and then she gave one of her short laughs. "You do not seem to need much assistance. But then, with your looks, that can be no surprise. And this gentleman?"

"It is a secret."

Sarah shrugged. "Please yourself, my child. But you will need a friend at Court, you above any I have ever known."

Lorna chewed her lip. "His name is Munro."

"A Scot?"

"In Swedish service."

This time Sarah's laugh was at last genuine, a peal of merriment which echoed from the high ceiling. "Oh, my dear, you are perfect. I imagine you have been sent from heaven especially to entertain me."

Lorna's mouth settled into the firm line only her mirror had ever hitherto seen. "I will marry him, my lady."

"He is the father of your babe?" Sarah still smiled.

Lorna flushed. "Why, I . . ."

"Aha. You are a busy little thing. A Swede. A Catholic? I'll not believe that."

"He is a Lutheran. But . . ."

To her surprise Sarah threw both arms around her shoulders and hugged her. "I love you, I love you, I love you," she said. "You are a delight. I do not know what I have done these ten years. And the Princess will love you too."

"You'll not confide my secret?" Lorna was aghast.

"Of course. You need more than just a friend, Lorna

Butler. You need a host of friends. The Queen will not be crossed. She still enjoys playing the monarch too well. But she may be persuaded. That will be Morley's province, with me at her elbow. Your duty is to do no more than look beautiful, which cannot be difficult, act beautiful, which is something I will teach you how to do, and be beautiful, which merely means to smile and keep your mouth shut."

Indeed the business of being, or rather, becoming a lady was so overwhelming, so interesting, and so exciting, Lorna had very little time to worry about her personal affairs. For the next six months she scarce knew whether she was on her head or her heels, but loved every moment of every day with no more than a slight fear that the activity, the constant round of schoolings, and the late nights would surely bring her to a miscarriage. A fear at which Sarah laughed, as she did at most of the possible problems of life. "My dear child," she said, "activity is the best state for a pregnant woman. For what is the greatest danger that can befall you? That your babe will twist and lie across your belly instead of in a proper position for exit. But constant movement on the part of the mother, now, ensures a proper assumption by the child. Oh, ask anyone."

Lorna preferred to take her word, as she took her word for everything else. For her apartments, which she could not believe at first, as they were only removed by a brief corridor and a private staircase from those of the Queen herself. Here was a bedchamber, which seemed as large as MacMahon's farm, draped in brocade, carpeted from wall to wall with thick rugs, and dominated by a tester which stood eight feet high and scarcely less wide, so that when the drapes had been drawn by an equally bemused Alice Mountfield, Lorna felt that she had entered a room within a room. The bedchamber provided not less of a paradise for Snow-drop, who revelled in the softness of the carpet and the mattress and the coverlets, and was only disappointed at the lack of insects or mice for her to pursue, but Sarah reminded Lorna that it was dead of winter, and there would be more than enough come summer.

But the bedchamber was only a part of her establishment. Opening to the left was a second chamber, in which Alice slept, together with the two maids appointed for her use, and beyond them was a privy, which flushed water at the pulling of a tasselled rope, much to Lorna's delight, for she had never seen such a thing before, while to the right was her sitting room, a splendid place of rose-coloured chintz, which glowed even in the pale December sunshine that drifted through the windows from the park outside. Here there were comfortable chairs, and a settee, and a spinet, which she did not know how to play, but which she was set to learning from an Austrian gentleman, somewhat old and crotchety, and a magnificent painting on the wall, representing Diana at the Hunt. She had never known such elegance, dreamed only of the day she could show it to Lennart.

Her duties, as lady in waiting to the Queen, were minimal. She was required, when Mary decided to retire, to assist in her undressing, but the Queen was generally early to bed. For the rest, she was summoned as and when Mary wished her company, which was usually when she was entertaining privately, or when she wished to play cards. Lorna's days were far more busily spent in learning to walk, with enormous books piled on her head, in learning to speak in what the Court considered correct English—which seemed to consist mainly of adding an oath to every remark—in reading the latest plays and broadsheets and ballads, that she might be able to hold her own in repartee, in learning to dance, in learning to ride sidesaddle, which she had never done—but this was abandoned the moment her belly began to swell—in learning to sit, in learning to stand, in learning to lounge, in learning to use her fan to attract or repel, in learning to use a glimpse into her décolletage to drive a man's mind entirely from whatever subject he had been discussing. She never went abroad, except as part of the Queen's household, and the Queen herself seldom went abroad, save for summer voyages down the Thames in the royal barge to Greenwich, where she was busily completing a palace commenced by her late uncle, King Charles II. Mary attended the play only once a month, professing to find it vulgar, whereas Lorna found it delightfully scandalous, not only on account of the language and because the actresses seemed perfectly prepared to reveal their legs if called upon to do so, but because she enjoyed the sensation of being stared at by several hundred people, especially as she knew that they were staring principally at her. All ladies wore masks to the theatre, but as the Queen traveled in her own coach with her own guards and sat in her own box no one ever had any doubt who she was, or who were the ladies accompanying her, especially the tall young woman with the titian hair.

The Queen's other enjoyment was in watching the gentlemen play at a game called pall mall, which Lorna for her part found utterly boring, as it consisted of trying to knock a wooden ball with a wooden mallet through a loop of rope suspended above the ground. All the young men at Court played at it, to the accompaniment of much laughter and swearing, perspiring and indeed visibly hating each other with as much venom as if they had been antagonists on a field of war.

To her surprise, apart from looking at men on the stage or at play, theirs was an entirely female life. Whatever the whispered suggestions of amours and flirtations in which all the ladies claimed to engage, Queen Mary herself was utterly proper. She waited in vain for her husband to visit her apartments, and the only sign of true emotion Lorna ever saw in her was when there came a knock on the royal door while she was being prepared for bed. Then the Queen would turn pale and flush in a single instant, and send her maids scurrying, and add perfume to the already heavy scent she wore, and all for naught, as it was invariably someone of no account. And then of course the King's responsibilities as Statholder, as well as leader of the coalition opposing Louis XIV, meant that he spent several months in every year in Holland, while the Queen ruled England. It was at these times that Lorna felt closest to her, for was she not in the same position, several hundred miles separated from Lennart, with not a letter received to renew his pledge of love. But in fact she did not wish to see him again for a while, as her belly began to grow, and as she became more nervous. And at least Sarah and the Princess Anne seemed to have done their work well, and Queen Mary no longer spoke of the imperative necessity to find her a husband.

Her principal pleasure, however, rested in the clothes with which she was inundated. Her first week in Kensington Palace seemed to be spent entirely in the hands of the royal dressmakers, and over the next couple of months her wardrobes slowly filled to capacity. There were satin gowns and silk gowns, there were velvet gowns and gold-cloth gowns, all in the richest and most dramatic of hues, intended to contrast the invariably pastel shades of her silk or taffeta petticoats.

She soon possessed twenty pairs of shoes, all with enormously high heels and equally excessively pointed toes, which rendered walking an art to be learned anew, but made once again of splendid materials, brocade or silk or satin, with either ribbon bows or a buckle decorated with a jewel.

For she now owned an enormous jewel box, also filled to capacity. There were earrings—for which she had to submit to having her lobes pierced with a needle —and necklaces, brooches, and finger rings, pendants of diamonds and rubies, sapphires and emeralds. She would stand in front of her mirrors by the hour, just watching them wink at her.

She spent equal hours seated beneath the hands of hairdressers, watching her magnificent straight red-gold hair being curled with hot irons and gigantic combs, to allow it to trickle in ringlets on to her shoulders. In fact the hair style enhanced the loveliness of her face by surrounding it with a suggestion of sophistication. Hats were not in vogue for women, and ladies going abroad secured their coiffures in hoods made of velvet or silk, attached to their pelisses, while indoors they either went bareheaded or wore a small lace cap, so small indeed, and set well back in the crown, that it was invisible from the front and did nothing to add or detract from the hair itself.

She was given a stable of horses and her own carriage. Who paid for all of these luxuries remained a mystery to her. "Why, you do," Sarah had said when she raised the matter, but she found this hard to believe, as she never actually seemed to possess any money. Whatever she wanted, she merely told Alice about it, and it appeared. Alice might be equally confused at this strange way of life, but was determined to enjoy it to the utmost.

Her private life was very little interfered with. The fact of her religion was communicated to Her Majesty, and apparently accepted without opposition. She soon discovered that there was a considerable number of Roman Catholic lords and ladies at Court. Officially anyone of that faith could not hold office, as the country was still agitated by the efforts of James the Second, Queen Mary's father, to restore Roman Catholicism as the state religion. But as long as a Catholic was content to practise his or her faith in private and to attend official functions as a good Anglican when called upon to do so, he was left very much alone in his personal devotions. There was a chapel within the palace, where Lorna attended mass every Sunday morning, very early and before the Queen had risen, and where she would steal away to confession at least two evenings during the week. She was become a perfect hypocrite, she felt, especially as the Queen often, with a childish sense of malice which she certainly possessed, insisted on the Countess of Morne attending her to her own devotions. But she excused herself by reminding herself that all this was necessary, first of all for her unborn child, who would surely inherit the earldom unless she was to lose favour, and secondly, for her eventual marriage with Lennart, to accomplish which she had no doubt she would need all the support she could find. Quite apart from the religious problems which would then be raised.

But if only he would write, or send a message through Baron Falkenhayn, the Swedish ambassador. She dreamed of him constantly, sometimes awoke to feel his member between her hands, where it had rested on that never-to-be-forgotten night, recalled every aspect of his smile, his touch, his voice, the feel of his body on hers.

Remembering Lennart was the easier as *she* had

almost no contact with the male sex at all. The Queen, with her quite remarkable views on morality—for a queen—seldom permitted men into her own apartments, and Lorna was very conscious of how close hers were to the royal bedchamber. Even had she been so inclined, which she was not. She spoke her confession to a priest named Father Simeon, old enough to be her true father, with a delightful habit of staring into space and scarcely seeming to listen, and therefore told him her secret thoughts and secret desires, and received a gentle reminder in each case that it was sinful to love a Lutheran, but certainly less sinful to love him at a great distance than to take men promiscuously to her bed. Father Simeon seemed to have no doubt at all that her girlish passion would pass as soon as her child was born.

When her child was born. Soon after the Christmas festivities were over—and this was the first Christmas the new King and Queen had been able to celebrate jointly in England—the swelling of her belly became too obvious to conceal. And then, strangely, she thought, Queen Mary appeared to lose interest in her. There was no diminution in the remarkable luxury in which she now lived—she was not even required to move from her apartments close to the Queen—but it was indicated to her that Her Majesty would rather she took extreme care of herself, and resume her attendance when she had been safely delivered.

"She is no more than jealous," Sarah declared. "How could she be otherwise? 'Tis said that William has visited her bed but half a dozen times in all their marriage." She lowered her voice to an arch whisper. "What do you expect? Her Majesty has this fatal tendency to laugh, and I have heard she will do so whenever he pushes it in, while as for foreplay, it reduces her to helpless convulsions."

Indeed Lorna had herself noted that the Queen, for all her facile explanations, seemed to have developed the habit of answering every problem with a laugh, which was certainly preferable to tears, but which suggested to everyone not an absolute intimate that she was of a very shallow disposition. As perhaps she was. She and her sister were children of James and Anne Hyde, daughter of the Earl of Clarendon. Clarendon himself was regarded as a very sagacious fellow, who had written copiously if in a most biased fashion concerning the Great Rebellion, as he called it, but no one had ever supposed his daughter to be terribly intelligent and it was rumoured that King James had been blackmailed into marrying her as the price of Clarendon's support of the efforts of his brother Charles II in regaining his throne. If so it had certainly been successful, for here was one of the Earl's granddaughters actually on the throne, co-regnant with Dutch William, and the other certain to succeed, in view of Mary's barrenness.

But if Mary, silly or not, disguised her weaknesses behind a peal of laughter, Anne did almost nothing to diminish her own dullness, and her husband, Prince George of Denmark, took such continual refuge in excessive eating and drinking that most days he was incapable of more constructive action than belching. So then, who would rule England when the present King and Queen died? Why, Sarah Churchill, to be sure, Anne's closest friend. Although this was a thought that clearly taxed the Queen. Lorna was quick enough to perceive that for all the apparent closeness between the royal sisters there was in fact considerable coolness.

"Oh, 'tis a childish matter," Sarah insisted. "Poor

Mistress Morley has no more than thirty thousand a year from the civil list. Why, *you* possess a greater income."

"Do I?" Lorna screamed in delight. "What is it, oh, do tell me, Sarah."

"I have no idea," the Countess of Marlborough said primly. "But it is a large amount, I can tell you that. Anne, poor dear Mrs. Morley, who is after all heiress to the throne of England, feels that she should possess more. She has demanded seventy thousand from the Commons. And would you believe it, Her Majesty is offended, and Dutch William is offended, that she should ask it of the Commons rather than of them. As if they could possibly meet the bill. Poor Mistress Morley was but desiring to save them from any embarrassment."

"Why do you call her Mrs. Morley?"

" 'Tis a game we play. What, would you have me constantly curtseying and mouthing Your Royal Highness when we are alone together? No, no, she is Mrs. Morley, as Prince George is Mr. Morley, as I am Mrs. Freeman, and my lord is Mr. Freeman."

"And how do you stand in the matter of her income, darling Sarah?" Lorna asked, practising the hypocrite as hard as ever.

Sarah gave one of those terrifying laughs of hers. "My *dear*, Mrs. Morley and I have been friends from girlhood. And, besides, she will be our next Queen."

Which seemed to Lorna to be taking rather a long view, as Queen Mary was but thirty years old and extremely healthy. But here was a cause for concern, as she now discovered herself a possible pawn in the intrigue that filled the Court. As the Queen had no use for her until she was delivered, she was entirely in the hands of the Princess and her friend. And to her dismay they appeared in her boudoir, one morning in the summer of 1691, accompanied by a man to whom she took an instant dislike, because he was a tall lean fellow whose eyes could not keep still, but roamed over her and her furniture and her drapes and her pictures, but most of all over her belly, time and again.

"Your time is near, dear Mrs. Butler," Anne declared.

"This is Monsieur Chamberlen," Sarah explained.

"My pleasure, sir," Lorna said in her most haughty tone.

"And mine, my lady," Chamberlen agreed, seizing her hand and covering it with kisses.

"Monsieur Chamberlen is the world's foremost accoucheur," Princess Anne explained. "Why, without him I would have lost Willie."

"Accoucheur?" Lorna inquired.

"Midwife is the common term," Sarah explained. "Male midwife."

"But . . ." Lorna stared at them aghast.

"Mr. Chamberlen wishes to examine you, Lorna," Princess Anne explained.

"To be sure all is well with you and the babe," Sarah said.

"There is nothing for you to be afraid of, Mistress Butler," Chamberlen said. "I do assure you."

"Mr. Chamberlen has invented an instrument which enables him to deliver the most difficult child," Sarah said. "Oh, do show it to us, Mr. Chamberlen."

"Well . . ." He opened his bag and took out what appeared to be a gigantic pair of tweezers, save that the two arms were flattened and rectangular.

Lorna stared at it in horror. "You'll not touch me with that," she declared.

"One hopes it will not be necessary, my dear lady,"

Chamberlen said. "But as you will understand, 'tis the babe's head which is the difficult part. Once that is free the rest follows with speed. This is the reason behind my forceps. I seize the babe's head between these two arms, they can do it no harm, I do assure you, and by gently pulling and turning at the same time I draw it clear, and there is your birth, accomplished with precision and safety."

"My God," Lorna said. "It sounds barbarous."

"Well, let us hope it will not be needed," Princess Anne decided. "Now, Lorna, if you will lie down, Mr. Chamberlen may proceed."

"But . . . he is a man," Lorna protested.

Sarah gave a shriek of laughter. "And was it not a man placed you in this position, in the first place?"

"Mr. Chamberlen has looked on so many women, my dear, he is no longer interested, I do promise you," Princess Anne said. "Haven't you, monsieur? Now come along, be a good girl."

Lorna sighed, and lay on the bed, and closed her eyes, as she had done when first assaulted by Butler. Her heart pounded and she was sure the flush extended throughout her body.

"Water," Chamberlen said. "I must have water."

She opened her eyes in alarm.

"Why, to wash my hands, my lady."

Sarah was snapping her fingers, and Alice was hurrying forward with a basin. Lorna closed her eyes again, and felt her skirts being raised, and a moment later a hand touched her belly. Prepared as she was she yet gave a start, and opened her eyes, to find Chamberlen smiling at her.

"My hand is cold. I apologise, my lady, indeed I do." His fingers kneaded her flesh, stroked down to her pelvis and her hair, and back up again. Then to her utter dismay she felt him parting her thighs, as Butler had done. She tensed her muscles to resist his touch and felt nothing, opened her eyes and realised he was peering at her, nose not six inches from her flesh. Oh, the scoundrel. Not even Butler had done that.

"Well?" the Princess demanded.

"Oh, she will have no trouble at all, madam," Chamberlen said. "She is a fine, healthy young woman, with good muscles and wide thighs." He gave her a little pat, and she glared at him in fury. "And the babe is lying in the best position, so far as I can ascertain. This will be a simple birth."

"But you will attend the Countess again," Sarah insisted.

"Again?" Lorna asked weakly, sitting up to straighten her skirts.

"Of course," the Princess said. "We must take no chances with so lovely a creature."

It occurred to Lorna that they were playing with her as a doll. And the thought of a man's hand on her naked groin brought back memory in a tremendous rush, and desire as well, and sent her to bed in a torment of wild dreams. For it was now eight months since she had seen Lennart, and not a word. Had he then been no more than a lecher, to whom she had given her body with innocent delight?

For the first time since coming to England she felt utterly lonely. Alice was not really the sort of woman one could use as a confidante in matters of that sort. Which left only Father Simeon.

"Outrageous," he said, walking with her in the garden, cloaks drawn tight to keep out the July rain. "I have heard of this fellow, Chamberlen. A charlatan if ever there was one, who preys upon defenceless women."

"He was introduced to me by Her Royal Highness."

"Indeed. As defenceless a woman as ever I saw, if you will pardon me, my lady. And supposing he is not a charlatan, what of this secret device of his?"

"You have heard of it?"

"He boasts of it, considers selling it at some inflated price, and then changes his mind and says no, he will retain it, and wait for a still better offer. If that is his concept of medical ethics, supposing his weapon can help afflicted women, then it says very little for his ethics in any other direction. And if, as you have confessed, his ministrations drive you to lewd thoughts, well, one must wonder if he is not a positive danger to society." He paused in his perambulation to gaze at her. "My lady?"

Lorna clutched her belly, and her knees touched with sheer fright. "Oh, my God, Father," she said. "Oh, my God. My time is here."

It was amazingly quick and easy. Lorna had always treated the very thought of the chair, of being held down in agony, as she had heard it described in St. Mary's, with disgust; but Chamberlen had new ideas on this also, and explained how in France great ladies retired to their couches for their delivery. Lorna was placed in her own bed, with Alice and Bridget and Patience to look after her, and Sarah to sit by her and engage in bright conversation, and, strangely, she was even happy to know that Chamberlen was there as well—charlatan or not, he exuded a great deal of confidence, which in this case was quite justified.

"I knew it," he cried. "With such a mother, how could it be otherwise?" He pretended to frown. "And I had no use for my forceps."

"For which I say, thank God," Lorna agreed, giving

her rosary a last stroke. Then the little girl was placed in the crook of her arm. "Her eyes," she said. "I cannot see the colour of her eyes."

"All babes' eyes are blue," Sarah pointed out.

"She looks just like Lennart," Lorna said. "Her eyes will be grey."

Sarah frowned. "Yours are green."

"And Captain Butler's were brown," Lorna shouted triumphantly. "But Lennart's are grey."

"You'd best keep that to yourself," Sarah recommended. "Or she will be known as a bastard. But a girl is the best thing for you. There can be no question now of your being Countess of Morne, and in your own right rather than merely caretaking it for some brat. What will you call her?"

"Kathleen," Lorna said, and smiled. "Kathleen Munro, no matter what."

"Aye, well, I'd not worry about that," Sarah recommended. "Until we see if the fever comes."

"The fever?"

" 'Tis a problem, after birth. And if it comes, you'll be in your grave. There is no known cure." She handed Lorna her rosary. "You'd best pray. But Monsieur Chamberlen has a way with the fever also."

"Water, my dear Countess," he explained, "clean water, for you . . ." he was busily bathing her, "and for me. I cannot explain why, but the fever seldom follows clean water."

She shivered and glared at him with a mixture of discomfort and embarrassment. But the fever did not come, and within a week he pronounced her free of danger.

The Queen herself attended the christening, at the private chapel; King William was campaigning. Two Catholic ladies and their husbands were secured as godparents, and Father Simeon performed the ceremony. It was the happiest day of Lorna's life, for now that she was sure of the father she had no doubts to what she must do. She wrote a long letter to Lennart, describing Kathleen minutely, swearing her own undying love, and delivered it to Falkenhayn who promised to see that it reached Stockholm as soon as possible. After which there was nothing to do but wait and be happy. Happiness was Kathleen. Lorna spent every moment the Queen allowed her from her duties—for she was now reinstated as a lady of the bedchamber—with the babe, and was only distressed when at the end of the second week she was confronted with a wet nurse.

"But she is my child," she insisted. "And must grow on my milk."

"What nonsense," Sarah declared. "Sixteen years old? My dear Lorna, you could be the mother of thirty children should you be the slightest bit unlucky, and would you feed them all? Those marvelous tits of yours would be trailing on the ground."

Lorna supposed she was right, although it cost her some painful days before her own milk dried, with ministrations from Bridget, the prettiest of the maids, gently to work the teats to remove the excess fluid, an operation at which Sarah also assisted. In fact as Lorna regained her figure and her strength, Sarah became her inseparable companion. It was possible to talk to her as to no other woman, for she possessed an almost masculine vulgarity of wit, and certainly a masculine forcefulness of character, and could toss away doubts and fears in a few brisk sentences. It was thus the more surprising for Lorna to return to her apartments one morning in the spring of 1692, carrying Kathleen up from her pram in the garden, and find her friend lying on her bed, weeping her heart out.

"Alice," she shouted. "Alice. Take the babe." She ran to the bed, knelt beside it. "Sarah? What has happened?"

Sarah sat up, dragged disordered hair from her forehead. "I am dismissed from the palace."

"Dismissed? But . . ."

"My lord Churchill has been accused of corresponding with the Court at St. Germain."

Which was the property given to the exiled James the Second by King Louis.

"But . . . accused?" Lorna said.

"Oh, you silly child, there is proof. You'll know Arabella, John's sister, was the King's mistress for years. Why, she mothered Berwick for him. The King. What am I saying. But . . . oh, my God." She gazed at the door.

Queen Mary stalked, rather than walked. Her sister trailed behind her.

"You, madam," the Queen said, pointing at Sarah, "are no longer welcome here. Take yourself off."

Sarah stared at her for a moment, an angry flush mingling with the tearstains on her cheeks, then she stood up, as did Lorna.

"Your Majesty," Anne protested. "Dear, dear sister, I am sure there is some logical explanation. . . ."

"Indeed there is," Mary declared. "Her husband will play both ends against the middle. Against you, as well, sister. Be sure Papa will forgive you no more than me should he ever regain his prerogatives. And you still wish to harbour this . . . viper in your bosom?"

"Your Majesty," Sarah began.

"Hold your miserable tongue," the Queen commanded. "And leave my house this instant. Count yourself fortunate there is no guard waiting to deposit you in the Tower."

"You'll not speak to my dear Freeman like that," Anne cried.

"Your dear Freeman," Mary said with heavy sarcasm.

"My friend," Anne insisted, flushing crimson in turn. "My best friend. My only friend, I do declare."

"Look to yourself," Mary said.

"Bah," Anne said. "You threaten me? You, a barren half-monarch?"

"Why, you . . ." Mary took a step forward, and for a terrible moment Lorna supposed she would strike her sister.

"Barren," Anne shouted. "I will be Queen. Nothing can stop that. I will be Queen."

Mary's breath hissed. "Then take your leave and wait, in patience. And take that . . . that creature with you."

"Madam," Sarah tried again.

"I will not have her speak," Mary shouted. "My lady Morne, summon a guard. Have her removed."

Lorna took a step towards the door, hesitated.

"That will not be necessary." Anne seized Sarah's arm, herself went to the door. "We shall not breathe this air again." The door of the apartment banged.

"Your Majesty," Lorna ventured.

"And you," Mary shouted, her arm once again extended. "How do I know you are not similarly corrupt? An Irish Papist . . ."

"I have never set foot in Ireland, ma'am," Lorna protested. "You may describe me as an American Papist, if you must, but I would be grieved to have you question my loyalty."

Mary gazed at her for some seconds longer, then suddenly her face dissolved, she sat on the bed, and burst into tears.

"Your Majesty," Lorna cried, hurrying to her side, to have her hand seized and pressed against the Queen's breast.

"Oh, it is so cruel," she wailed. "My own sister, so cruel. I have no friends, Lorna. I have nothing. A husband who will not grace my bed, a sister who prefers upstarts to me, a childless, miserable existence . . ."

"I am here, Your Majesty," Lorna said.

"You dear, sweet child. You must forgive me. I feel so desolated. And now this terrible Glencoe business . . ."

"Traitorous Scotsmen, Your Majesty," Lorna said soothingly, although in common with everyone else she had been shocked at the suggestion that King William had sanctioned the massacre of an entire clan for merely being late in taking the oath of allegiance.

The Queen raised her head. "You are my best support, Lorna. And here you will remain, promise me that. I will find you a husband, a father for your lovely daughter."

"Your Majesty," Lorna said. "You may believe I wish for nothing more. But I am already betrothed. . . ."

"To some itinerant Swede? Why has he not answered your letter? Oh, men are all careless, perfidious creatures. Forget him, Lorna, I beg of you."

"Should I do so, ma'am, I would beg to be allowed to remain no more than a widow," Lorna said.

Mary raised her head and suddenly smiled. "My faithful Lorna. Aye. We'll talk about it later."

She left the apartment, and Lorna could allow *herself* the luxury of stretching on the bed and shedding a few tears. The remembrance that she had indeed had no reply was unbearable. Especially as she now began to realise that Baron Falkenhayn was deliberately avoiding her, and it was more than her pride could bear to go behind him begging for a letter. So then, Father Derwent had been right at the very beginning.

And yet, she reasoned, Lennart had filled a central role in her life, in eradicating Butler and in fathering Kathleen. She should be grateful to him rather than merely becoming angry. On the other hand, Queen Mary was equally right, and it would be foolish to waste the rest of her life hoping for the return of a man who had no more interest in her.

Yet the thought of any other man filled her with disgust. No doubt she had lived her entire life in a single tumultuous week. She had sinned, most grievously, but then she had been equally sinned against. Now she would atone, for the rest of her life, in being a good mother, in being a good Catholic, in being a good woman, and in being a good servant to Her Majesty. She threw herself into her duties with all her energy, took great pains to entertain the Queen with her conversation, with her tales of life in Maryland, spent hours with Kathleen, watching her crawl and then walk, spent other hours learning the art of the spinet, sewing, and indulging in a new hobby, reading. There had been few books at MacMahons, and somehow, even less time. Here there was everything she could require. She read the playwrights Jonson and Marlowe and Shakespeare, the classical works of Spenser, the much frowned-upon diatribes of Milton, the spicy and topical poems of Dryden, and even enjoyed the scurrilous works of Defoe and Aphra Behn.

She occupied every day and well into every evening with a variety of nothings, resolutely putting aside every thought of men or of sex, allowing the stream of courtiers who would flirt with her no more than a gentle smile, so that it very rapidly became known that the Countess of Morne was simply not available, for all her beauty and for all the scandalous accounts of her background. Days, seasons passed, without her really being aware of them, except in the growing delight of Kathleen. She neither saw nor heard of Princess Anne nor of Sarah, who had together taken themselves off to Anne's residence at Berkeley House where they virtually set up an opposition Court to Kensington. No doubt she was confirmed as the Queen's creature, and therefore unacceptable. It scarcely seemed important. Princess Anne was only three years younger than her sister, and in Lorna's opinion the possibility of her ever succeeding to the throne was remote. It was therefore a shock for her to attend the Queen one morning, shortly after her own twentieth birthday, which took place on the fourth of December 1694, and find her a mass of sweat and shivering limbs, quite unable to move.

"Your Majesty," she cried. "Whatever is the matter?"

"My back," the Queen muttered. "God, how it hurts. My back . . ." She suddenly rose on her elbow, and quite without warning vomited on the floor.

"Your Majesty," Lorna screamed, her wail summoning the other maids. But Lorna was already running through the corridors in search of the Queen's physician, Dr. Radcliffe. For a moment she supposed, remembering her own symptoms, that the Queen might at last be pregnant, although she could not recall His Majesty attending her at any time during the previous few months. But the doctor knew the truth at once, and it was confirmed the next day, when the horrid pus-filled smallpox papules formed around her nose and mouth.

The ladies in waiting shrank to the far side of the room, terrified by their own exposure as much as by the implications for the Queen. Mary, indeed, soon demanded that they abandon her, for fear the infection would spread to them. Lorna alone stayed. She was afraid to leave the room at all, principally because she might carry the dread disease to Kathleen; she sent word to Alice to take the child away for the Christmas holidays.

Day by day, the Queen grew worse. And now at last William did come to his wife. The day following Boxing Day he stalked through the corridors of the palace, still wearing riding boots and heavy coat as he had come straight from Whitehall, and looked at her in silence. Her throat was so dry, her fever so high, she could hardly speak, and returned his gaze in mute longing. She was such a ghastly sight, her entire face and neck a mass of blisters, that Lorna was terrified he would show disgust, but his face remained impassive.

"You will be well, madam," he said. "Radcliffe tells me the crisis approaches. You will be well."

Her tongue showed for a moment as she desperately sought for saliva. "William . . ." she whispered.

"I am here, madam," he said. "And I will stay. You will be well." He raised his head, looked at the priest, the surgeons, then sat in the chair placed for him at the foot of the bed.

"Lorna . . ." Queen Mary whispered.

Lorna knelt beside the bed, steeled her nerves, and held the tortured hand.

"Lorna," she whispered. "Do not leave. I would not die alone."

"The King is here, Your Majesty. And you will not die," she said, tears streaming down her cheeks. "All the country prays for your recovery. There will be no Christmas celebrations until you are well again."

"There will be no Christmas celebrations," Mary whispered. "Do not let me die alone, Lorna."

"The King is here," Lorna repeated. "And he has sent for the Princess." She gave a start as the fingers closed on hers with sudden strength.

"No," Mary said. "I will not see her. I will not, you hear. I will not." She gave a sigh and closed her eyes.

Lorna gazed at King William, and they both turned to the doctor who stood on the far side of the bed.

"It is the crisis, Sire," Radcliffe said. "By tomorrow we will know, one way or the other. Will you stay with her?"

"You also, my lady Morne," William said.

The fingers were still tight on hers. She nodded. The candles were doused, the palace was silent, the watching crowds outside kept at a distance by the guards. The King did not speak. And in time Lorna slept, her head resting on the sheet beside the hand of her mistress. She slept until the fingers tightened on hers again, and then relaxed slightly, and almost immediately lost the fever heat, and grew quite cold.

Queen Mary the Second was dead.

# Chapter 5

*H*is Majesty will see you now, my lady." The major domo bowed as he spoke and struck the floor with his staff. The sound echoed in the corridor and set the guns to booming in Lorna's brain all over again. The guns, and the tramp of marching feet, the mournful dirge played by the band . . . she crossed herself as the door swung in.

William was alone, sitting at the head of his table, his chin resting on his hand. She sank into a curtsey, and felt the door close behind her.

"Rise, Countess."

Lorna obeyed. There was no grief in William's face, only tiredness. And now he was overtaken by a fit of coughing.

"Her Majesty often described you as her favourite amongst the ladies," he said.

"Her Majesty was very kind to me, Sire."

"And I have evidence of my own eyes that she was right. Come closer, Countess."

Lorna walked behind the chairs that surrounded the table.

"She asked me to give you a memento of hers. She supposed, I have no doubt correctly, that to leave you land or money would be an absurdity. Kneel."

Lorna obeyed, stared at his boots, felt her heart begin to pound and her skin to prickle with heat. The King's hands touched her hair for a moment, and then her neck, and she felt metal against her flesh and looked down. It was a gold chain, and at the end a gold replica of the crucified Jesus, resting on her bodice. She would have adjusted it herself, but the King, leaning forward, was himself lifting the crucifix free of the black velvet of her gown, and gently allowing it to drop between her breasts. For an unthinkable moment she thought his hands were about to follow, and raised her head in alarm. The hands were withdrawn, but as she looked into his face she realised that the thought had not been so unthinkable after all.

"Do you not like it?"

She controlled her breathing with an effort. "It is magnificent, Sire. But . . ."

"It is surprising, that a Protestant queen should possess a Catholic talisman?" He gave a brief, humourless smile. "Like all her family, Queen Mary was ambiguous, in many things."

"I will always wear it."

"Even in bed?"

The flush was back, burning at her cheeks. *Oh, God,* she thought. *Oh, God, help me.*

"I have heard it said, Countess, that you sleep alone, save for a cat. Have you no desire for male companionship?"

"Sire . . ."

"How old are you, Countess?"

"I am twenty, Your Majesty."

"And quite the most beautiful thing at this Court. And you would wither away in solitary self-communion? Baron Falkenhayn has told me all about this Swedish adventurer of yours. You are well rid of him. But the Countess of Morne should have a husband."

"Sire . . ." Again the quick flick of the tongue. "I fear marriage, Sire. My first experience of it was not a happy one."

"So I understand. You need have no fear of a match such as I would arrange. Your husband would be entirely subservient to you, would attend you only when you were not otherwise engaged. And I would have you be far more engaged in the life of the Court. Come closer."

Lorna hesitated, took a step. William leaned forward to seize her hand.

"This court has been divided too long. My wife was a noble and gallant lady. Her frivolity was no more than a mask, worn to disguise her true feelings. But that fear, that disguise of true feelings, extended to her bed."

Lorna inhaled. The fingers were tight on hers. "She was very lonely, Sire."

"And am I not very lonely?" He held out his other hand, and she hesitated, then extended hers. He grasped her fingers, slowly drew her forward. "I have also the cares of this government, of the government of Holland, of rebellions and traitors and wars hanging heavy above me. I have not the time for flirtation, for wooing, as a woman, as the Queen, certainly, would have had it." He gave another of his brief smiles. "No doubt you see before you a male characterisation of what you yourself will become, should you permit it, dried and withered. Women leave me unaffected, save where they are unusually beautiful, unusually desirable. You are those things, Lorna. I have watched you, walking the halls of this palace behind my wife, and I have looked at you, not at her. I have been swollen with desire after dining, and watching you at the far side of the table. Lorna . . ." His hand was round her waist, sliding over the back of her gown to caress her. "I could not speak before. You were a creature of my wife's. I can speak now, Lorna. You can make me very happy. You can make me a better man, Lorna. A better king." Both hands were behind her now, caressing her bottom as best they could through several layers of material, bringing her closer, so that her face was against his, and now his mouth was seeking her. "Oh, Lorna," he whispered. "If you knew how I have dreamed of parting these magnificent lips . . ."

Her mouth was open, and his tongue was inside. She was suddenly angry. Why should I submit? she asked herself. I am the Countess of Morne. I do not even like this man, much less love him. I consider he treated his wife abominably.

His hands slipped away from her gown, and he leaned back. Some of the animation had left his face. "You find me repulsive." His voice was again cold.

"Sire . . ." She licked her lips and tasted his saliva. "I am cursed, Sire. I cannot respond where I do not love."

"Do you not suppose that to reject a king may be a dangerous mistake?"

Her head came up. But it was a risk worth taking; at heart he was a gentleman. "No subject may reject her king, Sire. You may lead me to your bed, as you choose. But I'll not be able to satisfy you, Sire. It will remain rape."

His brows got together, and colour once again flared

in his cheeks. But this time it was anger. "And do you suppose you can remain here in such circumstances?"

"No, Sire, I . . ."

"You will leave Kensington today."

"Yes, Sire." She sucked air into her lungs. "I should like to go to Ireland."

"Ireland, by God. You are a traitor, after all."

"Sire?"

"All Irishmen, all Catholic Irishmen at the least, and their women are Jacobites at heart. I have heard it said you make no secret of that."

"Sire, I . . ." Another effort regained control of her breathing. "I am Countess of Morne. I have no more than a desire to see my property. My tenants."

His arm came out, his finger pointing. "You will not leave London. Ten miles, there is your limit. You have ample funds. Find yourself a house and an establishment within ten miles of this palace. And do not leave it, save to ride in this park."

"Sire . . . will that not still allow you to see me?"

His arms dropped. "The audience is over."

She remained standing before him. Having gained at least a partial victory, she would never have a better opportunity. "Sire, as I am not permitted to visit my estates, may I at the least receive an accounting of my affairs? I have received nothing in the four years I have lived here."

"Do you lack for anything?"

"No, Your Majesty. But as I do not know whether I am rich or poor, whether I have money on deposit or am in debt, I do not know what sort of establishment I may allow myself."

"The Countess of Morne concerned about debt?" His face twisted. "Well, then, there will be an accounting. You my purchase whatever sort of house, whatever sort of establishment you choose. But within ten miles of this palace. Remember that."

"But, my dear Lorna," Alice Mountfield protested. "No one can refuse a king."

"I do not love him," Lorna said. "I could not love him. It would be an act of prostitution. Father Simeon . . ."

The priest coughed. "You are a most honourable lady, my lady. Alas, in this world, honour is not always the path of advancement. . . ."

"Father!"

He shook his head. "I do not advocate a change in your decision, and I admire and congratulate your courage. But Alice is right. It is difficult to see how . . ."

"I may obtain advancement? I am Countess of Morne. Suppose His Majesty is not proposing marriage, and I can assure you he is not, I *can* advance no more."

"I was thinking less of advancement, my lady," Father Simeon said mildly, "than of maintaining yourself."

"Oh, bah," she said. "We shall be away from here tomorrow and out of His Majesty's mind the day after. He will find the bed warmer he desires soon enough."

"If I may say so, my lady, he is unlikely to find one as lovely as yourself."

Lorna gazed at him, chewing her lip. "I seek nothing from this Court, from this country, save my just deserts," she said. "My mind is made up. We shall go home."

"Home, my lady?"

"Maryland. MacMahons. Oh, fear not, dear friends, you will come with me. I will write Lord Calvert tomorrow and acquaint him of my intention."

"And who will acquaint His Majesty, my lady?"

Lorna hesitated. "Well, it may take a little time. I believe you are right, Father, and his desire to have me ride in the park is in the hope that I may change my mind. But as I will not change my mind, he will soon forget about me. In any event, Father, he is no longer a young man and is indeed far older than his age, in my opinion. We shall practise patience and make our plans." She gave them a bright smile. "And begin by finding ourselves a new lodging."

In fact she found she need go no farther afield than the village of Chelsea, where there was a manor house standing in five acres of land. And all within two miles of the palace, so she could not be more obedient to the royal command, as she made sure to write William and inform him. Alice was aghast, as she considered Hurd House far too humble a dwelling for one of the premier countesses of the land, but it was exactly suited to Lorna's tastes and ambitions. She left the staff to Alice, and it was augmented to half a dozen maids, a similar number of footmen, a butler named Morgan, a cook—Alice herself maintained the post of house-keeper—three scullery maids, two yard boys, an over-gardener and an undergardener, and five grooms for her horses and dogs, for she had started collecting and breeding spaniels. There was also Kathleen's nurse, Parkin, and Lorna's hairdresser, Bracknell.

The only rebuilding that was necessary was the addition and consecration of a chapel, but she had the entire house extensively redecorated and refurnished, indulging herself in chairs and tables made by André Buhl—and imported at great expense from France, for the war was now virtually over—in which materials such as tortoiseshell or mother-of-pearl were inlaid on ebonised wood to make exquisite designs. It was in fact a delicious sensation to be, for the very first time in her life, her own mistress. She rose when she liked and she retired when she liked; she ate what she liked and she drank what she liked. She read what she liked and she rode to the park in her carriage or on horseback when the weather was fine, again as she liked. Her delight was compounded by the arrival of Master Wilson, her steward, proving that the King was after all a man of his word. Wilson, a tall, thin fellow with a pronounced stoop, took up residence at Hurd House, and Lorna spent an utterly splendid May in going over her affairs with him. She had not known such money existed, as her rent roll from Ireland alone amounted to seventy-five thousand pounds a year, and Ireland continued in a state of total devastation, both from her war fought there in 1690 and from the continued opposition of Protestant and Catholic. She longed to visit her home, as she was beginning to consider it, and see for herself, and determined that whenever she did obtain permission to leave England, she would certainly stop at Morne in the course of her journey back to America.

She wrote to Lord Calvert and received a reply that the farm was well tenanted, but that the tenants would be very pleased to have their landlady living amongst them, and that had he the funds he would see to the construction of a suitable house for her in St. Mary's. The funds were dispatched. Spending money was Lorna's great joy, especially after Wilson convinced her that her English estates were bringing in another hundred thousand pounds per annum. "Considered at fourteen years' purchase," he said, pulling his lip, "that makes your ladyship worth roughly two and a half million pounds, and I do not include Hurd House."

Two and a half million pounds. She had not supposed there was so much money in the world. She lay on her bed that night, staring at the tent, listening to the soft whimper of the dogs clustered at the foot, idly stroking Snowdrop against her side, and tried to envisage what such a sum would look like, piled in gold coin. Would it reach the ceiling? Would it fill the room? She had no idea.

So, then, she thought, am I happy? Am I become a totally self-sufficient woman, wealthy, beautiful, well born, with nothing to do but live?

She sat up violently, and Snowdrop complained. But what was living? Where was the girl who had decided to take the worst that Butler could do to her rather than commit suicide? That girl had known how to live.

She left the bed and stalked the room. She continued to sleep naked, to Alice's distress, just as she continued to take cold baths, whenever possible. The Maryland farm girl was still in existence, somewhere. But the Countess of Morne had surely more to do with her life than count her money and change her clothes three times a day.

She stood before her mirror. Had she, then, forgotten altogether the touch of a man's hand? *Oh, no,* she thought. But had she, then, learned to prefer the touch of her own? There was a terrifying thought. But her hands were already stroking across her ribs, to cup underneath her breasts, and gently raise them, as Lennart had done. Oh, God, Lennart. How she remembered, how she dreamed, how she wanted. Anyone? No. The thought of the King filled her with repugnance. Why? Because he was old? Because he was the Queen's husband? Because she knew how cold his heart really was?

Well, then, marriage. But that thought filled her no less with dread. Marriage meant submission. She had not submitted to Lennart. He had been reluctant, and she had drawn him forward, her hands on his member. And then they had been equals at love. Well, then, find another equal? But how? How does one know a man can be equal, save by some magical communication? There, she thought, is a true definition of love. And she did not love, had not loved, could not love, save Lennart. Who was by now no doubt happily married to some buxom Swede, and remembered her only as an enjoyable night.

But, oh God, how she loved. She sank to her knees, still before her mirror, remembering, attempting to repeat, where she could, and then suddenly hating herself. For once again she had half lifted the lid of the Pandora's box she had discovered on that night so long ago. And been afraid to rip it off. Why? Because the woman who did that would not be the woman who had begun it?

Afraid. Afraid. Afraid. There was the truth. She was no more than afraid of everything.

"Afraid," she told Father Simeon. "And I suffer the torments of the damned, Father. The temptations of the damned."

"It would be surprising, my lady, did you not suffer, at once fear and temptation."

Her nostrils dilated as she stared at him. They were alone in the chapel. "My blood is too hot, Father. I would relieve it. I must, or I shall go mad. You shall scourge me."

His frown deepened. "Indeed, my lady, you *are* tormented."

"Now," she panted, reaching behind her to unfasten her gown. "You shall whip me until the blood runs. Do not refuse me this, Father. Or you will lose my soul."

He held her wrists, pulled her hands to the front. "Your soul is not in danger, sweet lady." His smile was crooked. "Although perhaps you seek to endanger mine. I will kneel beside you and pray with you."

"But it will come again," she shouted. "And again."

"Then will we pray again, my lady. And again. But, my lady, your salvation lies in marriage."

Undoubtedly he was right. Lorna began to entertain, holding select luncheon parties, on the lawn during the summer months, and indoors in the winter, to which she invited half a dozen lords and ladies, and at which she provided music so that they could dance and disport themselves to their hearts' content. And found that, contrary to her expectations, *she* began to enjoy herself very much. There was certainly enough to do, as Kathleen developed into a bright and intelligent child, and it was time to start her education, a task Lorna preferred to undertake herself at this early age.

She found the presence of a constantly differing stream of men, of all ages and sizes and requirements, vastly stimulating, and found flirting with them a great relief to the pressure which occasionally still overtook her in the middle of a lonely night. All of them wanted her; if they were married they sought her as a mistress, or in some cases both as a mistress and a prospective bride for their sons, and if they were unmarried they were dazzled equally by her beauty and the thought of the Morne millions. They sought to discover her alone, by calling at unusual hours, and would press her hand and sigh, and surreptitiously slip their arm around her waist to fondle her breast, and were reduced to desperation by the invariable arrival of Alice and Kathleen, summoned by Lorna's instruction that no gentleman caller should be permitted more than fifteen minutes alone with her before being interrupted.

Or they endeavoured to hold her close as they danced, allowing their hands to rove around, again in search of a heaving bosom, or they wrote her sonnets, or they waited for her daily ride in the park, and clustered around her carriage like a swarm of bees. One young man threatened suicide if she would not have him, and two more fought a duel after they had come calling at the same time.

"In fact, my lady," Father Simeon said severely, "it is beginning to be doubted whether you seriously intend to marry at all, or even to take a man into your bed, ever again, and are not just indulging an infamous game with all humanity."

He was the only person permitted to speak to her in this fashion, and even he could arouse her resentment, for she had practised to perfection the art of being icily angry.

Now she allowed him a smile. "My dear Father Simeon, you know my intention. I will return to Maryland, whenever in my judgment the King would be receptive to such a plan. Therefore my husband is required to be a frontiersman, at least in the prospect. And amongst these courtiers, why, I am coming to realize it will require a most diligent search."

"Then perhaps you should cast your net farther afield."

"Now really, Father," she protested. "I shall be marrying beneath my rank in any event, even by taking someone from Court. Would you have me tie myself to some lout?"

"Lorna Butler," he said, standing over her. "To lie to a priest, and more, to your confessor, is a grave sin."

"Lie?" she demanded. "Sometimes, Father, you go too far."

"Lie," he said. "Your entire life is a lie. You have enjoyed this house, this wealth, this independence, for two years, now. You are twenty-two years old. You are wasting the best part of a woman's life, in self-gratification."

"Self-gratification?" she protested. "Do you discover me naked with a man in the morning? Do you discover me lying at the foot of the stairs, drunk? Do you discover me trembling with fat from overeating?"

"Self-gratification," he repeated. "It can take many forms. The ones you describe are at least its more natural paths. But you, my lady, are gratifying nothing more than an enjoyment of being Countess of Morne. Of being the most beautiful woman in the kingdom. For God's sake, my lady, I would *rather* discover you naked in bed with a man. There were something actual, something living, something you may remember, even if with pain or disgust. But what can be more empty than to share nothing with anyone, save yourself? I repeat, you are twenty-two. You grow more lovely, day by day. But do you suppose this is an eternal, unchanging state of affairs? Every day you waste, in idle flirtation, in idle daydreaming, is indeed a day torn up and destroyed, with naught to show for it. Two years have passed like a snap of the fingers. Will not ten pass as quickly? Will you not discover a wrinkle when you are thirty-two, and know the end is in sight? Of all things, a woman's beauty is most fragile. It should be shared, it should be used, to increase the happiness of the world, to bring forth beautiful children. It should not be wielded as a mocking laugh, look but do not touch, admire but do not dare to possess. Why, madam, you are naught but a picture hanging on a wall, gathering dust."

Her anger was the more intense because every word he had said was so clearly true. She sought only to hurt him, as quickly and as brutally as possible. "Well, then, Simeon," she demanded, "would you not correct me, as you are my confessor? And who better than you could accomplish so much without the slightest risk of gossip."

He gazed at her for some seconds. "And as your beauty atrophies, my lady, so does your heart. No doubt that is inevitable." He bowed and left the room, and next day the house. A letter arrived to say that he had returned to the monastery from whence Sarah Churchill had brought him.

And Lorna felt more independent than ever. Perhaps Simeon had been after all a mistake. A confessor should be someone less forceful, less aggressive, and on a temporary basis. To remain with one priest for too long allowed him too much understanding, too much latitude in his ministration. After all, what did she have to confess, save her thoughts.

Indeed, because she could find no part of humanity to love, she found all of it easy to hate. Her flirtations grew more cruel, her arrogance more domineering, more harsh. Only to Kathleen, and to Alice, did she soften. To her servants she was a tyrant, no less than to her horses and her dogs. In all the world, only Snowdrop, who had shared those first long hours of solitude, of dreams, of hopes and of fears, of temptations, remained her true equal, her true confidante. It was as if she had suddenly discovered the brutality of Butler, the faithlessness of Lennart all over again, and present in every man who would approach her. Mankind's fury had made her what she was; her own fury, far more terrible, would leave them what they were, forever, their feeble minds blinded with the brilliance of the light she emanated. And womankind also. Her known estrangement from the King very rapidly brought her a letter from Berkeley House, expressing the sympathy of Mrs. Freeman on behalf of Mrs. Morley, and inviting her to call.

But it was all too clearly an intrigue; Marlborough still lurked, unable to obtain employment from an unforgiving king. Lorna wrote back that she was well satisfied with her present circumstances, but would be available should either Mrs. Freeman or Mrs. Morley choose to visit *her*.

She invariably slept in until nine, as she seldom retired much before midnight. She breakfasted in her boudoir, overlooking the gardens and the lawns, with Kathleen, now six years old—and a serious precocious child who daily seemed to grow more like her father, although she possessed Lorna's hair, in a somewhat darker shade—for company, as well, of course, as Snowdrop and the dogs. They ate eggs, and cream tarts, and apple dumplings, and drank a bottle of sack. To her here Alice brought the day's letters and any broadsheets that she might have accumulated during her ramblings into the city of the previous day, as well as a considerable amount of gossip. Alice also always shared a glass of wine, as Kathleen was generally quite tipsy on a single glass and Lorna very little better.

"From Berkeley House, my lady. Another invitation?"

"I'll not read it," Lorna declared. "They are up to their old tricks. Mistress Morley, indeed. What else?"

"Oooh, my lady. From Kensington Palace."

Lorna's head came up. During the past two years

she had encountered the King often enough when riding in Hyde Park, as she had been instructed to do. But he had never done more than incline his head most coldly. "What does it say?"

Alice slit the envelope, took out a sheet of parchment. "Stiff paper," she muttered. " 'Tis an invitation."

"His Majesty King William, The Third, of Great Britain France and Ireland, Statholder of Holland, commands the presence of Lady Lorna Butler, Countess of Morne, at a reception to be held at Kensington Palace on Monday, the seventeenth of October, 1697, at six."

Lorna stared at her housekeeper in total consternation. "Monday, the seventeenth of October?"

"Today, my lady."

"Holy Mother. The scoundrel. He but does it to torment me. How can I attend at such short notice?"

"How can you not attend, my lady?"

"My God," Lorna muttered. "Oh, my God. Mistress Bracknell. Fetch Mistress Bracknell." Her fingers drummed on the table. "Tell Harry to see to that harness. It was uncommonly dull. What time is it? Ten-thirty? Oh, my God. Seven hours. Prepare my bath. That will have to be done before Mistress Bracknell gets here. Don't just stand there, Alice. Move."

"Yes, my lady." Alice hurried for the door.

"Wait there," Lorna called, getting up. "Reception? What sort of a reception?"

"I have no idea, my lady." Alice smiled. "There is talk of a Russian embassy. . . ."

"Russian? Russian? My God, the ends of the earth. Alice. What am I to *wear*?"

"The gold, my lady?"

"Everyone has seen that before. Oh, Holy Mother, what am I to do? Oh, be off. Fetch Mistress Bracknell."

Alice disappeared. Kathleen finished her wine noisily. "What is happening, Mama? Are you being sent to the Tower?"

Lorna stopped her pacing to gaze at her. "Whatever are you discussing?"

" 'Tis what Nanny Parkin says, that all the people of our faith will be sent to the Tower before long."

"I'll have her whipped," Lorna decided. "I'll whip her myself. Sent to the Tower. What nonsense. I am summoned to Court, sweetheart. To Court."

To Court, after two years. And it could be no other than the King's own intention, especially as it apparently concerned nothing more than a barbaric embassy. Why, she could be insulted, really, at having been placed so low in the social scale. She decided to be insulted, and had Morgan write the reply instead of doing it herself.

But the King. She sat in her bath, while Alice scrubbed her back, and Mistress Bracknell prepared curling irons and the combs, keeping her eye on her employer as she did so; she had herself gathered Lorna's red-gold hair on the top of her head, and secured it with a bandeau; she had no intention of allowing even a strand of it get wet.

The King. He had sent for her, after letting her stew for two years, after refusing to acknowledge her existence or her letter. Well, then, that was fair enough. He had insulted her, and she had angered him. Now they could begin again, as friends, as equals, even, in private. There were all her problems falling into place, melting away. She would be radiant, her very best . . . in an old gown. Oh, the wretch.

She decided on drama rather than simplicity, wore her dark red brocade over a blue silk undershirt, with white neck and elbow frills, and deep blue velvet ribbon bows to hold back her overskirt and her sleeves. Around her neck she chose a single string of pearls, drawn tight the way the Queen had liked to wear it, and she matched it with pearl earrings. But for real effect she fastened the bodice of her gown with three enormous jewelled brooches, the pride of her collection; between her breasts there nestled a cluster of rubies, below her breasts a cluster of emeralds, and at her waist a cluster of sapphires.

Even Mistress Bracknell was pleased, and she was usually of the opinion that there was no gown ever created fit to set beside a coiffure of her creation. *So then,* she thought, *I go to meet my destiny.* She took a glass of wine before leaving the house, while she felt herself trembling all the way in the coach. Then she was again at that never-to-be-forgotten doorway, finding herself, strangely, apparently the only guest, although the major-domos were decked out in their best.

Her heart commenced to pound all over again. "Is His Majesty not entertaining tonight?" she inquired.

"Indeed he is, my lady," said the chamberlain. "There are several gentlemen within."

No doubt that was necessary. But if there were no other ladies, then was she not in effect invited to a tête à tête, which would develop into heaven knew what after the gentlemen had departed? She nodded, and the doors were opened.

"Lady Lorna Butler, Countess of Morne."

She paused in the doorway, to allow herself to be admired, and also to discover for herself jut whom she was about to encounter. The room was only half full and contained only men; half of these were courtiers, and she recognised most of them by sight. The other half were obviously the Russians of whom she had heard; they wore the same clothes as the Englishmen they copied, but wore them most uncertainly and uncomfortably, and to her amusement she saw one fellow, as he reached up for his hat, remove his entire wig as well to uncover a shaved head. They also wore a variety of moustaches, in contrast to the clean-shaven Englishmen. But it was their faces which were truly different, round rather than long, with heavy rather than thin features. Their faces and, she observed, as the men assembled to look at her, their sizes, for she saw to her astonishment that two of the company were dwarfs, hardly three feet tall, while another man was not less than four inches taller than six feet, and and towered above everyone in the room.

But now they all parted to allow the King himself to leave his chair to welcome her. "My dear Countess. It has been too long."

She sank into a deep curtsey, waited for his hands to raise her. "Indeed, Sire," she murmured. "I can have spent no more lonely two years in my life."

He frowned at her, as he was no doubt well aware of her parties, and her intrigues, and then extended his hand to walk her up the centre aisle. "These gentlemen are from Russia, my dear. They are touring Europe, learning our ways, and expressed the desire to meet the most beautiful woman in my kingdom."

"You flatter me, Sire."

"It is not in my nature," he said drily. "This young man in particular is interested in beautiful things. He speaks only French."

Lorna discovered they were before the giant, who was, she estimated, not much older than herself; his flesh was attractively burned by both wind and sun, and he wore a carefully trimmed little moustache. But as he beheld her immediately in front of him, he gave what appeared to be an involuntary grimace, which distorted his expression and left him quite hideous for a moment.

"Peter Mikhailovich," King William said, speaking French. "May I present the Countess of Morne."

To Lorna's amazement he did not even bow, but merely took her hand, and then, his face regaining its normal expression, placed his other hand on top of it. She glanced at the King, but he had stepped aside to engage in conversation.

She would have to extricate herself. "You are the Russian ambassador, Monsieur Mikhailovich?" she asked.

He shook his head. "Shipbuilding. You have a lovely voice, madam."

"Thank you. Shipbuilding?" She gave a little tug, but her hand was quite imprisoned.

"I am to learn. Ships, madam. Russia needs ships. And who builds better ships than the English? I had supposed your king exaggerated, when he described your beauty."

Another unsuccessful tug. "Thank you. You should refer to His Majesty as His Majesty. May I inquire your rank?"

The giant gave a booming laugh which gusted his breath around her head and echoed across the room. "I am secretary. Yes, I am secretary to the ambassador."

"Secretary?" His grip if anything was tightening. She turned her head right and left, for surely everyone would have been offended by that gush of vulgar noise, but it seemed to her that everyone had gone deaf; if anything, she would have supposed they were deliberately ignoring the couple in the centre of the room, each talking most animatedly to the man next to him. "Would you mind releasing me, master secretary?"

He ignored her request. "I was also told that you are the most arrogant and ill-tempered woman in England."

Lorna's chin dropped.

"Russian women are never arrogant," he said smiling. He had very white teeth. "Should they wish to be, we give them a taste of the knout."

Now she was definitely angry. "If you do not release me, sir, and this instant," she declared, raising her voice, "I shall be forced to seek assistance."

"But I have also been told," the young man continued, "that what you really wish is a hard cock up your hole."

Her mouth fell open again; her brain seemed paralysed.

"And that is good," he said thoughtfully. "Because I have a hard cock. Hard at the very sight of you, madam. And long. Why, I measure nine inches."

"You . . ." She panted and tugged.

"I will show you. I will let you measure." At last he released her and began unbuttoning his vest, apparently with the intention of removing his breeches there and then. Lorna's hand was free. She swung it with all her force, slashing it across his cheek, bringing his head up in an expression of sheer amazement.

She took a step backwards, turned to find the King. But William was no longer in the room. She stamped her foot with rage, ran for the door. The astonished major-domos hastily pulled it open, and she ran down the hall and on to the steps, quite forgetting her pelisse, wishing only to regain the safety of her carriage.

She got to sleep, eventually, with the aid of several glasses of brandy. She did not want to think. She dared not think, about the evening. Had the King meant only to insult her, to humiliate her? Could he be that hateful?

But what else could he have intended, to force her to submit to the obscene rudeness of some secretary here to learn about shipbuilding?

She awoke to the sound of her door opening, discovered that she had a headache, sat up, pushing hair from her eyes. "Who is it?" For it was scarcely daylight.

"Alice, my lady. Lorna. You must get up."

"Get up? Whatever for?"

"The King, my lady. His Majesty is downstairs."

"What? What did you say?" Lorna threw back the covers and leapt out of bed. "What time is it?"

"Eight o'clock, my lady."

"My God. The King. My bath, Alice. Quickly."

Alice was holding her cream undressing robe. "His Majesty wishes to see you, my lady. Now. He repeated the word 'now.' "

"Holy Mother." Lorna crossed herself, allowed the robe to be thrust over her arms, settled on her shoulders.

Alice seized her hair and brushed the tangles free.

"I must wash my face, at the least," Lorna protested.

"I have here a damp cloth, my lady."

Lorna wiped the sleep from her eyes, dampened her lips. "It is too unfair," she complained. "Calling here, without giving any notice . . ."

Alice was opening the bedroom door, her finger to her lips. Lorna gave a pout, went down the stairs, holding the train of her robe free of the steps, slowing up, geting her breathing under control. Her front hall was full; two guardsmen, two coachmen, two secretaries, her own butler, and three of her own footmen, all standing to attention.

"His Majesty is in the parlour, my lady," Morgan said, stepping forward to open the door.

"The parlour? He should be in the withdrawing room."

But the door was swinging in.

King William wore riding boots and a sword. "It was my choice, the smaller room," he said. "Would you close the door?"

She pushed it to, dropped to her knees.

"Rise," he said. "You left this behind, last night."

She rose, took the cloak from his hand. "I left in haste."

"So I understand. May I sit down?"

"Of course, Your Majesty." She hesitated, but he did not invite her to do likewise, so she remained standing, clasping her hands in front of her. And feeling her heart begin its perambulations again.

"I invited you to entertain my Russian guests."

Her head came up. "To be insulted by them, Sire?"

"A man, Lorna, or a woman, is insulted only when he chooses to be. It is generally a result of ignorance."

"Ignorance," she cried. "If you knew . . ."

"What he said? It has been related to me. Do you know, I believe he could be right, and that is all you *do* need. Having been taken advantage of, as a girl, now that you are in a position to pick and choose, you find yourself quite unable to make the decision. Yes, indeed, I had been told he is a most intelligent and perspicacious young man."

"That . . . that . . ."

"That Tsar, of Moscovy."

Her mouth fell open, and her knees gave way. She sat, unbidden, on the edge of a chair.

"Oh, indeed, Lorna." William uncrossed his knees, and sat up straight. "Peter, son of Michael, is actually

Peter, son of Alexis, and as I say, Tsar of Moscovy. Now, in the first place, Russia is a wild and barbaric country. It is to Peter's credit that he wishes to bring his vast empire into the fold of Western civilisation. But you will have observed that he is very young, and therefore perhaps hardly appreciates himself just what he is about. Certain it is that he can have little knowledge of the requirements of polite society."

Lorna continued to stare at him.

"And in the second place, he is an autocrat. In Russia his word is law." William sighed, suggesting a trace of envy. "He has no ministers to cajole, no parliament to convince. He decides, and it is done, or someone loses his head. It follows that he is accustomed to saying exactly what he thinks, to expressing exactly what he feels, without fear of contradiction. Your behaviour last night took him entirely by surprise. It has never happened to him before."

Lorna licked her lips. "Your Majesty . . ."

William smiled, and leaned back again. "And then, think of this. He paid you the greatest compliment a man may pay a woman. The Tsar of Moscovy expressed a wish to lie with you. And you are insulted."

Lorna had her breathing back. "Perhaps, had I been forewarned . . ."

"You would not have been natural. Peter likes other people to be as natural as himself. And believe it or not, having had the experience, the unique experience, for him, of a woman turning her back on him, of a woman striking him . . ." He leaned forward again. "Do you know what would have happened to you had you struck the Tsar in Russia?" He threw himself back in the chair. "Faith, neither do I. But no doubt by now we would have been hearing your screams all the way across Europe."

Lorna paled visibly.

"However," William went on, "as I was saying, you have intrigued him. Perhaps he sees in you a twin spirit. He is renting Evelyn's house at Deptford. He likes to be near the dockyards. You are invited to dinner. This very night."

Lorna discovered her jaw sagging again and hastily snapped it shut. "Sire . . ."

King William appeared to be studying the ceiling. "Try as I might," he said, "I can find no answer to the power, to the prospects, to the ambitions of Louis. I raise armies, and I am defeated. The reason is plain enough. My armies are hybrid, Germans, Dutchmen, Austrians, Englishmen, Scots, even some of your Irish. I had hopes of the Swedes and the Danes, but they would not join with us, and now that Charles is dead and succeeded by some boy, they will be of no use, anyway. While France, Louis, commands one nationality, but a nationality able to match any numbers I can produce, and all fighting in one language and for one ideal, however false that may be. Now we have signed a peace treaty. Louis is temporarily tired of the war. But he plans, and I know, that this be no more than a truce, to be ended the moment he is ready to resume hostilities. What would you have me do, Lorna? Prepare a surrender, which would certainly involve Holland? Or raise yet bigger and stronger armies, which in time must bring the French monster to heel? And where will I find those armies? The Turks? Or perhaps the Russians. The Rusians are at least Christians, if of a somewhat different complexion to either you or me."

"Sire . . ." Lorna stood up. "You are attending this dinner?"

"No. He wishes it to be an intimate affair."

She turned to face him, cheeks flaming. "Intimate? You are exposing me to rape."

"Oh, nonsense. I have spoken to him, told him that our customs, our manners, are a trifle different here to those obtaining in Moscow. I have secured his word that your womanhood shall be inviolate."

"His word," she muttered.

"And to reinforce his understanding of my intentions, you shall travel to Deptford in the royal barge, which will wait to bring you back."

"I . . . tonight is really too short a notice, Sire. I have no gown, I . . ."

"The Tsar has requested that you dress exactly as you did last night. He is a simple soul and wishes, perhaps, to start again and make a friend of you. So there is your problem solved. I have returned your cloak. You will leave the Westminster steps at four o'clock this afternoon."

She sat down again. And sighed. "Sire, I had supposed, I had hoped, I had prayed, that your invitation of last night meant that the quarrel between us was at an end." She raised her head, surprised at her own boldness.

"The quarrel, madam, was of your manufacture," William pointed out, then gave his winning smile. "But it is at an end, Lorna. And if you will act graciously towards the Tsar, then will I count you one of my dearest friends, and indeed supports. You may be sure of that." He extended his hand, and she slipped from her chair to the floor to kiss his fingers.

It was dark when the barge pulled into the dock at Deptford. This was not a part of London Lorna knew well, although she had passed it from time to time on her visits to Greenwich. All around her half-built vessels thrust their masts into the night, and the air was heavy with the scent of tar, and paint, and cordage.

A man waited for her on the dock, accompanied by a torchbearer and two other servants.

"Countess Morne," he said in French, bowing over her hand as he assisted her from the boat. "We are privileged."

She glanced at him in surprise, at once for his manners and his dress, for he was in uniform, a white coat and white breeches with black boots and a liberal profusion of gold braid, while in contrast to a baldric he wore a sword belt. But her surprise was centred mainly on the hat he was now replacing on his head, for while this was clearly a plain flat felt, as worn by the average English gentleman, although the brim was trimmed with braid, this brim had been pinned back in three places to give the effect of a triangle sitting on top of his hair, for a closer inspection convinced her that the luxuriant black tresses which rested on his shoulder were indeed his, and not a wig.

"Prince Vassily Bogoljubov, at your service."

In fact, she recalled having seen him the previous night, a moon-faced young man with a somewhat vacant smile. "But we had expected you alone," he said, peering at Alice as she left the barge.

"You'd not have me travel without my woman, Your Grace."

"Prince," he said. "Ah, your woman. Of course." He took Lorna's hand to escort her up the path from the dock, leaving Alice to walk behind with the Russian servants.

"Yes," she said. "I understand the word 'prince,' Your Grace."

"No, no," he said. "I am not of royal blood. I think our ranks are similar. In Russia, Prince."

"Ah," she said. "I apologise for my stupidity, my lord."

"How were you to know," he said gallantly. "My lady," and opened a door set in a high wall to admit them immediately to Evelyn's house, where a butler, clearly an Englishman, waited to take her cloak. And, strangely, seemed to tremble with fright at the sight of her.

"Monsieur Mikhailovich awaits you upstairs," Bogoljubov explained, and continued to hold her hand to walk her along a hallway, up a flight of stairs and through an antechamber towards a small withdrawing room, the strangest journey she had ever made in her life, for she was totally unprepared for her surroundings. The house was certainly of unusual richness, and quite compared with her own Hurd: The wainscotings were of the finest oak, decorated with clusters of exquisitely carved acanthus; the ceilings were painted, the floors were parqueted, and such drapes as remained in place were clearly of the finest brocade. But very few drapes actually remained, and those were cut and torn, while the floors were scored and the panelling was covered with bullet holes.

"Holy Mother," she said. "There has been a battle."

Inside as well as out, for a glance through a bay window, in which every pane of glass was either shattered or cracked to permit the chill autumnal air free access, indicated that the garden, which in summer had clearly been a wonderland of kaleidoscopic flower beds, delightful walks, shady nooks, fruitful orchards, and crowning the whole, a maze of marvellous intricacy, was in a similar state of disrepair. In fact, the place was an utter shambles.

But the Prince was smiling. "No, no," he said. "No battle."

She looked behind to discover what Alice thought, and was disturbed to find that she was alone; Alice had apparently been spirited below stairs. And now they were at the doors to the drawing room, where she paused in a consternation even greater than that she already felt, for the room before her suggested the home of a herd of pigs. Here too the drapes were torn and the windows were cracked, but in addition the carpet was soiled and the upholstery was cut and slashed, while over everything there arose a miasma of unwashed linen and indeed human urine.

Reclining on the remnants of the settee was Peter the Tsar himself, beside him another man, much smaller in every way, and with close-knit and somewhat unpleasant features while before them on what must once have been a Persian rug rolled and wrestled the two dwarfs she had observed at Kensington Palace the previous evening, apparently in deadly earnest, although she saw that they were happy enough to stop when their master clapped his hands.

"My lady," he cried, rising. "Never can this humble house have been so graced."

*Oh, God,* she thought. *Oh, God. I must leave.* But how to leave, without offending at once the Tsar and the King?

She sank into a curtsey, endeavouring at the same time to keep her balance and her skirts free of the floor. "It is my great pleasure, Your Majesty."

"Ha," he shouted. "Ha ha ha ha. My name is Peter. Peter Mikhailovich. Peter, madam. And you are my lady, for I am a humble secretary."

Bogoljubov gave her his arm to straighten.

"As you wish . . . Peter."

"Ha," he shouted. "Ha ha. She is good sport, after all, eh Pieman?" He gave the man standing beside him a push which threw him to the floor. "This is my friend, Alexander Menshikov. Alex, get up and bow to the Countess of Morne. He has no manners, my lady. Would you believe he once offered his pies for sale in the streets of Moscow?"

Lorna had her hand seized and kissed. "From which terrible fate my lord raised me," Menshikov said, in hardly more than a whisper, at the same time raising his eyes to stare at her.

"Wine," Peter shouted. "Wine for our guest. And you will sit here, my lady." He patted the couch behind him, and she sat down. "They tell me you come from far away across the sea, as far distant as is Russia across the land."

"I was born in America," she agreed, accepting a glass of wine from Menshikov, and commending her stomach to God as she sipped, for the glass had clearly not been washed for some time.

"You must tell me of it," he said. "To learn, to know . . . there is the object. To learn."

She found herself once again staring at him in amazement; for just a moment his voice had sunk into a thoughtful, reflective tone, and an expression of the most utter longing had crossed his face.

"I will certainly try, Peter," she said.

"After dinner," he decided. "Aye, that is the ticket. After dinner. Food," he bawled. "We shall eat this instant. My lady?" He took her hand and dragged her across the hall into a once magnificent dining room, with tables and sideboards of oak, and laden with crystal, but showing the same evidence of having been assaulted by a troop of madmen; there were splinters of crystal scattered on the floor from a previous debauch, which crackled beneath their feet.

The table was set for eight, the Tsar, Menshikov, the

two dwarfs, Prince Bogoljubov, two other Russians, and Lorna. Even her worst imagination had not supposed she would be entirely alone with them. But at least, as they were eating so soon, her escape would be equally soon made. And she now discovered that she would not be required to provide any conversation during the meal, for the Russians attacked the food in front of them—brought in by several serving girls, much to Lorna's surprise, rather than footmen—as if they had never eaten in their lives. The Court of King William had not been a particularly abstemious one, but she had never sat down to a meal quite like this, as there were several ribs of beef, four legs of lamb, a loin of veal trussed with bacon, eight rabbits, and half a dozen chickens, the whole assisted down by bread and beer, which promptly resurfaced in loud and odorous belches, while in between mouthfuls they sipped, or rather gulped by the goblet full, vast quantities of claret.

"You are not eating," Peter spluttered at her.

She tried her best smile. "A lady must look to her appetite, Peter," she explained. "Or she becomes fat."

"Ha," he shouted. "Ha ha. That must be true. For you are not as Russian women. They are all fat. Fat," he bawled. "A man knows not where to put his hands. But you . . ."

Hastily she drank some wine.

"Are all English women as you?" ·

"I have the honour to be Irish," she reminded him. "But you will find that Irish, and English, and, indeed, French women prefer to retain some control over their figures."

"So I have observed," he agreed. "These maids, they are like you also?"

"Why . . . I suppose they are. Although less by choice, perhaps."

"Ha," he said. "I would see what an English woman or an Irish looks like."

Her head turned in alarm. "His Majesty assured me . . ."

But Peter was clapping his hands. "Wine," he bawled. "This is too thin. Sherry. We shall have hot sherry. And Pieman," he shouted. "Fetch me one of those wenches. The Countess will explain her points."

Menshikov was out of the room in a moment, the dwarfs behind him. Lorna tried to get up, but she was feeling fairly unsteady herself from the constant glasses of wine being set in front of her.

"My lord," she protested. "Peter . . ."

"It will be sport," he shouted. "Pieman. Pieman. What are you about?"

Menshikov returned, half carrying, half dragging one of the serving girls, the youngest, a child of perhaps eighteen years old, who gave the lie to their earlier discussion, for she was distinctly plump. Menshikov had already pulled the cap from her head to allow her thin black hair to flop free, and the dwarfs had a leg each as they bore her to the table.

"Peter," Lorna shouted in desperation, a succession of nightmarish memories rising before her. But the Tsar ignored her, jumping to his feet in his excitement, and instead she felt a hand on her arm, and looked round to see Prince Bogoljubov, his face a picture of alarm, shaking his head and raising his finger to his lips. Perhaps she *was* overupset, she reasoned; two more of the girls had brought in an enormous cauldron of mulled sherry, which they placed on the table, gazed at their unlucky compatriot, giggled, and fled from the room.

Lorna leaned back in her chair and attempted to close her eyes, but was too fascinated by what was happening in front of her. For now all the Russians, saving only Bogoljubov, who remained seated beside her, seized the poor girl.

"Ow," she screamed in English. "Ow me God. Lemme go, sirs. Sirs, lemme go."

There was a succession of ripping noises as her apron and gown and shift were torn to shreds, and a moment later the naked girl was thumped on the table, half in and half out of the dishes, scattering gravy and bones and pieces of bread, shrieking again, although she was laughing now as well as someone upended a goblet of wine into her mouth. By now Peter was climbing on to the table itself, his friends beside him, to push and pull and poke the young woman, while Menshikov produced an enormous magnifying glass, with which they set about examining her inch by inch, hair by hair, orifice by orifice.

Lorna found herself rigid in her chair, at once with disgust and with fright, at the thought that it could easily be her lying there to undergo such an indignity, and, indeed, that it might yet be her, when they tired of the girl. She glanced at the prince, but if he was not actually taking part in the examination, he was totally absorbed in it. All of them were. And the door stood open. And only a few hundred yards away waited the King's barge and safety.

Cautiously she pushed back her chair, rose to her feet, turned to run. Bogoljubov discovered her intention and stood in front of her, so that she had to jump backwards. Her shoulder struck the edge of the steaming cauldron of wine, set it teetering for a moment, and as she gasped in horror, it crashed to the floor with an explosion like a pistol shot.

Which was followed by a moment of absolute silence, while the Russians looked up. And if Lorna was alarmed, she knew she had never seen anything to equal the pure terror on the faces in front of her. She gazed at the Tsar's back, for Peter was now kneeling absolutely straight, as if paralysed. Then he uttered an incredible howl of mingled fear and anger, before turning to face his imagined assailant.

"Sire," screamed Bogoljubov. But the Tsar was clearly at that moment quite mad. Lorna gave another gasp and dropped to her hands and knees, still staring at the apparition which loomed in front of her, for Peter's face was suffused, and his occasional twitchings had taken control of his features, so that every inch of purple flesh seemed to be cavorting with a muscular independence of its own, while his eyes rolled so that only the whites were visible, his breath heaved, and the tension of the huge muscles in his arms and shoulders was splitting the already frayed linen of his shirt.

She felt, rather than saw, the other members of the dinner party scattering for shelter behind chairs and sideboard, leaving the serving girl still spread-eagled in the centre of the table, uncertain as to what was going on. Then she threw herself to one side as well, forgetful at once of her dignity, her hair, her gown, or her jewels, anxious only to find shelter. She came to rest under the sideboard, watched Peter pick up the heavy oaken chair in which he had been sitting and snap it in two between his hands as if it had been made of straw. He then whipped his sword from his scabbard, and charged round and round the room, whooping and shouting and screaming, cutting and thrusting at the furniture, at the air, at the ceiling, and at any one his eye alighted on, so that everyone was howling and scampering to and fro, the maid leaving the table to flee for her life, and tripping as she did so to roll across the floor and come to rest against Lorna, who instinctively clutched the naked girl in her arms.

The awful dance lasted perhaps five minutes, and then Peter collapsed on the table, out of breath, the sword drooping from his hands.

Slowly the Russians began to sit up, and Lorna released the girl, who immediately crawled out from beneath the sideboard.

"No," Bogoljubov shouted, but he spoke in French and the girl was intent only on escaping. She ran to the door and seized the handle, and in so doing awoke Peter. He sat up, his sword pointing, his mouth covered in froth, shrieking orders in a high-pitched tone. Two of his men immediately ran after the girl, and one dived to seize her ankle and bring her heavily to the floor. The other held her wrist and between them they dragged her back and made her kneel before the Tsar, who made several passes with his blade across the pulsing white throat, while she shuddered and moaned.

"For God's sake," Lorna screamed, regaining her feet and seizing Peter by the shoulder. "Will you drive the child mad?"

His head turned, and he stared at her for some seconds, while her knees knocked, and she wondered if she had sealed her own death warrant. Then on a sudden the colour faded from his cheeks. "By no means, my lady," he said in an entirely normal and quiet tone of voice. "But look there."

Lorna glanced in the indicated direction, at the girl's mouth, which was open as she alternately screamed and begged and gasped for breath.

"Have you ever seen such rotten teeth?"

"I know nothing of teeth, my lord," she said. "Saving my own, which are in perfect condition."

"Ha," he said. "You never know. I will have to see. I have studied dentistry. I did so in Holland, but two months gone. We will have to have an extraction. Do you open her mouth, Pieman."

Menshikov grinned, and the dwarfs clapped their hands. The girl's jaws were forced apart, and a pair of gnawed bones inserted to hold them wide, while Peter took from his pocket a pair of enormous pincers, which reminded Lorna quite unpleasantly of Peter Chamberlen's forceps. These he inserted into the gasping aperture before him, cast this way and that, and at last appeared to fasten on what he sought, for there followed a frightful struggle, with the maid wrestling and fighting, and making as much noise as she could with her tongue restrained, while Peter knelt half upon her chest, tugging and pulling, and at last, in the midst of a gush of blood, removed the offending tooth. Whereupon the lamb bones were also removed and the girl allowed to sit up; she promptly gave vent to the full fury of her pain and wrath in a screaming series of curses; Lorna, sunk again to her knees at the horror of what she was watching, could only thank God that the girl was screaming in English, and Peter apparently was unaware of what she was saying.

Nor was he concerned by her fury, for he had regained his humour. He felt in his pocket again, stuck a gold coin between the teeth he had left her, pressed a bottle of wine into each hand, and gestured at the door. The girl heaved herself from the table and left, blood dribbling down her chin.

"There," Peter shouted, throwing himself into a chair. "A perfect extraction." He picked up the blood-stained tooth, looked at it against the light as another might have looked at a diamond. "Although perchance we removed the wrong one. Up, my lady. Up. You cannot spend the night on the floor."

Willing hands helped Lorna to her feet, and she attempted to straighten her gown. Her hair was a mess, and one of her brooches, the sapphire, had flown from her bodice, but she was not prepared to search for it now. "Sire," she said. "Peter. I am exhausted with the exhilaration of your entertainment. If you would permit me to take my leave . . ."

"Leave," he shouted, again starting to his feet. "It is not yet midnight. And there is much to be done. Entertainment? We have shown you no entertainment yet. Chariots. We shall play at chariots."

"Chariots?" she asked.

"Downstairs," Peter whooped. "Downstairs."

He seized Lorna's arm and hustled her down the stairs, the others following behind, yelling and screaming. They flooded out of the front door, Lorna having lost a shoe, and discovered three wheelbarrows waiting for them.

"The Countess is mine," Peter roared. "Do you have the dwarfs. You, Alex. And you, Bogoljubov." He seized Lorna's arm again. "Get in. Get in."

"My lord," she begged.

"In," he bawled, and swept her from her feet, one arm round her shoulders and the other under her thighs, to throw her into the wheelbarrow with a force which left her breathless. Immediately he seized the handles and started off, running straight across the garden, through flower beds and across lawns, through privet hedges and round trees. Lorna could do no more than moan and attempt to huddle as tight as she could, knees drawn up and arms around her head, as branch and thorn tore at her hair and her flesh and her gown, and while the night echoed to the screams and shouts of the other contestants in this strangest of races.

Round and round the garden they charged, several times, until the wheelbarrow containing Lorna struck a stone and seemed to leap into the air. She gave a shriek, but landed on her hands and knees in a rose-bush, scratched, but at least on soft earth. Immediately men were there to pull her out, and she saw the Tsar, lying full length beside her barrow.

"Holy Mother," she wailed. "He's not dead?" She did not know whether she was inquiring or hoping.

"No, no, my lady," said Prince Bogoljubov, setting her on her feet and attempting to dust her off. "He is but overtaken by liquor. But if you would make your escape, now is your moment."

"My lady?" Alice Mountfield hovered in the door-way.

Lorna sat up, clutched Snowdrop against her stomach. "Did you sleep?"

"Eventually, my lady."

"So did I." She was surprised. "What time is it?"

"Past noon, my lady." Alice came into the room, commenced to draw the drapes.

"Noon? Good heavens. Where is Kathleen?"

"In the garden with Parkin, my lady."

"I don't know how I'll face her." Lorna released the cat. "I don't know how I'll face anyone. My God. Did you see? Did you hear?"

"Yes, my lady." Alice stood by the bed, the tray waiting.

"That poor girl." Lorna held the cup in both hands, as she drank. "That poor, poor girl. He is mad, of course. I wonder if they are not all mad. But the Tsar most certainly." She handed back the cup, swung her legs out of bed. "My God, I am black and blue all over. And the King exposed me to that. I shall have something to say to him."

"Yes, my lady." Alice put down the tray, picked up the undressing robe. "There is a letter."

Lorna frowned at her. How her head hurt. She could not remember receiving a blow on it, but it could easily have happened during that madcap ride through the garden. On the other hand, it could just as easily be a result of all the liquor she had consumed. "From the palace?"

"Indirectly, my lady."

Lorna snatched the heavy envelope, picked up her paper knife from the table, slit it, took out a sheet of paper, and then another envelope. She read the paper first; it bore the royal coat of arms.

"My Dear Countess," William had written. "I find this utterly delightful, and greatly to our mutual advantage. You have my congratulations and my grateful blessing."

Her frown deepened, as she turned to the second envelope, which had been opened. It had been addressed, in French, and in a scrawling hand, to "The Lady Butler, Countess of Morne, in care of His Majesty King William the Third, King of England and Holland, France and Ireland, at Kensington House. For his eyes alone."

"My God, their ignorance," she muttered. "It would be laughable, were it not so cruel."

She inserted her fingers, drew out another folded sheet of paper. This bore the crest of an eagle, and was also in French.

"Your Majesty," the handwriting read. "My master, Peter Mikhailovich, whom you will know better as the Tsar Peter the First, Autocrat of all the Russias, bids me write to you to confess the unquenchable yearnings of my heart, in the hopes that you, as ruler of this realm and as protector of the Lady Butler, may assist me in achieving that which is dearer to me than life itself. My idea, my intention, my desire, my determination, is to make the lady mine, and to this end I here make formal application for her hand in marriage.

(Signed) Vassily Bogoljubov, Prince,
Captain in the Imperial Guard."

# Chapter 6

*H*is Majesty is at his papers," Sir John Capel explained.

"Tell him who it is," Lorna insisted.

"My dear Countess . . ."

"Then I will tell him myself." She strode across the antechamber, boots clicking on the parquet floor; she had come on horseback with only a groom in attendance, and wore her deep blue riding habit, a colour she well knew showed off her hair and her pale complexion to perfection.

"You cannot," Capel gasped, running behind her. But she was already opening the double doors to the study.

William sat at his desk, wearing a crimson undressing robe. He seemed to hang above the papers, for he wore his wig and the hair drooped. His faithful Dutchman, Bentinck, Duke of Portland, stood at his elbow.

Lorna hesitated, her courage already dissipating,

and sank into a deep curtsey as the King's head came up.

"Lorna?" He sounded genuinely surprised. "Capel?"

"The Countess insisted, Sire."

Lorna raised her head. "The matter is most urgent, Your Majesty."

"I have no doubt it is, to you," William agreed. "Well, rise, girl. Thank you, Sir John; you had best close the door."

Capel bowed and withdrew. Lorna regained her feet, took a few steps farther into the room.

"I wrote my congratulations," William said. "Now I can only repeat them. I understand your lover is ardent, and his master is equally anxious to be on his travels, and so I have issued instructions that a special licence is to be made ready to negate the necessity of having banns pronounced."

"Sire," Lorna cried. "Your humour has a cruel twist."

"Humour?" He was seized with a paroxysm of coughing which made his face grow unnaturally red. Lorna wondered if his back should not be slapped and looked hopefully at Portland, but the duke merely smiled at her.

"Humour," the King said at last, having regained his breath. "I wish I did possess the gift of humour."

"Sire," she said, taking a few more steps into the room, to bring herself almost to the desk itself. "You have entertained these people. You have seen them for what they are."

"A trifle primitive," William agreed. "Perhaps somewhat like those of your native America, by all accounts."

"Like . . . Sire, they are savages, you must see that. Last night, why, I would not have believed it possible had I not seen it with my own eyes. Evelyn's house, Sire? Once the loveliest in all England? It is a wreck. A pigsty, in which they live like pigs. Their servants are tormented, their idea of sport is to destroy everything in sight, their manners are those of blackamoors, their . . ."

"I am sure you generalise, my dear Countess," William said. "The young man, Prince Bogoljubov, seemed to me to be a very quiet and well-spoken fellow."

"Prince Bogoljubov," she cried. "Do you suppose it is really he who asks for my hand? 'Tis the Tsar."

"Ah," William said. "That could well be true. Although I doubt it is your hand he seeks. But what would you, Lorna? He cannot marry you, as he possesses a wife already, although I believe he keeps her locked away in a convent." He gave one of his half-envious sighs.

"Your Majesty," Lorna begged. "Of all his people he is the most savage. Perhaps you have not seen him when . . . oh, I cannot even say in a rage. It happens without warning."

"I have heard he is subject to fits of irrationality," William sighed. "Alas, poor lad. It is his background."

"And you would expose me to such a maniacal lust?"

"Oh, nonsense, Lorna. The young man is infatuated with you. Well, and why not? You are an infatuating creature. I will wager even Bentinck here has made advances. Eh, my lord?"

"I am a soldier, Sire," the duke pointed out. "A brief reconnoitre assured me the fortress was unassailable."

"Oh, well said. Indeed, Lorna, you have a reputation as being impregnable. Although your first husband certainly discovered a breach. Ha ha. Who said I could not make a joke."

Lorna glared at him. "In very poor taste, Your Majesty."

"Humour is often so," he said mildly. "Now listen to me. You are worrying quite unnecessarily. I will grant that it is Peter who really wishes you, but you may be sure that Bogoljubov is also in love with you, only the poor lad no doubt feels that you are as the sun, and can only be admired and never touched. You will make him your perfect slave, and as I do believe that is all you desire of any man, you should be very happy. As for Peter, well, I doubt you will succeed in conquering *him*. But if you do, England, the world, may well hold you in great gratitude. And if you do not, Lorna, yet will you have to suffer him for a very short while. His brain is never still, but flits from subject to subject, passion to passion. He will have lost interest in you in a month, and you may settle back into domestic bliss with your Prince."

Lorna stared at him, divided between outrage at what he proposed and anger at his suggestion she could not make the Tsar fall in love with her. But to be at the mercy of that monster . . . her mouth settled into a determined line.

"Your Majesty," she said. "I had assumed this entire masquerade was an attempt at humour. If it is not, then I must reassess my position. Sire, you may believe that I place your requirements, the requirements of the country above everything I possess, saving only my honour. You are asking me to prostitute myself, and not to a man, but to a madman. I would refuse either. When I marry again, it shall be for love. This coldness you think you see in me, this impregnability you choose to joke about, is because I have discovered no man in this kingdom worthy of my love. As yet. I am an optimist."

She paused for breath, and her knees touched each other. The King was frowning and Bentinck had ceased to smile.

"Your Majesty," she said. "I understand that I am offending against you, and deeply. Confine me to my house, Sire. Banish me from the kingdom, Sire. Brand me. Whip me. Cut off my head," she shouted, as he continued to gaze at her, without even winking. "I would rather die than go to that lunatic."

William sighed and rested his chin on his hands. "God knows how tired I am," he said. "My lungs ache, my head aches, I have fever which turns my blood to fire, night after night after night. Would you believe I am not yet fifty years of age, Lorna, and I suffer the torments of an old man?"

"Sire . . ."

"Oh, go to the devil," he said. "Go back to your Maryland. There. Is that not what you have sought, these last two years? Take yourself off, and do not let me see your face again."

"Sire." Her heart pounded so she thought it would burst. She had fought and won. Why had she not opposed him so openly before? Maryland. Home.

"Take the next available passage," he said. "Just begone. I will send someone for the child."

Lorna slowly straightened, the blood draining from her face. "Sire?" She could manage no more than a whisper.

"The Tsar has promised to aid me against the French," William said. "In return he has asked for the hand of the Countess of Morne. Well, he will have to be patient, but I am told your daughter will probably possess a beauty as perfect as your own. She will assume the title and the responsibilities of her rank, as you seem unable to do so. And who knows, it may be for the best. She will be educated in Russia, understand their ways, learn to love where you can only hate."

The room seemed to sway about her. "You cannot," she said. "You cannot take my child," she screamed.

"I can," he said coldly. "Or you can, with you, to Russia."

"You . . . you . . . you tyrant," she screamed. "You monster. You Caliban."

"You are quoting my dear sister-in-law's mistress," he said. "And as you are doing that, I will forgive the words."

Lorna dropped to her knees, clung to the edge of the desk. "Sire, have mercy on me." *Oh God,* she thought, *I am going to weep.* But she was too angry, too outraged for tears.

"I shall, Countess. When next I can afford such a luxury."

She attempted to dig her fingers into the wood, slowly pushed herself away from the desk, once more stood before him. *God,* she prayed, *give me strength.* "I will write the Prince Bogoljubov, Sire, expressing my devotion, my amazement that he should have chosen to admire one such as I, my grateful acceptance of his proposal."

The King leaned back in his chair and smiled at her. "Lorna, you are a treasure, the very prop of my old age."

"No doubt the Prince will show my letter to the Tsar and make him as happy," she said bitterly.

"I have no doubt of it." He turned to Bentinck. "My lord duke, pour some wine. We shall drink a toast, to the Princess Bogoljubov. My God, but it has a ring to it."

How memory flooded back, to a group of bedraggled horsemen and their captive, riding away from a burning homestead. But now was not the time for sentiment.

"Yes, Your Majesty," she said. "But as I am to be the Princess Bogoljubov, may I make a request?"

"You may."

"I should like to take my daughter."

"I shall insist upon it."

"And, as I have no more use for the title, I should like her made Countess of Morne, with a certainty that she will inherit, supposing she does not die on the Russian steppe."

William frowned. "I would prefer you to retain that title, Lorna. But I give you my word, it shall pass to your daughter on your death, or her children on hers. Will that not satisfy you?" He smiled. "We shall hold your estates, your wealth, in trust for you."

Lorna bowed. "You are more than generous, Sire."

Bentinck stood at her side, a glass in his hand. She raised her own, as the King raised his.

"To the Princess Bogoljubov. May Russia appreciate the great gift we bestow upon them," William said. "You may drink as well, Lorna, as you do not yet actually possess the title. Now, there are one or two other details. The Tsar is accompanied by his priests, of course, and they will attend you to instruct you in the Orthodox faith. This will have to be done quickly, if the marriage is to be celebrated by the end of the month."

Lorna's head came up so suddenly she spilled her wine. "No."

William's brows drew together. "I had supposed we had discarded refusals."

"I will not change my faith, Your Majesty."

He stared at her.

"No," she said again. "I have surrendered everything else. You cannot ask this of me, as well."

William leaned back again. He was too superb a diplomat not to know when to yield as well as to be hard. "You are right, of course. I admire you for it, Lorna. Oh, I admire you for everything. We shall insist on your own establishment. Your own priests, your own maids, your own secretaries. Oh, yes, indeed, Bentinck, why should we give these Russians everything? After all, as the Countess has just said, the promise of their assistance is at best intangible. Oh, do not fear, Lorna, we shall insist upon your rights. And now, my dear, will you not attend me at dinner? We have much to discuss."

Lorna sighed and put down her empty glass. "I would beg to be excused, Your Majesty."

"You have a prior engagement?"

"I have no engagement, Your Majesty." She did a deep curtsey. "I but intend to seek a corner, where I may weep in peace." She straightened. "No doubt it shall be for the last time."

But it had happened too suddenly for tears. She doubted she really understood what *had* happened yet, save that the world of physical security she had built around herself, through which those idle dreams of a perfect future she had always indulged had filtered like morning sunlight through a vale of trees, had suddenly been torn apart. As before.

She looked at the trees, the grass, the dwindling flowers of her garden. But need it be as dramatic, as drastic as that? She must leave this place. But then, she had left MacMahons. And still found Hurd House, at the end of it.

But Russia. She knew nothing of it at all, save that it was a country of deep snows and wild horsemen. But then, so were considerable parts of the North American continent.

And she knew, now, that the people were uncouth, hardly better than savages. But would they not the more readily respond to her culture, as they had too readily responded to her beauty? Had not Papa insisted, only a few days before his death, that she be happy? Do what must be done, he said, but be happy. And she had promised.

And she had gained a personal concession of tremendous importance. She dismounted, and the doors of the house opened before her. She strode inside, and Morgan was waiting to take her cloak. "Summon the servants," she said. "Everyone. I will see them in the dining room, in fifteen minutes."

She did not change, stamped into her study in her riding boots, sat before her desk.

Be happy. With Vassily Bogoljubov? She wrote as she had promised the King, in a quick, clear hand. Then threw herself back in the chair; she did not wish to read it again. Whatever the words read, it was a lie. It could be interpreted: "I, Lorna Butler, Countess of Morne, do hereby sign away all my rights and privileges and freedoms as a woman, into the keeping of a man I do not know, do not like, and could not possibly love."

She got up, paced the room, twisting her pen between her hands. But could surely dominate. Vassily Bogoljubov was no older, and possibly a little younger. He could be no wealthier. The title of Princess he would bestow upon her, however grand it might sound to English ears, he had himself confessed was no superior to her own in Russia. And he was a characterless young man.

He was also, when she came to think about it, by no means ugly. Indeed, he could even be described as pleasant featured, if not handsome. And he was certainly pleasant mannered, at least for a Russian. Of everyone last night, he alone could not be complained of, and he had seen to her escape, and that of Alice, with much care, had kissed her hand . . . with love? There was a start. If indeed he loved her . . . at first glance? But it was possible, at least in the imagination of playwrights and poets. Then did she possess a tremendous advantage to start with. A man in love could be controlled. A man in love was a prisoner.

Then was it possible he had merely obtained the Tsar's permission, and had not been instructed?

She sat back on to her chair, her fine white teeth chewing into the spine of her pen. There was the thought which had been banging on her consciousness all day. The Tsar. *Have mercy on my soul,* she thought. *No, not my soul. But Peter would have that as well, if he chose.*

A madman, with the power of life and death over all of his subjects. Of whom she would be one. *Oh, Mary,* she thought. *Oh, Holy Mother. Help me.*

She seized paper again, wrote quickly and vigorously, outlining the situation to Father Simeon, begging him to return to her house and undertake with her this voyage into the unknown, to perform the marriage, and then to share with her the looming dangers. Why should he, after the way she had treated him? But to face the Tsar, without support . . .

She thrust the papers away from her, made herself

sit straight. Simeon would come because, like most men who came into contact with her, he loved her. At least like a father. And there, surely was her answer. She must surround herself with love, an invisible barrier which even Peter would be unable to penetrate.

To penetrate. Oh, my God. Her head sank, and she supported her chin with her hands. Butler had penetrated. Seven years and more ago, and she could remember that first thrust as if it had been yesterday. That stab of pain. She could still feel his beard, tickling her thighs. And he had wanted nothing more. That kiss, that tickle, was the most intimate thing he had done to her, if she could ignore the penetration. And that was something which would have been done by her husband, and caused her pain, no matter how much his love. There was no love in penetration. Love was to be found in what happened before, in what happened after, in what happened in their minds during penetration. Not in the physical act.

Unless . . . she sat up again, recalled that terrifyingly beautiful split second in time, when she had felt . . . she did not know what. But she had felt it again with Lennart. And had endeavoured to recreate it again, for herself, with only partial success. Because she had never dared cross the threshold of physical pleasure to that extent, had withdrawn her hand as if burned, and gazed on those slender white fingers as if they had belonged to someone else, to some devil, some succubus, waiting to claim her soul for eternity.

She was out of her chair, striding to and fro, throwing one long leg in front of the other, scattering her skirts. Then that was not love either. Save it was shared . . . She shook her head to restore the clarity of her thought. Butler had sought nothing more than his own gratification. What had happened to her had been incidental, and as long as what had been happening to her was not in any way related or shared with what was happening to him he had been unable to possess her utterly. The same would go for any man. So, Peter would wish to penetrate. With a lance nine inches long. Oh, Holy Mother . . . Again her fingers made the sign of the Cross. Nine inches. But then, how did she know Butler and Lennart had not been nine inches? She had not measured them.

No doubt he boasted, in any event. He would wish to penetrate her. Think only of that, and then forget it.

Once again she sank into her chair. But would mere penetration satisfy a man like Peter? So then, perhaps he would want to kiss her as well. He might wish to kiss her from head to toe. How her heart pounded. But Butler had kissed her, as intimately as was possible. The Tsar could do no more.

Save that he might not rest content with kisses and penetration. She was back on her feet, holding on to the back of her chair. What else could he want, could he do? Explore her, as he had explored that unfortunate girl? *She* had not been injured. At least during the exploration. But she was a slut. No doubt all men assaulted her in that fashion. And could exploration be more intimate than a kiss?

She sat down again. She was driving herself as mad as the Tsar. That was no way to go about it. She was being utterly stupid, like a young girl instead of a mature widow. King William had himself said the Tsar was in haste to be again on his travels. And she was getting married at the end of next week. There would be her honeymoon, by which time the Russian entourage would be on its way, she knew not where. There would hardly be time for the slightest dalliance. It would take them months to regain Russia. There would be the moment of crisis. But by then, months after her marriage, she would be pregnant.

She sat straight, the enormity of the thought clouding her brain. Pregnant, by Vassily? The possibility had not occurred to her. Yet as she was going to be his wife, she would have to bear his child. But would she not enjoy more children? Kathleen had been no hardship to bear, and a joy to have. And Kathleen sorely needed some brothers and sisters. There it was. By the time she regained Russia, she would be pregnant, and the Tsar would be forced to wait. And by then, he would have lost interest, would have found some other pretty thing to fill his eye.

There was her salvation, in the simplest and most obvious terms, staring her in the face, just as she had been about to lose her head and collapse into tears.

She frowned. And by then, she must have completed her very first task, that of making Vassily Bogoljubov fall utterly and irrevocably in love with her.

She seized her letter of acceptance, tore it up, and rewrote it, using the words she had promised William, but adding at the end, "How I would dearly like the opportunity to convey my feelings in person, my lord."

She leaned back, feeling suddenly calm, heard the door open. "My lady?" Alice inquired. "The servants have all been summoned. I hope there is no difficulty with the King?"

"Difficulty, Alice?" Lorna got up, turned to face her. "Oh, no difficulty. We are going on a journey, you and I. To Russia."

"His Highness, Prince Vassily Bogoljubov," Morgan said, pronouncing each syllable with great emphasis.

"Stay close for five minutes, Father," Lorna said, and rose. She had dressed carefully for this occasion, wore but a single strand of pearls. Her skirt was indigo with an underskirt of cobalt blue; her bodice was rose madder while her sleeves were white. And she was distinctly nervous.

The Prince wore a uniform and appeared equally apprehensive. He removed his hat with a flourish and bowed, left hand on the hilt of his sword, but immediately it was creeping up to stroke his moustache, and she had a sudden wonder as to whether a moustache would tickle like a beard. "Madam," he said in French. "I am the most fortunate of men."

"You flatter me, Highness," she said, and extended her hand. His kiss was wet, and she kept her smile with difficulty. "I would have you meet my confessor, Father Simeon."

"Father." Bogoljubov shook hands.

"Father Simeon will be conducting the ceremony," Lorna explained.

Bogoljubov nodded.

"And we shall hold it in this house," Lorna said.

"Of course," said the Prince, and resumed gazing at Lorna.

She looked at the priest, who raised his eyebrows.

"Perhaps the Prince and I should have a talk," he suggested.

"Yes," Lorna said. "But not now. Why, we have had not a moment alone together since our betrothal. Morgan, some wine."

Father Simeon bowed and left the parlour. Morgan had received his instruction, and a tray with a bottle and two crystal goblets was instantly placed on the small table. Then he too withdrew, and the door was closed.

And Prince Bogoljubov continued to gaze at her. She felt desperation seizing hold of her mind.

"You'll take a glass?"

"I would like to."

She poured, held his out, her own fingers wrapped around the stem so that he had to touch them in order to take it. But he had not removed his gloves.

She sighed, raised her own. "To us, Highness."

"To us." He brushed his glass against hers, then drained it in a single gulp.

"Another?"

"Thank you."

She poured.

"And will you not sit down?"

"Thank you." He chose a straight chair and sat.

Lorna sipped her drink, placed it on the table, and sat on the settee, arranging her skirts as she did so. Bogoljubov continued to stare at her. She was not sure if he had blinked at all since entering the room.

"I . . . I know nothing of Russia," she said. "You will think me very ignorant."

"No one knows anything of Russia," the Prince said and drained his glass.

Lorna got up, pulled the bell rope, refilled the glass, and as an afterthought, left the nearly empty bottle beside him.

"But you will tell me of it," she said. "Ah, Morgan, another bottle." No doubt the Prince was merely shy.

Prince Bogoljubov smiled. "I will do better. I will show it to you, madam."

Was she making progress? She took another sip of wine, remained standing in front of him. "I should still like to know something about it."

The Prince appeared to consider. "It is very cold."

"Oh? Oh, dear."

"In winter. It is very hot, in summer."

"Oh." She gave a bright smile. "Then at least there

is variety. Where I was born, there was not so much variety. Have you heard, where I was born?"

"In the colony."

"Ah . . . yes, I suppose you could say that. In Maryland. That is in America. Have you been there?"

"No," said Prince Bogoljubov.

Lorna discovered her own glass was empty. But by now the second bottle was on the table. She poured, placed the bottle beside Bogoljubov. To her consternation he drank from the neck.

"Would . . . would you like to hear about it?"

"No," said Prince Bogoljubov.

"Ah." Lorna sat down, and did not trouble to arrange her skirts. She presumed she was shortly going to be as mad as everyone else around Peter.

Prince Bogoljubov finished the second bottle of wine, set it down. Lorna got up and pulled the bell rope. Morgan brought a third bottle of wine.

"Your people," Prince Bogoljubov said. "They are too many."

"Highness?"

"We are marrying in your church. That pleases you. You must please me also. Three. No more."

"Three?" she cried. "But I cannot possibly . . ."

"Three," he insisted.

She kept her temper. "Well . . . Father Simeon, Alice, Bridget . . . but what of Kathleen? I must take four. My daughter's nurse."

"Three," he said. "We will find you a nurse in Russia."

"Oh . . ." She drained her glass, refilled it, felt like smashing it on the floor.

"I love you," said Prince Bogoljubov.

Lorna dropped her glass by accident; it did not break. "I love you," said Prince Bogoljubov again.

"I shall make you a good husband. And you," he added confidently, "shall make me a good wife."

Lorna regained her glass, poured. "I shall certainly try to do so, Highness."

"I am not so large as His Majesty," the Prince said.

Lorna finished her fourth glass. "I would not expect it, Highness."

The Prince emptied wine down his throat. "We shall have many children."

"Oh, indeed," Lorna agreed.

"Mine is an old family," the Prince said.

"So are the MacMahons of Morne," Lorna said.

The prince stood up. "I should like to feel your breasts."

Lorna hastily closed her mouth.

The Prince stood in front of her. "I do not wish to tear your gown."

Lorna licked her lips and wished the room would stop swaying. But she also wished her glass was again full. "You will not," she said. "If you remove your gauntlets."

"Ah." He stripped off his gloves. "You are a very intelligent woman," he said conversationally.

"Thank you, Highness."

"In Russia there are no intelligent women."

"Oh, I'm sure . . . oh."

He had taken her by surprise, thrust his hands down her chest with such force he carried her bodice with it. Perhaps he wanted to be sure that she was flesh and blood. He squeezed her as he might have shaken her hand. Then he released her, stepped back.

"You have nice breasts. They are not soft."

Lorna found her mouth was open again. She closed it, got up, pulled on the bell rope.

"Is your bottom soft?"

"Ah . . . I do not think so," she said. "Would you like to feel it?"

"Yes," he said.

She supposed, that if things were not going quite according to plan, they were at least going fairly well.

"Kneel," he said.

"Oh . . ." She licked her lips. "It is bad luck to make an entry before the wedding."

"In Russia, also," he agreed.

She sighed with relief, knelt on the couch, and felt her skirts being lifted. Holy Mother, she thought. Let him be pleased. And gazed at Morgan, entering with his fourth bottle.

"My lady?"

"Put it down," she said. "Put it down."

Morgan obeyed. God alone knew what the servants would be discussing this night.

Once again the hearty squeeze, this time accompanied by some kneading. "They are good," he said. "Good. They smell good. You are clean."

His hands were gone, and she hastily pulled down her skirts.

"Russian women," he said sadly, "are not clean. Would you like to look at me?"

"No," she said firmly, getting off her knees. "It is bad fortune for a wife to look at her husband before the wedding night."

"Ah. I have not heard that, in Russia."

"The English are very superstitious," she said. "The Irish, even more so."

The Prince sat down, began on the fresh bottle. "Your hair," he said. "I have never seen anything like your hair. It is beautiful. I would like to touch your hair."

She supposed he was at the least establishing a

certain order of priorities. She knelt before him, stared at his sword. Once again he pulled and prodded, utterly destroyed her coiffure.

"But the hair on your belly," he said accusingly. "It is not the same colour."

*My God,* she thought, *he must have looked as closely as Chamberlen.* She extricated herself, knelt straight. "Is it in Russia?"

"Russian women," he said, "have black hair on their heads, black hair on their bodies. You have red hair on your head, and brown hair on your body."

"Pale brown," she protested. "It sometimes appears red."

"Why it that?"

"Ah . . . I have no idea. Highness, do you think I could call you Vassily?"

"No," he said.

"It is customary, in England, to call one's husband by his name. In private, of course."

"Highness," he said. "Or Prince."

"Ah. And you call me?"

"Madam. Or woman."

She managed another smile. "There hardly seems any point in having a name at all."

"How would we know you from your sister?"

"Ah. I never thought of that. I have no sister. I am a silly goose."

"No, no," he said. "You are intelligent. Russian women . . ."

"Are not intelligent." She could see an absolute riot of conversation opening in front of her, over the years. But to give up now . . . "Highness," she said. "There is another custom, in England, in Western Europe, that when two people are betrothed, they may kiss each other on the lips."

Which were presently occupied by the neck of the wine bottle. He put it down, gazed at her.

"May I?" she asked.

The Prince got up, the action making her over-balance to sit on the floor. "No," he said.

"I can't," Lorna said, staring at herself in the mirror. "I cannot, I cannot, I cannot. I will not."

It was the hundredth time she had said it. Perhaps she had wept, a hundred times as well, all in a matter of five days. But now it was too late to weep; Bridget was lacing her corset, bracing herself to drag it tight without actually pulling her mistress from her feet, causing Lorna's breasts to swell out of the top, the nipples to start up as blood rushed into them, ribs to constrict, the belly beneath to pout, the silky brown hair to spread. Why isn't it red?

"I felt the same way about Mr. Smiley," and Mistress Smiley, standing waiting with the first petticoat. "Didn't you feel the same way about Mr. Bracknell, Mistress Bracknell?"

"I was terrified," confessed Mistress Bracknell, arranging her instruments on the table before the second mirror.

"But it all came right in the end," Smiley said. "As it will for you, my lady. Aren't you done yet, girl?"

Bridget panted and tied the bows. Lorna released the post, raised her knees as high as she could, one after the other, lowered them again, and felt a little more comfortable.

"My lady is so beautiful," Mistress Bracknell said dreamily. "It must come right for her."

"Now, my lady, if you will lower your head." Lorna obeyed, and the petticoat was dropped over her head, smoothed on to her body.

"The man is a boor," she grumbled. "Not even a boor. A totally feelingless . . . thing."

"Perchance he was more afraid of you, than you of him." Smiley adjusted the second petticoat.

"I was not in the least afraid of him, Smiley," Lorna said. "I but supposed, as I am to live with the creature, that we might get to know each other first. Get to know each other? I might as well wed a tree." *With branches,* she thought bitterly. "What is that noise?"

"'Tis the guests arriving, your ladyship," Bridget said.

"The guests. Oh, Holy Mother. Smiley, haste."

"No haste, my lady," Smiley said, adjusting the last petticoat. "'Tis no fortune for a bride to be early for her wedding. Mistress Bracknell, my lady is yours."

"Here we are, my lady." Bracknell held the chair for her, smoothed the titian hair, only recently dry from its thorough washing. "Oh, you must keep them waiting."

"But the King . . ."

"Even the King, on such an occasion," Bracknell said.

She gazed at Mistress Bracknell, lovingly setting the ringlets. "A drink," she said. "I must have a drink. Smiley . . ."

Smiley looked at Bracknell. "It might be no bad idea, Mistress Bracknell. It will bring colour to her cheeks."

"I will see to it," Bridget said.

"Privily, child," Smiley snapped. "Don't go screaming it all over the house."

The door opened, to admit a tremendous hubbub, and also Frances, Duchess of Richmond, her matron of honour.

"Fanny," Lorna gasped. "Whatever is happening?"

Bracknell seized her head to set it straight again. "My lady, please."

"They are coming in their hundreds." Fanny was scarcely less excited than her friend.

"The Marlboroughs? The Princess?"

"The Earl and Countess are here. Not her Royal Highness."

She had not really expected her to come. After all, why should she? "The Russians?"

"Not as yet, my dear."

"Perhaps they will not come." Her head turned. "Oh, Fanny, perhaps they will not."

"My lady," Bracknell protested, once again setting her head straight. "And what a suggestion, on your wedding day."

"And after all my work," Smiley remarked.

"Oh, if they would not come," Lorna said, half to herself.

"Then would you be the laughing stock of all London," Bracknell pointed out. "All Europe, no doubt."

"And that would be the greatest blessing that could be bestowed upon me," she said. The hair was all but ready; only the headdress remained. Made of white lace on a wire frame, it stood nearly a foot high and would reach the small of her back; as she was celebrating her second marriage, and as it was a mixed ceremony, she had decided against a train. And beneath the lace and the glowing red-gold hair, the face. A mature face, now, she thought. Not even the ringlets could diminish the high pale forehead, which seemed only accentuated by the neatly penciled eyebrows. Below all was solemnity, the long, pointed chin, the smooth cheeks. The wide mouth suggested determination, the deep green eyes suggested confidence. The small, straight nose was the delicious incongruity which made the whole human and irresistible. Oh, yes. She was irresistible. And that was what they all thought of her. Even, presumably, the King. There was not one of them supposed even for an instant the trembling creature that lurked behind that green thicket.

Well, then, did such a creature exist? As the girl survived the worst of Butler, could not the woman survive the worst of Vassily Bogoljubov? Or Peter the Tsar?

Bridget stood at her elbow with a glass of wine on a silver tray, and she took it, hesitated, then drank it at a gulp. She might as well get used to Russian manners. And she was rewarded with a most delightful sensation of heat tracing its way down her chest, while, as Smiley had prophesied, colour promptly flared in her cheeks.

Bracknell was at last satisfied that the commode was at once straight and firmly set on its bedding of hair. "There," she said. "Now be careful, do, my lady. No sudden jerks. Mistress Smiley, you will be careful."

"I am always careful," Smiley said primly, lifting the gown as if it had been made of solid gold. "My lady?"

Lorna crossed the room slowly, keeping her head absolutely straight as she had been taught by Sarah Churchill. She stepped into the gown, and the satin was raised up and settled around and under her breasts by Mistress Smiley, while Alice and Bridget hastily commenced fastening the back.

"There," Smiley said. "My lady?"

Lorna gazed at herself. The gown was white satin, with a bodice and underskirt of white lace to match her headdress, as her sleeve ruffles and neck edgings were also white lace. But as she was not a virgin she had allowed herself a little colour; the bows securing her hair, and the bows holding back her skirt were in blue velvet. She had confined her jewellery to her gold crucifix, which Fanny was at this moment securing about her neck.

"Lorna," she whispered. "You look simply superb. Nothing suits you like white, unless it be black. It really is a crime for you ever to wear colour."

"Oh, fie on you," she muttered, and watched heat again seeping into her cheeks. Because in fact she *was* a virgin, to all intents and purposes. It was seven years since that never-to-be-forgotten night in St. Mary's. But whatever she was, there could be no more delay. She was fully dressed, and her attendants were standing back and clasping their hands and whispering to each other. And the hubbub from downstairs was rising through the floor.

And now there was a tap on the door. "Come."

Morgan, wearing his best maroon velvet coat. "His Majesty is here, my lady. And the Russian gentlemen."

"Oh," she said, and continued to gaze at herself in the mirror. She crossed herself, was fascinated by that beautiful, resolute, utterly calm face. *It cannot be me,* she thought. *It cannot be me.*

"Mama." Kathleen, dressed in a replica of her own gown, and carrying an enormous bouquet of late roses.

"Careful now." She stooped, not bending, but descending in as straight a line as possible to kiss the child on her cheek. "Are you ready?"

"Oh, yes, Mama. Mr. Morgan says the King is here, Mama. Oh, isn't it exciting."

Lorna straightened with the same care. Two kings, did they but know it. When last had a private house in England sheltered two kings at the same time?

"Then we had best not keep them waiting," she said. "Ladies, my thanks, a thousand times. Mr. Wilson will attend to you."

They clapped, and she walked through the door, and on to the gallery. Morgan waited, his staff in his hand. Father Simeon had decreed that there should be no music; he intended to miss no opportunity of letting the Russians know that they were receiving a favour, as much from Lorna's religion as from Lorna herself. She stopped, and he waited, and the noise from below grew. "My lady?" he asked.

"Faithful Morgan," she said. And in truth, she felt exactly as if she were going to the block, the same sudden sense of intimacy with everyone around her, because she and they shared so terrible a secret. She inhaled, until she thought her lungs would burst through the corset, and stepped forward. "You may announce me," she said.

The staff pounded the floor. "Lady Lorna Butler, Countess of Morne," Morgan bawled.

*For the last time,* she thought, and began her descent, Kathleen and Fanny close behind.

The King waited at the foot of the stairs, dressed in a scarlet coat with matching breeches and stockings, a white lace cravat and with white lace at his sleeves and ruffles, and wearing a blue silk sword belt. His gloves were white, and he took her arm as she reached him.

"Your Majesty." She gave a half curtsey.

"Courage, Lorna." he murmured. "All will be well. No man could do less than love you, after a single glance."

The hall was full of people. She knew them all, and yet at this moment she knew none of them. In the drawing room the crowd was even thicker; she was surrounded with the scents of perfumes and pomades, the rustle of taffeta, the shuffling of feet; the absence of music was uncanny, as no one was speaking.

She looked straight ahead of her, supported by the King's arm, while the assembly bowed and curtsied to their monarch. In front of her was the altar and Father Simeon, wearing black with purple accessories, his cap on his head and his book between his hands. And to his right were the Russians, turning now to face them. They all wore their white uniforms, even Peter himself, easily distinguishable by his height; she realised with vague surprise that he was best man.

She arrived before the altar, and Vassily, looking as solemn as ever, was waiting to take her hand. She gave him a half smile, but received no answering recognition from him. *Oh, God,* she thought. *Oh, Holy Mother. I will need You both, now and for the rest of my life.*

She concentrated, and heard nothing. She saw Father Simeon's lips moving, and did not know what he was saying. She was aware of the pressure of Vassily's fingers on hers, but did not relate it to the man beside her. She was more aware of heat, of sweat beginning to trickle down her legs, and the month was October. She wanted to lie down, but in the open air, if that were possible.

Father Simeon was asking her a question, and she said, "Yes." Then her fingers were being extended, and the gold band was being forced on to the third finger of her left hand. It seemed too tight, and she realised with a pang of near horror that she would never get it off again. She was a prisoner for life.

"You may kiss the bride," Father Simeon suggested. Lorna turned up her head, looked at Vassily's descending towards her. Still there was no humour there, no sign even of pleasure. His mouth brushed hers, and his fingers touched her arm, for just a moment, then they were separated by noisy hands, slapping and tugging, hugging and squeezing, by rushing breaths and shouted congratulations, by slobbered kisses and sly pinches. Lorna found herself opposite the Tsar himself, for just a moment; his huge arm went round her shoulders to give her a hug, and he smiled at her, the obvious pleasure in his face making him appear almost charming, for a moment. Then she was swept on into the rush, to discover Sarah Churchill.

"A Princess," the Countess remarked. "You use a long ladder, sweet child. Let us hope it does not sink into the Russian snows."

"My congratulations, Lorna," the Earl said, as stiffly as usual. "I have heard there is no stopping these Russian fellows. At least in bed."

Then she was back beside at once Vassily and the King, and there were cries for silence, and the speeches began. She gazed at the faces in front of her, some smiling, some serious, some jealous, some admiring. She heard little of what William said, until he raised his glass, and shouted, "So then, I give you Lorna of Morne, Princess Bogoljubov."

The cheers roared around her like an ocean wave, and she glanced at Vassily, but William had been speaking in English, and he preserved a stony impassivity. Someone whispered to him, no doubt in Russian, for he seemed to awake as from a sleep—a reassuring thought that he was as bemused as she— and then delivered a brief speech himself, but as he spoke in Russian, no one did more than smile politely.

The speeches done, Wilson gave the signal to the musicians, and the fiddles struck up, while Morgan and his army of footmen began circulating with the wine, and there were cries for the bride and groom to lead the dance. Lorna held Vassily's hand, and he looked at her inquiringly.

"We must dance," she explained, in French.

"Dance? What is this, dance?"

"It is called the minuet," she said. "I will show you."

"Show me? You?"

He followed her into the hastily cleared space in the centre of the floor, while the crowd clapped and shouted their encouragement, and followed her to the end, while the other dancers formed their partnerships and came behind, then stood at attention when they turned to make their arch, which earned him great applause, and for the first time he smiled. But soon she had other partners, a succession of them, and the house shook as they cavorted to and fro, and drank wine, and perspired, and she lost her headdress, a collapsing ruin of lace and wire, and tried to convince herself she was happy, or at least that she was enjoying herself, that she was not in fact a trembling jelly at the thought of what was rushing at her like a runaway coach and four with her bound to the road in front of it and unable to move even a muscle.

Until Fanny Richmond, at the previously selected hour, appeared in the doorway at the very moment the band, also previously instructed, came to a crashing halt, which left nothing but panting breaths to fill the room.

"Your Majesty," Fanny declared in a loud voice. "My lords, ladies, gentlemen, we have amused ourselves long enough. Time now for the serious business of the evening to begin."

They gave a whoop which reminded Lorna of the noise the Susquehannocks had made when enjoying themselves, or equally, no doubt, when about to set off on the warpath, and surged around their respective preys, the men seizing Vassily by the arms and legs and frog-marching him towards the chamber set aside for his use, the women, with equal enthusiasm and lack of decorum, seizing Lorna and carrying her towards the stairs and thence up them.

*Holy Mother,* she thought, endeavouring to keep a smile on her face and even to laugh at their rallies, do not let me burst into tears. *Holy Mother, do let me fall asleep now and wake up tomorrow morning, when it will be all over.*

But it would not all be over, tomorrow morning. It would all scarce have begun.

The maidservants were there too, laughing and clapping their hands and cheering; they had been given wine to drink and would now have the pleasure of seeing their betters acting their own roles. For Lorna was entirely surrounded by countesses as they removed her jewellery, tore the gown from her back as if they had indeed been marauding Indians, removed her underskirt and petticoats and corset and shift with a similar hasty brutality, twirled her around, naked, drenched her in perfume, smothered her in powder, made her bend this way and that while they attended to armpit and groin—"For depend upon it," someone shrieked to the accompaniment of a gale of laughter, "these Russians are thorough fellows"—destroying in seconds all of Bracknell's careful work in order to smooth the titian hair down her back, and at last dropping the satin nightgown over her head, and smoothing it as well, over shoulders and around breasts, down her thighs and patting her bottom, while others turned back the coverlets and plumped up the pillows, arranging them so that she would have to sit up, and then seizing her arms and legs to lift her bodily from the floor, and place her in the centre of the bed.

"Up, up," Fanny commanded. "She is too low. He will think her afraid."

*Think me afraid*, Lorna thought. *Oh, God, will he not know me, afraid?*

She was sitting up, her back against the pile of pillows, the coverlet folded across her lap. They were pulling at the nightgown again, so that she thought they must certainly tear it, to expose as much breast as possible and yet leave the actual nipple concealed, and they were taking her hair again, to spread it on the pillows like a shawl.

And at last standing back with a sudden decision which left her breathless.

"There," Fanny declared. "Ladies, you have worked with a will. We can do no more. My lady Wharton?"

Lady Wharton curtsied, and hurried to the door, while the others pushed back from the bed, forming a mass to either side in front of the dressing tables and windows.

Lady Wharton opened the door. "My lords," she shouted. "Her Highness awaits her husband."

There was a roar from the other end of the house; the runaway coach was coming closer. Lorna made herself sit still, made herself control her breathing, discovered that her legs were spreading, insensibly, under the coverlet, and hastily brought them together again, pressed against one another. What had caused that? Memory? Anticipation? Did she want what was about to happen? She might as well want it, as it was going to happen, whether she liked it or not. There. That was better. It was going to happen, and she was going to enjoy it. No, no. She was going to love it. It was going to be the most memorable night of her life.

Vassily would complete the cycle begun by Butler and so nearly brought to fruition by Lennart. He was going to transport her beyond that ecstasy barrier at which she had halted so often, and in doing that, secure her love, her desire, forever more, so that she would want no other condition in life, save to be his wife.

She looked at the door, eyes wide, as the men burst in, to be greeted by cheers from the women. Vassily wore a white nightshirt which reached his ankles, and was being half pushed and half carried. That was custom. There was no way of telling whether he would have come of his own accord, whether he would have come reluctantly or enthusiastically.

"Your bride," someone shouted, and she gazed at her husband's face. His mouth worked and his cheeks were pale. He was afraid. As she was afraid. So then, there was a mutual sharing from the very start. Hands pulled back the coverlet, other hands seized her ankles to drag her down the bed. Her nightgown rode up over her legs, and she wanted to kick; but that would expose her even further.

The pillows were wrenched from beneath her head, and now Vassily was being lifted from the floor, and placed beside her. His breath rushed at her, and she saw to her alarm that there were tears in his eyes. Then his body was placed on hers, and his head hit the sheet beside her.

"Cover them up," Fanny commanded.

The sheets and coverlets came up to their shoulders.

"Haste, now, haste," someone bawled. "There is wine to be drunk."

"Will they not go?" Vassily muttered.

"They wish to see the consummation," she said into his ear. He too smelt of perfume.

"I cannot," he said. "I cannot."

Her hands were beneath the coverlets and could not be seen. She touched his thighs and he shuddered. She attempted to find his member and felt his body being pressed against hers, but there was no hardness there.

"The thrust," they screamed, ranging around the bed, stamping and cheering. "The thrust."

"Leave us," she shouted. "Leave us," she screamed. *Oh, Holy Mother,* she prayed, *give him strength.*

He moved, on her. Surely that would bring an erection. But he moaned, and she could feel moisture on her ear.

"Leave us," she shouted. "It is done."

No doubt Fanny Richmond, who had drunk little, caught some of the disgust, some of the fear in her voice.

"It is done," she shouted, her voice high and clear. "Leave them, it is done." She shepherded people to the door, and Lorna lay still, trying to keep her breathing even beneath the weight of the man, trying to smile, to look happy. But, oh, what have I married?

The crowd poured through the door, laughing and gossiping, their own ardour aroused by the very sport which had ruined Vassily. Assignations were made, squeezes were exchanged in anticipation of more to follow. Gradually the noise and the smells died, and Lorna could open her eyes. Only Fanny Richmond remained, standing by the bed.

"God bless you, Lorna, and keep you," she said, and turned away. The door closed, and the room was quiet, the candles flaring as the air steadied.

Vassily gave a stifled sob, rolled away from her.

Lorna sat up. "I am sorry, my lord Prince," she said. "In Russia it is not so?"

"No." His eyes were tight shut.

Lorna hesitated. She should lean above him now.

She should allow her hair to brush his face, her mouth to brush his lips. She should remove her nightdress and raise his shirt, and apply her naked thighs, her naked hands, to his member. Had she not done all of that to Lennart, and been rewarded?

"The room is close," she said, and got out of bed. The nightgown was sheer, and surely he could watch her if he chose. She crossed the floor slowly, throwing her legs one in front of the other, breathing deeply, feeling the material gather at bottom and breast. She reached the casement and pushed it open. The night air was cold and raised her nipples as it raised every pore on her body into chilled tumescence. She turned back, to face the bed.

His eyes were still shut.

Noise gusted up from below. The guests were leaving, carriages being harnessed, voices bidding farewell. Kathleen had already gone, with Snowdrop, to Frances Richmond's house for this night.

And her husband's eyes were shut.

"Would my lord sleep alone?" she asked, feeling anger begin to stir in her belly. Whether commanded to it or not, he had a part to play, as had she, and no one could have been more commanded than herself.

Vassily sat up suddenly, eyes wide, listening. "God have mercy on my soul," he gabbled.

Lorna frowned at him, and then also heard the creak outside the door. She turned, heart pounding, breath rasping. "No," she whispered. *It cannot be,* she prayed. *Not this night, of all nights. Not so soon.*

But the handle was turning, the door swinging in, to allow Peter the Tsar to enter.

# Chapter 7

*L*orna found herself against the window, the cold air playing on her back. She wondered what would happen to her were she to throw the casement wide and jump through.

The Tsar was speaking to Vassily in Russian. The Prince made no reply or even acknowledgement that he had heard, other than to get out of the bed and go to the door.

"No," Lorna said. "You cannot. Your Majesty, you cannot so humiliate a man."

The bedroom door closed.

"Peter," Peter said. "To you, Peter."

"Peter." She left the window, crossed the room. "Peter, please. This is our wedding night. There is no more sacred moment in a marriage."

Peter took her hands. "Who is to know?" He leaned forward, kissed her on the tip of the nose, and she lost all of her breath. Love, from Peter of Russia, could surely only ever be brutal, ugly, debased. Surely. And, incredibly, he was sober.

"Well . . ." she muttered. "Everyone."

"The guests have gone, and he will go to a house I have especially selected for him."

Her head rocked back. "You have sent my husband to a whore, on his wedding night?"

"It is all he deserves, Lorna. Believe me." He was drawing her slowly towards him. "So you see, there is naught for you to worry about."

"Rumour . . ."

"Will scarce overtake him. Or us. We leave England tomorrow."

"The servants . . ."

She was in his arms, bracing herself against the enormous crushing power she anticipated at any moment. And was held softly against his chest, while his tongue made a circle of her lips, before he kissed each of her eyes in turn. "I have sent the servants home, There is no one here at all. Come. I will show you."

He held her hand, opened the door, led her on to the gallery. The house was silent. In the distance they heard the sound of hooves, receding. Vassily? Oh, God, she thought. Vassily. How could she ever face him again? How could she ever risk being alone with him, again?

Peter moved to the stairs, and she pulled against him. "I have no slippers."

"For me, no slippers," he said. "Your feet should be bare, Lorna. They are too beautiful for slippers."

"The floor is cold."

He smiled. "Then shall I carry you?"

Again she was breathless. "No, it is not that cold."

She walked beside him down the stairs, her hand loose in the cavern of his fingers.

"This is a good house," he remarked. "Well built. I have studied architecture, in Germany. Two months ago. Russian houses are not good. But I will build them good houses. I will build them a city." His face twisted and she stopped in alarm. "But we are surrounded by the Swedes." Then he smiled. "No politics."

He turned into the disordered withdrawing room. It was quite warm, as the fires had burned low but not yet gone out.

"You have been happy here," Peter said.

"Yes," she said.

He led her across the room, and down the corridor to the chapel. Now the air was chill, and at the door she stopped.

He frowned. "Is this not your church?"

"It is where I worship. But it *is* a church, Peter."

"And cannot be entered?"

"Not by people with thoughts of the flesh."

"Of the flesh," he mused, and gave another smile, at the same time pulling her forward. "The church," he said, "is an organised conspiracy. A state within a state."

"Your Majesty," she gasped, instinctively looking at the roof, half expecting it to crack.

"It is worse in Russia." He stood before the altar. "Here, things are better ordered. But it is still too powerful. I will change it. I have studied the matter."

She waited to be told where, but he did not continue.

"You seek to change the face of the world," she said.

"The face of Russia, certainly." This time his smile was crooked. "And then, who knows? The world is not so very large. Take off your nightgown."

"Here?" she cried. "I cannot."

"Because God shall not see your body? Did He not create it in the first place?"

"But . . . there is the whole house. . . ."

"You are afraid to walk naked through your own house? You should not be afraid to do that, Lorna."

"But . . . it is obscene."

His frown this time appeared genuine. "Your body is obscene? I would have described it as beautiful." His face relaxed. "And I have not seen it yet." He held up his finger. "Ah. You conceive that sex, between us, will be obscene. I will not touch you, Lorna, within the confines of this chapel. You have my oath. But it is a beautiful chapel. That is the best thing that can be said about religion; it is housed in beautiful places. Then why cannot a beautiful woman stand beautifully, in a beautiful place of worship?"

His gaze paralysed her brain. *What does he seek?* she wondered. *What does he really mean to do to me?* And yet, as had happened with Butler, her fear was slowly being encroached by curiosity, by wonder, even anticipation. She lifted the nightgown over her head, threw it on the floor, inhaling as she did so and sucking her belly flat.

"How insignificant this church becomes," he said, and stretched out his hand.

"You promised."

"And I always keep my promise." He gave a sudden gust of laughter. "Unless it pleases me not to."

She stepped backwards, and he shook his head.

"To you, Lorna, I will keep my word. I but wish to look at this." With his forefinger he hooked the crucifix from its nest between her breasts, raised it up. "You seek protection, on your wedding night?"

"Should I not? On such a wedding night? The cross was given me by her late Majesty."

"Ah." He let it go, and it fell back into place. "It is a happy cross. Come." He held out his hand, and after a moment she took his fingers, walked with him back through the house. Walked naked, through her house. Had she never wanted to do that, in her lonely midnight hours, and been afraid to? Was that Peter's secret, that he would not fear, refused to fear? But the maniac who had turned on the crashing wine pot in the house at Deptford had been afraid. Had been terrified. *Holy Mother,* she thought, *the maniac.*

He led her past the staircase and towards the pantries. "Can you cook?"

"I . . ." She had not cooked, since leaving MacMahons. "Yes. But not like this."

"Why not?"

"Well . . . I . . ."

"I like you naked," he said. "I like to watch you move. To cover your body is a sin. Cook me eggs."

He sat at the kitchen table, rested his chin on his hand. Lorna opened the cupboard, found the eggs, stooped to peer at the range. "The fire needs stoking," she said.

"Then do so."

She glanced at him, seized the poker, thrust it in, and, again, felt sweat start out on her face and shoulders as the heat rose. She was acutely conscious of him, just behind her, watching her. She closed the door, seized the bucket of water Cook had drawn before going home, emptied some in a saucepan with an effort, panting now, pushed the saucepan over the grate, scattered salt, broke the eggs into the water.

"You are an expert cook," he said. "Where is the wine?"

She straightened. "In the cellar."

"Then fetch some," he suggested. "Two bottles."

Lorna glanced at the slowly poaching eggs, at the Tsar, sighed, and crossed the kitchen floor. This was stone and distinctly chill. She stumbled down the wooden steps, seized the first two bottles she could find, returned to the kitchen, shivering.

"Beautiful," Peter said. "The eggs are done."

She placed the bottles on the table, served the eggs, removed the stoppers. "You are not eating," Peter said.

"I am not hungry."

"But you will drink." He pushed a bottle across the table, began stuffing food into his mouth.

Lorna hesitated. But the goblets were in the pantry, and he had already drunk from the neck. He was her King. Her Tsar. Her Autocrat. She lifted the bottle, took a gulp, felt the liquid burning her chest.

"Now," Peter said. "You may undress me."

"Un . . . undress you? Here?"

"You are obsessed with your surroundings. Your surroundings are me." Peter crammed more eggs into his mouth, washed them down with wine. "I enjoy being undressed while I eat. Start with my boots."

She hesitated, then knelt before him.

"No, no," he said. "They will not come off that way."

She sighed, got up, turned round and seized his leg between her hands, straddling it. He placed the other boot on her bottom, and pushed, very gently. She was surprised to discover that he wore no stockings.

She placed the boot on the floor, took the other leg. She found it strange how intimate they had become, on a moment, and he had not yet actually touched her, with his hands. Now she felt his bare toes on her flesh, and a moment later the other boot came free.

She began to breathe more heavily, as she came closer, unfastened his shirt.

"When last did you know a man?" he asked.

"I . . . that is surely my concern," she protested.

"It is mine," he said, drinking some wine. "Now. How can I make you happy, unless I know your condition?"

"My condition? Make me happy?" She eased the shirt from his shoulders. He could not be meaning what she was afraid he meant. Afraid?

She folded the shirt on a chair. He had a magnificent torso, an enormous barrel of sunburned muscle, with only a light coating of hair.

"When?" Peter asked.

Only his breeches remained. Cautiously she released his belt. "Seven years."

"Seven years?" he shouted, and she straightened.

"My husband was killed seven years ago," she explained.

"You must have been a child."

"I was fifteen."

"And never since? What did they do, shut you in a convent?"

"I . . ." But there really was no use in being embarrassed with this man. Obviously he intended to turn her inside out, body and soul, as he had turned the serving girl inside out. She could only hope he would leave her her teeth. "I was pregnant," she said. "And then . . . I had no taste for it."

"No taste for it." He finished the wine, lay back.

She knelt before him again, began to ease the breeches down his thighs; be obligingly lifted his rump to allow them to pass. She panted, and felt the blood rushing to her cheeks. She had no idea what to expect, what undergarments she would encounter . . . and was horrified to see that there were no undergarments at all.

"Then you amuse yourself, with your fingers."

She stared at him. "Self-abuse is a sin."

"How can anything pleasurable be a sin? Pleasure is universal, universally enjoyed."

She stopped dragging, to catch her breath; she could see hair. Nine inches. She could not imagine, nine inches. "My lord Tsar," she said. "It may give you a great deal of pleasure to chop off people's heads, but surely it cannot be pleasurable to them."

"A good point," he agreed. "As a matter of fact, it does give me great pleasure to chop off heads. I can think of nothing I prefer doing. Well, almost nothing. Why have you stopped?"

"I . . ." She bit her lip.

"You were married," he reminded her. "It is but a question of degree." He stood up, shook himself, and the breeches settled around his ankles. Nine inches. She found herself rocking back on her haunches.

"Well?" he demanded. "Am I not beautiful?"

Her mouth opened, and then shut again. But it was beautiful. "Yes, my lord."

"We are both beautiful. Therefore we shall be beautiful together. You may touch me."

"My lord?" Her voice rose an octave.

"Have you never touched a man?"

"Yes, my lord. But . . ."

"It was accidental? Or incidental? Do you know . . . ?" He sat down again, keeping his legs wide. "Women are the most selfish, the most intolerant creatures? They never suppose that a man might wish to be loved, as they wish to be."

"I had supposed a man found his pleasure in loving a woman, my lord. Not in being loved by a woman, except as a return."

"And you are wrong. A man's best lover is another man. He at least will know what is best done. Come now, Lorna. Use your hands, your lips, your body." He smiled at her. "It will not bite you."

She inhaled slowly, closed her eyes.

"And keep your eyes open," he commanded.

She obeyed, hurled herself forward, buried her face in his groin, felt his thighs closing on her shoulders.

"But do not bite," he said. "I would not feel it now, but later it would be painful. And I am clean. I bathed today, Lorna, for you. Do you not like the smell of my pomade?"

She could not speak. She was obsessed with a sense of guilt. But it was a delicious sense of guilt.

"You are right, of course," Peter mused. "Much pleasure is one-sided, is even sheer misery to the person on whom it is inflicted. But you are having pleasure, Lorna, and so am I. There can be no sin. And so, when you handle yourself to orgasm, that can be no sin. *You* are committing the deed, the pleasurable deed, and *you* are receiving pleasure from it."

She got herself free, overbalanced, and sat on the floor. How could she ever look at him? But she was looking at him. And no longer even panting. Her body seemed alight, transported, she scarce felt the floor, and she *was* feeling that spreading desire extending from her groin, pumping through her arteries, while at the same time her brain was perfectly clear. She felt suspended in place and time, with only Peter for company, with no one else in the world to care about. "Your philosophy, Sire," she said, "is that of a devil."

"Or of a god," he suggested. "At least, those of the Greeks, and not this Christian moralist."

"My lord," she gasped, scrambling to her feet.

"I blaspheme? I do so constantly. No doubt, when He is tired of it, He will seek an accounting. Then there will be a tussle, I do assure you. Come here."

She came closer, and he sat her on his lap.

"If you were to die," he whispered in her ear, "without ever having known orgasm, you would never have lived."

His hands were beneath her, behind her, before her; he seemed all fingers. But what fingers, gently stroking. And not only fingers, she realised. She threw both arms round his neck, panted, thought her heart was setting about breaking its way out through her chest and gave a moan, which turned into a shriek as he suddenly took his hands away and stood up, lifting her in his arms.

"No," she wailed. "You cannot stop."

"Ecstasy postponed, for a short while, is ecstasy doubled," he said, and began to climb the stairs. "I will take you in your own bed."

She could not keep still. Her body seethed. She kicked her legs and twisted against his chest. She held him tight round the neck and raised herself to scrape her nipples against his chin. She prayed for his hands somehow to return. She moaned and nibbled at his ear, and he kissed her mouth.

The bedroom door stood open. She expected to be thrown, and was laid, with the utmost gentleness on the pillows. She thrust her hands down, to seize his member, to pull it and caress it, and he shook his head. "You have done enough."

Her hands flopped away. She spread her legs as wide as she could, and waited for the thrust she had so feared, and felt instead the gentle caress which reminded her of Lennart. She panted, the flooding ecstasy rising, her eyes wide, gazing at his smiling face, but he was panting now as well, and his cheeks were pink, although he still watched her, kept his mind busy, timing his thrust. Because suddenly she knew that there would be a thrust, when he was ready.

And there it was. She screamed, a long howling whoop of the sheerest pleasure. The sound of her voice echoed round the room and came back to hammer at her pounding ears. Her body seemed to collapse, heartbeat, breathing, mind, muscular ability all losing their power at the same moment.

And then the sound faded, and the room was quiet.

She lay in the crook of his arm, to be caressed. Her eyes were shut. She did not wish to think, to understand; she was content to feel the fingers running lightly over her back, sliding through her hair, stroking her nipples. She longed for them to return between her legs, but did not know how to ask. This man was a monster. But he had made her happy and could do so again, whenever he chose. *Oh, Holy Mother,* she thought, *let him choose.*

"Are you still afraid of me, Lorna?"

"Of you, Sire?" Her eyes flopped open. He was too intelligent to be fooled. "Should I not fear the Autocrat of all the Russias?"

He smiled and kissed her nose. "I meant the man, not the institution. The madman."

"Sire?"

"Oh, that is what they say of me, Lorna. You will have heard it. You will have thought it, yourself, during that little romp the other night."

"Sire," she protested.

"I am what I am," he said softly, perhaps half to himself. "I am Tsar of all Russia, Lorna. Can you conceive the size of the domains which call me master? But can you conceive, either, the trials and perils of such a position of omnipotence?"

He had rolled on to his back, and his fingers were gone. She sighed. But he clearly wished to talk, clearly was going to talk. She rested her head on his shoulder, her leg across his thighs; this way she could feel his member beneath her, and know when it stirred.

"You probably don't know," Peter said, "that my father, the Tsar Alexis, may God rest his soul, being disappointed in the offspring of his first wife, who produced for him nothing but girls or half wits, sought a second wife late in life, and so died when I was but a child. The regency passed to my mother and her family, but was usurped by my half sister, Sophia, a spirited slut, certainly, who, I swear, dreamed of making *herself* Autocrat of all Russia, as if my subjects would ever have stood for the dominance of a woman. Be that as it may, she inspired the soldiers of the Moscow garrison, the Streltsi, we call them, a turbulent mob, to follow her standard, assaulted the Kremlin itself, and made herself mistress of the state. I watched it happen, Lorna, as a boy of ten, standing by my mother's side. I watched my uncles and my ministers thrown from the upstairs balcony onto a sea of pikes, and I watched their still warm bodies torn limb from limb by the frenzied mob. Can you wonder that I ofttimes awake at night screaming?"

"Peter," she whispered, interested despite herself. She kissed his chin. "I wonder I find you here, alive and well, and in control of your destiny."

To her dismay he threw himself from the bed and paced the room, a magnificent sight, but out of her reach.

"It took much time and patience. For years I played the boy, when I was already all but a full-grown man, waiting and watching. I shared the throne with my half brother, Ivan, a mindless imbecile, while Sophia stood in the shadows behind us and told us what to say through a small door she had cut in the back of our chair. And all the time I planned. For I know my people well enough. One by one the commanders chose to follow me rather than my sister. And she, poor wretch, was reduced to seeking my assassination. I led her a merry dance, Lorna, fled her hired murderers, wearing nothing more than my shirt."

She raised herself on her elbow, and he came back to sit beside her, smooth hair from her forehead. "But now you are secure upon your throne, surely," she said. "Or you would never have dared risk this lengthy absence from your kingdom."

"Oh, my throne is safe enough," he agreed. "Sophia is incarcerated in a convent and will remain there. But indeed I only understood the true nature of my problems after the end of my personal conflict." He waved his arm. "You, living in this tiny island, cannot conceive the vastness which is Russia. It is as huge as all the rest of Europe assembled, and has a population to match, in size, but steeped in such superstition and backwardness as I could never relate to you. Suffice to say that even the noblemen of my realm, we call them boyars, are more ignorant than the lowest English peasant. And their women are far, far worse."

She put her arms round his waist, nuzzled him. "You are as intelligent as any man I have ever met."

"It was the fortune of my mother, long before she met the Tsar, my father, to be educated in the house of a Scottish lady, who by the merest chance had married a Muscovite. She thus imbibed some knowledge of the outside world, and more important, she discovered a desire for more, which she imparted to me. But you see me now, twenty-five years of age, Lorna, and still seeking the completion of my education. To teach all of Russia the arts of civilisation, that is my goal."

*Another Scot,* she thought dreamily, once again closing her eyes as his penis rose to stroke beneath her chin, apparently without his being aware of it. They seem to spread around the world, leaving their influence behind them.

"And yet," Peter muttered, "what can I, one man with but a mortal span of life at his disposal, hope to accomplish, cut off as we Russians are behind a line of hostile nations?" He was away again, leaving her sprawled on her face. "To travel out of Russia, we must first apply for passports from foreign capitals. That in itself is a national insult. I tell you, Lorna, I considered our predicament as insoluble, as all my predecessors accepted their situations with hopeless equanimity, until the day I saw my first ship, sailing proudly upon the sea, granting its captain a freedom neither I nor any of my subjects have ever possessed. This was at a port called Archangel, in the far north. But for more than half of every year it lies frozen, and so is of no use. We are encompassed elsewhere by the Swedes and the Turks. I tried conclusions with the Ottomans only a couple of years ago, and gained the port of Azov, on the Black Sea. There was the first triumph of my reign, Lorna. So we have our port at last. But a mean, miserable place it is, and worse, it is several hundred miles from Moscow, and hard in the middle of hostile nations, the Turks themselves, and the Cossacks, who pay lip service to my rule and hate and fear me. My dream is of a new seaport nearer to home. A new capital city, indeed, for I will confess to you that if I never again saw the Kremlin for as long as I live, I should shed no tear. The Baltic, that is Russia's natural doorway. I would open a window on the West, up there in Livonia."

She frowned, despite her lack of interest. "The Baltic belongs to Sweden."

"So it does. And Sweden is the greatest military power in the world. The thought haunts me, day and night. But only a few months past I received news of a most remarkable intelligence. Charles of Sweden is dead."

"So I have heard," she said. "But . . ."

"Do you not understand? Charles was a warrior worthy of belonging to the family of the great Gustavus. Now I am faced only by his successor. Oh, his name is also Charles, the Twelfth to bear it. The Swedes are not the most imaginative of races. But he is no more than fifteen years of age. Fifteen. It seems to me that my earlier misfortunes were but a trial, and that I am destined to rule Russia in its most fortunate period."

Russia and Sweden at war? She was a Russian now. But what did she owe Lennart, in any event? Save Kathleen. And a memory. But the memory had just been obliterated.

Nor could it be allowed to return. She threw her arms round his waist again, hugging him this time. "Why must men," she asked, "think only of war, when there are so much pleasanter ways of passing the time?"

Eventually she slept, a dreamless sleep of utter exhaustion, utter satiation. Never had she felt so completely at ease. She had the old desire to spread her legs, spread her arms, nestle her body farther and farther into the sheets, but now she could indulge it, wallowing in the softness, reaching for the man in her half-awakened state, and slowly beginning to frown as she found nothing.

Yet there was someone in the room. She rolled over and sat up, blinking in the sudden daylight, for the drapes had been drawn, staring at Vassily, fully dressed and standing by the window.

"You look well pleased, madam," he remarked.

Her tongue circled her lips.

"Oh, His Majesty has left," Vassily said. "In fact, I doubt not that by now he has left the country."

Her brain was still dull. "Left the country?"

"Oh, we shall be following. But by a different route. His Majesty is taking ship for Venice, and thence Vienna. He wishes you in Moscow by the time he reaches there, and so has instructed us to accompany the main party across Europe."

"Across Europe?"

"We cannot proceed by the sea, my lady. We are on terms of hostility with Sweden, and they control the Baltic. You will enjoy crossing Europe. Although you might have enjoyed it more in the summer. Will you not rise? There is little time."

She pushed back the coverlet, draped her legs over the side of the bed, felt rather than saw his gaze. *Holy Mother,* she thought. *He must not want me now. I could not stand that.* "Are my servants returned?"

"Yes, madam. Those you are taking with you. They wait to pack your belongings."

"I must have a bath," she said.

"Indeed, madam, I can smell you from here. But you will have to do without, for the time. There is a tide we must catch, and the coach is waiting."

She stood up, ran her fingers into her hair, peered at herself in the mirror. She had done that before, and wondered at the absence of change. And this morning? The face had not changed, but there was a laziness about the eyes, about the mouth. As indeed there was a laziness about her entire body. Her muscles seemed disconnected, unable to co-ordinate.

She turned to find her clothes, felt him behind her, and checked. Fingers closed on her arm, and she made herself keep still, with an effort. "Did he make you scream?" he whispered. "With pain? Or with pleasure?"

She inhaled slowly, cautiously. The fingers were tightening and turning her, to face him.

"Would you scream, for me?" he asked. "With pleasure?"

But why be afraid of him? She was the Tsar's mistress. She was inviolate. "Indeed I would, my lord," she said. "If you pleased me enough."

He pushed her towards the bed. Presumably she need not even submit. But he was her husband. His rights were legal. Her knees touched the mattress and she sat, his fingers still tight on her arm. She stared at his breeches, at the bulge. Then he drove the fingers of his right hand into her hair, forcing her head back, so that her eyes widened and seemed to start from their sockets, and her mouth dropped open.

"Then scream," he said. "I want to hear you scream."

"You . . ." She attempted to move, and he forced her back, until she was lying, and he knelt above her.

"Scream, as you screamed for the Tsar."

She sucked air into her lungs and expelled it as loudly as she could. The wailing cry hurtled up to the ceiling, drifted round and round, died slowly.

His face twisted. "Aye," he said. "That is your scream."

She stared at him in awful understanding. He had gone nowhere last night. He had spent the entire night outside, watching. And he had heard her scream.

The fingers were relaxing on her hair, leaving her arm. And she wanted to weep, for him. She sat up. "Vassily. Now. Please. Or it will be . . ." She bit her lip.

"Too late, madam?" He walked to the door. "You are the Tsar's whore. For the present. I will send your maids to you."

"Ra, ra, ra," shouted the coachman. The crack of his whip echoed even through the rain. But the coach was beginning that long, slow, and now so familiar slide.

"Ooooh," squealed Alice. "Ooooh."

Bridget gripped the window and panted.

"Not another one," Kathleen remarked with studied sophistication.

Lorna found herself holding Snowdrop against her belly. It was hope rather than certainty; she was no more than a week overdue. Peter's child. It could be no other.

The coach gave a lurch and came to a halt. Rain pounded on the roof. It had not ceased raining since they had left their ship at Boulogne, and if the roads in France had been bad, the roads here in Bavaria were nothing more than rivers with rutted beds.

"Highness?" Alice was relieved that they had not actually turned over, as had happened three days ago. "Lorna? You're not ill?"

Lorna shook her head and peered through the window at the people. The November afternoon was already dark, and the rain teemed down, but they materialised around the stricken coach like ghosts. *Too apt a simile,* she thought. It was very cold inside the carriage, and she and her companions wore fur. She could not conceive what it must be like outside, at least lacking the proper clothing. But these men and women wore rags, and their flesh was blue. And there were children too. One was held up to the window, while it wailed, and its parents shouted.

"Bridget, draw the blinds," Alice commanded. "Oh, it is sheer purgatory."

"Highness?" Bridget hesitated, as Lorna was still staring.

"Give them something," Lorna said.

"Lorna," Alice protested. "They'll wreck the coach."

"Give them something."

Alice hesitated, then fumbled in her bag. But the escort had returned.

"Ooora, oora, oora," they shouted, drawing their swords and urging their horses through the knee-deep mud and water, splashing and kicking. "Ooorra."

The people fled, screaming. And no doubt cursing. Alice sighed with relief, and refastened her bag.

Lorna gazed at Vassily. He preferred to ride with his men than share the carriage with her. Enough that he had to share their sleeping quarters, whatever that might be. And did it matter? They obeyed the Tsar. And she was happy to do so. Peter, Peter, Peter. To love a Tsar. To have a Tsar love you. But that was irrelevant. To love Peter, to have Peter love you. Peter the draughtsman. Peter the lover. Peter the Tsar was but an extension of that.

He pushed his head into the window. "The carriage is stuck, and it is getting dark. We will need an entire team of horses. But there is a village, only half a mile away. With an inn. I have sent ahead to reserve it."

"Are those people from the village?"

He shrugged. "They'll not trouble us. They lack the strength." He smiled. "And *they* claim to have won the war."

The door opened, and she gazed at the mud, and sighed. She thought she would never rid her nostrils of the smell of mud. But Vassily had dismounted and waited for her, his boots disappeared to the ankle. She moved forward, still holding Snowdrop, and he gripped her under the shoulders, swung his other arm under her knees. Why, he had not touched her so intimately since the day he had come to call. She frowned. But he had touched her then. And had seemed to wish to do more.

He placed her on the saddle, mounted behind her; Snowdrop complained at the wet. Other men were waiting to do the same for Kathleen and Bridget and Alice, while in the coaches behind Father Simeon the rest of the passangers were also being disembarked. Vassily gave his horse the most gentle of touches with his heel, and it picked its way through the mud. All of his horses seemed to know exactly what to do under every circumstance; she had never seen such a horseman.

But then, she reflected, leaning against his chest, she had never seen Peter ride. But Vassily was so gentle with his horses, perhaps he was a gentle man. She had no reason to suppose otherwise; he had never harmed her. But how do you tell your husband, with whom you have never slept, that you think you are pregnant?

Yet he had to be told. Moscow, they said, was at least three months distant, in winter. Only Peter the Tsar would have commanded them to undertake such a journey in winter. As he never recognised physical obstacles, he refused to permit others to do so. But three months of jolting and sliding and occasionally capsizing would certainly induce a miscarriage. And it was Peter's child.

"There." He pointed a gauntleted finger at the glow of lights. "You will soon be warm and dry."

She dabbed rainwater from her face; there was no wind, yet the drizzle seemed capable of getting underneath her fur hood to dampen her hair. His hand, returning from its gesture, rested for a moment on her waist, and then slid round her thigh. She should not have felt it at all through the thick fur of her pelisse. He had been pressing.

She chewed her lip, was overtaken by her decision, as had happened so often in the past. "Vassily," she said.

"It is not far." Their hooves were already striking cobbles.

"I cannot continue," she said.

"I will obtain you a bath," he said. Because, remarkably, he studied to please her, without ever touching her. "You will enjoy that, Princess. You have not had a bath in a week."

"I would enjoy that very much," she said. "But, Highness, I cannot continue. I dare not."

"These people will not harm us," he said. "They are too poor, we are too strong. And besides, we have a safe conduct from the King. From the Emperor, in fact."

"I do not fear the people," she said. "I fear the roads."

"We will get through." Was that a squeeze?

The inn was immediately in front of them. The guardsmen he had sent ahead had dismounted and waited by the door, stiffly to attention. The innkeeper and his wives and daughters stood in the rain to greet their distinguished guests. The rest of the villagers clustered on the far side of the street, eyeing the richness of the carriages, the gleaming steel of the escorts' drawn swords.

"I have no doubt of that," Lorna said. "But *I* cannot continue, Highness. I am pregnant."

The horse halted, and Vassily dismounted. He held up his hands, and she slipped forward, felt his fingers closing on her ribs, and was set on the squelching mud. "Did you hear me?" she asked.

He turned away, stamped into the light, gave his

orders. He spoke German fluently. The innkeeper bowed and scurried off, accompanied by his daughters. His wife curtsied to Lorna, who gave her a brief nod. *Oh, Holy Mother,* she thought, *what have I done?*

She stepped into shelter, threw back her hood, looked down at the water and mud sliding from her boots on to the floor. But the inn was warm; a fire blazed. Although the innkeeper and his family appeared hardly less starved than the people outside. No doubt they were this night exhausting their entire remaining stock of fuel to please their princely guests.

"Another inn," Kathleen remarked with supreme boredom, stamping her little feet. "I am soaked through, Mama."

"Aye, well, stand before the fire." Lorna accompanied her across the room, felt the heat begin to seep into her flesh. She placed Snowdrop on the floor, and the cat scurried for the hearth. Bridget assisted her from her pelisse.

"Supper is ready," Vassily said. The table had been laid for them all. "You do not mind eating with the servants?"

"Why should I mind?" She sank on to the bench seat, and one of the girls hastily filled her tankard with foaming beer. Snowdrop, dry and warm, leapt on her lap and hooked a fragment of rabbit from her plate.

"There is no wine." Vassily sat opposite. Kathleen was already attacking the stew.

"Beer is sufficient." Lorna drank. She felt not in the least hungry. Indeed, she seldom felt hungry when in the company of the Russians. They assaulted every meal as if they had never eaten, and stuffed themselves until she was surrounded by belches. Vassily was the best of the lot, but even his manners were appalling. And Kathleen was clearly studying to be as Russian as possible. Which, she supposed, was a very sensible point of view. She drank beer and gazed at her husband; the girl hastily refilled their mugs.

"I have arranged a bath for you," he said. "I do not know what it will be like." He filled his mouth, ballooned his cheeks, chewed noisily.

Lorna drank some more beer. She no longer knew what to say to him. She heard a clatter and turned her head, watched the tin tub being carried up the stairs. "Then I will go now," she said. "If you will excuse me, Highness."

"You have not eaten."

"I am not hungry." She tucked Snowdrop under her arm and got up, and Bridget hastily rose also, to hurry behind her mistress, following the straining young men, shouting at them, but of course they understood not a word of what was said.

The bedchamber contained only a tester and a single table. "My lady," Bridget said. "You cannot sleep here."

"I doubt there is better," Lorna said and raised her arms to be undressed.

"It is outrageous." Bridget worked very quickly; her fingers seemed to twinkle. "There is not even a glass." She knew how her mistress liked to watch herself being undressed. Snowdrop explored the room and promptly found a cockroach; she had not, after all, had much dinner.

"Tonight, I am grateful for that." Lorna was wrapped in her robe, and sat on the bed, watched the maid filling the tub. "That will do, Biddy. I would like you to see to Miss Kathleen's bed, and that she washes."

She stepped out of the robe, sank into the hot water, gave a sigh. Bridget was still gathering her hair on the top of her head, securing it with the bandeau. "But who will attend you, mistress?"

"Ask His Highness to attend me."

"His . . ." Bridget's chin dropped.

"Go on, girl. He will not bite you. Or beat you."

The door closed, and she lay back to soak. Blessed relaxation. She could feel her muscles unwinding, her flesh prickled with the heat. And inside? Peter's child. A future Tsar of Russia, perhaps.

The door opened, closed again with a bang. "I am a prince," Vassily complained. "You do not send for a prince. Not even the Tsar's whore sends for a prince."

"I must speak with you," she said. "I am pregnant."

He came round the front of the tub, looked down at her. It was the first time he had looked at her, naked, since their first morning, and that was three weeks ago. But she felt no embarrassment. She felt nothing about him at all, save pity.

"If I go on with this journey," she said, "I may have a miscarriage."

"You cannot stay here," he pointed out.

"I could go back into France," she said. "We were invited to visit Versailles."

"You shall not go to Versailles," he said. "It is a political matter." He turned away, took off his sword belt. "King Louis would put Leczynski on the Polish throne. The Tsar favours Augustus of Saxony. And Augustus has been elected. There could be war at any moment. That is why we had to hasten across France. You could not stay there for months."

"Louis cannot afford another war so soon," she said.

"You know nothing of politics," he pointed out. "Women know nothing of politics. You cannot go to France, and you cannot stay here. Bavaria is in French pay."

She sighed. "Will you assist me?"

He had taken off his coat. Now he came across the room, extended his hands, raised her from the tub. Instantly she was chilled; the fire in the room was low. His eyes were sad.

"It is Peter's child," she said.

"He will assume so," he agreed, and handed her the towel. She wrapped it round her shoulders, stood in front of the fire, gazed at the flickering flames, knew he was immediately behind her. "Did you hold his cock?" he asked.

She started to turn, checked herself.

"He likes that," Vassily remarked. "I have held his cock."

She could not stop herself. She turned, her mouth wide with horror.

Vassily smiled at her. "The Tsar is a man of wide tastes, Lorna. Will you hold my cock, too?"

# Chapter 8

*L*orna sat on the bed, careless of the moisture which still clung to her body. "I don't believe you," she muttered. But Peter's words, Peter's desires, indeed came back to her.

"Or you would hate him."

Her head came up. "Why should I hate him? He is Tsar." And there it was. The Tsar did what he wished. And he had made her happy. So perhaps he could not love her the way she could so easily love him, perhaps loved him already. But he had made her happy, and would do so again. And he was the father of her child. "I love him," she said.

Vassily gazed at her, and she watched with horror as his entire face broke up, the mouth turning down, the chin sagging, the tears rolling out of his eyes to drip down his cheeks. "Then you hate me," he wailed.

Lorna leapt to her feet, ran for the door, turned the key, leaned against it, panting.

Vassily watched her, curiosity restoring some dignity to his features. "I thought you were running away."

"From you?" She was genuinely surprised. "You are my husband. I but wished to be sure no one saw you cry."

The tears continued. They were so quiet. But she had never seen a man weep. "You are so lovely," he said. "I would so love to love you. To have you love me."

She left the door, crossed the floor slowly. Her mind was such a raging tumult she did not know which thoughts to attempt to isolate. The spreading feeling was back in her belly, for the first time since Peter had left her bed. What had William said, so discerningly. That she wished only to make men her slaves?

She reached the bedside, stood before him. "I am your wife."

"And you carry the Tsar's babe."

"I do not know that," she said. "I think it is possible. I hope it is possible. It would insure my . . . our favour forever. Would it not?"

He remained staring at her pubes. She thrust her fingers into his hair, pushed his head back. "You could not harm the child, anyway."

He put up his hands, gripped her wrists so tightly that she released his hair. He turned, slipping to his knees beside the bed, buried his head in his hands, muttered in Russian.

She realised he was praying and realised too what was his trouble. She knelt beside him. "Vassily? You have never known a woman?"

His head started to turn, and then buried itself in the bedclothes once again. *What is to become of me,* she thought, *caught up between a madman and a child?* But the madman had made her happy, had earned her love. Why should not the child do the same?

She reached round his shoulders to release his belt, and then to unfasten his coat. He shuddered and kept his head hidden, but allowed his arms to be pulled back so that she could slip the coat from his shoulders. She did the same for the shirt, left him naked from the waist up. He had no such physique as Peter, was almost narrow chested. But he had more hair, and he was a man. She tickled his nipples into erectness, and when he turned, kissed his mouth. He pushed against her, but she had locked her arms on his neck, and his own hands had to touch her body, and slide up to her breasts, before dropping away again, as if burnt.

She sighed and released him. "My lord," she said. "I would help you."

She held his hands, and he got to his feet. The tears had dried, leaving stains on his cheeks, and he gazed at her with a remarkable longing. *Like a child,* she thought, *like a child.*

She released his breeches, pushed him on to the bed, removed his boots and pants. Not nine inches. Oh, indeed not. But hard enough and fat enough to satisfy her, could she ever get it inside. And he wished it held, as she had held Peter's. She lowered her head, and he sat up straight, hugging her against him. She sank on to his lap, used her hands, and felt his fingers scraping about her body, sliding down to her thighs, but going behind to squeeze and massage her bottom. Peter had hardly touched her bottom. But King William had wanted only that. So then, here was experience. And one she could appreciate, because she felt absolutely no passion for him. Just a private delight that her body was being stroked, being used, as Father Simeon had said, for what it had been intended.

She kissed his eyes, his nose, his mouth again, tried to turn away from him, slipped from his fingers and lay on her back, legs wide. He began to lower himself, and then checked.

"Vassily." She sat up, reaching for him again with her fingers.

He gasped for breath. "On your knees, Lorna. Please."

She frowned at him. "I'll not be sodomised."

"No." He shook his head violently. "But please . . ."

She hesitated, but she was not afraid of him, knew that she could end it whenever she chose. She turned on her knees, braced her elbows on the mattress, felt his hands on her buttocks, tensed and relaxed. The thrust was hard, but delightful at the same time. Not even Peter had so filled her, so sent passion racing away from her groin. But this was not Peter, and it was his first time. There was no more than a single thrust, and then she was carrying his entire weight on her back as he collapsed in a spasm of heat. Leaving her no more than aroused, she thought. But without bitterness. It was a start, and there would be others. Now.

She allowed her elbows to give way, and sank into the mattress, the man's weight smothering her, his lips against her ear.

"Now we are married," she whispered. "But, Vassily, I must find somewhere to wait, for the birth of my child."

His teeth closed on her lobe, gently, and he sighed. "Dresden," he said. "The Court of Augustus. There are our friends. We will go to Dresden."


He rode his horse alongside, bent from the saddle to peer through the window of the carriage. "Over the next rise. You will see it." He spoke Russian. Over the previous month he had devoted most of his time to teaching her his language.

"And I will say thank God for that," she said in English. She could understand Russian better than she could speak it. It was three weeks since the Bavarian inn, and now there could be no doubt at all; she remembered the sensation, the nausea, from the *Centaur* too well. Indeed, her only comfort as regards the child in her belly was that the motion of the coach was not so very different to that of the ship, and Kathleen had been at once an easy birth and a healthy child.

Her condition apart, however, Lorna was well pleased. She did not suppose he loved her, in a strong physical sense. Her body seemed to interest him, and at times arouse him, but he was more interested in what she might do for him; as she had always considered the male member the most fascinating part of a man's body, she was happy to sleep with his between her hands. She loved to explore him, watch him stir into life, slowly become erect and fill with blood, squirm with pleasure, like a girl.

His lovemaking remained perfunctory; he would far rather be handled than come to orgasm within her. Yet even this suited her mood of the moment to perfection. She could not help but suppose that had Vassily been able to reproduce in her the shuddering ecstasy that Peter had accomplished, it *would* harm the child, and indeed to watch with some detachment the same process taking place in a man, and through the agency of her own fingers, was itself a tremendously exciting pleasure. It seemed to her that a future of loving Vassily, when she chose, of being loved by Peter, when he chose, and no doubt of attracting a swarm of lesser men around her, as she had done at Hurd House, with her children to care for and educate, would provide her with a very full and satisfying life.

*So then, where was the simple girl who had roamed*

*MacMahons, seeking only the love of a single man?
Why,* she thought, as she smiled at Kathleen, awakening from a deep sleep on the seat opposite, *that simple
girl had also become a great lady, who sought her
pleasures where she chose.*

The cavalcade was stopping, as her carriage, in the
lead, had halted in the midst of a cluster of guardsmen,
to look down on the valley through which the River
Elbe had cut its bed, and on the City of Dresden, the
home of the Electors of Saxony for over four hundred
years. And despite her pleasantly personal thoughts,
Lorna leaned out of the window in delight at the scene
below her, for the Altstadt, on the south and west
banks of the river, suggested nothing less than a sea
of green copper roofs, from which rose a variety of
spires and towers and cupolas, to remind her of an
illustration of a fairy city which she had come across
in one of her books at Hurd.

To be sure, the streets, as inspected through the telescope offered by Vassily, looked narrow and dark, and
even from the distance she could make out the discolouration in the water where the sewers discharged
into the river. It occurred to her that in cities one
could seek either beauty or air, but not both; Dresden
had been growing, obviously recently, and the Neustadt
on the eastern bank was much better laid out, as a city,
but the houses seemed quite lacking in distinction.

She handed back the telescope. "They are expecting
us," Vassily said. "I have sent a messenger ahead."
He smiled at her. "By tonight you will be in comfort."

He raised his hand, and the troop moved forward,
down the hill and into a splendid pleasure park, the
Grosse Garten, Vassily explained—he seemed to be
entirely familiar with this place, which made sense if
Saxony was supported by Russian money and the prom-

ise of Russian power. Here the snow was thick on the ground once again, and it was necessary to slow, and here they encountered a group of horsemen and horsewomen, merely out for a ride, it seemed, but dressed with a richness which made Lorna feel quite shabby.

The Russian party was stopped, and to Lorna's surprise, Vassily rode out in front of his men, at the same time removing his hat and bowing over the saddle as he came up to the leader of the German party; she frowned as she realised that this was a woman, and quite the most beautiful woman she had ever seen, her own reflection included. She was not a girl; Lorna decided she was past thirty, which was the only crumb of comfort she could discern. Her features were rounded and possessed a perfect symmetry; in repose they might have seemed a trifle too soft, but this was corrected by the intensity of her gaze, which Lorna was left quite breathless to discover was now turning on her, following her greeting of Vassily, and which made her want to shrink back into the recesses of the carriage. Her hair, which flowed out from beneath her tricorne hat, apparently undressed save for some velvet bows, was a magnificent deep brown, and her close-fitting habit left no doubt that her figure was comparable with her face. While above all there was a presence, a confidence which put even Sarah Churchill to shame.

She approached the carriage and smiled, thereby doubling her beauty. "Princess Bogoljubov," she said in French. "Welcome to Dresden. I could not believe the news, that this rogue had finally married. But a glance at you explains it all."

Lorna inhaled, threw back the fur hood which concealed her own hair, and glanced at Vassily, in search of some directive as to their respective ranks.

"I would have you meet the Countess Aurora Konigsmarck, madam," Vassily said. "My wife, the Princess Bogoljubov."

The Countess thrust her gloved hand through the window, and Lorna squeezed it. The Countess looked a little surprised, and then smiled again, and withdrew her hand. "My lord Augustus awaits you, my child," she said. "But afterwards, why then you and I may get to know one another, as you are to spend some time with us."

Lorna could only stare at her, as a great deal of the gossip at Queen Mary's Court had concerned this remarkable Swedish family, the young man whose affair with Sophia Dorothea, Electress of Hanover, had rocked the bedchambers of Europe, had caused her to be locked away by her unforgiving husband, and equally Konigsmarck's sister, whose charm and beauty, it was said, had almost made Augustus the Strong turn away from the other members of his harem.

The Countess waved her entourage forward. Vassily waited for them to pass, and then signalled his own troop to continue, and Lorna could sit back and fan herself, glaring at Kathleen, who seemed inclined to laugh. They crossed the park and rode into the courtyard of the Georgenschloss, next to the river, where guardsmen in red coats with green facings, and wearing enormous red grenadier bonnets, stood to attention, and grooms hurried forward to open the doors of the carriages and assist them to the ground.

Vassily was already speaking to one of the majordomos, in German, and now came back to where Lorna waited. "His Majesty is expecting us."

"I should prefer to have the opportunity to change my clothes," she said, "before attending him."

"He expects us now," Vassily insisted. "It seems that there is news. Grave news. Your people will be shown your apartments. Hurry along, child . . ." This to Kathleen, while at the same time he removed a protesting Snowdrop from Lorna's arms and gave her to Bridget.

"Grave news?" she inquired.

"I can discover no more than that. Come." He escorted her up the steps while the guardsmen clicked to attention, and the major-domo hurried in front of them to have the doors opened as they approached. The castle was in fact even more sumptuously decorated than Kensington; some of the carved wood on the balustrades and on the panellings was quite exquisite, while the paintings on the ceiling were considerably more indecent. But Lorna was marched along at such a speed she had no time to inspect properly, and before she could even catch her breath the door was opening at the end of the great hallway, and they were being ushered into the reception chamber, some fifty feet long and very nearly as wide, but presently empty save for the two men who waited on the dais at the end, one standing, a short, swarthy fellow, and the other, seated, but now rising to his feet as they approached, a perfect mountain of a human being, taller than Peter the Tsar, she realised, and broader and stouter, not old, but already with heavy jowls, which drooped from his chin in accompaniment to the full wig he wore. His coat and breeches were red velvet, she estimated, but they and his shirt and vest were disordered as if he had not changed them overnight.

She lowered herself into a deep curtsey at the foot of the dais, while the King made a remark in German, which was answered by Vassily, also bowing very deep.

She heard his feet approaching. "Rise, my dear," he said in imperfect French.

She raised her head and found his arms outstretched.

She gave him her hands and was lifted to her feet. She might have been a feather.

"Beautiful," he said. "Utterly beautiful. Prince Bogoljubov, you do not deserve her. You of all people. 'Tis a waste. A waste, by God, sir, of God's bounty." He gave a bellow of laughter.

Vassily stood to attention, apparently undisturbed by the sally, although Lorna could feel her cheeks burning.

"I was told there was grave news, Sire," Vassily said, continuing to speak French.

"Grave news." Augustus turned, still holding Lorna's hand, and escorted her back up the steps. "There has been a revolt."

"Revolt, Sire?"

"In Russia. The Streltsi."

"Sire?" Vassily cried.

"Sire?" Lorna also stopped, and turned to face him.

"While the cat's away," Augustus said. "But what a cat."

"Where is the Tsar, Your Majesty?" Lorna cried.

Augustus smiled, as if her concern was answering a question he had posed himself. "In Moscow, I have no doubt. The news was given to him in Vienna, and he hurried home, riding day and night." He chuckled. "He passed through here, but pausing to change horses."

"And he is safe?"

"Oh, he is safe enough."

"And the revolt, Sire?" Vassily inquired.

"Is crushed. They say Moscow's streets run red with blood. Most of it being shed by Peter himself. But my dear Prince, he requires all his most trusted aides at his side, and immediately. I am instructed to send you to him the moment you ride into Dresden. There is a horse waiting."

"But . . ." Vassily looked at Lorna, his mouth open.

Augustus smiled at him. "Your charming wife will remain here. She cannot possibly continue in such haste. No, no, she must await the birth of her child, must she not? You had best say good-bye."

"But . . ." It was Lorna's turn to stare at Vassily. She had not anticipated being abandoned to the care of total strangers.

"Your people will stay with you, of course," Vassily said. "But I must attend the Tsar." He took her hands, raised them to his lips. "Madam, this past month has been the happiest of my life. You may believe I intend no flattery. I shall await your arrival in Moscow with an ever pounding heart."

"Why, my lord," Lorna said. "Believe me that my thoughts will be with you, now and always."

He kissed her fingers, released them, stood back, saluted the King, and hurried from the room.

Augustus sat down with a sigh. "A detestable fellow," he remarked. "And unnatural to boot. But you, my dear, I swear you have been sent here by some kindly angel entirely to remove my boredom. I can wait no longer. Puss, girl. Puss."

"Sire?"

"Your skirts, girl. Up with them. I would see if your pussy equals the rest of you."

Lorna retreated down the steps; she was too utterly surprised even to feel anger. "Your Majesty," she protested. "I came here to seek shelter and comfort. . . ."

"And you shall have, the best comfort and shelter that may be provided," the King promised. "Your skirts, girl. Up with them."

Lorna reached the lower level, discovered that her fingers were indeed twined in her gown, as she had been first taught by her mother. "Your Majesty, I am pregnant."

"You do not look pregnant to me," Augustus declared. "Eh, Kunert?"

The other man smiled. "No doubt the Princess is still in an early stage, Sire."

"Oh, indeed. Up, girl. Up."

Lorna continued to retreat. Now the surprise was wearing off, and she was aware of a rash of sweat breaking out on her shoulders. But it was anger, more than fear. This creature, after the Tsar? "I must protest, Your Majesty. I . . . I must refuse."

"What? You'd refuse a king a reasonable request?"

"Reasonable," she cried. "With . . . with another man present?"

"Ah." Augustus heaved himself to his feet. "Kunert sees with my eyes, hears with my ears. On occasion he speaks with my mouth. You may forget he is here."

"Forget . . ." Lorna turned and ran for the door, seized the great handles, and twisted them to no avail.

"They are locked," Augustus said, coming down the steps. "The doors are always locked when I am closeted with a lady."

Lorna turned to face them, panting, back pressed against the panels. "Sire, I belong to the Tsar."

"So I had assumed. You could not possibly belong to that perverted oaf. But Peter and I, why, we share everything. We have always done so, we will always do so. And having received the Tsar, my dear child, you will find me only an improvement. That I do promise you."

Lorna glanced from left to right, seeking some

escape. But Kunert had also descended the steps, and was walking some distance away from his master.

"Well, then," Augustus said. "As you will not humour me, we must have at you. It will be sport, eh?"

She opened her mouth to scream, closed it again. That would be senseless and humiliating. Equally would it be humiliating to be raped on the floor. "Wait," she gasped. "I will obey Your Majesty."

"Up then, up," he cried, standing in front of her, his face crimson with excitement.

"Under protest."

"Of course, of course, my dear. Everyone carries out my orders, under protest."

Lorna sighed, closed her eyes, seized her skirts, and slowly raised them.

"Higher, girl, higher."

She scooped them to her breast, stood as still as she could, aware of the sudden chill raising her flesh in goose-pimples.

"By God," Augustus remarked. "What perfection. What superb perfection." She knew what would follow, instinctively, and tensed her muscles to remain still. Surprisingly, he touched her with but a single finger, stroking it lightly across her belly, at the very edge of the hairline, and then down each valley of her groin, again lightly, tickling her but also inducing a very pleasant sensation, so that her eyes opened despite herself, and she felt her cheeks flaming. She need not have worried. Both men were bending to peer at her.

"A perfect vee, Your Majesty. A perfect vee," Kunert remarked. "Why, it is superior to the Countess's."

"Then I should inspect her for myself," remarked Aurora Konigsmarck.

The two men straightened and turned in embarrassment. Lorna, no less embarrassed, hastily dropped her skirts. The Countess had apparently entered from a private doorway behind the throne, and had crossed the room on tiptoe. Her face was composed, but there were pink spots in her cheeks.

"Madam," the King protested, continuing to speak French. "This habit of yours of sneaking about the palace is unseemingly."

"Had you been less absorbed in your sport, Sire, you would certainly have heard me," Aurora pointed out.

"And what do you here?"

"Why, having seen Prince Bogoljubov ride off," she said, "I thought it best that I should attend Your Majesty in order to prevent a catastrophe."

"Catastrophe?" the King shouted. "With so beautiful an object? Show her, Princess. Up, girl, up."

Lorna gave Aurora an imploring look, and the Countess's smile became warmer.

"You may leave your skirts where they are, Princess."

"She's not diseased?" The King sounded utterly despondent. "You'll not say such a creature is diseased?"

"Of course not, Sire. But she is with child. That is why she is here, to await her delivery."

"Child? Bah. 'Tis but a scheme to avoid her husband. That Bogoljubov? He has not that much seed in his entire body."

"By the Tsar, Sire," Aurora said gently. "The Princess is high in His Majesty's favour."

"So she claimed," Augustus agreed. "But . . . it is Peter's child?"

Lorna hesitated. "I . . . I understand it to be so, Sire."

"And your lance, Your Majesty," Aurora said, kissing him on the cheek, "so long, so powerful, flooding the infant, may well do it an injury."

He glanced at her, frowning, then turned and walked back across the room. "I am cursed with ill fortune. To have so delectable a creature, here in my palace . . ."

Aurora took Lorna's arms and escorted her towards the private doorway. "You may look on the Princess, Sire, as and when you choose, as she shall share my apartments. For the rest, you may be sure I shall do my poor best to make up for your misfortune in that direction." She sank into a deep curtsey before the door, and Lorna followed her example. Then they were through the door and in a little corridor, and she could allow herself to gasp in sheer relief.

"My lady Konigsmarck," she said. "I am in your debt for life. I do not know how to set about thanking you."

Aurora smiled at her. "Then do not try. Indeed, there is nothing to thank me for, Princess. What, have you in Gussie's bed? Then indeed would I be a careless wench. But you shall stay in my apartments." She squeezed Lorna's hand. "That way I may keep an eye on you."

"I do assure you, Countess," Lorna protested, "that His Majesty would have had to force me."

"He would have enjoyed that, I have no doubt at all," Aurora remarked without emotion. "Oh, you came here as a guest, seeking his protection until your child is born. Alas, my dear, none of those would have counted when placed beside his lust. He is well known for that, as well as for his avarice, his cruelty, and indeed his cowardice. It has been said that his only redeeming feature is the size of his weapon."

"But . . ." Lorna shook her head in mystification.

"I remain with him?" Aurora gave a little laugh. "I love him, my dear. How shall we explain that? I see him for what he is, and yet I know that whenever next he comes to my bed I shall be transported with delight, and as I also please him, why, you find me here in the lap of luxury, far superior to anything I could possibly achieve in my native Sweden."

"Sweden," Lorna muttered. Of course, this woman would have been born there. As a girl she might even have known Lennart. But what an absurd thought, for her to recommence brooding on Lennart. Even had he not so cruelly deserted her, was she not now the wife of a prince and the mistress of a tsar?

"You have been there?" Aurora inquired, continuing to lead the way down a succession of corridors and up a series of staircases, all apparently concealed somewhere in the walls of the castle.

"No," Lorna said.

"But you wish to? You are interested?"

"Yes. No, why should I be?" Lorna said. "I but know of it as the enemy of Russia. I was thinking that I feel the same way about the Tsar as you do about the King."

"The Tsar." Aurora stopped and turned to face her. "How well do you know him?"

"Well, I . . ." Lorna flushed.

"He is the father of your child. That is scarce an intimate acquaintance, if you will excuse me. You know he is quite mad?"

"Madam," Lorna said. "If you mean that he is given to fits of anger and fits of depression, he has explained them to me. Their cause is found in the events of his childhood."

"No doubt," Aurora said. "As your common madman becomes so by being dropped on his head as a babe. Yet is he dangerous to everything around him, and Peter is no different. I would beg you to be careful." She continued her walk. "And do not suppose that popinjay of a husband will ever protect you."

"I would not expect him to," Lorna said, keeping her temper under control with difficulty. "We are both servants of the Tsar."

Aurora stopped once more, this time before a velvet-draped door. "I would not quarrel with you, Princess," she said, her hand on Lorna's arm. "I wish us to be friends. They call me the most beautiful woman in Europe. Clearly they have not seen enough of you. And being of such joint eminence we are, again jointly, the perquisites of probably the two most vicious men in all Europe. There is a cause for mutual regard, not mutual enmity. Mutual pity, if you like." She smiled, and Lorna's anger dissipated. Aurora's arms went round her neck, and to her surprise she kissed her on the mouth, although chastely enough. "Inside this door, let us forget about men, and concern ourselves with being women and mothers."

The door opened, and she found herself in a large and light room, clearly situated in one of the wings of this vast place, and comfortably furnished. And here, to her delight, waited Alice and Bridget, while Kathleen came bounding across the floor to throw herself into her arms.

"Mama, isn't it nice? Isn't he sweet?"

Lorna followed her gaze, to the centre of the floor, where a little boy, who could hardly have been more than two played with his bricks, arranging them into what appeared to be fortifications, then levelling them again.

"His name is Maurice." Aurora swept the child from the floor and held him up. "This is the Princess Bogoljubov, Maurice. She will be our friend."

The boy stared at her with large, solemn eyes.

"He is mine, by Augustus," Aurora explained. "And he will be a prince. Gussie has promised. Maurice of Saxony. There is a good title, do you think?"

"I envy you, Countess. At once the safe delivery and the healthy child, not to mention the title." And what will Peter call mine, she wondered?

Aurora laughed, set the boy back on the floor, and gave her a hug. "You will have all three, Lorna. Now come, I will show you your own apartments."

"I am accompanied by my confessor," Lorna said. "And my cat."

Aurora gave another laugh, crossed the room, and opened another door, which gave access to a wide, carpeted corridor, off which several more apartments opened. *"Voilà!"*

Lorna heard the mew and hurried forward. Snowdrop had taken up her position in the centre of the quilt. Father Simeon stood by the bed.

"I will leave you, to settle in," Aurora said. "You will dine with me, in two hours, Princess?" She bowed and left the room.

"Oh, it is elegant, Highness, elegant," Bridget said.

Alice was prowling the room. "Rich enough," she said. "But these Germans, I have heard they are uncouth fellows."

"Are we going to stay here long, Mama?" Kathleen demanded.

Lorna sat on the bed. She felt exhausted. Snowdrop crawled on to her lap. "For several months, sweet. Well, Father, what do you think?"

"It is better than a Bavarian inn, my lady. I cannot say I am relieved by the tales they tell of this King's amatory prowess."

Lorna smiled and squeezed his hand. "But I, and

therefore we, are protected, by the Konigsmarck's jealousy. Our sojourn here will be an opportunity for us to rest. That can be no bad thing."

In fact she found Dresden inexpressibly boring. King Augustus lived an extremely active life, hunting several times a week, and requiring to be accompanied by his ladies, for he more often than not spent the night in one of the various lodges he had built himself. Lorna could not of course take part in these, even had she wished, but the removal of the entire Court for days on end left her bereft of company, apart from her servants; very few of the Saxons spoke understandable French, and none of them knew English. This handicap extended to the various entertainments provided within the palace itself, when the Court was in residence, and even more seriously, to the books in the library. Fortunately Vassily had left half a dozen of his guards, to see to her safety when she could eventually continue her journey, and the lieutenant in command, named Lissitsin, was an intelligent fellow, with whom she could practice her Russian.

But he was neither charming, nor witty, nor especially forthcoming about Russia itself. It seemed to Lorna that she was cut off from all human intercourse, save with Aurora, who proceeded through life with determined ebullience. She indeed was the very best of companions, eager to talk, about Saxony, about middle-European politics, about her late brother's famous escapade, and equally eager to listen, to Lorna's tales of life at the Court of Queen Mary and on a Maryland homestead. But apart from the hunt and her duties as hostess for the King, Aurora's time was also considerably taken up by her responsibilities as the royal mistress. She certainly enjoyed herself, but Lorna wondered for how long her health would stand up to it, for on a morning after Augustus had visited her bed she would be in a state of total exhaustion, her thighs, inside and out, covered with teeth marks, her shoulders black and blue, her lips puffy, her breasts too tender to touch. Lorna could only thank God that so effective a barrier stood between herself and a similar fate.

She longed for news, but this, when it came, was scanty. Every month she received a letter from Vassily, but as each one was a repeat of the one before, she soon ceased to look forward to it. The wording was exact:

PRINCESS,
Your husband sends you greetings, and trusts that you are well. He is well. The Tsar is well. Things go well.

PRINCE BOGOLJUBOV.

She answered the first one equally formally, but attempted more in the second.

"I am so lonely, my dearest," she wrote. "I know nothing of what goes on outside this dreary palace, and even less of what happens within. My body yearns for the touch of your hand, my hands yearn once again to enclose that delicious morsel of flesh that is our mutual happiness. Can you not come to me, my sweet, for at least a short season? The months stretch before me with terrible monotony."

He did not alter the wording of his reply.

Aurora attempted to reassure her. "There are great political moves afoot," she explained. "And no doubt he is in constant attendance on the Tsar. They plan to deal once and for all with Sweden."

"They?" Lorna inquired.

"Ah, well, you must know, my dear, that for a hundred years Sweden has been riding roughshod over all its neighbors. It has conquered Norway, invaded Denmark time and again, seized Pomerania, dictated terms to Poland, sealed off the Russians from the Baltic. Ah, you can have no concept what it is like to live in close proximity to such a power. Why, not even Louis is so grasping, so determined to aggrandise himself."

"But you are Swedish."

"I am Saxon, by adoption. One can possess only one country. Just as you are now a Russian, and would do well to remember that. You'll find no passion from them, except perhaps in bed. And not even there from your Vassily. Oh, you may have stirred him once or twice. But you know his tastes are perverted?"

"Of course," Lorna said. "Although I would have described them as catholic."

"A man," Aurora said sternly, "who once prefers his tool to be wrapped in fingers rather than your own sweet thighs is lost. That is my opinion, anyway, and you may be sure that I have considerably more experience than you. I do not mean to insult your husband. I do not mean that he is any less a man. I do not mean he may be less gallant, less brave, or less ambitious and successful. Indeed, history leads us to suppose that he may well become more so. I am but putting the matter from a female point of view. To such a man, we can never be anything more *than* females, second best, a vehicle for producing his children, for managing his house, perhaps, and for occasional visitations. Not for continual lust, and even more, continual love. And where that happens, a woman finds it very difficult to maintain herself upon terms of equality."

"I do not agree at all," Lorna said. "Cannot the woman equally supply the fingers he desires?"

Aurora's eyebrows arched. "My God. Perhaps I have not so much the greater experience. You have done this?"

"I am his wife," Lorna said primly, and picked up her needlework. But in fact Aurora's lecture was extremely depressing. She could not help but remember Vassily's hint concerning Peter himself, which she had dismissed at the time. But surely, had Peter enjoyed their night together as much as she had done, he would have shown some suggestion of love. Instead she had no proof that he had even thought of her again, for a moment. And life in Russia, without Peter's love, did not bear considering.

By now winter was finished, and spring had arrived, much warmer and drier than an English spring. But for Lorna it meant an increase in boredom, for by now her belly was swollen—she conceived it entirely possible that her child would share the same birthday as Kathleen—and Augustus no longer invited her to his parties. Aurora did her best and would take her to one of the curtained galleries overlooking the grand ballroom where she might at least oversee the glittering throng, listen to the music and watch the dancing, but this was a pale substitute for the real thing. Yet she always went. To be left alone in her apartments, with only Alice's grumbling, Bridget's chattering, Kathleen's desire to play endless games, Father Simeon's patient smile, would have driven her mad.

And it was while sitting in her private box, looking down on a ball in the early summer of 1698, that she found herself staring at Lennart Munro.

For a moment Lorna supposed she must be dreaming. Then she seized the curtains and pulled them aside to see better. His uniform had changed. The drab buff had disappeared, and in its place he wore a rich blue coat, over a gold-coloured vest, with matching cross and waist belts supporting a gold hilted sword, while there were gold lace edgings to his buff gauntlets. Highly polished black boots completed his dress, together with a tricorne hat in the same blue as his coat, but edged with gold braid. He was not dancing, but stood with a group of similarly dressed officers, conversing with red-coated Saxon life guards, and making a tremendous splash of colour, even in the midst of the brilliant hues worn by the dancing ladies and their escorts.

And then he looked up and saw her. Hastily she drew back, allowing the curtain to fall into place, while her heart pounded and her entire body broke out in a sweat; she left the box, stumbled along the corridors to regain her own apartments. She had supposed him forever gone—from her life, from her memory, from her heart. But the sight of him . . . it suddenly occurred to her that when she had written Vassily she had in fact been writing Lennart, as she would have wished to do so, had they been lovers. But now . . .

She regained her apartment, closed the door behind her. The hour was late and the palace quiet; the faintest sound of the music from the ballroom lingered on the air. Bridget had retired, as had Father Simeon; Alice was asleep in her chair, Snowdrop curled on her lap. Neither woke.

Lorna tiptoed into Kathleen's bedchamber, looked down at the sleeping girl. Lennart's daughter. There could be no doubt. There had never been any doubt in her heart, but in fact with every year Kathleen looked more and more like her father, tempering the MacMahon beauty with a certain boldness which suggested that she would be a handsome rather than a lovely woman.

And her father was downstairs.

Lorna sat beside the bed, still gazing at the child. What to do? She had never spoken of him to Kathleen, and Kathleen had never inquired. No doubt she supposed that her father had been named Butler, as she had no inkling of what had happened on those fateful two days in Maryland. But she would inquire, eventually.

To meet him again, and now. Her hands settled on her belly. She had wanted the child. But now she wished she was not pregnant at this moment. How she wished . . . her head jerked as she heard the outer door open. She was on her feet in an instant, turned to face the nursery door as if expecting disaster to overtake her, watched Aurora standing there.

"Will you come with me?"

"No," Lorna said. "No."

"An interest in Sweden," Aurora murmured. "Instantly repressed. And now I find you staring at your child. There is someone would speak with you. He came hastening to my side, virtually wrenched me from the floor."

Lorna's tongue circled her lips. "I cannot."

"Is he Kathleen's father?"

Lorna flushed.

"If you do not come, Lorna, you will regret it all your life."

"But . . . look at me."

"You are lovelier than ever. More limited, certainly, but that may be to the good. Lennart is most certainly a gentleman."

"Lennart? You know his name?"

"We were friends as children. Come, Lorna."

She held out both her arms, and Lorna went to her, allowed herself to be led through the outer room, along the corridor, and into Aurora's own apartments. Her thoughts whirled. What to say? What to do? What attitude to take? He had deserted her. There could be no argument about that. He was the guilty one, not she. He must know that. He must . . .

The door was swinging in, and Aurora was waiting for her to enter. Lennart stood in the centre of the room. He had removed his hat, and his cheeks were flushed.

"Colonel Lennart Munro, of His Majesty King Charles the Twelfth's Drabant guards, Princess Vassily Bogoljubov," Aurora said and stepped outside, closing the door behind her.

They gazed at each other.

"Colonel?" Lorna inquired. "You are prospering at your chosen profession." She was amazed at the evenness of her voice.

"Princess?" he inquired. "And you are married. To a *Russian?*"

"Should I not, sir? Or would you have me remain a widow for all of my life?"

"On the contrary, madam," he said, and she realised that he was preserving an equal coolness. "I had supposed you wed these past seven years to some English nobleman."

She frowned at him. "You had supposed, sir? Faith, it would have taken you but a few lines put to paper to discover the truth of it."

"Lines to paper?" He took a step closer. "Highness, your humour has a cruel twist. What did you do with all of those words. Burn them unread?"

"Words?" she whispered. "Words? Oh, my God." Her knees gave way, and she sat. "You wrote me?"

"Will you pretend not to know of it?"

"Tell me," she said. "Tell me," she begged. "What you wrote."

His turn to frown. "Why, Highness, I wrote you my undying love, time and again. I wrote you of my parents' sickness, begged you to wait but a few months, until I could settle my affairs and come to you. And received no reply. Not a line."

"Oh, my God," she whispered. "Oh, my God." Queen Mary, smiling at her childish indulgence. And no doubt reading the letters before having them destroyed. Oh, certainly Sarah and Princess Anne had also been in the secret. How they must have laughed at her. "We were betrayed," she said.

"But . . ." He knelt at her side. "You . . ."

"Wrote. Time and again. I gave my letters to Count Falkenhayn. Who no doubt destroyed them."

"By God," he said. "When I get home . . ."

"He acted under orders, I have no doubt." She hesitated, placed her hand over his. "We were betrayed," she said again. "No doubt it was never meant to be."

"Never?" he cried. "And here we have met again, in such strange circumstances. I'll never believe that, Lorna." He took her face between his hands. "Not if I live to be a thousand." He drew her towards him very gently, kissed her on the lips.

She held his hand, led him along the corridor, into the privacy of her own apartment, across the withdrawing chamber and into the nursery. "'She is seven years old next week," she whispered.

"Seven?" He bent over the cot, blood rushing into his cheeks.

"Her eyes are grey, Lennart," Lorna said.

He stared at the child, then slowly straightened.

"I have called her Kathleen Munro."

He looked around the room, and she seized his hand once more, drew him into her own bedchamber, closed and locked the door.

"We leave in three days' time," he said. "You'll accompany us, Lorna."

She sat on the bed, sighed. "Do you play cards, Lennart?"

He frowned. "I have held a hand."

"And do you rail, when you receive a deuce instead of an ace, and say, if only I had been dealt an ace? Or do you play the hand you are dealt, and hope for a better one, in due course."

"Lorna . . ." He sat beside her, held her hand.

"I am married, Lennart."

"You cannot love him. Prince Bogoljubov? Vassily Bogoljubov? I have heard it said . . ."

"That he is a pervert? He is my husband, Lennart. In every way."

"He is the father of the child in your belly?"

She shook her head.

"Aha. What did I say? He is incapable."

"He had no opportunity, Lennart. The child is Peter's."

This time the frown was deep and concerned. "The Tsar's? That madman?"

"He has never been other than kind with me."

Slowly his fingers released her, and he stood up. "You are become a royal whore."

With an effort she kept her face composed, her voice even. "If you believe that, then there is nothing more to say. I understand now a great deal that puzzled me in the past. I am very beautiful, they say. I am very wealthy, I know. These things make me valuable. Too valuable, apparently, to be squandered upon a Swedish soldier, for this is how King William and Queen Mary considered it. So I was sold, to the highest bidder. The Tsar saw me and wanted me. The marriage was arranged whether I would or no. And the Tsar claimed what he wished, that very night."

"Lorna . . ." He was beside her again, reaching for her hands.

"So, my beauty sealed a pact of friendship between England and Russia, and my money, held in trust for my children, should they ever return to reclaim it, will in the meantime swell King William's coffers for his never-ending war with France. It has all worked out very neatly, for everyone."

"And left you a slave to the most barbarous monarch, who rules the most barbarous people in the world."

She smiled at him. "I would hope to civilise them, to some extent. And what would you have me do? I swore certain oaths, agreed to certain proposals. And I am to be again a mother—of a child who could one day be Tsar of Russia."

His face twisted. "You have become ambitious."

"And you have become cruel."

"Lorna . . . forgive me." He pulled her to him, kissed her forehead, her nose, her eyes, her chin, her lips, stroked her hair, lowered his head to kiss her belly. "I love you, Lorna. In seven years, I have not thought twice of any other woman. I love you and only you. If I am cruel, 'tis my love makes me so. Lorna . . ."

"And I love you, Lennart. But for the sake of my children, of my honour, of my inheritance which I hold but for them, I must carry out my duty. And pray for deliverance, in the course of time. And should that ever happen, and you still want me, I will come to you. I swear it, Lennart."

"Want you? I will want you on your deathbed, my darling. But, deliverance . . . do you not know why we are here, why we are leaving in such haste?"

She shook her head.

"We are an embassy," he said. "A last attempt to persuade Augustus to surrender the throne of Poland, which he obtained by fraud and deceit. Believe me, we are here despite the wishes of our king. He would have none of it. But as he is an honest man, he agreed to this last attempt to prevent war. And we have been told to leave the kingdom. This Augustus rides above himself."

"And there will be war? My God, you will be crushed."

His frown was back, deeper than ever. "A Swedish army, crushed?"

"Your king is only a boy."

"Ah. Do not join the mistaken world and suppose that will matter. This boy was spawned at the mouth of a cannon, with a sword in his hand. Poland will be crushed, and should your Tsar come to its assistance, Russia will equally be crushed. I fear for your safety. King Charles already has his mind set on burning Moscow, at some near date."

"Then I shall await your coming."

He stood up in frustration. "Do you not understand? Have you any idea what a war can be like? You will be considered a Russian. . . ."

"I am a Russian, Lennart, by marriage. You would not have me a traitor into the bargain?"

He chewed his lip. "I shall not see you again, Lorna. Ever. I fear it."

She remained seated. "Then will I have to exist upon your memory, upon the memory of this night, and of that other night so long ago. Believe that I will always treasure those two memories, Lennart. Above all others."

"But you will not change your mind and elope with me now."

"I cannot," she whispered. "As God is my witness, I cannot."

# Chapter 9

*H*e left the room, and Lorna could give herself up to tears. The following day she remained in her bed-chamber, declaring a headache. Next morning Aurora visited her to say that the Swedish embassy was leaving.

"What else could I *do?*" Lorna wailed.

"In your condition, why, nothing," Aurora smiled.

"Oh, I meant . . . he would have had me elope with him. Leave everything. I am married. . . ."

"Oh, indeed," Aurora agreed. "It would have been a heinous sin."

"But one you would have committed?"

"Ah. If I loved, no doubt, yes."

*If I loved.* Lorna sank on to the bed. *Oh, Holy Mother, to be able to know.* But was she then, so much at the mercy of her body? To spend the rest of her life in the company of no one but Lennart would be sheer bliss . . . but only if he could send her through that transport of joy she had known with Peter, looked forward to knowing again, the moment her babe was born and she could rejoin the Tsar. To abandon Peter for a better man in every way, save in bed, would be disaster. She knew that, now. But suppose Lennart were a better man, or at least an equal man, in bed? Then was she damned forever. Oh, curse the swelling in her belly. Were it not for that, she could have discovered.

But were it not for that, she would never have seen him again. Never even known the agony of decision. Then doubly curse the swelling.

"Anyway," Aurora pointed out. "You will scarce see him again. There will certainly be war."

"Which he is certain Sweden will win."

Aurora sighed. "They are a very confident people. I am one of them, remember? But it is impossible to suppose they will defeat the numbers being brought against them. I am also privy to Augustus' secret councils. Anyway," she said brightly, "it is unlikely that Lennart will survive."

"What? What did you say?" Lorna jumped to her feet.

"He is a Drabant guardsman. Do you not know what that means?"

"He wears a magnificent uniform."

"And that guarantees his safety? The Swedish army, of all armies, my dear girl, is there to fight, not to display itself. The Drabants are the bodyguard of the King himself. Every man in it is a commissioned officer. Why, in the regiment itself, Lennart is no more than a sergeant, for all his rank. Their duty is to die for their King's safety, and as it is the tradition that a Swedish king leads his men into the thickest part of the fight, at all times, the casualties among the Drabants are higher than in any other regiment."

"Oh, God." Lorna sat down again. She grasped her

belly as the pain began. "No," she shouted. "It cannot be. It is not yet time. And I have not been examined."

"Still, we had best prepare," Aurora said, suddenly very efficient. "I will summon Madame Bluthner and have the chair brought up."

"Madame Bluthner?" Lorna gasped, the pains now suddenly intense. "The chair? I have a bed . . ."

"My dear Lorna, you cannot give birth in a bed."

"I can," Lorna shouted. "I have. You'll not put me in the chair. 'Tis barbarous."

"Alice," Aurora shouted, hurrying to the door. "Bridget. Summon my people. Your mistress has lost her mind. She would lie in her bed."

"But Countess," Alice protested. "The babe, Kathleen, was born in a bed."

Aurora peered at her. "My God," she said. "What a backward country this England of yours must be. Have you no chairs?"

"Do you not understand?" Lorna cried. "It is an advance. The French began it. An advance."

"The French," Aurora said scornfully. "We do not talk of the French in Dresden. Alice, summon my people this instant or I will have you whipped." She smiled at Lorna. "You have naught to be afraid of, my dear. You are in good hands, here."

It appeared she meant literally, even if she was certainly mistaken about the "good." Lorna was changed into a voluminous nightgown, by which time both Madame Bluthner and the chair had made their appearance. Madame Bluthner wore a moustache and had no recent acquaintance with water that Lorna could see, but presumably she knew her business, at least as regards the chair. This was placed in the centre of the room, and Lorna was seated in it, and pushed about to make sure her buttocks were embedded on either side of the hole. Her wrists were placed one on each arm, and then tied down with velvet ribbons. She anticipated a similar fate for her ankles, but to her disgust these were not tied; instead two of the Countess Konigsmarck's maids took charge of an ankle each. They were big, strong girls, and anchored her firmly to the floor, pulling her legs as far apart as they could, so that her thighs ate into the sides of the chair. But this pain seemed trifling with what was happening inside her belly, for now the cramps were coming regularly.

"Help me," she gasped, sweat running down her cheeks. Oh, what would she give for a glimpse of Chamberlen's smiling, confident face. "Oh, we shall, Highness, we shall," Bluthner agreed. She had been busily arranging the skirts of the nightgown on the outside of the char.

"Pull it up," Lorna wailed. "Pull it up. You'll not be able to see."

"To see?" Bluthner cried.

"Why, Lorna," Aurora protested. "We cannot look. That is indecent."

"And besides, Highness, a birth is the work of God," Bluthner said piously. "We do not seek to understand His wonders, only to assist them. Assist, assist."

Lorna's jaw dropped in utter horror as she was surrounded by a dozen of the maids—Alice and Bridget were gathered on the far side of the room, equally aghast—the chair was seized, as were her shoulders, and the whole lifted a foot into the air and then dropped again with a crash, while the two girls retained their hold on her ankles, so that she thought she would at once be pulled right through the hole and at the same time have her spine driven through the top of her head.

"No," she screamed. "No."

"The moment is near," Bluthner shouted, having worked herself into a fine frenzy of excitement. "Shake her, shake her."

"Oh, God," Lorna shrieked as another shattering crash tore through her body.

Again and again went the bump, then they stopped, mainly because they had run out of breath. Tears ran down her cheeks to mingle with the sweat, and she moaned in agony. "Look, for God's sake, look," she begged.

Instead her face was dried with a towel, and she was given something to drink, and after a while she was shaken again. But by then time ceased to matter, pain ceased to matter. She was aware that candles were being lit, and she remembered having started labour in the morning. She was aware of other people in the room, of Augustus himself, and supposed she must be dreaming, even when she heard Aurora saying, apparently to her, "He does love to watch women in labour."

She was aware of long hours when the shaking had ceased, because the women appeared to be sleeping or dozing. Then it was daylight again, and the cramps were more severe than ever. And the girls were back to seize the chair. She collected her thoughts, her determination, with an immense effort. "Touch me," she screamed, "and I'll . . ." She was overtaken by a spasm she had to assume was her last. No woman could survive such pain. But the next was less severe, and the next. "Oh, God," she gasped. "Take the babe. Take the babe."

She felt hands lifting her skirt, and then lost consciousness, for only a few seconds. But when she next opened her eyes she had been laid on her bed, and now at last her skirts were being rolled to her waist, and Bluthner, sleeves pushed back, face gleaming with determined energy, was preparing to see to her.

"Take her away," she shouted. "Get her away."

"But, my dear Lorna," Aurora protested.

"If she touches me I'll kill her," Lorna screamed. "I'll kill her. I swear it."

"Well," Bluthner declared.

"You are beside yourself," Aurora said sympathetically. "Why, there is no one better than Bluthner. Of all the births she has attended, no more than half the mothers have died from the fever."

"Half?" Lorna shrieked. "I swear it. If she touches me, I'll kill her." She sat up, weak as she felt.

"Well," Bluthner declared. "I'll not stay a moment longer."

"Now see what you've done," Aurora complained. "She is insulted. And who's to care for your wound?"

"Alice," Lorna muttered. "Alice. And wash your hands, Alice. Remember Mr. Chamberlen."

Alice's hands were soft and clean. And the pain was gone, leaving only an ache. She went to sleep. And sat up again in stark horror.

"My babe," she screamed.

"Here it is," Aurora said reassuringly. "An enormous child. You must thank God that he was premature. Another couple of weeks and you'd not have managed it."

"It?" Lorna looked down at the wizened face. Peter's child. Which explained its size.

"He," Aurora smiled.

"A boy. For the Tsar." Lorna leaned back with a sigh. "I shall call him Alexis. Alexis Petrovich Romanov."

"The Tsar already has a son called Alexis."

"What?" Lorna cried.

"By his wife, Eudoxia Lopukhina. But rumour has it he cares little for the boy. I recommend that you name yours Michael. Michael Petrovich."

"Michael?"

" 'Tis the name of his grandfather, the founder of the Romanov greatness. He will be well pleased."

Well pleased. If she could only reach him. And while summer lasted. She dreaded the thought of having to spend another winter in Dresden. But at the same time she knew she could not possibly take Michael on a lengthy journey until he was at least two months old.

And soon there was a more pressing urgency. Once again she did not contract puerperal fever, with the result that within a fortnight she was as strong as ever and the idol of the Court, which invariably assembled in her boudoir, cramming the room to the door, to watch her feed the babe. Most eager of her attendants was Augustus himself, and he insisted, to the accompaniment of loud applause, in drying the teat when the child was removed. He also elected himself godfather, as Aurora stood godmother, when Prince Michael was christened.

Lorna thanked him most gratefully and bolted her bedroom door at night, while Alice maintained a watch in the outer room. But she was well aware that should he intend to come to her there was very little she could do. She was less visitor than prisoner, and, she reflected bitterly, a royal whore was a royal whore. Nor was it a subject she felt she could discuss with Aurora, and was therefore surprised when one morning in the early autumn, Aurora decided to discuss it with her. "Do you not suppose, my sweet Lorna," she remarked, as they sat over their needlework, "that you should be considering reaching Moscow before the onset of winter?"

"Nothing would please me more," she confessed, "did I know how to set about procuring the means of travel and the necessary passports."

"I shall see to those for you," Aurora promised. "What, a young mother, separated from at once her husband and the father of her child? It cannot be."

Lorna ignored the sarcasm, concentrated on stitching the imperial insignia into Michael's nightgowns. That noontime she smiled even more graciously on the King, too graciously, as it turned out, for when Bridget came for the babe he waved the room empty without actually leaving himself.

"Oh, lucky babe," he said, kneeling beside her chair. Even kneeling his head reached above hers.

"He has a tremendous appetite," Lorna said. "And the strongest of gums. I look forward to weaning him to a nurse, indeed I do."

"And can we not provide a nurse for him, here in Saxony? There are no more buxom women in the world." He closed one eye. "Saving perhaps in your native Maryland." Alice handed him the damp cloth, and he gently stroked her aureole. The touch could not help but induce a response, and she had known no sex now for some nine months. And like Peter, he was extraordinarily gentle, while she had Aurora's word for it that he was an accomplished lover. Yet the thought of him filled her with disgust. She could not tell why.

"He must have only one, Sire," she said. And watched his head sinking. Her knees were pressed together.

His hand was inside the loose bodice of her robe, and he was lifting the breast from underneath, as Lennart had done. *Lennart.* He kissed the breast, gave the teat a little suck. "Happy babe," he murmured, resting his head on her flesh. "How your heart pounds, sweet Lorna. I cannot let you go. You are magnificent. Magnificent. And your problem is easily solved. If your child must have a single nurse, then she shall be a Saxon, and you will remain here until he is weaned from *her*."

Two years? she thought. "Sire . . ." His head was turning again, the bodice of her own gown now completely opened, nuzzling the damp flesh in the valley, to her utter dismay taking the crucifix into his mouth and sucking it before spitting it out; she could feel his saliva trickling down her stomach, or was it merely horror sweat? "As he is a Russian, Sire, should his nurse not also be Russian?" As ever, she was surprised by the evenness of her voice.

"Foolishness," he mumbled. She stiffened as she felt his fingers, having slid beneath the hem of her robe, move across her instep to discover her ankle. "Magnificent," he said again. "So cold. So impassive. So haughty. To feel you warm, Lorna, my love, to watch you writhe with pleasure, to hear you cry out with joy, a man could know nothing finer."

His hand slipped round her calf, kneading the flesh. Cold, she thought. Impassive. Shall I cry out now, with terror? She gazed at Alice, whose face was a study of disapproval. Help me, she mouthed.

Alice coughed, and the King's head raised. "Woman? What are you doing here?"

"Someone comes, Sire."

"Someone . . . send them away."

"I suspect it is the Countess Konigsmarck."

Augustus withdrew his hand, heaved himself to his feet; the front of his breeches bulged. " 'Tis best we do not excite her. But, Princess, I can wait no longer. This night. This very night. Midnight. Leave your door open." He glared at Alice. "Open, woman, or I shall break it down."

He left the room. "Oh, my God," Lorna said. "Oh, my God. What can we do?"

"What *can* we do?" Alice repeated. "Lorna, were it not best to . . ."

"No," Lorna said. "I could not. There is a quality about him . . . ugh." The outer door was again opening. She gazed at Aurora. "Was it really you?"

Aurora frowned at her. "Was it really me doing what?"

"Ah . . . never mind. I have had a tiring morning."

"So I understand." Aurora sat beside her. "And you are going to have a tiring night. You leave at ten."

"At ten? But . . . the King?"

"Knows nothing of it. Here are your passports, and a berlin will be waiting for you at the eastern gate; you will ride through the night. It is no more than twenty-four hours to the Polish border, and thence no more than a week to Smolensk."

"Across Poland?" Lorna was aghast. "What of the King?"

Aurora smiled. "Indeed he will be angry. My advice to you would be never to set foot in Saxony again, or Poland either, while Gussie remains on the throne." She got up. "Now haste, girl. Your people must make all ready without seeming to. You have six hours."

"But you do not understand," Lorna cried. "The King is attending me this very night. At midnight. He will send in pursuit."

"He will not," Aurora assured her. "I shall be here, instead of you. Oh, I may have to agree with him you are a treacherous and perfidious young woman, but at the least I shall occupy his time. I promise you, Lorna, that by the time Gussie thinks to chase after you, you will be safe to Smolensk."

Smolensk. Lorna leaned from the window of her carriage, despite the drizzling rain shrouding the landscape. For there it was, towering on the crags above the Dnieper. Russia. Her first glimpse of the country she had adopted. Which was to be hers, perhaps, in the person of her son. Who slept, noisily sucking his thumb, in Kathleen's arms. Kathleen had indeed adopted him almost as a son herself.

The carriage slithered to a halt, and the ferry was being made ready. And Lieutenant Lissitsin was holding the door for her and standing to attention. "We leave you here, Princess, to return to our duty."

She extended her hand, and he kissed it. "You have been the best of companions, Lieutenant," she said, adjusting her hood before stepping on to the cobbles. The Polish peasants were gathered behind the coaches, peering at the Russian party as best they might, restrained by the guardsmen. "Have you sent ahead?"

"I have, my lady. The Tsar awaits you."

"Ah." She walked down the ramp, Snowdrop snuggling her head into the fur pelisse, gazed across the river once again. Beyond the town there was a forest, clinging to the river, stretching into the hills. She had not seen a real forest since leaving America; the European varieties were too clearly hunting parks. Russia, shrouded in rain mist. That was how it should be. A mighty land, stretching no man could say how far into the east. Peter had said she could not conceive the size of his domains. This day she could, just. And this day she would see Peter again. After a year, almost to the day. She should feel afraid. She should be trembling. She could think only, thank God, for my safe deliverance.

"Highness."

She smiled at the young man, smartly dressed in a green coat and a red bonnet, with black boots.

"Captain Nicolai Bogdanovich, at your service, Highness."

"My pleasure, Captain." She took his hand, was escorted across the plank and on to the wooden raft, watching the bubbling brown waters of the river rushing by.

"It is safe, I hope, Lorna," Father Simeon whispered as he joined her.

"I am sure it is, or it would not have been sent. Careful now, sweetheart." This to Kathleen but Bogdanovich was assisting her as well, before turning his attention to Bridget, who was now in charge of Michael.

"What of our boxes?"

"The ferry will return for them, Highness," Bogdanovich said. "I have no doubt you are in haste to set foot on Russian soil."

"I am," she agreed, and walked across the raft to the far side as the crew began their poling to free it from the bank, while the huge rope cables commenced to emerge from the water, dripping, clanking through the windlasses on board although they were actually being drawn from the distant shore.

The house of the city came closer; she could make out the gaunt skeleton of the cathedral, high above her now, still in the process of construction. And now, beyond the town itself, she could see the army encampment. She wrinkled her nose. She could smell it, too, drifting toward her on the breeze.

The raft came into the shore, and she frowned in

dismay, for it was difficult to tell where river ended and land began, save that the river looked somewhat cleaner than the oozing mud. She glanced at the captain, but he seemed not the slightest bit disturbed, had the gangplank run ashore, and went down it, immediately sinking to his ankles.

Lorna sighed—in honour of the occasion she was wearing one of her best blue satin gowns—hoisted her skirts to her knees, and followed. He did not offer her his arm this time, but was busy giving orders in Russian to the soldiers, from their uniforms clearly of his own regiment. They waited, separating her from a crowd of dismal-looking people, dressed in shabby outer garments which could hardly be called cloaks, for she could discern no buttons or pockets, and for the most part, she discovered as one of them moved, barefoot in the clinging mud.

"Lorna," Alice wailed, and she turned, to see the soldiers escorting the rest of her party away to the right. Including Michael.

"Is that where we go?" she asked.

Bogdanovich smiled. "Your people are being taken to your palace, Highness."

Lorna looked up the hill at the town. None of the buildings looked particularly like a palace to her. "And I stay here?"

"No, no, Highness. You are to be taken straight to the Tsar. This way."

He squelched through the mud, following the more level ground, and heading, she realised, for the military encampment. Lorna squelched behind him; she would actually rather present Peter with his sin in private, and after their reunion had been consummated. They rounded a corner to come upon a square, in which there was gathered a crowd of people. She stopped and arranged her features in a smile, only to discover that they were not waiting for her, nor even looking at her, but at what was taking place in the square itself. Bogdanovich shouted and cursed at them, and they parted to let them through, where she halted again, in sheer horror. For in the centre of the crowd there was a gallows, from which hung the body of a man, his face already black, to suggest that he had hung there for some time. But she had seen hanged men before. Directly beneath the corpse, buried in the mud so that only her head was visible, was a woman, young and pretty enough, despite her disordered hair, and she was alive, although clearly so weak with thirst and hunger that she could do no more than gaze at the man's boots, which swung twelve inches above her head.

"My God." Lorna crossed herself. "What crime can they have committed?"

"The crime of adultery," Bogdanovich said severely. "The lady Tatiana is the wife of a boyar, discovered in a criminal liaison with her coachman, who you see hanged above her."

"And she will be left there to die of exposure?"

"It is the law," Bogdanovich said. "Although if she is fortunate the mob will soon grow tired of her and stone her to death. Come, the Tsar is waiting."

He was already pushing through people at the far side of the square, and she almost ran behind him, forgetting her skirts and allowing them to trail in the mud as she crossed herself. Adultery! *Holy Mother,* she prayed. *What manner of people are these? Peter. Oh, Peter.*

The houses were thinning, and they were close to the camp. The stench of open latrines and unwashed bodies and horse manure seemed to fill the air. She thought it had taken up permanent residence in her nostrils. And still the drizzle pattered down from a solid grey sky; she was wet through, and could not even summon a smile at the guards who came to attention, as best they could, for extricating their boots from the mud was a lengthy operation.

Most of the army seemed to be camped in the open, but there was a cluster of wooden huts, close to the town, and it was towards these that Bogdanovich was leading, to stop before the largest. Here a sentry, wearing a similar uniform to the captain's, save that he carried a musket, stood to attention, and here too there was a flagpole with a standard drooping in the rain. The sentry saluted the captain, who ignored him, opened the door, and ushered Lorna into a cloud of smoke, at once from the huge open fire in the corner, as well as from the pipes which almost everyone appeared to be using.

She found herself coughing and gasping, and for a moment unable to see. When she recovered, she saw the room was littered with garbage, and the furniture, such as it was, was cracked and scarred; the whole place immediately reminded her of that once magnificent house in Deptford where she had first been entertained by the Tsar, and a moment later she discovered the two dwarfs, and then Menshikov, staring at her with that half sneer as ever, and then Peter himself, reclining in the corner in the midst of his midday meal, and drinking wine from a pewter mug.

"Sire," she cried, and started across the room to pause in dismay. "Sire?"

For while it was certainly Peter, it was not the man of her wedding night. This face was bloated and twitching, as it had on their first meeting, or when the cauldron of wine had dropped behind his back, and the eyes were bloodshot, while there was no softness at the mouth.

His hand came out, pointing. "That woman is a Saxon whore," he shouted.

"Sire?" she asked again, her knees bumping together.

"Who insults my presence," he screamed. "The knout. Let her feel the knout. She has long needed the knout."

Lorna's jaw dropped in amazement, and before she could recover herself Menshikov had given the signal and three men had leapt forward, two to seize her arms while the other jerked her pelisse from her shoulders, pulled it from her back, and then dug his fingers into the neck of her gown to rip it away.

"My lord," she shouted, gasping for breath.

For Menshikov now stood in front of her, smiling, to tear her petticoats and leave her naked from the waist up.

"Peter," she screamed. "My love."

"She blasphemes," Menshikov yelled. "She insults the Tsar." He seized her throat, so that she thought he was about to throttle her, and sank to her knees, but his fingers were moving up to grip the base of her jaw and force her mouth open, while Mensikov gave a chuckle, darted his hand inside, and seized her tongue, at the same time using his other hand to draw a hunting knife from his belt. "She spoke your name, my lord Tsar. Let me cut it out."

Lorna was afraid to move, for fear that he would indeed tear it out, so tight was his grip. She could only stare at the Tsar and at the knout, which was now produced and dangled before her eyes. It resembled a cat of nine tails, save that each tail was tipped with steel. The thought of that biting into her flesh was quite incomprehensible. Her brain seemed to go blank and she almost fainted.

Peter heaved himself to his feet. "Leave her tongue," he said. "Or she will not be able to scream."

Menshikov hesitated, then gave a squeeze and withdrew his hand. Lorna's jaws snapped shut, but she could not speak, at once with fear and with pain, for she certainly felt strained. She could only stare at Peter, who now stood before her, his legs, encased as usual in huge black boots, spread wide.

"But I will flog her myself," he said.

Menshikov grinned and snapped an order, and the men holding her hands stepped away from her and sank to their knees, carrying her with them so that she was forced to arch her back. *It cannot happen,* she prayed. She knew that one stroke of that ghastly instrument would turn her, mentally as well as physically, into a complete wreck.

"It would be a total waste," said a soft voice from the farthest corner of the room, pronouncing each word with great care to suggest that her Russian was no more than Lorna's. Lorna's head swung to see, emerging from the smoke, a girl even younger than herself, she estimated, with a pleasant rather than lovely face, but a voluptuous body, even when displayed in a Russian caftan, and bareheaded, but this was to her advantage, as it showed off her quite magnificent rich brown hair. She looked a typical peasant of yeoman stock, but that she was more than that was obvious, for her quiet words made Peter check, and immediately his twitchings grew less violent, and some of the colour left his cheeks.

"Truly I had forgot your presence, Martha," he said. "But 'tis no concern of yours. Rather should you hate her. She has been to my bed, bewitched me with her beauty."

Martha came closer. "She is Prince Bogoljubov's

wife?" She smiled at Lorna. "For once the men did not exaggerate. Believe me, lord Peter, take away this girl's beauty and you will most certainly regret it. Why . . ." She gave his arm a squeeze. "You will grow tired of me, soon enough, my lord. But of this one, never."

Lorna trembled as the Tsar once again looked at her, and his mouth gave another twitch.

"Women," he bellowed. "I do not understand them. I know not why I humour you, you Livonian whore."

Martha snapped her fingers, and the men released Lorna's arms. Martha herself took her hand to help her up. "Because I am a Livonian whore," she pointed out. "And as that is all the Princess is accused of, you must humour her also. And really, Peterkin, I have warned you before, you risk your health with these sudden outbursts."

Lorna felt her jaw sagging again and hastily closed it, for the Tsar's anger had disappeared as if Martha had been his mother, and he looked almost contrite.

"So now, my lords, if you will excuse us," Martha said, "the Princess Bogoljubov and I will retire."

Martha threw her arm around Lorna's shoulders and escorted her to a door set in the rear of the room, which gave access to what could be described as a bed-chamber; the bed itself was scarcely more than a pallet, and the only other furniture was an open privy and a table, on which there was a bottle and a tin mug. There were no rugs on the floor and no drapes at the single window, but that was so stained it made no difference to their privacy, while the fire roaring in the grate had the air heavy with smoke.

Martha closed and locked the door behind her, released Lorna, and went to the table to fill the mug. Lorna sat on the bed, careless of her torn dress, of the mud sliding down her boots to gather on the floor. She felt utterly exhausted, but there was more, a lurking despair which was seeping at her consciousness and which she was afraid to recognise. She had plunged all the way across Europe to this?

Martha held out the mug, and she took a sip. She had expected wine, but this was an almost tasteless white liquid that burned her throat.

"Vodka," Martha explained. "It will be good for you."

Lorna held the cup in both hands, took another sip, and shuddered. "If I could understand," she muttered.

Martha sat beside her. "Understand? Are you not his mistress?"

Heat gathered in Lorna's cheeks, and she drank some more vodka. "We slept together but once."

"But you knew of his moods, surely. And alas, he has been much worse since his return to Russia, or so Alex tells me. It was the Streltsi. He trusted them, and they rebelled. And then . . ." She sighed. "He was so angry, so afraid, perhaps, for he is a very frightened man, he saw to their executions himself. With his own hands, he sliced away their tools, pulled out their toenails, ripped out their tongues, gouged out their eyes, and finally cut off their heads. His own hands . . ."

Lorna drank some more vodka, discovered the mug was empty. The room became brighter. But her brain would not lighten. "I had thought he loved me," she whispered.

"Why, I am sure he does." Martha smoothed hair from Lorna's forehead, and then, to her total surprise and consternation, lowered her head and kissed her on the left breast. "What, not love these? He would indeed have to be demented."

"But . . ." Lorna shivered.

Martha got up, took the cup from her fingers, refilled it, and drank herself before passing it back. "Oh, he loves me as well. There is a mystery."

"Oh, I . . ."

"Do not dissemble. I am good in bed. You must study that. But I have had the advantage. I am, you see, nothing more than a whore. A captive whore. I am not even a Russian. I am a Livonian. Almost a Swede, and there is no human being Peter hates more than a Swede."

Lorna gazed at her.

"While you are a countess in your own right," Martha smiled. "And a mother. And utterly lovely."

"I am . . ." Lorna bit off the words. She had no more desire for Peter to recognise Michael as his son. Not at this moment.

"While I . . ." Martha shrugged. "My name is Skavronskaya. My man was a soldier, who was killed in a skirmish with the Russian border guards. I was a prize of war, Highness. I was dragged to the camp, and taken by Prince Menshikov himself."

"The pieman?"

Martha gave a delightful tinkle of laughter. "The same. I made him happy. So when next the Tsar was in camp, Alex sent me to him for the night." Her shoulders rose and fell. "I made him happy, also. He is happy when he is with me."

She spoke with complete simplicity, complete honesty. And complete accuracy, Lorna realised, remembering the way Peter's anger had dissipated.

"And do you not feel jealousy towards another?"

Martha lay back, her hands beneath her head. Once again to Lorna's total surprise, she swung her mudstained boots on to the mattress. "I think I have no cause for jealousy. You are far more beautiful than I,

Princess. But you will not make him happy. I do not know if you could make any man happy."

Lorna frowned at her. "I do not understand your philosophy, madam."

Martha smiled. "It is very simple. You are too much your own woman. You have every right to be, surely. You are beautiful. I have heard that in your own country you are very wealthy. I can see for myself that you are intelligent and strong-willed. You are a woman any man would wish to take to his bed, for the sake of conquering you. But would you ever forego your own satisfaction, to give him his?"

"Why, I . . ." Lorna flushed. She was going to claim that she had, indeed, done so. At least with Vassily. But had she, totally and utterly? Or had she just been aware of disappointment? And Vassily? Where was Vassily?

"And would you ever sacrifice your pride to gratify his, Princess?" Martha asked softly. "So, we shall be friends. We shall complement each other." Her eyebrows raised as there came a sudden violent bang on the door. "As now. You had best unlock it, or he will surely break it down."

Lorna got up, crossed the floor, listened to another series of bangs on the door. She gathered her torn bodice together with her left hand, turned the key with her right, stepped back. She was aware of fear, rumbling in her belly, but also of anticipation. She had seen Peter act the monster before. And she had known him act the lover, before.

He entered, kicked the door shut behind him, did not immediately seem to notice her. Lorna turned, and discovered that Martha had also risen, and was undressing as rapidly as possible. Indeed, as she watched, her shift, for she seemed to wear no petticoats, dropped to the floor. She was not a beautiful woman to Lorna's eyes, for her waist was too thick, and her legs were heavy; but she had magnificent breasts, at once much larger than her own, Lorna realised, and still high and firm—she could hardly be more than twenty. And she was a Russian woman, as Vassily had described, for all her protests; the mass of curling dark brown hair which drooped past her shoulders was more than matched by the curling dark brown on her groin.

"My lord," she said.

Peter ignored her in turn, looked at Lorna.

"My lord," she hastily added.

"You are not undressed," he growled.

"My lord?" She looked at Martha and was given a frantic waggle of the eyebrows. "I shall attend to it immediately."

She tore at her clothes, her heart commencing to pound. What could he intend? What new hell—or what new heaven—was he about to drag her through?

Peter threw himself on the bed, and Martha knelt beside him to remove his boots. "The news is ill," he grumbled.

"My lord?" they asked together. Martha, her back to the Tsar now as she straddled his leg, looked and smiled.

"The Danes," he said. "They would not wait. They have gone to war before I am ready. Before Augustus is ready. Oh, they are a foolish people."

Martha dropped one boot to the floor, began work on the other. Lorna stepped out of her last petticoat; sat down to remove her own boots, fingers picking their way through the dried mud.

"Perchance they will do the task for you, my lord," Martha suggested.

"Perchance." He gave her a kick which sent her and the boot to the floor. She never lost her smile. "They are shattered. Charles dictates peace before Copenhagen. In Copenhagen, God knows. That boy," he shouted, sitting up, a trace of froth showing at the corner of his mouth.

Lorna dropped her second boot, rolled down her stockings, garters and all. She dared not think. Dared not anticipate. For the first time in her life.

Martha sat on the bed, put her arms round the Tsar's neck, hugged him against that enormous bosom. "Danes," she said. "Only Danes. He has not yet fought Russians, my lord."

"I will crush him like a nut," Peter said. "A boy. He can know nothing of soldiering. Nothing, do you hear?" as if they were prepared to argue. He gazed at Lorna, slowly crossing the room, extended a hand behind Martha's back. She ran to him, for fear he would again lose his temper, had her left breast seized to draw her to the bed. "I had forgot your beauty," he said in a lower tone. "Did I suppose Augustus had known it. . . ."

"Never, my lord," she whispered, terrified.

He drew her closer, and Martha obligingly slipped out of the way. Peter lay back, at last releasing her breast to slide his arm round her back, and she lay on his naked chest. Gently she felt Martha moving her legs so that she could release his breeches. He gazed at her from a distance of four inches. His breath was stale, as he had not washed for perhaps a week, but she was little better after her journey across Poland. And he was Peter, the Tsar. His tongue came out, and for a moment she hesitated, uncertain what he wanted. Then she leaned forward and took it between her lips, sucking it into her mouth, feeling the passion swell in her belly as it had not done since that night in Hurd, racing away from her very womb, it seemed, to trace its way down her legs and arms and make even her finger-tips tingle. For she felt Martha's hand on her bottom as well, spreading her legs, and a moment later she was impaled upon his member, raised and guided by Martha's hands.

She gasped, with the sheer pleasure of it, the almost agonising delight, which was as much mental as physical, for surely she was now damned forever, but eager only to raise and lower her thighs, sliding them up and down that unforgettable lance, knowing the growing ecstasy she had not experienced for over a year, burst-ing into a cry as she broke out in a rush of sweat, allow-ing her head to droop, his tongue to slip from her mouth. She wanted to lie there forever. She did not wish him even to look at her again. She wanted him only to be there, his member inside her, for he had not yet climaxed, and she would come again.

But already she was being moved, withdrawn and gently pushed to one side, to make room for Martha. Peter's head went with her, and he wanted her mouth again. She slid down the side of his thigh onto the mattress, realised she had left a leg behind, and that it was now pinned between his thighs and Martha's, realized too that Martha was licking her cheek in an attempt to reach the Tsar's mouth. I should hate her, she thought. I should loathe her. Love is a private affair, between man and woman.

But was she not the outsider here? In any event, she was too tired, too pleasantly weary, too delightfully exhausted, to hate anyone. She allowed Peter's mouth to go, closed her eyes, felt fingers thrust into her hair gently to knead her scalp and then suddenly tighten with passion, realised to her amazement that they belonged to Martha, and yet felt no repugnance, even more to her surprise.

Then the room was quiet, save for their breaths, which mingled. *So,* she thought, *perhaps it always takes two women to satisfy this man.* As he was larger than life in every other sense she did not suppose that was unreasonable. But what an odd world it was, to be sure. Lorna, Countess of Morne, the Princess Bogoljubov, and Martha Skavronskaya, Livonian camp follower, sharing bed, a passion, with Peter, Tsar of Muscovy. *Is this to be my life?* she thought. It was an inconceivable thought, that she had actually been placed in a harem without realising it. A thought which should fill her with horror, and which instead at this moment only filled her with lazy delight.

There was a sudden howl from beside her, and an upheaval which threw her off the bed and landed her sitting on the floor. Martha had apparently landed on the other side, and the Tsar was alone in the bed, sitting up, pointing at the closed door, frothing at the mouth, his face purple, shrieking in a quite unintelligible tongue. And now he was getting up, and the bed was too low to the floor to crawl beneath. Lorna rolled on her belly, hid her head in her arms. *Oh, God,* she thought. *The harem of a madman.*

# Chapter 10

*L* orna became aware that the maniacal howling had ceased, and that instead there was a banging on the door. Huddled against the side of the bed, she watched the Tsar's bare feet swing to the floor, inches from her nose. *What am I to do? What were they all to do?* But she had wanted only to be near this man again, had submerged all the possible misery of her future in the delight of this man's love. Without that, she was damned.

And had he not restored that delight, only a few moments gone? But now she dreaded it. Suppose he were to have one of those attacks while inside her?

"Well, come," Peter bawled, still sitting on the bed. He bent down, slapped her on the bottom. "And you, get up. A princess cannot roll around on the floor in company."

She pushed herself up, kneeling beside the bed, watched the door swing in.

"Up," Peter commanded.

"I have no clothes, Your Majesty," she whispered.

"And you are ashamed of your body? Not that body, Lorna." He glared at the door. "Well?"

It was Menshikov. His gaze drifted to the right, where Martha was already up and sitting carelessly on the table, legs apart, and then to his left, Lorna sat on the edge of the bed, half turned away from him, knees pressed together and arms folded across her breasts. His eyes gleamed. "A messenger, Sire."

"Send him in."

Menshikov snapped his fingers, and a very tired, travel-stained man entered, pulling off his woolen cap as he did so, dragging his fingers through his thick black beard.

Thick black beard. Lorna watched in horror as the colour drained from Peter's face and as rapidly flooded it again. The Tsar was on his feet, naked body quivering, hand outflung. "That man is an insult. He challenges my authority."

"My lord Tsar," the man began.

"Guards," Peter shrieked, running across the room, seizing the offending beard, and jerking the man to his knees. "Guards. Bring me a knife."

The man's mouth opened and shut, and he gaped at his ruler. But the room was already filling with men from outside, seizing the fellow's arms and legs, holding him still, while someone else pressed a sharp knife into Peter's hands. Lorna could only stare at them in terror, almost forgetting to shield herself.

"Beards," Peter shrieked, sawing the knife to and fro, seizing handfuls of hair and tossing them over his shoulder. One landed on Lorna's lap, but she was not prepared to move it at this moment. "Only barbarians wear beards," Peter bawled, cutting away. "I will not have it. I will not have it." He paused from exhaustion, threw the knife in a corner, sank on to the bed, panting. His victim's chin looked as if assaulted by an army of rats. "Take him out and have him shaved."

"But his message, Sire," Menshikov suggested.

Peter glowered at the shivering man. "Well? Well, out with it."

"From the north, Sire," he gasped. "I come from General Repnin. He has interrogated a Swedish prisoner, Sire. The Swedish king leaves Denmark, Sire, and sails for Livonia. They say he is accompanied by a mighty army."

"How mighty?" Peter's voice was almost soft.

"Eight, ten thousand men, Sire."

"Eight thousand? Ten thousand?" Peter gave one of his sudden bellows of laughter. "I have twenty thousand in camp here alone. And Repnin has twenty more. Ten thousand? That boy? We will go to war. Should he set foot on Livonian soil, we shall go to war." He left the bed, paraded the room. "We shall crush him. The army marches in the hour. Have my horse saddled." He whirled on the two women. "Do not just sit there, whores. Dress me."

Lorna sucked air into her lungs, scrambled to her feet, began gathering his clothes, acutely conscious of the open door, of the eyes beyond. He extended his arms and she pulled on his shirt; Martha was already inserting his feet into his boots. Lorna panted, buckled his breeches, felt his hands closing on her breasts. "You shall go to Moscow," he said. "You will be safe there, until I return." He slid his hand down her belly to give her pubes a gentle squeeze which left her breathless, heaved himself up, strode through the doorway.

Menshikov followed, closing the door behind him.

"He likes you," Martha said, sitting beside her. "Did he not make you happy, just now?"

Lorna's head jerked. "I . . . yes."

"I knew it. And I made *him* happy. You are not angry about that?"

Lorna shook her head.

Martha put her arm round her shoulders, squeezed her against herself. "We make a good team, you and I. We shall be friends. More than friends. Much more than friends. We are already. The Tsar's women."

Lorna's head turned to gape at her, and Martha kissed her on the mouth. *Like Aurora Konigsmarck,* she thought. But not in the least like Aurora Konigsmarck. For Martha's mouth was open, and her wet tongue drifted across Lorna's lips. Then she drew back her head and smiled at her. "Much more than friends," she said. "Besides, Prince Bogoljubov is in Moscow. Your husband."

"Help me, Father," Lorna begged. "Help me." She raised her head, frowning at him. "Or do you suppose I am merely being served my just deserts?"

Father Simeon sighed. "If you feel that, my child, there is nothing I can do for you."

She rose from her knees, skirts swirling. "But would it not be just?" she demanded. "Did you not once say I was using my beauty, my womanhood, as a weapon? So now, my weapon has been wrenched away from me, thrown on the ground, for all to oversee, for all to trample upon, the plaything of a madman."

"I suspect you are overtired, Princess," he said mildly. "And overwrought. After all, you . . . ah, knew the Tsar before. You knew of his moods, his excesses. . . ."

She turned to face him violently, hair joining the whirl of material. "I knew a man. Oh, given to fits of rage. What man is not? But a man who loved me. Who gave evidence of it in everything he did. A man who talked gently and interestingly, when in my company. Who studied to please me. And who knew how to please me. This . . . this is a madman, who occasionally has fits of sanity. Believe me, Father. You have not seen him."

"Yet is he the father of your son. Surely that . . ."

"He does not know and he must not know. Vassily apparently merely told everyone I remained in Dresden to be delivered, let them assume the child was his. No doubt," she said bitterly, "he took pleasure in this, illustrating his manhood. But I am grateful for that now. The Tsar must not know." She sank to her knees. "Promise me that, Father. No matter what happens. No matter what tortures are inflicted upon me, Peter must never know Michael is his son."

Father Simeon frowned at her. "Of course you shall be obeyed, my dear," he said. "But I wish I could understand your reasoning."

"This . . . this madman, who holds all our lives in the palm of his hand," she whispered. "He would take Michael away. I know it. He would first of all turn him into a replica of himself, make him as mad as himself, I have no doubt, he will debauch him into unnatural habits as he has done to so many others, and he will carry him off to war as soon as he can walk, and no doubt have him killed."

Father Simeon frowned. "You do not *know* all this. You are supposing."

"I know it, Father. I know the man."

"And suppose you become pregnant again?"

"Never." She surged back to her feet.

Father Simeon coughed. "Of course, I do not pretend to know a great deal about these matters. . . ."

"I could not stand it," she declared. "The thought

of that agony again . . . I'd go mad. 'Tis that confounds me. Father . . ."

He held her hands. "Princess."

His flesh was dry and firm. And soothing. Some of the anxiety left her spirit.

"Princess," he said again. "We knew when you were forced to embark upon this career that it would have its difficult times. But now the Tsar is departed upon a campaign, which may well occupy some time. And you are going to your husband. . . ."

"That pervert?"

"I had supposed you and the Prince had established some rapport, Highness."

She sighed. "I suppose we did. A year ago. Will it still be there? Will he not have found another? A man, you may be sure. A boy. My God, the things I am forced to say. Two years ago I would not have supposed them possible."

"Two years ago, Highness, you were still a girl. Now you are a woman."

"Oh, yes? And do not suppose Vassily will be of any use to me when it comes to opposing the Tsar."

"Undoubtedly it is to *your* strength that we must all look, Highness," Father Simeon said. "But your strength is considerable."

"Mine? I am but a woman."

"That has nothing at all to do with it. I do not speak of the muscles in your arms, although even those are considerable, were you but to use them. I speak of the strength in your mind. My sweet Princess, you have been given a very hard road to walk, yet you have but to keep faith with yourself and with God, and you will arrive at your journey's end, however difficult it may be to see that end at this moment. And more, Princess. Your responsibility, the need for your courage and your determination, is greater than you suppose. I do not speak of myself. My life is at the disposal of God and He will call for it whenever He chooses. But there is Kathleen and Michael and Alice and Bridget, all dependent upon your survival, upon your favour, indeed, with the Tsar. Can you conceive their fate, Highness, should the barrier of your beauty, your courage, your appeal be removed?"

She frowned at him. *And all I ever wanted to do,* she thought, *was ride my mare across the Maryland hills. God in Heaven, what made You single me out for such an adventure?*

Her knees gave way, and she sat. The room in their "palace" contained but two chairs, in any event; there were no carpets on the floor, no drapes at the windows. And it was cold, despite the burning fires. She could understand why Peter preferred to live in a hut. "But there is yet more," she whispered. "More, and I think, worse, Father. This is a land where no Christian concept seems to hold, at least at Court. Father, this woman of whom I spoke, with whom I shared the Tsar's bed, this . . ." She broke off and watched the door open.

"Our carriages are waiting." Martha Skavronskaya wore a white fur cloak and a white fur hat, and looked absolutely entrancing. "We must be on our way. Moscow. I can hardly wait. I have never been there. And now, sweet Lorna, to go there with *you*. I can hardly wait."

"Truly," Martha complained, peering through the window of the berlin. "Can there be a more desolate country in the world?"

Lorna supposed she was right, and she was determined not to look out of the window at all, for fear she would suffer snow blindness. Indeed, every day seemed colder than the previous one, and the country was at once the poorest and most desolate she had ever encountered, and, in addition, was populated by the most sullen of people—even when compared with the Bavarians—for in those hamlets through which they passed, and at which they stopped for the night, they received not a smile. A glance at the imperial insignia on their wagons, at the guardsmen who rode beside them, was sufficient to send the moujiks scurrying for the far side of the street, there to stand and stare and whisper.

At least the quite unspeakable cold, as well as the constantly growing exhaustion, for part of every day was spent stamping through thigh-deep snow as the men fought and strained to free the wagons and carriages—the wheels had been removed and they travelled on skis, and yet were liable to slide into every ditch—precluded the appearance of any other problem. They never removed even their fur cloaks, but merely wrapped themselves the more securely to sleep, while in the evenings they were in addition so exhausted it was difficult to do more than eat before their eyes drooped shut. Certainly they shared their beds, Martha and her maid, Lorna, Kathleen, Michael, and Snowdrop huddled between them, Alice and Bridget, all crowded together, drawing mutual warmth, mutual support from each other. Poor Father Simeon had to sleep with the escorts, in a slurry of steaming leather and vodka-laden breaths. The guardsmen seemed to live on vodka; whenever she looked at one of them he was either taking out his flask or restoring it to his saddlebag. Often enough they swayed in the saddle, but not one ever fell off. They were in any event superb horsemen, but an additional reason lay in the savage brutality of Russian military discipline; one unfortunate who scattered snow across the ladies was immediately, despite Lorna's protests, stripped naked and whipped behind the carriage for over a mile. In which circumstances, she supposed, the blows of the cane kept him alive, for otherwise he must surely have frozen to death.

In the beginning Martha, as might have been expected, was gay as ever, full of quips, stroking Kathleen's hair, which aroused considerable dismay in Lorna's mind, and embracing and caressing Lorna herself, as they made their way slowly across these interminable frozen wastes. She was so charming, so happy in herself, so utterly innocent of any conscience and thus of any doubts that in enjoying herself she was doing nothing more than the Will of God, that it was impossible not to admire her and indeed like her enormously. Certainly one could not be embarrassed with her. So they had together shared the Tsar's bed and his embrace, an utterly horrifying thought if looked at in Lord Calvert's parlour in St. Marys, or even in Queen Mary's parlour in Kensington, but somehow entirely natural in this purgatory which was Russia. And certainly she seemed to be indicating that when a man was not available they could as well enjoy each other, again an inconceivable thought anywhere than in this endless snow and ice and cold. Lorna was too tired even to consider the matter further. It was a bridge to be crossed when they were again warm, and bathed, and comfortable. Supposing that ever happened.

But even Martha's ebullience had diminished over the past three days. Now she pushed the blinds farther aside to lean out and hail the captain of their escort. "Petrovsky," she bawled, for she was no respecter of titles. "Where is this Moscow of yours? Or does it exist only in your imagination?"

"Why, look there, my lady Skavronskaya," he suggested, reining his horse beside the carriage.

"Moscow? Ooh, let me see." Kathleen crawled on to Martha's lap the better to look, and even Lorna managed to rouse herself from her lethargy, to gaze down the hillside and feel an immediate sense of disappointment, for below her there was nothing better than a large village, and one which seemed under fire, there was so much smoke drifting in the air.

"There is a battle?" Martha inquired.

"No, no, Highness," Petrovsky said. "It is merely a house burning. Or a street. In Moscow there is a fire every day of the year. The city is built of wood, you see, and the moujiks are careless when they seek warmth."

Lorna sighed and drew her cloak tighter around herself. It would be ridiculous to have survived all this discomfort and then be set alight, she thought.

But things improved when the cavalcade had slithered down the hillside and approached the Kremlin, the central fortress, which was situated on the banks of the Moscow River and approached through a vast cobbled area which Petrovsky told them was named Krasnaya Ploschad, meaning Red, or Brave, Square. Across these cobbles they clattered, scattering snow, and through tremendous gates set in walls some sixty feet high and at least twenty thick, to find themselves in the midst of a quite wonderful town of palaces and churches, decorated in, to Lorna, a unique fashion, for instead of spires there were great gilded globes, which sparkled and shone in the winter sunlight like burnished onions.

"No fire will reach you here, Highness," Petrovsky

assured them, as he opened the carriage door to assist them down.

"There's a relief," Martha agreed, first out. Lorna followed, listened to her boots clumping on the stone, and to others, running towards her from the nearest doorway, and turned, arranging her features into a smile, to greet her husband.

Vassily checked, and equally, she could see him arranging his smile. But his effort was an endeavour to diminish his initial pleasure. Her heartbeat quickened. Could he really have missed her?

She extended her hands, and he seized them, to smother them with kisses, pulling back the gloves to reach her flesh. "My lord," she murmured. "It has been so long."

"So long," he agreed. "So long." He straightened, still holding her hands. "I had been so afraid. . . ." He checked himself.

Her smile was genuine pleasure, at last. "That I would not come?"

"That you might have changed, in some way. That your beauty . . . but it is no matter. Your beauty is unchangeable, incomparable. . . ."

"Prince Bogoljubov?" Martha cried, slapping him on the shoulder. "Can it really be you?"

He bowed in her direction, still holding Lorna's hands. "Madam Skavronskaya." And frowned, at Bridget, being assisted from the coach, Michael in her arms. Now at last his fingers slackened. "And is that . . . ?"

It was Lorna's turn to squeeze. "Your son, my lord. Michael."

"My . . ." He glanced at her. "But . . ."

Lorna was watching Martha; the faintest of lines appeared between the Skavronskaya's eyes. "Your son, my lord," she insisted. "See? Does he not look like you?"

Bridget brought the babe closer.

"Like you, I think," Vassily said. "Kathleen. Welcome to Russia."

Kathleen gave a little curtsey. "I am glad to be here, my lord Papa," she said, this being the name she had herself invented for him. "I had supposed us lost forever in the snow."

"And she is but seven years old," Vassily said wonderingly. "With all the sophistication of a great lady."

"What do you expect?" Martha said slyly, "in view of her mother. Do we spend the day standing here in the cold?"

"Forgive me, madam. Forgive me, ladies. I am so overwhelmed at being reunited with my family. Your apartments are awaiting you. Madam."

He offered Lorna his arm, and she accompanied him through the high-vaulted doorway and into a plain stone corridor. Her heart began to sink. But then they were climbing wide wooden steps and entering an upper apartment of quite remarkable contrasts; the floors were unpolished wood, lacking in carpets or rugs— their boots crashed dully on the bare surface. But the drapes were in crimson and gold, and the occasional tables were laden with ornaments in what she first supposed to be brass or copper, but then realised were actually of pure gold. Here were representations of peacocks, each wing studded with glittering emeralds, eyes nothing less than glowing rubies, goblets and jugs in the same precious metal, weapon cases in which each tulwar's hilt was a blaze of sapphires. While on the walls there were pictures in frames of equal value and painted in colours of matching brilliance, but entirely, she discovered, of religious subjects, and in an ancient perspective-lacking style which had nothing in common with the genius of Lely. Soldiers stood to attention, wearing the white uniforms of the imperial guards, and now they were climbing more stairs, mounting high into the palace, so that she could see over the walls as they passed the windows at the snow-littered huts of the city itself, proceeding through the same remarkable contrast of discomfort and wealth.

On the third floor the two parties were separated, to proceed to their own quarters, although these were connected by a private corridor, much as Lorna had been connected to the Queen in Kensington. Her own apartment consisted of a dozen rooms, a nursery for the children, a parlour, a dining room, her own kitchen and scullery—for which she had her own staff, of some half-dozen Russians, three men and three women —bedchambers for Bridget and Alice and Father Simeon, a room which had been set aside as a Roman Catholic chapel, with an altar, but otherwise left plain for Father Simeon to arrange as he chose, a library of Western books mingled with Russian, she saw to her delight and growing amazement, and finally, her own bedchamber, in which a fire blazed, and there waited a large tester, smothered in pillows and warm quilts and rugs, and even more imposing, an enormous dressing table, occupying most of one wall, a mass of mirrors and drawers, and boxes of powders and salves, and bottles of perfume, every one in gold or silver, while her hairbrushes were studded with diamonds.

And all this on a plain wooden floor, an undecorated ceiling, with not a carpet to be seen, while the moment she set Snowdrop on the floor, the cat gave a squawk of delight and unearthed a mouse from under the bed, chasing it across the floor to a hole in the wall, and crouching there in patient anticipation of the coming feast.

She listened to the door closing and turned. Vassily had come into the room. "You are pleased?"

"I am overwhelmed. But . . . you did all of this?"

He flushed and shook his head. "I do not command so much, madam. At least inside the Kremlin. My family has estates, which I should be pleased to show you when the winter is over, and should affairs of state permit it."

"Then it was Peter?" She turned again, looked around the room. A madman. An utter degenerate. Who would, in his rage, have whipped her to death. But who, in his love, had set aside so much splendour for her personal use. She sank on to the bed, and then started up again; Vassily was still standing there, and the tears were glistening in his eyes.

"Vassily," she cried. "My lord Prince." She ran across the room, seized his hands. "Forgive me. I should love to see your estates. I can hardly wait. I am no more than overwhelmed." She raised her shoulders, let them fall again. "This . . . this magnificence. I expected nothing like it. I . . . I did not know what to expect."

"You thought we lived in huts?"

"I . . ." She bit her lip. "The Tsar is certainly doing so, at the moment." She attempted to smile.

"And so must I," Vassily said.

"You are not going?" Her voice was genuinely alarmed.

"I have orders to join the army, yes. War with Sweden may break out at any moment."

"I know. But . . ." She began to retreat across the room, still holding his hands, taking him with her. "You cannot just abandon me, here."

He frowned. "I will return to you, as soon as possible. You cannot be abandoned in your own home, Princess. This is your home, now. The Tsar decrees it."

The backs of her thighs touched the bed, and she sat again. *My home,* she thought. *My home. Here I will live, until I die. This magnificent prison is mine, forever. I am become a caged animal, to be displayed for the pleasure, for the titillation of the Tsar.*

"You are unhappy?"

She raised her head. Had she not known, this is what it would be eventually? Without agreeing to recognise it? But now it was here. And she had certainly expected far worse. She smiled at him. "I am merely still overwhelmed, I think. But it is not my home, Vassily. Surely it is *our* home."

"You are too kind, madam." His face was stiff. "I may attend you only when the Tsar is not in residence. And now this matter of his son. You have not told him?"

"I let him continue to believe *your* tale, my lord." He blushed. "I . . ."

She smiled at him. "I need no explanations. I am your wife. And the Tsar is not in residence now, Vassily," she said, drawing him closer. "And you have but a short while."

"I leave tomorrow." He sat beside her, colour once again flooding his face. "Oh, my love," he whispered. "If you know how I have dreamed of you, of your fingers. . . ." He squeezed them. "I must confess."

"No," she said. "No confessions."

"Yes," he said fiercely. "I must. I have sought others. And they have laughed at me or cursed at me. Lorna . . ."

"You poor child," she whispered. "You poor, sweet child." She took him in her arms, reached for his lips with her own, but his face slid past her, although his cheek remained pressed close.

"Now you are here, my dearest wife," he whispered. "Now you are here."

She could see herself in the mirror. *Now have the doors shut behind me, forever and ever and ever*, she thought. *You see me here, extended on the rack, between the lust of a madman and the lust of a pervert. And I would not run with Lennart Munro, to happiness.*

The face stared back at her, composed, confident, beautiful. Which would conquer, she wondered? Would her face collapse into the frightened creature it sheltered? Or would the frightened creature ever rise to the heights of certainty indicated by that flat, wide mouth, those glinting green eyes?

"Lorna," he whispered. "As you are back . . ."

"As I am back, sweetheart," she said, "my hands are yours, my lord."

"But what do you *do?*" Martha Skavronskaya sat on one of her divans, legs curled beneath her, and drank tea, hot and sweet and black, from an enormous silver goblet.

Lorna, seated in an armchair beside her, sipped more cautiously. In England tea had been a luxury, only occasionally indulged; here in Moscow it seemed to be drunk more than wine. The samovar was bubbling away in the corner, normally with a maidservant in attendance. This morning the servant had been dismissed, which was a cause for some alarm. "We make love," she said primly.

"But does he push it in? Does he wish to?"

"He . . ." Lorna buried her face in her cup. "It is not right to pry into another's bed."

"But we are friends," Martha cried, uncoiling her

legs to get up. "And I am curious. And you have just told me," she said with a shriek of laughter.

"I have not," Lorna said crossly. "Of course he pushes it in."

"Ah. As he would into another man." She sighed. "I have never known that. It must be delightful. Peter would do it, were I to suggest it. But with that tool, he might do me an injury."

"He most certainly would. And I have never known it either. Vassily . . . he merely prefers to kneel. It is . . ."

Martha gave another shriek of laughter. "What he is used to. But that is delicious. He can hold your titties at the same time. Oh, yes. That is my favourite." Another sigh. "Peter cares little for it. He is too big. To enter me from the rear he must bend his back too much." She knelt beside Lorna. "But now he is gone. They are both gone, far away, to fight the Swedes. There is just you and me, Lorna, to solace each other until they come back."

Lorna deliberately clamped her knees together. She had seen this crisis rushing towards her for over a week, and had as yet formed no clear plan as how best to meet it. Because she wished it to happen? Her heart pounded, to be sure. She had never touched another woman's body, in all her life. And Martha was so lovely, so enormously voluptuous, so overpoweringly happy, she could scarce do less than spread happiness all about her. What had Papa said, Be happy? As she was here, and as she would remain here, moments of happiness, of pure physical pleasure were all that she could possibly seek.

"And I will make you happy, dearest Lorna," Martha said, untying the strings of her bodice. "I have never known a woman like you. I have never known such

carriage, such sheer dignity, even in bed. Do you know
. . ." She giggled. "I think the Tsar is a little afraid of
you. I think he was afraid to see you again, which is
why he worked himself into such a fuss."

*Holy Mother,* Lorna thought. *The Tsar, afraid of
me? William, thinking I mean only to enslave men.*
That was what she strove after, certainly. She could
feel it, lurking in her mind, lurking in her body. She
awoke at night, sometimes, and sweated at the memory
of how she had willed Lennart into killing Butler, without a thought of remorse. For that cur? But she had
wanted only his death, his utter dismissal from her life.
That had been the true Lorna, the Lorna she wished
to be, all the time.

The bodice was loose, and Martha's hand was inside,
so soft, so gentle. Far more gentle than the best of men,
far more titillating, as she knew it was the caress of the
breast which counted more than the often irritating tug
on the nipple, which was what all men seemed to suppose she wanted.

"They are so perfect," Martha said, raising her head,
tongue extended to touch her own. "And you have
twice given suck. Life is an unfair business. Mine are
so large . . ." Her eyes glowed. "Lorna, raise your
skirts. Better yet, take them off altogether. Let me see
you, Lorna. I had no time before. Let me kiss you,
Lorna, and you will kiss me, and we will be happy.
We need each other, to be happy, Lorna, to resist
Peter. Lorna . . ."

Lorna kissed her, almost savagely, sucking her tongue
into her mouth. She sweated and felt the desire in her
belly. Oh, how happy they could be, with no fear of
pregnancy, no fear of anger, no fear of misunderstand-
ing. And in Russia there could be no crime. These
people did not seem to understand any difference be-

tween right and wrong, between desire and fulfillment. And she was a Russian now.

Martha's mouth slipped away, and her skirts were being pushed above her knees. Martha's hands were there, caressing her thighs, seeking the damp warmth between. And oh, how damp it was. Never, she supposed, had she wanted so badly, because never had she been so sure there need be no fear, no possibility of regret. Then would the future stretch in front of her, of slowly growing old, of slowly mellowing, of slowly losing her beauty, as Father Simeon had said, in total self-gratification.

Then would Lorna MacMahon finally have disappeared from the face of the earth, and the Princess Bogoljubov would have become a reality.

Martha's head had disappeared, and she felt a soft tugging on her pubes. And stood up, so violently Martha lost her balance and fell over. The Princess Bogoljubov could never be a reality. The Princess Bogoljubov was a purgatory, in which she was presently forced to exist. To consider it as being the substance for the rest of her life would be to damn herself, here and for all eternity.

"Lorna? I did not hurt you?"

"I . . ." Lorna stepped back. Her body seemed to be a seething mass of desire. She could hardly recognise it as her own. "I cannot."

"Cannot? Cannot enjoy pleasure?" Martha was genuinely bewildered.

"Cannot, cannot, cannot," Lorna shouted. She ran to the door, hesitated there, looking over her shoulder at the woman on the floor. *My God,* she thought. *What have I done? This woman is my friend. Perhaps my only friend, in all Russia. And I want her love, just as I want to give her mine.*

But she wanted to be Lorna MacMahon more. "I *will* not," she said, and closed the door.

Michael came first. "Happy birthday, Mama." He spoke English perfectly, but slowly; the language was only used in Lorna's private apartments.

She hugged him against her. "Thank you, sweetheart." At eight years of age it grew daily less and less likely that this tall, already well-shouldered little boy could possibly be Vassily's son, supposing anyone ever chose to think about it. In fact, he was *her* son, in every way, the delicate features, the composed, serious face, the green eyes. Only in his hair, dark brown and lank, was he a Russian. She would not count his intelligence, because surely hers matched the Tsar's.

But he was the Tsar's. It showed, if only to her, in the occasional imperiousness of his stare, his interest in guns and swords and horses, his eagerness to listen to adult conversation. Would it ever also show in frothing lips and shrieking voice? This was her obsessive nightmare.

Kathleen was next. "Happy birthday, Mama." She stooped to kiss her mother on the forehead, and receive a squeeze of the hand. Or suppose anyone ever chose to notice so much beauty? Lorna tried to remember herself at fifteen. It seemed memory only began, at fifteen. When the year had begun she had been a child, with Patrick Burke just beginning to move into her orbit. When it had ended she had been a widow, the world spinning about her ears. Had it ever ceased to do that?

So, at fifteen Kathleen was a tall, strong young woman with straight auburn hair and grey eyes, an unusual combination. A MacMahon, with Lennart Munro's face. Having her in daily attendance was at once a delight and a torture. Lorna did not wish to forget Lennart; he remained an impossible dream. But she did not enjoy being reminded of how that dream could have been a reality, had she been less ambitious, less caught up in the ecstasy of loving a Tsar.

She smiled past her children at Bridget and Father Simeon. Bridget had not changed at all, save to grow fat. Father Simeon leaned on his stick. But, rheumatism apart, he had not changed a great deal either.

"Every birthday, Highness, you grow more lovely," Bridget said.

"Oh, away with you, flatterer," Lorna said. "Away with all of you. I'll join you in a moment. Stay, Father. Do you not suppose I should confess, on my birthday?"

The doors closed behind the children and their nurse. "Supposing you had anything to confess, Highness."

She had turned back, to stare at her mirror. She, herself, her own beauty, her own self-possession, in the widest term, composed her entire world. *I am thirty-two years old,* she thought. "Do you remember, Father, what you once threatened me with, on my thirty-second birthday?"

"And I was wrong, my lady." He stood behind her. "There is not a wrinkle on your face. One cannot suppose there ever will be, a wrinkle on that face."

"Because I have leaned too far the other way," she said, half to herself. "I am wasting myself, no less here, than I did at Hurd."

"How can you say that, my lady?" he protested. "You are happily married . . ."

*To a pervert I see but three times a year,* she thought.

". . . you have two splendid children, you are a good mother, and even more, you are a good woman, and

in such surroundings, my lady, that were the most remarkable thing of all."

She got up, and he held her pelisse for her. He knew
where she was going, for she went there every day. He
opened the inner door for her, followed her down the
spiral staircase, his stick tapping. He would be next to
die, she supposed. Happy, to be sure. He had his books,
he had his meditations, he had his papers, for he worked
hard at some interminable tome, a comparison between
the Roman and Orthodox religions, he had the children
to instruct, he could look forward to his summer ride
in the country as the family travelled away from the
heat and stench of Moscow to the almost pleasant surroundings of the Bogoljubov estates.

And after Father Simeon, herself. There was an inconceivable thought. But she was next oldest. He
opened the door for her, and the cold struck at her.
She drew her cloak tighter, pulled the hood lower over
her forehead, crunched the snow beneath her boots.
She stood before the two graves. Alice Mountfield,
Snowdrop, the cat. What a journey those two had had,
from a burning homestead in Maryland, across the
wide Atlantic, through the intrigues of Kensington and
Hurd, across Europe, through the dissipation of Dresden, to die in the Russian snow, full of years, as Father
Simeon had said on each occcasion, and full of life.
They had been full of life.

The tears started, and she turned back inside before
they could freeze on her cheeks, climbed the stairs
again. So then, she was full of years now, and full of
life too. But it was an inverted, perverted life. In the
beginning she had been full of self-righteousness. To
satisfy her own desires had been entirely reasonable,
as she had refused to sink even deeper into the Russian
pit. Besides, she had felt that her purgatory would be

short-lived. War had commenced, and the decision was near. She had thought it had come, the night Peter had ridden into this palace, shrieking his agony to the world. He had besieged the town of Narva, with forty thousand men. And to him had come the boy, Charles the Twelfth, incredibly commanding only eight thousand, even more incredibly, leading an attack in the midst of a snowstorm, against every rule of warfare. If the Russians had fled, it had only been behind their Tsar. As Peter well knew. He had ranged the palace like the madman he was, cutting at icons with his sword, slapping men and women to the floor. He had burst through the doors of her apartment and gazed at her, standing before him in her nightgown, and, incredibly, he had burst into tears.

She could not forget that night, because it was the last time he had shared her bed. Thus it was the last time a man had brought her to orgasm. Why? Because he had moaned his fear, his terror, at the blue and yellow hordes swarming at his heels, as he supposed. As she had supposed, too. She had lain with that giant figure in her arms, that giant head hugged to her breasts, and gazed at the ceiling, and almost heard the Swedish guns battering at the walls. Lennart was coming to her rescue.

But instead Charles had invaded Poland, and had been there ever since. Augustus and his army had fled in disorder back into Saxony. But Charles had remained in Poland. For nearly seven years. As she had remained in Russia, for eight years.

She discovered herself alone. Father Simeon had recognised her mood for introspection and had left, silently, to amuse the children until their mother was ready to celebrate her birthday.

She sat on her bed, gazed at herself in the mirror.

Her favourite occupation. And her most futile one. She gazed at a picture. The most beautiful picture she could imagine, the most beautiful picture she had ever seen. And like all pictures, she gathered dust. Peter had been too ashamed to return to her bed. When he could spare the time for Moscow, nowadays, he went straight to Martha. When he could spare the time. He continued to campaign, in Livonia, with some success when ordinary generals were opposed to him, with total failure, without even waiting to try his fortune, whenever the dreaded word was received that Charles himself was on the march towards him.

But he *was* achieving some success. He had conquered a portion of land, swamp would be a better word, at the mouth of the River Neva, and was there building the city he had promised himself, Petersburg. By all accounts it was a dismal place. But she would still have liked to see it. Martha had been taken up there, last summer. The Princess Bogoljubov had not been invited, had instead made her annual pilgrimage to her husband's estates.

So then, why did she wait? Why was she not now riding west across the steppes, while she retained her strength, while her children were still hers to command? Could she still suppose Peter would send behind her, bring her back in pain and disgrace? Did he care that much? Did she wait for Vassily, on his rare furloughs from his command, again to weep in her arms and seek her ministrations? Were there no *men* in Russia? Oh, undoubtedly there were, but she wanted none of them. She walked too uncertain a tightrope as it was, her body crying out for love, crying out for Martha to forgive her, to allow her more than a cold smile when they passed in a corridor, or met on a state occasion. But her mind rejected the thought immediately, just as her ambition had long abandoned the dream of becoming Russian herself, of perhaps playing a role in making this country, these people, a part of the civilised world. With Peter's encouragement she had attempted, in the beginning, to reveal to the boyars the delights of a Western ball. They had come, bringing their wives and daughters from the seclusion Russian manners demanded, because their Tsar had commanded them, and the Kremlin had blazed with light and trembled with music. But the music had been an accumulation of discords, and the dancers had been clumsily embarrassed. On a second occasion, in Peter's absence, they had not come at all, and since then they had done their best to pretend the Princess Bogoljubov did not exist. Russia was Russia, and it was too immense for her.

So she must maintain herself, a woman of foreign culture, foreign civilisation, foreign dignity, and foreign decency in the midst of this vast degeneracy. She practised it constantly, allowed herself no vodka and but a single glass of wine at supper time, ate sparingly, lost herself in her books and her tapestries, at which she was becoming expert, in personally supervising her kitchens, in educating Kathleen and Michael, and in waiting.

For the Swedes? For Lennart? She did not even know if he was alive, and if he was, that boyish oath taken so long ago must necessarily be forgotten. When he thought of her, it must be with contempt, that for all her professed love she had placed her ambition higher, had refused to risk all for a life of happiness. How he would smile did he know her true estate.

Or did she wait, merely for Peter's death? Was she not, for all her determined self-possession, just like the rest, the Tsar's creature, even if a neglected one, knowing that she was helpless while that enormous, tortured, terrified personality stalked the land, tearing down and building up, scattering his own fear and his own fate far and wide. No one could dream and no one could suppose to act on his or her own, while Peter lived. And die he must, eventually. King William was dead, his weakening health finally ruined by a broken collar-bone suffered in a fall from his horse. Anne now ruled England, and was ruled by her Mistress Freeman, daily growing more powerful and more arrogant, too, by all accounts, as her husband achieved a military fame almost to equal that of Charles of Sweden.

Sarah Churchill had waited, long enough and in sufficiently unpromising circumstances, to achieve her goal. So, then, it was necessary for Lorna to prepare for another patient year, to watch the winter roll away into the spring rain, and the summer heat, to pack her boxes once again and ready herself for the annual migration across the steppes to the Bogoljubov estates, to see the children's spirits lift as they looked forward to their holiday, to meander round her own bedchamber immediately before departing to make sure nothing was forgotten, to turn, absently, as the door opened behind her, supposing it to be Bridget, and to gaze at her husband in surprise.

"Vassily?"

His uniform was disordered, and she supposed he might be drunk. Certainly his eyes were bloodshot.

"We had no word of your coming."

He lurched across the room, sat on the bed, panted. She knelt beside him.

"You are not wounded?"

"Wounded? You amuse yourself, Highness. I am dismissed."

"Dismissed? Your command?"

"For incompetence." He rose, strode the room. "Incompetence. He dismisses men left and centre. He executes some. And who is most incompetent of all? Who trembles with fear at the sound of a Swedish cannon? Who leads the flight from every field?"

"My lord," she cried, seizing his hand as he whirled past to bring him to a halt. "For God's sake be careful what you say."

"Say?" He looked down at her, blinking. "Bah. It cannot matter, now. The man is a disaster. He leads Russia to her utter ruin. He has lost more battles than any general in history. He has alienated his people with his senseless reforms. But now, now the moment is at hand." He sank to his knees beside her. "There is word that Poland is finally pacified, that Charles means to settle this business once and for all. That he is accumulating the biggest army Sweden has ever put in the field. That he means to march on Moscow."

Lorna stared at him, her jaw dropping. At last? After so many years? It could not be true. "Rumour," she said.

"Fact," Vassily insisted. "And this time, indeed, he will not be stopped. Not by Russian armies. Not by Peter. Only by negotiation."

"By surrender, you mean? Peter will not surrender. He may be a coward, but he is a stubborn one."

Vassily leaned forward, kissed her on the nose. "He is mad, and therefore unfit to rule."

"My lord." She was aghast, looked from left to right, as if expecting guards to materialise from the very walls.

"And so must be . . ." He bit his lip, lowered his voice. "You will see. It is all arranged. You will see."

"You are mad," she whispered. "To oppose the Tsar? To dream of . . ." She could not form the words.

"Of deposing him," Vassily said. "Nothing more than that. Come. You are an important part of our plan."

He had seized her hand and was dragging her across the room.

"Me?" she cried, attempting to stop herself. "I could not."

"You must." He paused at the door. "Do you not realise he grows more insane by the day. More unable to control himself or those around him, save by ordering their execution. You think you are safe because he has slept with you? You are in more danger than anyone. Why, he has a mistress in camp. Had, I should say. He loved her dearly, and she was a pretty child. But one night he had a fit and strangled her while he lay on her belly. That could happen to you, Lorna."

"Oh, my God," she said. But the door was open, and her children were peering at her.

"Mama? Papa?" Kathleen inquired. "Are we not leaving?"

"Are you coming with us, Papa?" Michael asked.

"No. Yes. Just now. There is something we must do first."

"Do?" Lorna cried. "Now?"

"Hush." He was leading her out of the apartment and down her private corridor, panting, face flushed. *How could anyone so unstable ever hope to be a conspirator,* she thought. *And what a force to conspire against.*

"The Streltsi," she said. "Do you not remember the Streltsi?" She remembered her own belly rolling when she had been told what Peter had done to them—and with his own hands.

"Hush," he said again. "Just follow me."

Clearly she was endangering them both by refusing, so she obeyed, down a honeycomb of narrow passageways and draughty staircases, until they emerged into one of the innumerable courtyards into which this maze of palaces was divided. This they crossed, to enter another door, and resume their investigation of the secrets of the Kremlin. Nor did they see another soul, and might have been making their way through a palace of the dead, until they arrived at yet another door, which this time was locked. Here Vassily tapped, in a peculiar series of knocks, whereupon the door was immediately opened by a young boy wearing a nightshirt. He gazed at Vassily, then at Lorna, allowed them in, and closed and bolted the door behind them. Then he left the darkened room, which was a small withdrawing chamber, furnished with a solitary chair, and lit by a single candle.

"Vassily," Lorna whispered. "What is this madness?"

"Hush," he said again. "And kneel."

He himself set the example, and Lorna did likewise, keeping her eyes on the door, which now opened to reveal a youth scarce older than the boy who had admitted them, also dressed for bed, although his clothes were somewhat richer, and clearly suffering from a lung complaint, for his long red nose dripped mucus. All in all, with his thin limbs and tight, secretive face, he was a most unprepossessing sight. Nor did Lorna much care for either the tone or the thin timbre of the voice which inquired, "Is this the woman?"

"My wife, the Princess Bogoljubov, Your Highness," Vassily said. "An English lady."

"I am Irish, Your Highness," Lorna protested.

The boy smiled and revealed teeth no better than the rest of him. "Perchance you know who I am?"

It certainly was not difficult to guess, although Lorna had never beheld the Tsarevitch in her life; he seldom visited Moscow. "Your name is Alexis Petrovich, Your Highness."

"You do not like me," he said petulantly.

"Who am I, Your Highness, to be other than exalted by your presence?"

"She dissembles like a Frenchwoman," Alexis grumbled. "You may rise. Boy, fetch some wine."

The boy bowed and left the room, while the Tsarevitch sat in the only chair. Clearly he did not believe in practising the geniality of his father. But Lorna was glad just to get to her feet; the floor was uncommonly hard. She did not dare think. Thought could only be practical after she had regained her own bedchamber.

"You are my father's woman," Alexis said. "One of them."

She did not hesitate. "I have had that honour, Highness."

"But he has treated you badly, I am informed. Which is why I have brought you here. Tell me if this is so."

"It is not my place to complain of the actions of the Tsar, Highness."

"It is to me. By coming here at all, you have incurred his gravest displeasure, should he ever learn of it. That decision is mine. So now, speak."

Another circle of her lips. "The Tsar has not visited my bed for some time, Highness."

"He has deserted you for others. He is faithless. You must hate him very much." He took a glass of wine from the boy, and young as he was, drained it in a breath. "Drink," he invited.

Lorna had a feeling that she had stumbled into a very deep pit, from which she would indeed be fortunate to discover an exit. "I scarce know where to direct my hatred, Highness," she confessed. "It seems to me that I am the victim of most unhappy circumstances."

"There are no circumstances in Russia that are not inspired by the Tsar," Alexis said, a trace of fire suddenly in his voice which for the first time suggested that she was truly in the presence of the Romanov heir. "Know you aught of Russian affairs, Princess?"

"Little more than the Tsar has himself told me, Highness."

The Tsarevitch smiled. "But he has not discussed *me*. I fear I am something of a disappointment to my father, Princess. But then, so is my poor mother. She married the Tsar in accordance with my grandmother's wishes, when he was yet a boy, as you see me now. He never cared for her, shut her up in a convent, and now but waits for her to die. Which, alas, is not likely to be long delayed. As for me, because I have not the senseless brutality of his own nature, and would rather listen to a harp than play at soldiers, or sketch than lash about me with the knout, he assumes that I must be diseased, and has as much to do with me as with my mother. But I will be the next ruler of Russia, Princess Bogoljubov. Think upon that."

As indeed she had been doing, for the first time in her life wondering at the institution of kingship, which would allow the destinies of this immense nation to pass from one set of hands to another so unlike.

"If, indeed, there is a Russia left to rule," Alexis said bitterly. "My father cares for no man save himself, brooks no opposition to his schemes. He will bankrupt the exchequer. I have this on good authority. He has already alienated the common people and the boyars, by his insatiable taxes and his absurd reforms. Now he quarrels with the Patriarch and with Mazeppa at the same time. Soon he will not have a friend in Russia, save for his drinking companions and his dwarfs."

"And the woman Skavronskaya," Vassily said softly.

"And his whore," Alexis said bitterly. "And all the while he carries on this unending war with the Swedes, who but wait the right moment to crush him and the state out of existence. These are hideous crimes, Princess. Which are but compounded by the idea that he should prefer a Livonian slut to a beauty such as you."

An absurd flattery which merely increased her dislike of him. But there would be no point in taking offense. "Highness, I know not what to say. What do you wish of me?"

"I wish your friendship, Princess Bogoljubov," Alexis said. "I wish your help. Russia needs your help."

"*My* help, Highness?"

"It has been decided, no doubt by Heaven itself, that you shall have the opportunity to save us all from the mad tyrant. You and you alone, Princess Bogoljubov."

Lorna decided against commenting on a son who could thus refer to his father. "You flatter me, Highness."

"It is not in my nature." Alexis said. "But you know my father only too well. To topple such a giant can be no easy task. Yet it must be done, while there is yet time. My mother is ill, perchance dying. The moment she is dead, I know it well, the Tsar will marry again, and look for another son to reign in my stead. His father did the same."

"Highness," Lorna gasped. "You speak of revolution."

"I am not so deluded, Princess, as to suppose that a youth of eighteen could possibly challenge the Tsar in the open field. But were he removed from the throne then things would indeed be different."

"You plan assassination, Highness?" Lorna was incredulous. "Of your own father?"

"Think you I am a common murderer, Princess? Or would require your assistance for such a deed? I seek to confine my father where he can do no harm, to us or to our country. But confining such a man as the Tsar is no easy task. Wherever he goes he is accompanied by guards, by his dwarfs, by his creatures. Save only when in bed with a woman."

"But, Highness . . ." Her brain spun. "He no longer seeks my bed."

"Because of his insensate lust for the Skavronskaya. But supposing she were not here, when he next returns?"

"Not here, Highness?"

Alexis smiled. "That shall be my concern. Then you may depend upon it, the Tsar, my father, home from the wars, with no Martha available, will certainly turn once again to you. Now, I am well aware that he fears assassination to such an extent that he locks every door behind himself, and that were we to attempt to force an entry our plans might well miscarry. But supposing, after you had in every way satisfied his lust, he lay in deep sleep upon your bed, and you then arose and unlocked the door, quietly, and thus admitted us to his presence, why, then I think it could be done."

She stared at him. "My lord Prince . . ."

"You will do it. Good. It is your only means of saving your own life, as well as that of your children. Ah, your children. I am told your daughter very nearly possesses the beauty of her mother and will soon be of marriageable age."

*Oh, Holy Mother,* she thought.

"And I will need a wife, Princess. The moment I become Tsar. A beautiful wife, an intelligent wife, a wife I can trust." He smiled. "A wife whose mother I can trust. Think about that." He stood up, stretched out his hand, and touched her under the chin. "You would not be so stupid as to consider betraying me, Princess. In any way. You would be betraying your own husband and indeed yourself. My father would certainly listen to my claim that you are slandering me over yours that I planned his deposition. As I have just told you, he regards me as too passive to plan anything. So keep yourself, Princess, beautiful and enticing for his return to Moscow. It cannot be long delayed now."

# Chapter 11

*L*orna awoke from a deep sleep to the sound of Michael wailing. She sat up in bed, drawing her coverlets about her shoulders. It was again cold. After the longest, hottest summer she could recall. But it had not merely been the heat, the frustration of the children at not being able to leave Moscow for the country. It had been the daily threat of total disaster, hanging above her, above them all.

Vassily moved restlessly. "What is it?"

"Michael. Sleep." She pushed back the coverlet, dropped her legs out of bed, fumbled for her slippers. It was also the first long period she had ever spent sharing a bed with her husband. After just over ten years of marriage. There was an interesting thought. But even that had been less successful than she would have supposed and hoped. He still yearned for the touch of her fingers, as she still found sufficient pleasure in having his body at her mercy. He had even, during this year, learned to satisfy her, in a fumbling and uncertain fashion. But their moments, of joy no less than misery, were overshadowed by the enormity of what he hoped, what they planned.

*So, then, if she planned, what did she hope?* She wrapped herself in her robe, padded along the corridor to her son's room. She could no longer hope. She could only pray. They would attempt to arrest the Tsar in her bed, after she had lulled him to sleep, and after she had unlocked the door. No doubt he would strangle her there and then. But suppose they took him prisoner before he could accomplish that, he would wait, with a deadly and terrifying hatred, until she was again in his power. Because she would again be in his power. She knew this. The generals, the army, the very people of Russia might have grown to hate their unstable tyrant, but at least he pointed a course, and generals, soldiers, people, at all times and in all ages, wished to have a course pointed for them. They would tire of the inept dreams of Alexis Romanov far sooner than they had tired of the occasional ravings of his father.

So then, run to Martha with the tale? Suppose Martha would not merely laugh at her? Alexis was right there. He was the Tsar's son, she was nothing more than a discarded whore. She remembered the knout being shaken in front of her naked shoulders and shuddered at the thought. She felt like a woman caught in a bog, sinking slowly and certainly into oblivion, knowing only that the end would be particularly unpleasant. But that end could involve her own children as well, screaming their agony beside her. But surely she was suffering no more than just punishment for her years of blasphemy, her years of self-confidence. Her years of—what had Father Simeon called it?—self-gratification. Holy Mother, Father Simeon would undoubtedly be involved in her downfall as well.

So what could she pray for? That Peter might drop dead of a seizure or a Swedish bullet, before his return to Moscow? She could conceive of nothing else sufficient to save her. But even that would not save Kathleen. Kathleen, married to that snivelling, unstable boy? But Kathleen, Tsarina of Russia? With all the hideous intrigue and mistreatment, ending certainly in imprisonment in a convent, that would be entailed?

In her agony she had turned to the dream she had always held in reserve, had proposed escape to Vassily. And been crushed. Escape, he said, was impossible. Even if the Tsar did not fetch them back, where could they go? South were the Turks who hated all Russians. West were the Swedes who were their enemies. *Not mine,* she had wanted to shout. *Not mine.* But how to reach them, through four hundred miles of Russian territory, through the entire Russian army, without the support and guidance of a man?

She opened the nursery door, stood above Michael's cot. His eyes were wide. "What ails you, sweetheart?"

"I heard a noise, Mama. Men, coming to get me."

It was a recurring nightmare, perhaps inherited from his father. She rested her hand on his forehead. "You are safe here, my sweet," she lied. "There can be no men. Now sleep, and tomorrow we will play a game." She stood straight, and his eyes closed, leaving his face peaceful. She turned away, stepped through the door into the corridor, closed the door behind her, turned, and gazed at Peter the Tsar.

She found herself pressed against the wall. "My lord Tsar," she whispered. Her heart seemed to be chasing her stomach, which itself seemed to be trying to drop between her legs. For now she saw that he was not alone, but had several armed men at his back. And she saw too, even in the gloom, the hideous contortions of his face which meant that he was in the grip of one of his frenzies.

Yet his voice was controlled and quiet. "Utter a sound, and you will die," he said. "You will all die. Take her."

"Sire," she whispered, and found her arms gripped. "Sire," she begged, but he had turned away, was entering her bedchamber, his men at his back, saving only the two who had seized her and were now pushing her towards the outer door of the apartment. She wanted to scream, she wanted at least to shout, to warn them. But her throat was dry, and she could not doubt that he would carry out his threat.

The door was open, and she was half dragged, half pushed into the candlelit hallway. Now she could look at her captors, to discover that they were not wearing military uniform, but rather loose jackets belted at their waists, and fur caps, and damp boots. They had not shaved in at least twenty-four hours, and were altogether two of the least attractive men she had ever seen.

"Please," she said. "Will you tell me . . ."

One of the men released her long enough to close his fist and drive it into her stomach. All the breath was forced from her lungs, and she fell to her knees, and would have collapsed on to her face had he not seized her hair, jerking her head back, adding to the agony spreading through her body. "No talking," he said.

The other man shoved her, so that she did fall, still gasping for breath. She got her arms up to protect her head and face, anticipating the worst, but was rolled rather than kicked, along the corridor and to the head of the stairs. Here she grasped the bannisters with desperate courage, but they were on her again, pulling her fingers free, dragging her to her feet, thrusting her down the stairs. And again. And again. She lost track of her whereabouts as her body became nothing but a mass of bruises and her head spun and ached at the same time. After about her third tumble she made no further effort to resist them, and they picked her up like a sack, one of them throwing her over his shoulder. *Full circle,* she thought, tears beginning to stream out of her eyes and across her forehead and into her hair, which trailed on the floor behind them. *Full circle. She had survived Butler. But that had been seventeen years ago. Had she so much resilience left, so much determination, so much anger?*

She was surrounded by stench, and realised they had left the candles, the golden ornaments, the icons behind. Now torches flared from brackets in the walls, and the walls themselves dripped slime. They were below the Kremlin, in the maze of dungeons about which men spoke only in whispers. It was here Peter had tortured the Streltsi before dragging them out to a public execution. *Oh, God,* she prayed. *The Streltsi. Holy Mother, come to my rescue.*

She hit the floor again, cold stone, with a smattering of straw. She was surrounded by the stink of damp, of rats, of unwashed human bodies, of human excreta, and, above everything else, of human fear. Yet there were only five people in the room; her captors had been joined by three other men, very similar in dress and in appearance, standing above her, looking down at her, grinning.

"Maybe we could tickle her up a little," one of them said.

She realised her nightgown was torn and concealed very little of her. She had not noticed that before, had not cared about it. Now she attempted to draw up her legs, and received a kick in the buttock. "Lie still," another man growled.

"We'd best wait," said a third. "She's the Tsar's doxy. He'll want to do the stretching."

*The stretching.* She moved her head, discovering at once the windlass of the rack, which occupied the centre of the room. And discovering that there was indeed another person in here with her; the boy who attended the Tsarevitch hung by his wrists from the wall opposite, naked, his body a mass of bruises and scorch marks, most of them, she realized with sickening alarm, having occurred between his navel and his knees; his genitals were a drooping horror.

*Oh, God, help me,* she thought. She found she was shouting before she was aware of it. "Help me," she screamed, and was rewarded with a gust of laughter, which as quickly died, for Peter the Tsar was in the room and accompanied by a crowd.

"Mama," Kathleen screamed. "Mama."

"Mama," Michael wailed.

Vassily kept silent; his face was white, and he retched as he looked at the dangling boy. Father Simeon was also silent; he had not been allowed to bring his stick, and had apparently been thrown down most of the stairs. Bridget wept noisily.

Peter stood above her, huge legs spread. "Get her up," he growled, his face still twisting.

She was seized by the shoulders and dragged to her feet, turned by her captor to face the boy.

"Wake him up," Peter commanded.

A bucket of water was hurled at the naked boy. The boy jerked and shivered, opened his eyes, and began to weep. Lorna found fingers biting into her arms as she was forced across the room, to stand immediately before that tortured white body. *I am going to vomit,* she thought. *For the first time since leaving the* Centaur, *I am going to vomit.* She had not vomited even when carrying Michael. *Michael, oh God, Michael. But did she dare, now, when the Tsar was lost to all reason?*

"Is she the woman?" Peter bellowed.

The boy opened his eyes, gasped for breath, gazed at Lorna. His head moved up and down, and he sighed.

"Speak," Peter screamed at him, seizing him by the hair, to bang his head against the wall. "Speak."

The boy drooped further, if that were possible. The Tsar frowned and looked closer. "Bah," he said, releasing the hair, allowing the head once again to bang the wall. "He is dead. But he nodded."

Peter's face was close to hers, his lips drawn back in a smile. "You stand accused of treason, Princess. Oh, aye, it would be you. Now we are going to hear you scream. We are going to tear every last breath out of your body. Your so beautiful body, Lorna. Your body which has driven men mad with desire. We are going to drive you mad, with pain." His mouth widened still further. "When we have finished with your family." He snapped his fingers. "Secure her, and . . ." His eyes roamed over the room. "Begin with that one. It will be sport."

Lorna's arms were again seized and she was dragged against the wall, forced to her knees, and her wrists clampsed into iron brackets bolted to the stone floor, so that she could kneel, with her back arched, or sit, leaning sideways most uncomfortably, or eventually, no doubt, lie full length upon the cold stone. *Oh, my God,* she thought. *Lie, upon this floor. But will they not drive me to that?*

"Mama," Kathleen wailed, and her head jerked. For the moment she had been too absorbed in what was happening to herself. Now she saw the nightgown being torn from her daughter's body, whereupon she was released to fall to the floor in a huddle, while the gaolers stood around her, glancing at their Tsar for further instructions, but clearly supposing that they were not to proceed with any torture at this moment.

At this moment, Lorna's heart gave a leap into her throat, and she nearly choked. Why had she never taken sufficient notice of her own daughter, save to wonder at her innocence? Because she suddenly realised that here was a beauty even more likely than her own to appeal to Peter. Kathleen was more strongly built; already at fifteen her breasts were larger, with big nipples, now chilled into tumescence by the cold. Her auburn hair more matched the thatch on her belly. Her legs were not as long, but here again in their heavier muscles she more resembled Martha than her mother, and her thighs retained the slenderness of a girl's to give her a perfect figure.

"What beauty," Peter remarked, his voice almost quiet. He stooped, drove his fingers into the thick red brown hair, tilted that strong, handsome face back. Kathleen stared at him, and Lorna could almost see her composing her mind for what was about to happen. " 'Tis not to be destroyed, without reason." He gave a gust of laughter. "Without sampling, at the least. No, no. Perhaps the Princess loves her husband also. Stretch him on the rack. There is always the boy, as well."

The guardsmen descended on Vassily, stripped him naked, stretched him on the rack, arms extended above his head, back pressed against the rollers, feet secured to the ropes which were controlled by the windlass. His eyes were wide, his muscles tensed. But he uttered not a word. He did not lack for courage. But then, Lorna had never supposed that. She watched Kathleen being secured to handcuffs like her own, but on the far side of the room. Mother and daughter stared at each other, Kathleen's eyes a mute message of appeal. She looked to her to save them all. And why should she not, as her mother's had been the strength which had protected them for all of their lives. Even Vassily was looking to her, as Peter stood above him, smiling, reaching down to take penis and testicles in his hand and squeeze, bringing a gasp which turned into a shriek, causing his body to arch away from the drums.

"What?" Peter bellowed. "Have you no taste for it any more, dear friend? That comes from being married to a witch. But you'd best enjoy it. You'll not have them, when I am done."

Vassily wailed, at last, a thin sound rising to the ceiling. Lorna realised she could wait no longer. They were her people, her family. "Sire," she screamed.

"Gag that bitch," Peter snapped.

"Sire," she screamed. "What of the Tsarevitch?"

There was a sudden silence in the room, save for Bridget's sobs and Vassily's gasps. Peter had his back to her, but now he turned slowly.

"You accuse us of conspiracy?" Lorna cried, her voice stronger. As in the cabin of Butler's ship, once she had started there was no point in stopping—it was freedom or death, and for them all. "Where is the one who led us, who commanded our loyalty, on pain of death?"

Peter's face was horrible to behold; each muscle seemed to have a will of its own, every vein seemed to have turned into a throbbing artery. "You dare to accuse my son?" he whispered. "My son?" he screamed. "My son?" he howled. His arm came out, the finger pointing. "My only son? Take her. Take her," he screamed. "I want her . . . I want her skinned. Skin her alive. Slowly. I want to hear her scream. I want this room to sound forevermore with her screams." His voice dropped. "I want her skin to hang over my bed."

The men came forward. Lorna gasped for breath.

"Mama," Michael wailed.

They were kneeling to release her irons. "Your son," she shouted. "But not your only son. *There* is your son, my lord Tsar. *There* is the future prop of your throne."

Her irons fell away, and she rubbed her hands over her wrists. But the men had not seized her arms, as yet. They were watching their master.

"For that," Peter whispered, his voice terrible, "I will have you salted when they have taken your skin."

Strangely, she was no longer afraid. There was a limit to fear. "Think, Sire," she said. It was not a request, more a command. "Think," she shouted. "I was wed on October twenty-fifth, 1697. You came to my bed that night. Michael was born on June twenty-seventh, 1698. No more than eight months."

He frowned at her. Even through the tortured madness of his mind she could see his brain working.

"You know my situation," she cried. "My husband did not come to my bed for three weeks after my wedding. I swear that, my lord. So will Vassily."

"He would," Peter muttered. "And you."

"Then look at the child," she shouted. "Can you not recognise yourself?" And prayed.

The gaolers hastily released Michael, at the same time giving him a gentle push on the shoulder. He stumbled forward, gazing at the Tsar with wide eyes. And Peter slowly lowered himself, to kneel before the boy, arms stretched wide. Michael hesitated, glanced at his mother. Lorna gave a brief nod, and he allowed himself into that embrace. Which yet held him off for a moment while Peter stared into his eyes. Lorna supposed everyone in the dungeon was holding his breath; there was not a sound to be heard, for the space of almost a minute.

Then Peter uttered one of his most terrifying howls. "My son," he screamed. He swept Michael from the floor, held him high above his head. "My son."

She was aware only of exhaustion. She was too tired to think, wanted only to sit in her tub forever, and have Kathleen gently massage her shoulders and back, feel the heat rise about her, seep through her flesh and into her heart and chest and belly. Thought was impossible. Because thought meant the future, and the future was impossible. She leaned back, and her head rested on her daughter's breast. She looked up, through the cloud of her hair, and into her daughter's eyes. They had shared, with their minds, the enormity of what had been about to happen to them. What would they have to share, in the future?

"Mama," Kathleen said. It was the first time she had spoken since their return to their apartment.

Lorna shook her head.

"But, Mama . . ."

"Later. When I have rested. When we have both rested."

"But . . ." Kathleen's head jerked and turned to look at the door.

*So soon?* Lorna thought. She had thought that before, about this man. So she should not be surprised now. She should not be afraid. And to her surprise, she discovered that she was not afraid. She hated him now. Her feelings for him had always been a compound of hatred, and fear, and lust. Now it was only hate. He had taken her to the edge of eternity, and draped her head over it, and she had looked down into the pit. No mere mortal man could terrify her, after that.

But Kathleen, if also forced to look, was still too young to have seen. Lorna leapt out of the bath, scattering water. "Quickly."

"Mama?"

"He must not find you. You must . . ." She looked around the room, chewing her lip. There was no concealment. And she could hear those heavy footsteps coming closer. "Your bed," she said. Only the wildest gamble could succeed now. "Your bed, and bind a cloth between your legs, as you would. And do not open your eyes. Promise me."

Kathleen hesitated, then nodded, and ran for her room. Lorna sighed, and sank back into her tub, and listened to the door opening. *Only hate,* she thought. *Only hate.*

He stood in front of her, his face calm.

"Sire," she said. "What have you done with my son?"

"Ha," he said. "*my* son, Princess." He knelt beside her. "I should have you flogged for concealing that fact these years. The Tsar's son, brought up like some common boyar?"

"Brought up to be an English gentleman, my lord," she said, meeting his gaze.

"Bah." He straightened, turned away. "He will be a weakling. What, with Bogoljubov as a father. Weakling. I am surrounded by weaklings," he bawled, shaking his fists at the ceiling. And then whirling to face her. "Where is your daughter?"

"In her bed, Sire," Lorna said, keeping her voice even, and slowly rising from her tub, to stand before him, water dribbling down her shoulders and back, gathering in a pool between her legs, crucifix settled between her breasts.

"Ha-ha," he shouted and turned for the door. He pulled it open, gazed at the girl. Her eyes were shut, her face calm.

"Unconscious, Sire," Lorna said. "I have given her a sleeping draught."

"Unconscious? Sleeping draught? What matter? I wish only to feel her."

He reached forward, jerked the covers away, leaving the girl exposed. Kathleen never moved. *My daughter,* Lorna thought. *Kathleen MacMahon.*

"And menstruating, my lord," she said. "The shock no doubt brought on her period in advance of its time."

He paused, looking over his shoulder.

"So you must make do with me, my lord," Lorna said. "I am awake." *And I am no weakling,* she thought, with sudden pleasure. *I have met the Tsar upon equal terms, and not yet been defeated. My brain is as good as his, my body as healthy. My mind is as strong, or perhaps stronger.*

He glowered at her. "I desire something young," he said. "And fresh."

She sucked air into her lungs and squared her shoulders. Her breasts had begun to sag, but only slightly. They could still challenge a man. And the drying water was inflaming the nipples. Where was the girl who had flaunted herself in front of her glass, in the Maryland farmhouse? Why, she was still here. She had always been here. *I am Lorna MacMahon.* Nothing more was necessary.

"I am still young, Sire," she said. "And as you have not sought my bed these five years, I am no doubt fresh, as well."

He came closer, his frown fading. "You have a great deal of spirit, Lorna," he said. "I knew this, when first we met. You slapped my face."

"I thought you a secretary, Sire." Her heart was starting to pound, and she was determined it would not do so. Hate. Only hate.

He stood before her. "Would that I were," he said, his voice almost soft. "Then I could earn your love. To earn your love, Lorna, a man would have to be a man. Do you love me, Lorna?"

Her head went back, and she gazed into his eyes. *Now*, she thought. He wishes only to hear a lie, and who knows what doors may be opened to you. And will you be able to pass through a single one of them? *"I hate you, Sire,"* she whispered. *"I hate you, with all the love at my command."*

So then, where does hate end, and love begin? At a place in the mind so close to each other that there is no distinguishing mark. And what does hate or love, in its truest sense, have to do with the business of physical enjoyment?

She lay, with her head on his shoulders, her red-gold hair drifting across his chest; her left leg was thrown across his thighs, and from time to time his member tickled her as it sought to rise, and then subsided again. He was exhausted. Peter, the Tsar, was exhausted, had been exhausted, by Lorna of Morne. She had sought to do that deliberately, had permitted herself no moment of weakness. And because it had been so long, she had indeed been young and fresh. She had howled her pleasure, left her teeth marks on his thighs. As she herself seemed one long bruise. But she had exhausted the Tsar. How many women, she wondered, could lay claim to that.

As he would discover, if she retained anything to give. His hand was down her back, and now it drifted past her buttock, caressing, gently pulling, inserting, stroking. There was nothing but pain, down there, nothing but exhaustion. But she writhed and moaned. *I am Lorna MacMahon. I have been taken to the moment of death by this man, and more than once. And I have survived. And now I have reduced him to impotence. For only a few minutes, perhaps. But it had been done.*

She sank her teeth into his chin as part of her false ecstasy, sucked the wound. "Would you again, my lord Tsar?"

The fingers left her, slapping her bottom. "You are a witch. Aye, there it is."

"I am a woman who knows how to love, my lord," she said. "A woman you taught. Perhaps too well."

"Witch," he grumbled, his eyes closed.

"Will you give me back my son, Sire?"

"No," he said. "He is already too old for a woman's care. He must learn to fight, and ride, and use his weapons."

"And kill," she said. "And maim. And drink himself insensible."

"The man who would rule Russia must do all things, better than anyone else."

"You speak of barbarism," she said.

"And you have lost the control of your tongue," he said, sitting up, rolling her away from him.

She lay on her back, legs spread wide, arms outflung, pillowed in her hair. She felt lazy, disjointed, and sore. As after her first night with this man. This monster. And now there was only hate. Hate and determination. She had been a plaything, a pawn, for too long. Now she knew why she had waited, in this magnificent prison, for nine years. It had been to have this man once again in her bed; it had been the hope that he might become a regular visitor. Of all men, none could match Peter the Tsar. And now it had happened, and she no longer cared. Vassily had refused to let her escape before. But when he had been close to death, Vassily had turned to her, as had they all, and she had saved them. As she would save them again. It was as if something in her brain, some steel trap, perhaps, had snapped, shutting out fear, uncertainty, indecision, apprehension, leaving her cold and determined, and herself. Lorna MacMahon. And for the Tsar, only hate.

As he saw. He threw back his head and guffawed. "Oh, you are a woman, now, Lorna. Why do your eyes not burn, they smoulder so? Green eyes. Cat's eyes. They point the way to your witch's brain." He threw himself forward, on to his hands and knees, head drooping. Instinctively she tensed, and then forced herself to relax. He did not bite, but instead sucked, seeming to gather all of her groin into that cavernous mouth, to feel her writhe once again. Then he was up, towering over her. "I wish your daughter. I wish you both." He smiled at her. "I will share your bed, the three of us. There will be sport. You can teach her and me at the same time."

She watched him, keeping herself still, keeping herself flaccid.

"I must go," he said. "West. I must go to Smolensk. Charles waits there, with his army, for the ground to harden sufficiently. He would invade Russia, in the winter. They say he is mad." Again the bellow of laughter. "They say I am mad. What a meeting that will be. Two madmen, in the snow." His laughter died, and he paraded the room. "But I will win. I will crush him like a nut."

She spoke without meaning to. "As you did before, Sire?"

He leapt for the bed, so that she drew up her legs and attempted to sit. But he seized her ankle, dragged her down the mattress; she slid off the end and landed on the floor with a jar which went right through her head. "You think I fear him?" he shrieked, his foot raised.

She rolled to one side, and it crashed where she had been sitting. He gave a shriek of agony and sat himself on the bed, his face dissolving, his shoulders humping as he wept. "I am not afraid," he moaned. "I am not afraid of a boy. How can *I* fear a boy?"

Lorna used the coverlet to pull herself to her feet, kneel beside him. *Charles,* she thought. *The Swedish army.* Coming to tear down this entire rotten edifice, this entire pyramid of brutality and lust and madness and hatred. And with Charles, his Drabant guards, marching with him into battle. Would they care, for a royal whore, fleeing from her master?

Perhaps not. But they would care for Lorna Mac-Mahon, Countess of Morne. She would make them care. She put her arms round Peter's neck, hugged him against her breasts. "You are not afraid, Sire," she said. "You have but to meet him, face to face. There can be no doubt of the outcome. And when you return, why, Kathleen and I will be waiting for you. By then, Sire, by then, my daughter will know how to make you happy. You have my word."

The guardsman opened the door. He was always there. So, her victory had been less complete than she had thought. She was now, truly, in a prison. Waiting for the monster to return and absorb Kathleen into his fetid lair.

*But a prison to which she possessed a key,* she thought. *If she also possessed the courage and the determination.* "Her Highness, the Princess Skavronskaya."

Lorna stood up. She had dismissed Kathleen, as well as Bridget and Father Simeon, waited by herself. She wore a simple undressing robe, and her hair was loose. It was so long since it had been properly dressed that the last of the ringlets had dissolved, and she might have been back in Maryland again. But now was not the time for weakness.

Martha entered, smiled at her, took in the room with a glance. "Princess. I had hardly looked to find you in possession of a skin."

"Will you be seated." Lorna herself poured tea. "No doubt you have been informed as to how I remain in possession of my life and my position."

Martha took the silver cup, inhaled. "I am surprised His Majesty accepts so clear a subterfuge."

Lorna sat down opposite her rival. "He accepts it, Princess Skavronskaya, because he wishes it to be true."

Martha sniffed and drank some tea. "Our lord is perturbed regarding your attempt to implicate the Tsarevitch in your plot. . . ."

"What plot?"

Martha glanced at her, sipped some more tea. "And thus he is seeking perhaps an alternative. I observe that he retains guards upon your doors. Nor do I see you walking in the garden."

"I would hardly do so in any event," Lorna pointed out. "With winter upon us. His Majesty grows daily more and more suspicious of everyone."

"Not of me."

"Of you in time," Lorna pointed out. "I doubt, with a suspicious man, there can be room for more than one permanent royal mistress. I very much fear one of us will fall by the wayside."

"As you have already so nearly done," Martha observed. "As you are the one with guards on her doors."

"As I have survived," Lorna said. "As I am the mother of his son."

"As you are considerably older than I, Princess Bogoljubov."

Lorna allowed her a cold smile. "As I have a daughter who is considerably younger, and whom the Tsar already wishes to possess."

Martha frowned at her, put down the empty goblet. "Did you invite me here to compare our respective prospects?"

Lorna got up and poured. "As a means to an end, Highness. I have discovered that my position can be considered an enviable one. The Tsar desires me, desires my daughter, desires my son. Oh, there are guards on my door. But that is because he is unable to forget that I conspired with the Tsarevitch, as did my husband."

"And that is a cause for congratulation?"

"We have survived his initial anger," Lorna said. "And will regain his best favour. He is well aware that he has been unable, over all these years, to break my spirit, as perhaps he has broken . . ." She smiled at Martha. ". . . other spirits. He is afraid I may desert him."

Martha's head came up.

"As you have said," Lorna continued. "Our relationship remains abrasive. Yet it is a relationship he cannot resist. It is only resistable by distance."

Martha drank tea thoughtfully.

"As now," Lorna said. "Now he campaigns. But he will return. And it is generally supposed that we are moving into the climax of this war. After this campaign I imagine His Majesty will desire a long rest, here in Moscow. With the ladies of his heart."

Martha's breath hissed. "He may never return. He may be killed in battle."

"Indeed he may," Lorna agreed. "And then what will happen, do you think? Alexis will be Tsar. It was his plan, in this conspiracy of ours, to have you murdered before attempting to secure the person of his father."

Martha's hands went to her throat.

"Whereas I am a fellow conspirator," Lorna said. "Should His Majesty die, I would expect to be the greatest lady in the land. I would expect my daughter to be Tsarina. It has been proposed."

"You . . . I do not believe you," Martha whispered.

Lorna smiled at her. "What will you do, Princess? Ask the Tsarevitch?"

"You . . ." Martha licked her lips. "Why do you tell me this?"

"I am pointing out to you the precariousness of your position," Lorna said.

"Why?"

"Because I am unhappy here, and you are happy. I would leave. I have long dreamed of that. But to go where, I have always asked myself? Submit myself to the insults of a Turkish harem? Place myself at the mercy of Augustus of Saxony? Neither seemed a possible solution. But place myself in the power of the King of Sweden, and I will not only be safe, I will be treated according to my rank."

Martha's jaw dropped. "You tell *me* this?"

"I am baring my heart to you, sweet Martha, as you would have had me do so long ago. I hate and loathe and abhor the Tsar. Once he could make me the happiest woman in the world. Now I know him too well, and he fills me with disgust."

"Now you *will* be skinned alive," Martha said.

"The thought of him bedding my daughter makes me wish to vomit," Lorna continued, speaking quietly.

"And the thought of him taking my son to make into a replica of himself fills me with horror."

"You . . . I will be there to see it," Martha promised.

"To see what, Princess? There are no ears in these walls. And the Tsar will expect you to concoct such a story concerning me. He has warned me of it."

The colour began to drain from Martha's face.

"So I can tell you what I wish, in private," Lorna said. "And I am telling you this. But there is more, Princess. The Tsarina's health is failing. 'Tis this fact that led the Tsarevitch to conspire. He feels that should his mother die, his father may well turn to one of the two women who have been a comfort to him these past years."

"He will turn to me," Martha said. "He loves me. I could be Tsarina."

"So could I," Lorna lied. "Prince Bogoljubov would be no obstacle. And I am the mother of Peter's son. Dare you take that risk, Martha? Do you not realise that your interest, your only hope of survival, in fact, coincides with my desire, my ambition, perhaps my only hope of survival?"

"You wish to join the Swedish army? That is several hundred miles away."

"But coming closer. The Tsar concentrates on Smolensk. We will travel south of there," Lorna said. "I have mapped it out. Vassily knows the country; he has campaigned in it. And it is winter. There will be few people about."

"Thus you will perish," Martha said.

"Should that concern you?" Lorna asked. "But I am constrained by my guards. I cannot conspire, without their being aware of it, without word being sent to the Tsar. I need your help."

"My help," Martha said, half to herself.

"I need horses. I need food for the journey of at least two months. I need weapons. And most of all I need my son. I leave it to you how these things are obtained, but you had best make haste. It is now, while the Tsar is on this campaign, or it will be never. I feel it in my bones."

Martha's turn to smile. "I see your plan, Princess. You no doubt suppose he will turn on me when he finds you gone."

"I will provide against that, Martha," Lorna said. "By leaving you a letter, in which I take full responsibility for my action. Peter knows my writing."

"And his so-called son?"

"Michael is mine. Any fool, save a besotted father, can see that. You may explain how I lied, how Vassily lied. Of course he came to my bed, within hours of the Tsar leaving it. While I was still wet with desire. I screamed with the joy of it. This is well remembered."

Martha's frown had returned. "You play for very high stakes."

"I play for my life, Martha. And that of my children. Should we be recaptured, then I would expect to die. Indeed, I fully intend to kill us all, then myself, should such a contingency arise. Failing that, we will either perish in the snow or gain the Swedish army. In all those cases you will be rid of me forever, sure that the Tsar will ever hate even my memory."

Martha finished her tea, got up, roamed the apartment, fingered ornaments, looked out of the window.

"Your husband knows of this plan?"

"No. But he will come with us, now. I will tell him when I am ready."

Martha turned suddenly. "You will not survive, Lorna. No one could survive such a journey, in winter, in a country at war."

"I will not remain here. So the choice is a simple one."

"That simple," Martha said thoughtfully. And held out her hands. "You have more courage than I."

Lorna's head came up. "I am Lorna MacMahon."

# *Chapter 12*

*H*ist."

Lorna opened her eyes. She had been deeply asleep, deeply dreaming. For a moment she could not remember of what. But it had been of sunlit fields, and she had been riding Paleface over the gently sloping countryside towards the trees, where her father and her brothers were clearing land. It was a dream she had enjoyed often, this past week. It was a dream towards which she was reaching. Towards which she should have reached, with similar determination, long ago.

She sat up. Martha stood in the doorway, a flickering candle in her hand. "Haste," she said.

Lorna shook Vassily's shoulder. "Wake up." She dropped her legs out of the bed, found her slippers, pulled her robe around her shoulders; the fires had burned low, and the air was chill. "What time is it?"

"One o'clock," Martha said.

"And where is Michael?"

"In your drawing room."

Lorna stepped past her, went quietly along the corridor, looked down at the boy. "Mama?" His voice rose during the word. "Oh, Mama." He sat up to throw his arms round her neck. He was fully dressed, even to his fur coat.

She sat beside him, hugged him against her. "Hush, dearest," she whispered. "You must wait, just a little while." She kissed his forehead, stood up again.

"There is not much time," Martha said. "My man will not hold the horses forever."

"Just time to dress," Lorna said. How her heart pounded. And yet she did not sweat. She was perfectly calm. Perhaps she had been waiting for this moment, knowing it must come, for all the ten years since her marriage.

Martha followed her along the corridor. "And there is news," she said. "The Swedes have left Warsaw. They march on the border. Forty-five thousand men."

Lorna paused, to glance over her shoulder. "Surely an exaggeration?"

"They say, forty-five thousand. They say Charles means to destroy Moscow."

"He does." Lennart had promised that, nine years ago.

"And you flee," Martha said. "You might as well wait."

To be destroyed, by Peter the madman, in a last explosion of mayhem? "You do that," she said, and opened Kathleen's bedchamber door. "Sweetheart. Wake up. Get dressed. Your warmest clothes."

"Mama?" Kathleen sat up, holding the quilt to her breast.

"Quickly," Lorna said. "And pack only what can be contained in a single bag. Only what you most treasure. Haste, now."

She went on, to awake Bridget, and then Father Simeon. "Father," she whispered. "We are leaving this place."

He was wide awake in a moment. "My lady? You are sure what you do?"

"I am sure we can risk no other encounter with the madman," she said. "Haste, Father."

He hesitated. "Highness, Lorna. I am an old man. I will be a hindrance. And, besides, my work is here for me to finish. . . ."

"And do you suppose Peter will permit that?" she demanded fiercely. "You are strong enough for this journey, Father. It is our escape or our death. Haste. There are horses waiting."

She went back into the corridor. Martha's arms were folded. "Ten minutes," she said.

"Then help me dress." She opened her bedroom door, found Vassily, still sitting up in bed, taking off his nightcap to scratch his head.

"What is happening?" he asked. "Has the Tsar returned?"

"Not yet." Lorna took off her nightgown, dropped a satin shift over her head, reached for the woolen petticoat she wore in winter. "We are leaving. Haste, my lord. Please."

Vassily continued to gape at her. "Leaving? The Tsar has sent for us?"

"No," Lorna said, praying for patience, adjusting her stockings. "We are leaving, Vassily. We are riding away from this place."

"But . . . where will we go?"

"Southwest. To the Swedes."

"The Swedes? They are our enemies. And, besides, our armies lie between us and the Swedes."

"That is why we are going south of west," Lorna

explained, amazed at the evenness of her voice. She settled her favourite blue riding habit, fastened her bodice;
Martha, unwilling to risk recognition, had stepped into
the darkness at the far side of the room. "You will show
us the way. We will skirt the Russian armies, and ride
into Charles's camp, and surrender ourselves."

"But . . . that is treason," he cried.

"Be quiet," she shouted. "My lord Prince, can you
possibly consider remaining here, torn between the Tsar
and his son?"

"We cannot leave." Vassily threw back the covers
and scrambled out of bed, nightshirt flying. "I will not
let you."

Lorna pulled on her boots. "My lord Prince, will you
condemn me, my children, yourself, to the rack? It will
happen again. It must, knowing the Tsar."

"We cannot desert him," Vassily said. "Besides, we
would certainly be taken, and then . . . then . . ."

"Five minutes," Martha said.

Vassily turned to face her. "Who is that?" he demanded. "Conspiracy. I am surrounded by traitors.
Guards . . ."

Lorna looked around the room, found the heavy
brass warming pan, waiting next to the bed. It was still
full of coals, even if they had burned cold. She picked
it up in both hands, took a deep breath, and swung it
with all her force.

Vassily gave a sigh and fell forward. His knees hit
the bed, and he fell across it.

"Mother of God." Martha shrugged the hood from
her hair, came forward.

Lorna remained standing in the centre of the room,
the warming pan still in her hands. "Is he dead?"

Martha glanced at her, then bent over the man. She

frowned, touched his temple with the first two fingers of her hand. "Would you have him dead?"

"No." She laid down the pan. "He would have recognised you."

"Oh, indeed, I am grateful, Lorna. But what will you do now?" She straightened. "You cannot take him with you."

"If he is not dead, he can be no more than bruised."

"He will never forgive you for that blow, Lorna. And this means you cannot go. You have no guide."

Lorna chewed her lip. "I must go," she said. "You have just said he will never forgive me. Would you have me stay? Between their love, he and the Tsar have made my life sufficient of a misery as it is. Can you imagine my situation with them both hating me? Help me."

She began to tear the sheets into strips.

"In which case," Martha pointed out, "it would be better to finish the business."

"He is my husband." She pulled his hands behind him, secured his wrists.

"Wives have murdered their husbands before."

"I have never murdered anyone," she said. "And I do not propose to start now." She secured Vassily's ankles, hesitated, rolled him on his back. His eyes were shut, his mouth was open. "Nor will you, Martha. Swear it."

Martha shrugged. "As you stopped him from seeing my face, I have nothing to fear from him." She watched Lorna balling some more of the sheet to force into his mouth, secure it there with another strip. "But you are still being very foolish. He will send after you."

"My people do not come in until dawn, and they will certainly not think to disturb the Prince until well into the morning. We shall be far away, by then."

"He will send after you," Martha said again.

Lorna pushed Vassily straight on the bed, arranged his head on the pillows, covered him with the quilt. He appeared to be sleeping, but now his eyelids flickered.

"Leave the room," she said. "Pursuit is a risk we must take." She drew the drapes around the bed, turned to inspect the room, put on her blue tricorne and settled it over her hair, picked up her white fur pelisse with its fur hood and soft scarf, pulled on her fur gloves. She could carry nothing, save her most precious jewels, a change of linen, and the bag of money Martha had procured.

She listened to the bed creak as he moved. But once again there could be no hesitation, no turning back, from this road she had chosen. Martha waited in the doorway. She stepped outside, closed the door. Kathleen and Michael, Bridget and Father Simeon were gathered in the parlour, already wearing their furs.

"Mama?" Kathleen yawned. "What is happening, Mama?"

"Shhhh. And follow me."

Martha was at the door to the connecting passage, and they made their way along it. She was prowling the secret corridors of the Kremlin for the last time, Lorna thought. She wanted to shout for joy. She felt like a prisoner, after nine years in a cell, finally watching the door open to freedom.

They went through Martha's apartment, down another staircase, along another passageway, and down yet another staircase. At the foot the door stood open, and the freezing air drifted up to them. Here there were eight horses, two of them pack animals.

"Weapons?" Lorna asked.

"Here." There were four muskets, in holsters, and four pistols, and four hunting knives. "Powder and ball." Martha showed her.

"But, my lady," Father Simeon protested. "Who will use these things?"

"We will, if we have to," Lorna said. "Mount up." At least she should be grateful to Peter for one thing, she thought; Michael was already a superb horseman.

The groom assisted them; his face remained concealed. Lorna felt Martha's fingers on her arm. "The letter."

Lorna gave it to her, and she tucked it into her bodice. "Will you not read it?"

Martha smiled. "I trust you, Lorna. You of all people." She hesitated. "Without a guide, you have no hope. You know that."

"I have no hope here either, Martha."

Martha sighed, and then reached up and kissed her on the cheek. "When first we met, I said you are too much your own woman, to be happy. Were you ever able just to lie back and *be* a woman. . . ."

"I will be happy," Lorna said fiercely. "But in my own way. I will not become no more than a creature." She held Martha's face, kissed her on the lips. "Happiness is not, cannot be, unadulterated pleasure. If you do not follow a path, ride through life towards a goal, know how to select from the good things that are offered to you just as you must learn to decide which of the bad things must be avoided, then, as you say, you are someone else's creature. My fault is that I lost sight of my goal for too long."

Martha smiled. "Your trouble is, Highness, that you are too brave, too determined, too self-willed."

The groom was waiting. Lorna allowed him to grasp her knee and raise her into the saddle. She sat astride, for this journey. How long was it since she had done that? She looked down at the woman. "I am Lorna MacMahon."

Lorna drew rein, shaded her eyes. Once she had been afraid to look from the windows of her coach, in case the brilliant white of the snow should drive her blind. This afternoon it scintillated, glinting in the sun. But it was to the sun that she looked. The sun set in the southwest in January.

"Can we not stop, Mama?" Michael asked. "I am so tired. So cold."

"So hungry," Kathleen said.

Their faces were invisible, wrapped behind their scarves beneath their fur hoods. Only their breaths steamed out of the material to show they were there. Lorna turned to look at the others. Neither Father Simeon nor Bridget had anything to say. They were following their mistress, as they had always followed their mistress. As the Father had once said, they took her strength for granted.

She looked back along the road. Thus far the journey had been simple enough, because of the road. But for that reason, their route would be simple enough to follow. They had walked their horses through the streets of Moscow in the dark, without a challenge. Who would go abroad on a January night? Certainly, who would wish to leave the warmth and security of a city to plunge on to the steppe. The cold, the snow, was at once their ally and their most deadly enemy.

But the country behind them was empty, an endless expanse of glistening white. As the country to either side was empty, save for the trees. As the country ahead was empty, save for the wood they approached.

"We will stop in the wood," she said. She was more exhausted than any of them. More than any of them, she knew what they challenged, what they risked, what were the odds against their escape.

They urged the weary horses onwards, gained the shelter of the trees. The sun was dropping fast. In another hour it would be dark and even colder.

Lorna slid from her saddle to the ground, stamped her feet to restore circulation. "Now," she said. "Haste. Kathleen, collect all the dry wood you can find. Michael, you have been taught campaigning. Clear away the snow and prepare a fire. Bridget, unpack the horses, bring the food into the circle here. As soon as Prince Michael makes his flame, you may heat us some tea. Then we will erect the tent."

Father Simeon was last down. His knees gave way, and he sat on the snow. "And have you no instructions for me, my lady?"

She squeezed his shoulder. "Yes. That you sit and recover."

"But, my lady, will not a fire reveal us to any pursuers?"

"It may, if they are close enough. On the other hand, without a fire, Father, we may all be frozen to death by morning."

He shook his head in wonderment. "How simple it seems to be, to make a decision."

*Simple,* she thought, collecting the horses' bridles, attaching them together before driving her stakes into the frozen earth, each stroke of the mallet echoing in the stillness. *Oh, yes, once having made the decision, to take one's life into one's own keeping, all others were simple enough.*

She attached their nosebags, gave them a stroke. They were her most precious possession, at the end, a few tired horses. "Sleep well," she whispered, and turned back to her companions, to smile at their industry. The snow had already been cleared, dried wood had already been piled, smoke was already issuing into the afternoon twilight. And Bridget was nursing her samovar with a mother's care.

"How far do we travel?" Michael asked, sipping tea.

"I think about a month," Lorna said. "It will be an adventure, in the snow."

Remarkably, it had not yet occurred to him to ask where they were going or why.

They erected the tent, spread their blankets, slept one against the other, Michael in the middle, Lorna and Kathleen to either side of him, Bridget next to Kathleen, and Father Simeon next to Lorna. Body warmth spread from one to the other, and the fire glowed, throwing off its heat. The horses stamped contentedly. A month. They had food, and tea, and wine, for two. In two months they would be at the Polish border. Surely. That slow-moving cavalcade had only taken three weeks to travel from Smolensk to Moscow.

And at the Polish border she would find the Swedes. She must. She had not thought beyond that.

She slept heavily, awoke with a start, listened to the horses whinnying with terror.

"Mama?" Kathleen was also awake, and her voice trembled. "What is it, Mama?"

Lorna sat up, threw open the flap. The fire had burned low, and she estimated it was some time after midnight. The night was clear, and through the leafless branches above them she could see the glitter of the stars. But here in the wood it was very dark. The air was still and scented. And the scent was fetid. And now she could see the glowing eyes, beyond the horses. She pushed her head out, looked over her shoulder. Other eyes. They were surrounded. And now she could hear them moan.

"Mama?" Michael woke.

"My lady," Bridget whispered. "Wolves. Oh, my God, my lady."

"We cannot wait for their attack," Lorna said. "Now listen to me. Michael, Kathleen. Reload as soon as I have fired. Father Simeon, Bridget, take a pistol apiece in case they come too close."

"But, my lady . . ." Father Simeon protested.

"It is our lives or theirs, Father." She rose to her knees, crawled into the open, settled herself, picked up the first musket. She had been considered a good shot, on MacMahons. But that was eighteen years ago. Yet the range was not more than thirty yards, and closing. The horses were going mad with fear. And the eyes were distinct enough.

She fitted the butt to her shoulder, levelled the heavy piece, stared along the barrel. "Have the next one ready," she commanded. *And please God,* she prayed, *let this one not misfire.*

She squeezed the trigger, and the stock exploded against her shoulder. There came a howl from the circle of eyes, followed by screaming whimpers, and deep-seated snarling.

Father Simeon crossed himself.

"Next," Lorna snapped, fitting the butt to her aching shoulder. The eyes were gone, mostly turning on their stricken companion. But they had to be taught a lesson, driven far away, or there would be no rest for the humans. She found another glowing pair of red eyes, and fired, and was again rewarded. The third musket was pressed into her hand, and she fired again. The night air filled with a screaming, howling, sickening cacophony. Lorna fired the fourth musket, and the first was being returned to her hands. The horses screamed, the wolves howled, the dying moaned. The humans were silent, save for the explosions of the muskets. Lorna fired twelve shots, each piece three times, and then collapsed on to her belly, hand pressed to her bruised shoulder, breath panting, belly rumbling. But the eyes were gone.

Dawn revealed five mangled carcasses, red-brown in the snow, torn to pieces by their companions. "Oh, good shooting, Mama," Michael cried, jumping up and down. He at least was enjoying himself.

Bridget and Father Simeon exchanged glances. They knew nothing of the Maryland frontier, were no doubt realising for the first time that after better than ten years they still knew nothing of the woman to whom they had attached their lives.

"We had best be moving," Lorna said. "Those carcasses will prove beyond doubt that we were here." She helped them saddle their horses, swept snow over the blackened earth where they had lit the fire, swung into the saddle, and looked back along the road. Suppose men were there, would she have the courage, the determination, to fire into *them?* Her companions would expect it now.

But the road behind lay empty.

They rode, into the snow. The wolves clung to their flank, but well in the distance, and that night, though they heard the howling all around them and the horses were restless, they saw no eyes. And still there was no sign of pursuit.

On the twelfth day Lorna concluded that there was not going to be a pursuit. She did not know whether to thank God or Martha. No doubt it was a combination of the two. And that afternoon they saw smoke in front of them.

"What do you think of it, Mama?" Kathleen drew rein alongside her.

Lorna stared into the distance. The smoke hung in

the air like a pall, drifting in the stillness, for so far they had been no less fortunate with their weather than with their flight. "It was a village," she said, and urged her horse forward, but stopped them when they came in sight of the smouldering houses. There was no stench, because of the cold. But she did not know what they would find. "Wait here," she said, and walked her horse forward.

Not a house stood. This was no careless act of vandalism. And not a creature stirred. But there were no dead bodies, either, not even of animals. She halted in the square, gazed at what must once have been a church. And heard movement.

She turned, reaching for the pistol in her saddle holster, gazed at the moujik, who had crept from behind a pile of smouldering rubble. He gaped at her. "Highness?" There could be no gainsaying the richness of her furs, of her horse trappings.

"Who did this?" Lorna asked.

"The soldiers, Highness. Orders from Prince Menshikov."

She frowned at him. "Prince Menshikov? Prince Scheremetyev commands the southern flank."

"No more, my lady. Prince Menshikov has been given command over him, because, it is said, Prince Scheremetyev would stand and fight. But the Tsar retreats. And he has given orders that no village, no animals are to be left where the Swedes may discover them. All are to be destroyed or driven off."

"What of Smolensk?"

"Smolensk burns, my lady. The Swedes are coming, my lady. They will kill us all."

*The Swedes,* she thought, her heart pounding, her brain suddenly seeming to be filled with warmth. Perhaps she had not supposed she would succeed. Perhaps, in her heart, she had known she was committing suicide and murder, leading her family into the snow, to die of cold. *Remember, Kath, you and the child must not be taken alive. So, could the Susquehannocks be more horrible than Peter the Tsar? And now she had succeeded. The Swedes were coming, and they must be near, if this village was burned.*

She awoke from her daydream. The man was very close.

"Highness," he said, and she saw saliva dribbling from his lips, instantly to freeze on his chin. "Highness, we are starving. They have taken all our food. Highness . . ." His gaze was sliding away from her, and she turned her head. From the trees beyond the village came people. Men and women, children, some forty of them. Starving. *Oh God,* she thought. "Highness," his fingers were actually on her skirt, biting through the material, and into her flesh, and his tongue was out, poking the air. "Highness . . ." His grip tightened, and she realised he was going to drag her from the saddle. Her leg was pinned; she whipped the pistol from its holster and struck him across the head, sending him tumbling to the ground. From the approaching people there rose a wail.

"Ride," Lorna shouted. "Ride," she screamed. "Ride!"

Kathleen struck Michael's horse across the rump, Bridget did the same for Father Simeon. She also led the pack animals, and they came charging along the street, scattering snow. Lorna made herself wait, for the villagers were running and slipping, panting, breaths clouding the air, and they were armed with knives and axes.

"Ride," she screamed as they came up to her. "Do not stop, for anything."

They scattered past her. A man reached the road, waving an axe. Lorna levelled her pistol and fired. He gave a cry and tumbled backwards. I have never murdered anyone, she had boasted to Martha. Now it seemed the most natural thing in the world. She turned her horse, slapped it on the rump, urged it forward. Behind her there came wailing shrieks, and something struck her on the back. For a terrifying moment she thought she had been shot, but it was only a clod of earth. Then they were out the far side and into the open, but they missed the road, and one of the pack animals had lost its footing, and went tumbling over, neighing its terror.

Lorna drew rein, as did Kathleen. The others continued to flounder through the snow. But the villagers had seen what had happened also, and were running again, howling.

"No time," Lorna gasped. "Ride."

"But the food, Mama . . ." Tea was soaking from Bridget's samovar into the white.

"We must do without. Ride."

They rode together, hastening through the snow towards the others. Progress was slow, but there was no more pursuit. The villagers had stopped to loot the baggage.

Father Simeon's face was gray. "Would it not have been better to let them have it?"

Lorna's mouth was set in a hard line. "They would have taken it all. They would have taken us, as well. Animals or humans, Father, it is them or us. Until we reach the Swedes."

"My lady," Bridget whispered. "There is no more tea."

Lorna straightened slowly. Her legs ached and her shoulders ached; her back ached and her bottom ached; her belly ached and her head ached. No doubt they all suffered equally, although Michael and Kathleen remained determinedly cheerful. "Finish folding the tent," she commanded, and walked with Bridget to the packs. Her boots crunched in the crisp morning snow. She had no feeling down there, which was probably just as well. Three weeks, and she had not removed a single article of clothing, much less her boots. She dared not let any of them attempt even a change of linen, for fear of frostbite. "What else is short?"

"There is nothing, my lady. Some biscuits."

Lorna sighed, stared at the trees, and the snow, and the brilliant blue of the sky. Most of all, her eyes ached. *Where* were the Swedes? Perhaps they were there and she could not see them. Menshikov had been too anxious, too eager to reduce Russia to smouldering ruin. That was typical of the man, as it was typical of his master.

"Well, then," she said. "We will make do with biscuits, until we find some food." She could shoot a wolf. But even the wolves had abandoned them. And that supposed they could force themselves to eat the flesh of a wolf. They were not yet that hungry.

She walked to where Father Simeon knelt, beside him. He spent much time in prayer nowadays, and otherwise spoke little. "Bridget told me."

"I had expected to reach the Swedes before now, Father. But they cannot be far away."

"Are they there at all, Highness? Do we travel the right way?"

"The Swedes are there, Father, and we follow the sun, towards them. I promise you that."

"Lorna." He held her arm as she would have risen. "Why do you not leave me? Whatever you have left, it can be divided between four better than five."

"Do not be absurd," she said. "We . . . we will kill a horse, when it becomes necessary."

"Then you will have one horse the less," he pointed out. "Lorna, it would be quick, and painless, and right. I am old. Too old for a journey such as this. I shall not survive, anyway."

"What nonsense," she said, and kissed him on the cheek. "Where I go, you go, Father. You are the keeper of my soul, remember?" She gave him a bright smile. "And the possessor of all my most dreadful secrets. I dare not let you out of my sight. Let us make haste."

They mounted—the children had already stowed the tent—and rode, following the path of the sun. Lorna chewed her lip beneath her scarf. Perhaps she was being overcautious. Perhaps they should turn due west. Surely the Russians had long evacuated this area. Perhaps she was riding past the Swedes. Perhaps . . .

"Mama," Kathleen cried.

She turned, instinctively reaching for her musket, looked at Father Simeon. His horse had fallen behind the others, and he drooped. She turned, rode back to him. "Father?"

He raised his head, smiled, and then fell forward, hung for a moment on his horse's neck, and tumbled out of the saddle.

"The Lord have mercy on us," Bridget said.

Lorna dismounted, but knew before her boots touched the ground. "Ride on," she said. "Make camp in that wood, over there." They could just see the trees; the wood was in a dip.

"We cannot leave you, Mama," Kathleen objected.

"You are not leaving me, goose. I will catch up with you. Ride on."

Kathleen hesitated, then nodded, and turned her horse. Michael and Bridget followed obediently. *Presumably*, Lorna thought, *should anything happen to me,*

*Kathleen will be capable of taking them to safety. Kathleen MacMahon.*

Should anything happen to her. She knelt beside the priest, rolled him on his back, wiped snow from his nose and eyes and lips. His flesh was already blue. How much had his strength been vital to her own survival? Strangely, she had no desire to weep. She had stripped herself of all emotion to take her children to safety. And she had known Father Simeon could not survive, even as he had known himself. No doubt she had murdered him, as she was murdering them all.

She took the spade from her saddle pack, cleared the snow, began to scrape. It was slow, painful work; the ground was like solid stone. She hacked away, discarding her scarf the better to breathe, actually feeling sweat in her armpits. She paused, for breath, looked for her children. But they had disappeared, into the dip, into the trees. Not that she would have any difficulty in finding them; their tracks remained in the snow.

She resumed work, digging and scraping. It was good to feel the blood pulsing through her veins. *I shall survive,* she thought fiercely. *I will see that Michael and Kathleen survive as well. And Bridget. I shall survive.*

She dropped to her knees. She could dig no more, and he would lie secure, she thought, at least for the winter. And in the spring, someone would find him, supposing anyone ever came this way again. She pulled him into the shallow grave, heaped earth and snow over him until only his face remained exposed. She made the sign of the cross, and bowed her head. "Be gentle with him, oh God," she prayed. "He was a good man, and a faithful one." She covered the face, leaned back on her heels, raised her head, and saw two horsemen.

For a moment she supposed they might be a mirage. They wore white coats, and black hats, and were motionless, watching her. Then her heart leapt into her throat. *Swedes. They had to be Swedes. Oh, poor Father Simeon. He had died but a few minutes too soon.*

The men walked their horses towards her, descending the slight slope. How tired she was. She wanted to do nothing but look at them, until they reached her, and told her she was safe. She stared at them, as they approached, and could see the flash of their teeth as they smiled. Their horses stopped, only feet away, and they looked down at her.

"Are you mad?" one asked, in Russian. "Do you not know the Swedes are close?"

Slowly Lorna reached her feet; her muscles seemed to be paralysed, with fear more than cold or exhaustion. She turned her head, to find her horse, her muskets, and her pistols. But the animal had wandered some feet away. And these were not peasants. They were soldiers, better armed than herself. In addition to their muskets and their swords, they even wore bayonets on their right hips, suggesting that they were dragoons.

"Are you dumb?" asked the second man. He pointed at the tracks leading away into the snow. "Where have the others gone?"

Lorna dragged her scarf up to hide her mouth and nose. "There are no others," she said.

The men frowned at her.

"I . . . I seek the Tsar," she said. "I am . . ."

"The Princess Bogoljubov," said the first man. "Holy Christ."

The second man grinned. "The Tsar seeks *you*, Highness. It is said, he sleeps with the knout in his hand, waiting for you to come to him."

"I . . ." Lorna took a step backwards.

"But he supposes you dead," said the first man, and dismounted. "As you have managed to disappear, without trace, he supposes you lost in the snow."

Lorna halted. She knew they were ready for her to run, and the second man had also dismounted. "Then you could let me go," she said. "I have money. No one would ever know."

They exchanged glances. "No one," said the second man, "can ever know." His gaze drifted down her body. "They say she is the most beautiful woman in all Russia."

*Oh, God,* she thought. *Oh, Holy Mother.* But how tired she was. Her legs gave way, and she sank to her knees. They would arrange her, as they chose.

Their boots came closer, crunching in the snow. *Lie still,* she thought. *And they will not hurt you. But they mean to kill you, when they are satisfied.*

A gloved hand touched her scarf, jerked it away from her face. She could not stop herself raising her head, to look at the glowing eyes, the parted lips, the stubble of beard on his chin. "Are you not going to beg?" the lips asked.

"Holy Christ," said the other man, and held her shoulder, to push her over. Her head struck the snow and lay still. She felt the chill on her legs, and turned to look at him. He knelt, and his breeches were already dropped. His member was erect, blood-filled even in the freezing air. "Holy Christ," he said again. "Have you ever seen such beauty?"

The other man knelt by her hair, dug his fingers into her tricorne to pull it off, removed his gloves to drive his fingers into the neck of her gown, and she heard it rip. *I shall freeze,* she thought. *I shall freeze.*

Her body was still warm from the exertion. She felt the touch of icy fingers, the sudden caress of the glans on her thighs. She was rolled on her back and flopped, arms flung wide, legs spread. He knelt between, saliva flooding his mouth. She wished he would kiss her, suck her, bite her. She was too dry, and otherwise he would hurt her. His body came closer, and she felt pain. He would hurt her.

The second man was almost lying beside her face. His fingers were pulling at the breasts, squeezing the nipples and he was kissing her mouth, her eyes, her nose, her chin. His companion thudded on her belly, and again, his head bumping on his companion's hand, lost beneath the bodice of her gown. And now she was wet; he must have been deprived of a woman for a long time. The pain began to ease,

"Aaaaah," breathed the man. His lips sucked at her neck. "Your turn, comrade. Your turn."

"Soon," said the man. "I have come already. Just touching her, I have come. Soon."

He sucked at her nose. No man had ever done that before. *So then,* she thought, *I have had a new experience, while being raped, by two soldiers. And now they are spent, and I must wait, until they wish it again. I shall freeze. What a silly thought, whether she froze or whether they merely cut her throat, when they were finished.*

But they were spent. The first man moved slightly; he was still inside her, but she could feel him shrinking. His sword was resting on her ankle. He had not even troubled to take off his weapons. But then, neither had his companion.

And they were spent. But she was so tired. Too tired, to live? It did not seem to matter any more.

But Michael and Kathleen and Bridget were waiting for her, in the hollow. They might grow worried and decide to come back. Kathleen, spread-eagled in the snow, her skirt flung above her waist. They would find her no less beautiful. And they would find her whether *she* lay here and died, or not. They would certainly follow the tracks.

Slowly she moved her arms inward. The fingers had

stopped tugging at her nipples, the member was lying flaccid on her thigh. Soon they would grow cold and wish her again. Her gloved fingers touched steel and slithered up the scabbard. She found the hilt of the bayonet, tightened her fingers. The moment she started to withdraw it, he would know. It would have to be done quickly and decisively, as she had shot the villager. But the villager had no more existence for her than the wolves. This man's hand lay on her breast.

She gasped, drew the bayonet. His head jerked, and his fingers squeezed at the same time. Her gasp became one of pain, and she drove the blade sideways, amazed to discover no resistance. For a dreadful moment she thought she had missed him altogether, then she saw his head, arching back on his neck above her, mouth wide, the wailing scream escaping into the afternoon sky.

His companion jerked away, rising to his hands and knees. Lorna withdrew the bayonet; she had driven it just below the rib cage, and the man was rolling away from her, writhing and screaming. The second man shook his head as if to clear his thoughts, lunged for her with both hands. But she had brought back the weapon, and he fell on it. Blood spurted from his chest, cascaded over her gown, dribbled on to the snow. His weight again crashed onto her belly, but she was already pushing him away, turning and rising to her knees in the same instant, still clutching the bayonet.

The first man rolled on the snow. "Please," he gasped. "Help me." Blood oozed from his side, soaked his fingers where he clutched himself.

Lorna reached her feet, and her skirts fell past her knees and settled around her boots.

"Help me," the man gasped.

Lorna stepped backwards, refastened her bodice as best she could. Her pelisse still clung to her shoulders, and she pulled it close, looked around for her hat, which had rolled across the snow, stopped and picked it up, still watching the man. But he could no longer speak, although his mouth remained open and his eyes. She settled the tricorne on her head, brought up her scarf to cover her face, realised he was dead. She dropped the bayonet.

Their horses waited patiently, some fifty yards away. She held their reins, walked towards her own, suddenly trembling, knees touching, heart pounding. She gripped the reins, mounted, followed the tracks. She did not look back.

"Oh, Mama," Kathleen said. They had already lit a fire. "You look exhausted. Is poor Father Simeon buried?"

They could not see the blood beneath her pelisse. "Yes," Lorna said. "Father Simeon is buried."

"But where did you find these horses, Mama?" Michael asked. "These are soldiers' horses."

"I found them," Lorna said. "And the Swedes are close. Mount up."

That night it rained, a downpour of frightening intensity, which was even able to penetrate the skin of the tent and drip on to their faces. Lorna was afraid that it would be followed by a frost, but instead the next day remained almost warm, with the result that the snow showed signs of melting, and they proceeded on their way through a bog, which suddenly ended in a very real river.

"Mama?" Kathleen asked, as her horse halted.

"It must be crossed, sweetheart," Lorna said. It was the first time she had spoken since regaining them the previous night. No doubt they put her mood down to the death of her friend and confessor. Which was as well. They should not suspect her despair. It had little

to do with the rape itself. She had been raped before. It
had to do with the timing. Father Simeon had been
introduced into her life at the start of her sojourn at
Kensington, at the start of her upwards surge. He had
died, and the one thing she had truly feared throughout
the journey had come to pass. Did that mean there was
no fortune left to her? Well, then, perhaps she would
drown on this river crossing.

But Michael was already urging his horse into the
fast-flowing stream, and she must hasten forward herself to draw alongside him, and protect him if necessary,
should his horse slip. The water was very cold, and it
seeped over the tops of her boots to drench her feet.
But it did not reach her thighs, soak her crotch. No
doubt the evidence of what had happened to her remained.

"On," she shouted. "On," as their horses seemed
inclined to sheer away from the bubbling water and
turn downstream. She dragged her own mount's head
straight, and Michael did the same. They forced their
animals up the far bank, Kathleen and Bridget behind
them, and were checked by a quite startling noise,
which had them turning this way and that before Lorna
realised that it had been caused by the cocking of some
fifty muskets. They were, in fact, completely surrounded
by musketeers, clad in blue coats and yellow vests, and
with blue hats on their heads.

Lorna wanted to scream for joy, although there was
little friendship in the Swedes' faces. But they had
quickly discerned that there were no men with the party,
and in fact she had a momentary pang of alarm, for as
regards women they could hardly be any better off than
the men she had yesterday killed. But to her relief an
officer immediately stepped from their ranks. "What do
you here, woman?" He spoke Russian.

She pulled her scarf from her face. But she had already decided her best plan. "I am the Princess Bogoljubov. I seek His Majesty King Charles."

The man frowned at her. "You are Russian."

"I am Irish, sir," she said. "I happen to be married to a Russian. But you see me here seeking refuge from the Tsar, sir. My companions are my son and daughter, and my maid."

The captain hesitated, and then gave orders in Swedish. Four of his musketeers came forward to seize their bridles and lead the horses, while the rest resumed their positions, concealed in the trees overlooking the river.

"I am so hungry, Mama," Michael said.

"We will soon be fed, sweetheart," she said. "These people are our friends."

"Friends, Mama? Are they not our enemies?"

"Hush," Lorna said. There was no time to explain things now. And now, perhaps, it no longer mattered.

The trees thinned, and they came upon the encampment, a succession of orderly rows of tents, before and around which she estimated there were several thousand men, both horse and foot. But what a contrast between this camp and her only previous military experience. Unlike the Russians around Smolensk every man in the Swedish camp was hard at work, polishing either his equipment or his weapons, nor did they seem particularly interested in the sudden appearance of three women, allowing the intruders hardly a glance before continuing their work. Of anyone wearing the distinctive uniform of the Drabants there was no immediate sign, but as they approached a larger tent set in the very centre of the encampment, her heart began to pound as she made out two of them on sentry duty.

Neither was Lennart, however, and a moment later they were being signalled to dismount.

A man was summoned by the officer to beckon Kathleen and Michael and Bridget. "Where do you take them?" Lorna demanded.

"To the women," the officer replied. So there were some females in this camp.

"You asked to see the King," the officer said, lifting the flap of the tent for her. She hesitated, then ducked her head and stepped into the warmth of the tent, to find herself in the company of several men who were in the midst of their midday meal, seated around a trestle table, but turning as she turned. Two were general officers, from the splendour of their uniforms, another was a distinguished-looking civilian who was clearly the famous Chancellor, Count Karl Piper—for she was well acquainted with the various Swedish leaders as there was very little other topic of conversation in the Kremlin. There was also a scattering of secretaries and orderlies, and two young men, a boy who she estimated could not be more than nineteen, fresh faced and eager. She identified him as Prince Emmanuel Maximilian of Württemberg, well known as Prince Charles's inseparable companion, and indeed as a veteran of some five years' service already.

But Lorna's attention was entirely taken by the other young man in the tent, for this, she knew, could be none other than the King himself, Charles the Twelfth of Sweden.

He rose at her entry, to her surprise, and revealed himself to be tall, six feet, and quite remarkably slender, with a waist she thought many a woman might envy. His hands were unusually small, and his black thigh boots looked incongruous, with their tiny feet. His face was oval and a trifle plump, in the most marked contrast to the rest of him; his smooth complexion was burned a deep brown by the winds of so many years campaigning, but his hardy life had in no way dimmed the vigour of his brilliant blue eyes, which were extraordinarily large, as was his nose. He wore no wig, and his brown hair was beginning to recede, suggesting that once the ageing process set in, it might gather pace. His clothes lacked all decoration and were merely those of an ordinary soldier. Most remarkable of all, in Lorna's experience of monarchs, although the assembly were eating meat and drinking beer with great gusto, which made her mouth water, the King's fare appeared to be a piece of bread and a tankard of plain water. Indeed, anyone less like a reincarnation of Alexander and Hannibal combined, and even less, the sort of man likely to frighten Peter the Tsar, she could not imagine.

"Your name and rank," he inquired, speaking quietly and without preamble in Russian.

"Lorna of Morne, Princess Bogoljubov."

He frowned. "You are English?"

"Irish, Your Majesty."

"But, nevertheless, bearing a Russian name," he remarked. "Are you with Prince Scheremetyev's army?"

"No, indeed, Your Majesty," she said. "My family and I are fugitives from Moscow, from the wrath of the Tsar."

His frown deepened. "From Moscow? I am told you have a child with you."

"My son. My daughter, also, Your Majesty. And my maid."

"And you have crossed half Russia, in winter." He glanced at his companions, made a remark in Swedish. "Where is your husband?"

"He remains in Moscow, Your Majesty." Her heart began to pound. She could discern no trace of sympathy or even interest in his face. She could not possibly have made another total misjudgement in her choice of man to whom to turn. Life could not be that unkind, surely.

"And still you flee," he said, half to himself.

"It is the simplest matter in the world to incur the disfavour of the Tsar, Your Majesty," she said. "At times he is quite deranged."

He stared at her. "No doubt one's betters oft seem so," he pointed out. "Well, madam, I dislike the attendance of women on armies at the best of times, but as you are here, you will have to stay. I can do you no honour as regards your rank, however. You will have a place in the commissariat wagons, where you will find others of your sex. They will care for you, give you something to eat and drink . . ." He had observed the way her eyes had drifted to the food. ". . . and a change of clothing. They will also care for your people."

Lorna discovered herself becoming angry. No doubt it was a result of hunger as much as exhaustion, as much as resentment at his apparent disinterest in her as a woman. "Are we then your prisoners, Your Majesty?"

"By no means, Princess. Indeed it seems to me that you must necessarily share my antipathy to the Russians, having been forced to flee their company. But if you march with us, you will be obtaining the opportunity to avenge yourself. It is my intention to settle my long difference with the Tsar in that very palace of the Kremlin from which you have just come. In fact, it occurs to me that you may be of some use to me, as a scout. Have you not just passed through the entire Russian army?"

"I have spent the past three weeks, endeavouring to avoid the Russian army, Your Majesty." Now she wished he *would* let her go; exhaustion seemed to be creeping up her legs, inch by inch. But here was a possible way to gain his favour, and however she might resent his attitude his favour was essential. "However,

I can offer you two pieces of information, one good, the other bad."

"The bad first," Charles said.

"Well, then, Your Majesty, it is this. The Tsar has been rendered so apprehensive by the news of your imminent appearance before the walls of the Kremlin, that he has endeavoured to slow down your advance by making it impossible for your men or your horses to obtain sustenance. In short, over a considerable area, stretching as far as the city of Smolensk, I understand, there is not a building, not an ear of corn left standing, and not a cow, and scarce a human other than soldiers, left alive."

"The devil," he commented. "Peter would so treat his own people?"

"It is no more than we already know of the tyrant, Your Majesty," said one of the general officers, a splendidly dressed man, whose abnormally long and sharp nose told Lorna that he must be Field Marshal Count Rchnskold, regarded as the most talented of the Swedish commanders after their King; to the Russian generals he was known as Old Nosy.

"Well, then," Charles said. "We must obtain our necessaries from the Russian army itself, which, indeed, has always been my intention. For I am quite sure *they* do not go on short rations. And your second, happier piece of information?"

"It is that General Scheremetyev, although still commanding an army corps, is no longer general of the army opposed to you. He has been replaced by Prince Menshikov."

The King stared at her for an incredulous moment. "The pie seller?"

"The same, Your Majesty."

"That is good news indeed, Princess." At last his expression softened. "You will dine with me very soon, when I may more properly express my thanks. Now you had best attend your family." Once again he looked at her clothes. "And your toilet." He sat down again, to suggest that the interview was at an end.

Lorna stood her ground. She would never have a better opportunity. "Your Majesty, if I may make an inquiry . . ."

The King, already seated, turned his head. "Yes?"

"I am acquainted with an officer in your army, Sire. Colonel Lennart Munro."

The King's head came up. "Lennart Munro? General Munro?"

"General, Your Majesty?"

The King snapped his fingers, and one of the orderlies stepped outside. "I am sure General Munro will be pleased to greet you, Princess Bogoljubov. You may go with the attendant."

"I thank you, Sire," she said, and sank into a deep curtsey, from which she only with difficulty regained her feet. It was not only exhaustion, now. Her heart surged about her chest until she felt almost sick. Lennart was alive, and well, and, indeed, prospering more than ever. And within a few feet of her.

And closer than that. For as she stepped through the tent, she saw him coming towards her.

# Chapter 13

*L*ennart," she cried, running forward, arms outstretched.

"Lorna," he shouted, and then checked, and glanced at the man accompanying her in some embarrassment. "Princess Bogoljubov." The animation left his face, and it became impassive, almost cold.

She stopped also, only feet away. "Lennart?" she whispered.

He extended his hand. "I had heard that a Russian lady had been brought in, Highness," he said, in Russian. "And wondered if it could be you."

She gave him her hand, and he raised it to his lips. "You wondered," she said slowly in English, "if it could be me?"

He straightened. "And now, of course, I am overjoyed to see you here, Highness." He continued to speak Russian. "No doubt, at some suitable moment, you will tell me how you came to survive a journey across Russia, in the dead of winter. Your children are well?"

She inhaled, felt her nostrils expand. *Oh, God,* she thought. *Oh, Holy Mother. Am I totally damned?* "My children are very well, General," she said, also speaking Russian. "They are here, with me."

"I would have expected nothing less, Highness," he said. "I look forward to meeting them, when you have changed your clothing. You will excuse me, Highness?" He bowed and walked on.

Lorna gazed behind him. Oh, God,· she thought again. At least in Moscow there had been hate, and sometimes love, and always passion.

"If you will accompany me, Highness," said the man at her elbow, in Russian.

"Of course." She picked up her skirts. "Do any wives accompany the army?"

"Some, Highness. We are engaged upon a long campaign."

"Ah. The general's wife is here? General Munro?"

"No, no, Highness. General Munro is not married. Here are the women's quarters."

The tent flap was being opened, and Michael and Kathleen were calling to her. They were sharing an enormous wooden tub filled with hot water, to which Lorna was now also escorted by the Swedish women, all golden hair and heaving breasts. *Not married,* she thought. *But determined to treat her with the coldness she deserved. The Tsar's whore.*

The women were gabbling in Swedish, which she did not understand. But she could understand their concern, as they removed her pelisse and saw the dried blood on her gown. As they had her stripped naked within seconds they very rapidly understood that the blood was not her own, but they remained so excited by their discovery that at least she did not have to explain the bruises on her thighs. And a moment later Michael had been removed, and she was enjoying the tub.

"Mama?" Kathleen asked. "What happened?"

"It is of no concern," Lorna said. "We are safe now."

"Safe?" Kathleen cried. "These people are savages."

"They are friends," Lorna assured her.

"Friends?" Michael demanded, as two of the women began draping him in clothes far too large for him. "Are we not prisoners?"

"In a sense we are," Lorna agreed. "But all will be well, Michael. I promise you."

And a moment later he lost interest in the safety or not of their surroundings as he was seated at a trestle table and presented with hot food and a mug of beer. *All will be well,* she thought bitterly. But what right had she to be bitter? This man had asked her to go to him, as she had promised to do, that night in St. Mary's. And she had refused, reaching for a pinnacle too dazzling to be rejected. As Aurora Konigsmarck had said, she had not loved sufficiently. And now it was too late.

She was dried, and dressed, in a simple grey gown with a wide white collar, reminiscent of the garb adopted by the people called Quakers she had occasionally seen in England. For a hat she was given a black tricorne, but there were no boots of her size, and so she had to use her own battered pair. Kathleen and Bridget were similarly dressed, so that as the beer began to bite at their senses they could not help but laugh at each other.

"You look a perfect sight, Mama," Kathleen shouted.

"On the contrary," Lorna objected. "I think our new clothes suit us." For their hair had been left loose, and Kathleen, at the least, made a very pretty picture. "I wish I had a glass."

To see what? She knew the face, and now she knew that the face had, indeed, won its conflict with the mind. Those calm, beautiful, and utterly determined features no more than reflected the brain behind, the steel spring which would even kill if necessary. Which had killed three times. Or was she flattering herself? Had she not also killed Father Simeon, by forcing him to undertake this journey at all?

For what purpose? Total rejection at the end of it?

"Mama?" Kathleen asked. "What is going to happen to us?"

"Happen? Why, we are going to campaign, it appears, with the Swedes."

"And then what, my lady?" Bridget wanted to know.

"Then? Why . . ." She drank some beer. Sleep. All she wanted was sleep. She had thought herself exhausted before, and knew now she had been no more than pleasantly tired. "Why, that depends on when and how the campaign ends, I have no doubt. Now, I must retire. We must all have a rest. I could not keep my eyes open with my fingers." She smiled at the sergeant's wife who was watching over them like a mother hen, and made the necessary sign of closing her hands together and laying them on her cheek. The woman cackled happily and escorted them to the wagon which had been provided for their use. Here there were blankets and peace. My God, after so long, she had at the least found peace. Lorna's eyes were shut almost before she had settled Michael. She slept, at the back of the wagon, a deep and dreamless coma such as she had not known for too long, and awoke, to a sudden alarm, because a hand had been put through the canvas flap to squeeze her arm. She sat up, panting, and gazed at Lennart Munro.

"Lennart?" she whispered, for a moment supposing herself dreaming. The night air was cold and drifted across her face like an icy hand.

He released her, and stepped back, and the flap returned to place. Hastily she dragged on her boots, reached for her cloak, opened the flap and peered through. The night was quiet, save for the soughing of the wind; occasionally a horse neighed, and regularly the guard called their hours. Lemnart stood just behind the wagon and in its shade. She dropped her legs over the back, and he stepped forward to lift her down.

"Lorna," he whispered. "Oh, my God, Lorna." He spoke English.

She was in his arms, her arms around his back, hugging him tighter than she had ever held anything in her life before. It was Lennart, and he was alive and well and holding her against him. It was seventeen years, it was a lifetime, of dreaming suddenly come true, as he kissed her forehead, each eye, her nose, her chin, and then found her mouth.

"Lennart?" she asked, holding her head back to look at him.

"Bogoljubov," he said. "Where is he?"

"In Moscow." She caught her breath at the expression which crossed his face. "But I have left him, Lennart. Now and forever. I have left the Tsar. I should have done so before, but . . ." She chewed her lip, but would not lie to him. "A combination of weakness and fear kept me there. But no longer, my sweet. If you still want me, I am yours forever."

"Want you?" His voice was loud, and he looked around himself in fear. "Do you not know how long I have wanted you, my darling?"

"But then . . . this afternoon . . ."

"There is our problem," he said. "This King of mine, this Charles the Twelfth, oh, do not mistake me, Lorna, I worship the ground on which he walks. I have never known such a man, such a soldier, such a leader. There is not a man in this army would not happily sacrifice himself for the King. But how does one achieve such stature, Lorna? He has not a fault, save possibly rashness. He does not take wine, and he regards women as belonging in the home, and as a wife. There are women with this army; you have seem them. But they must be married. You come to him already married. He will not send you away, because he is as chivalrous as he is brave. But he would execute the man who dallied with you, and were he to suppose the dalliance was your desire, then he *would* certainly send you away and into the snow, to die. If there is a word he does not recognise, it is compromise."

"My God," she said. "But what do you risk, in coming here?"

He smiled. "My life, certainly. But I would risk that for you, dear heart, without consideration, did it not involve your life as well. And did it not . . ." He hesitated.

"Involve a betrayal of this man you have come so to admire," she said.

"I but had to make you understand, that this afternoon I was no more than acting. That, having waited for so long . . ."

"As I have waited, Lennart," she said. "Well, then, we shall wait some more. After so long, after so much . . ." She forced a smile herself, for all that her eyes were filled with tears. "Another week, another month, another year were nothing."

"And then?"

"Who knows? Vassily may be killed. He should be

dead, now. I should have killed him, before I left. He deserved it, to be sure."

"Lorna!"

"Oh, I did not, Lennart. I *have* killed. I would have you know that. But it has been in my defence, in defence of my family. Never in cold blood. And never even for love of another."

"And suppose he does not die?"

She hesitated, then squeezed his arm. "This campaign must result in the total destruction of the Russian army, the Russian state. This is what your King intends, what I have no doubt he will achieve. Then surely you can end your soldiering, and love me, and your daughter instead."

"It would be criminal."

"Criminal?" she asked, and kissed him on the lips. "Could there be crime, between you and me? It is all the people who have conspired to keep us apart who have been criminal." She pulled back to look at him. "You invited me to share your life, husband or no, once before."

He sighed. "If I could make you understand, my sweet. We are in the middle of a campaign. A campaign which means life or death to all of us here, and more, perhaps, to our very country. There can be no time for dalliance, no time for any thoughts other than those of war, and death, and destruction, until this is ended."

She listened. Within the wagon all was quiet, save for the heavy breathing of Bridget. She turned into his arms, and discovered that her heart had quietened, as her brain had cooled. "Do you not suppose it is a matter of life and death for me as well, Lennart?"

"Of course it is, my sweet. But . . ."

She slipped both arms up to his neck. "You saved

my life once," she said. "For be sure I would have killed myself had Butler killed you. Then I thought us betrothed, as I carried your child inside my belly. But we were cruelly separated, and I became wed to another. I am no longer, Lennart. That we are legally bound is nothing more than an encumbrance, like mud around my ankles, out of which I shall pull myself at the earliest possible moment. It is no longer a matter of honour. It was never a matter of my heart. But, Lennart, I am a passionate woman, eager for love, eager to be loved. Lennart, you have every reason to hate me, for my refusal to elope with you from Dresden. You will never know how many times I have regretted that decision. If you hate me for that, say so, now. If you do not, love me, now. I can wait no longer. If my life in the future is to be without love, then I wish to *know* now."

"Hate you, Lorna? Hate you?" At last his hands, closing on her ribs, slid up to her shoulders. "You are the only person, the only thing, I have ever loved, could ever love."

"Lennart . . ." *But how tragic*, she thought, *that I cannot tell this man* why *I must have his love, now,* why *I must know, that he and I will be happy.* Then why did she not dare? Because he was incapable of understanding? Or because she only feared that he was.

She turned away, and his fingers scraped round her waist and found her breasts, gently, holding them from underneath as he had done before, as she had wanted him to do again. She wanted to shriek with joy as the passion began to build, rippling out from her belly. Stones in a pond. But this would be the last stone ever to enter there.

She fumbled for the flap, released it, and his fingers slackened. "We cannot go in there," he whispered.

"They are heavy sleepers." She leaned her head back, on his shoulder, to kiss him on the cheek. "And we have nothing more to say, Lennart. Only to do."

The darkness and the silence made them young lovers, all over again, children seeking the first great adventure of their lives. And were they not?

He held her thighs to give her a push up, and then crawled beside her. His sword struck the wooden tailgate, and they clung to eath other, but neither Michael nor Bridget nor Kathleen stirred. She released his belt, laid the weapon beside her. "Me first," she whispered. Tonight had to be like that, a consummation of everything she had ever known, ever dreamed. His fingers slid over her nightgown and she dropped her cloak, found her thighs. She rose to her knees, and he raised the material over her head, mouth coming forward gently to suck at the flesh in her neck, and then drifting away, to raise her right arm and kiss the pit below, suck at the down. Oh, God, she thought. Oh, Holy Mother. No one has ever done that to me, before. It will be all right. It will be good. It will be the best, ever.

She kicked off one boot, and he pulled off the other, to stop as they heard the march of a measured tread.

They stayed absolutely still, both kneeling now, and she could feel his hardness against her thigh, all the way through his breeches. But the sentry merely did his about turn, close to the wagon, and marched off again.

Their breaths exploded together, and she turned in his arms, naked, kneeling against him, feeling his hands on her buttocks now as he sighed into her mouth, as his fingers slid over her flesh, parting, finding their way between, and was suddenly terrified at the thought that Lennart, having been without a woman for so long, might be as quick as Vassily, on his first occasion.

"Now you," she whispered, and pushed him down, straddling his leg to take off his boots, waiting for the print of his cold toes on her back as he pushed the second time, and wanting to scream with joy as they touched her. She almost forgot his jacket, so eager was she to reach for and discover his member, remembering how surprised she had been, on her first meeting, to find it limp where it should already have been hard. But no doubts tonight; it leapt at her, and when she lowered her head to kiss him he gave a gasp, so that she thought she had already lost him. Nor could the moment be far away. She chewed her lips, remembered a suggestion Martha had once made to her, during their interminable discussions as to the best ways of making love. From the rear of the wagon there hung a skin of water, and the night was very cold. She thrust her hand through the flap, found the water, allowed her hand to enter to the wrist, nearly gasped with the sudden shock, and then closed her fingers on his penis.

"Aaaah." He tried to sit up, and she gently pushed him back, kissed his lips.

"You will stay," she said. "And want."

And oh, how he wanted. Now he did sit up, forcing her back in turn. She had been going to ask him to do this, and now she need speak not a word. He kissed her toes, slipped from her ankles to her knees to her thighs. Lie still, she thought. How often had she thought that. Lie still, and they will not hurt you, and in time they will go away. So this night, lie still, and he will not hurry. Lie still, and who knows . . .?

But she knew. It needed no more than the caress of his tongue to send the passion streaming away, bring the scream of pleasure tearing up to her throat, to be stifled in a gasp. For how long had she waited, for that, from this man.

But he was kneeling above her anxiously. "Lorna? You are disgusted with me."

"No," she said. "I love you. Lennart . . ."

"But you are sweating, my darling."

"With passion, only with passion."

His body descended on her, and his mouth reached for hers, then he was away again. "I will need more water," he said.

She wanted to scream with joy. In seconds they had stepped across that invisible, but immense gulf that separates one human being from the other, had come together, making a nonsense of time and space and discomfort and fear and hope and ambition, to have their minds meet, in what they wished, in what they would have. They were equals, in love, as she had always wanted. And where that had happened once, it must happen again. And again. And again.

She bathed him, and fell to kissing him in turn, reaching a second orgasm in the mere fact of touching him, lying on his belly to feel the chilled member against her groin, moaning with pleasure, thrusting her face into his neck, feeling his fingers rippling through her hair to stroke her scalp. And then at last it was time, for them to come together, for her to recall and once again enjoy that caressing movement, slowly, and limited in entry, gradually building up, to a series of deep stabs which had her heart, her chest, her belly, her mind soaring away into the night sky, sent her breath gasping through her opened mouth and widened nostrils, to mingle with his rushing towards her. This then was what she had waited seventeen years to know.

This was happiness.

She was so happy she wanted to sing. Certainly she no longer wanted to sleep, for all her exhaustion. Lennart loved her. He had waited for her. And he would wait for her. All the long seventeen years that had separated them had been nothing but a purgatory, preparing her for the heaven that lay beyond, preparing her, too, to be a woman of whom any man could be proud. She was that. She knew it, and was proud of it.

And the end was near. She had come from Moscow in less than a month. The army could take very little longer. Surely. For they were on the march before dawn the next morning, re-fording the very river across which she and the children had swum the previous day, forging onwards, filled with the confidence that must come to any force marching behind a commander who has not only never lost a battle, but who has invariably gained his victory at absurd odds, concerned only, it seemed, with the fear that they might take Moscow without having had the opportunity of destroying the Russian army in the field.

That they might take Moscow. Suppose they ever got there. The sudden thaw in early February was followed by a return to the cold, and for a week they marched, slowly but surely. Then it began to rain again. It rained throughout March and it rained throughout April, and the rain became heavier in May and even heavier in June, and the Swedish army became increasingly bogged down, their wagons unable to move unless whole regiments were pulling and pushing. They lived in a sea of mud, which seemed to fill their nostrils, get into their hair, colour every meal. And Lorna suddenly became afraid. Not of the weather. Summers in Russia were often like this, as she reminded both Lennart and the King. Charles, indeed, cared absolutely nothing for the rain, save that it held up his march, and Lennart was a man rejuvenated, able to spare her little time—deliberately, so that his King should not suspect their liaison—but going about his duties with tremendous enthusiasm, and always managing to pass by her wagon at least once in every day, to give her a smile and a wave of his hand, to enjoy the sight of her, to allow her to enjoy the sight of him.

"Oh, I do like him," Michael said one day. "Of all the boors, he is the only one I will not have the Tsar, my father, kill."

Lorna smiled, and hugged him against her. *Poor boy. He could have been Tsar,* she thought. But she never doubted she had done the right thing, and she would glance at Kathleen, who looked at Lennart with a frown whenever she saw him, as she knew what *she* looked like, well enough.

But her fear lurked. Here was the finest army the world had ever seen, so it was claimed, and so she was prepared to believe. But it was an army intended to fight. And instead it was wallowing onwards like some sea creature left stranded by the tide and seeking only to regain the security of its depths. And dwindling, as the sickness inevitable where large bodies of men move together existing on rations accumulated some time before began to drift through the ranks. *Suppose,* she thought, *Peter is not mad, and seeks only to let us march forever, until the last of us dies on the steppe.* But that would mean sacrificing Moscow. And no Tsar could risk the loss of his Holy City. Not even Peter.

She found herself spending more and more time in the company of the King, talking about the Tsar. For Charles was himself starting to wonder whether he would ever manage to catch hold of his adversary. He made her recount everything she could remember about him, everything she could remember about Menshikov, everything she could remember about Russian military discipline and Russian military method, supposing they had any. It was a duty she enjoyed well enough, not only because Lennart was more often than not in attendance, but because she was making herself valuable to this single-minded young man who held all of their futures in the palm of his hand. Charles was certainly not mad, although she would willingly concede, after only a week in his company, that he was obsessed with the destruction of Russia, which he saw as a looming menace which in time would dominate all Europe unless strangled at birth. And being sane, he would in the course of time, when he had won his great victory, be amenable to reason, and she hoped, be anxious to reward her for the part she had played in his triumph.

And in early July, they came to the River Vabitsch. River crosings were the only chance they ever enjoyed of actually encountering Russians, for small detachments were invariably left behind to do what damage they could as the Swedish wagons slowly plodded across the fords, and Charles had taken up sending picked bodies of men ahead of the main army to clear the way and maintain a bridgehead on the farther bank. Competion was high amongst his officers for these commands, which were occasionally costly. When they had crossed the Beresina, Prince Emmanuel had received a severe wound, and had been forced to ride in a wagon for three weeks.

This river appeared to be no different. Even as the army pitched its tents in and around the little village of Holovzin, the rattle of musketry was heard.

"Another battle," Kathleen grumbled. "Is there no end of them?" She was busily lighting the fire in front of their wagon, for she had become the most dedicated frontierswoman. *And why not,* Lorna asked herself? Not only was it in her blood, but if all went well it was a life to which she would eventually return.

"Those aren't battles," Michael said scornfully. "Battles are big things, with lots of men. Those are skirmishes."

"At which men get killed, nonetheless," Lorna pointed out. She hated to hear him in any way sound like the Tsar. And looked up as an orderly tramped through the mud towards her.

"Princess Bogoljubov. His Majesty requests your company to dinner."

"Willingly, sir." She stood up, reached for her cloak. How strange, to dine with a king, and not even ask for time to have a bath, have her hair prepared, have her gowns and her jewels laid out. She wondered if she would ever be able to grace a drawing room again.

"Princess Bogoljubov." The King sat at a table in the open, accompanied by Piper, Rehnskold, Prince Emmanuel, now fully recovered, and Lennart. "How splendid your presence makes the evening." He held a chair for her, next to himself. "Now tell us, did you cross this river on your way?"

"We did indeed, Your Majesty," Lorna said. "But it was frozen over."

"Ah." He poured wine for her. He was himself, as usual, drinking water. "And did you . . ." He looked up as an aide approached.

The man spoke in Swedish, and Lorna could only attempt to interpret what was happening by his actions, and by the reactions of the Swedes. For the young man pointed north and south, and the King's eyes suddenly gleamed, while he threw back his head and laughed like the boy he was. A snap of his fingers produced a map, which was laid on the table, cups and bottles pushed aside, while Charles prodded with his finger, again, and again, and then leaned back, and smiled at them all.

"Your Majesty?" she asked. "May I inquire the reason for your pleasure?"

"You may, Princess," he said. "It appears that our patrols have been fired upon for a distance of several miles each side of this ford."

"But . . ." She gasped for breath.

"Oh, indeed," he smiled. "It means that this can be no mere rearguard action, like the others, but that the Russians army is there, waiting for us to attempt to cross."

"Oh, my God," she said and crossed herself. "And you will cross?"

"I came here to destroy these people."

"But . . . they are entrenched, with a river between. How can you?"

"Look." He prodded the map. "Here is the river, and here is Holovzin, where we are. The ford is opposite, the Russians stretch all the way along the bank. But see where the ford crosses and meets the other side? The ground is no better than a marsh. Therefore it is not defended. My information suggests that it lies between the Russian centre and their right wing."

"But, Your Majesty," she protested. "May that not be a trap, to lure you across, so that they may fall on you while you are limited by the ground?"

"I am sure it is," he agreed. "Supposing I am limited by the ground. Were that the only point I might hesitate. But my scouts report something else of interest. There." He prodded the map again. "That little line is a tributary of the main river, and it again cuts the Russian position, between, I estimate, the centre and the left. What does that mean, Princess?"

"Why, I . . ." She glanced at Lennart, licked her lips.

"It means," Charles said gently, "that we are faced by not one army, but by three. That is the fault in their strategy. They hope to close on us, struggling through the marsh. But, Princess, suppose, having gained the bank, we turn left and launch our force on their right wing? Do you not see that their centre will be delayed in coming up behind us by that very marsh? While their left, to come into the battle, must cross that second river. Supposing we defeat the right wing quickly enough, we may destroy the other two one by one."

"But, sire," she protested. "They will see you crossing the river. How may you reach the other side without their knowing?"

He gave another laugh and got up. "We shall wait for darkness, and we shall do it in silence. It is a risk, Princess. But war is a choice of risks. Now you will excuse us. Gentlemen, to your posts. Midnight."

They saluted, hurried off. Lorna stood up, gazed at Lennart. "Oh, my love," she whispered, forming the words with her mouth. "What will you do?"

He smiled at her. "I shall follow the King, sweetheart."

Follow the King. She peered out of the back of her wagon at the gathering darkness. She had allowed herself to be lulled into a false sense of security by the lack of action these last four months. But Lennart was a Drabant guard. More, he was commander of the regiment. Wherever the King went, it was Lennart's duty to be at his side.

"They will be defeated, Mama," Michael said confidently. "By tonight we shall be reunited with Papa."

She glanced down at him. No doubt she was being the most arrant of all cowards in not telling him the truth. But she did not dare. Suppose they *were* defeated, and they did indeed face Peter by dawn?

"Bed," she said. "It is late. Biddy."

Michael was dragged away to the front of the wagon.

"Rain," Kathleen whispered, as the soft patter commenced on the roof.

"That may be to the good," Lorna said. "It will deaden sound."

"Will we lose, Mama?"

"We?"

"Are these not our only hope?"

"Aye." She squeezed her daughter's hand. "You know we cannot be recaptured?"

"I know that, Mama."

"Well, then . . . oh, God above, I cannot stay here and wait. Come." For all around them there was a great stealthy whispering of sound, as the army was roused, without drum or bugle, but by the touch of a sergeant's hand on each shoulder, and prepared itself. It was quite dark now, the twilight being shrouded by the low clouds and the drizzling rain. They pulled their cloaks around themselves, dropped from the back of the wagon, and stole across the village, ignored by the busy men, obscured by the wet and the gathering darkness, and came suddenly to the end of the houses, to discover the main Swedish force, that which would lead the assault, gathered in an enormous group around their King and his generals, and muttering a verse of the hymn "Our Hope and Trust Is in the Lord." The low murmur of sound drifted through the rain and made Lorna's knees tremble. There was a solemn dedication here she had never known before, a determination, to conquer or die. Suddenly some of the true spirit of this army communicated itself to her, and she realised the secret of their victories, their belief in themselves not less than in their remarkable leader.

Remarkable indeed. For the prayer was ended, and Charles, without a word, turned and walked through

the throng, not drawing his sword, but carrying instead
a cane in his right hand, with which he occasionally
touched the ground. Lennart walked at his heels, with
the other members of the staff behind him. She supposed they were going to take their places at the banks
of the river to oversee the crossing, and her heart descended into her belly with an enormous thump as
she saw them not hesitate for a moment, but descend
the bank and commence wading the river, almost immediately being lost to sight in the rain and the darkness.

"They say he leads into every battle," Kathleen
whispered. "And has never even been wounded."

But what of those at his side? She squeezed Kathleen's hand, and they crawled forward to a position
on the bank itself, where they could oversee the long
blue and yellow line slowly entering the water, each
man holding his musket above his head. How slowly
they moved, for by now it was long past midnight and
to her horror she could see a sudden lightening of the
gloom. But as yet there had been not a sound from
the farther bank, nothing to indicate that the Russians
knew what was happening.

"Mama." Kathleen gripped her shoulder. They could
see trees. And at the same time a single shot echoed
on the morning air. To be followed by an explosion
of noise which sent them both sprawling to the ground
in terror. They lay on their bellies and watched the
water flying into darting foam to either side of the long
column. But now that they could make out the farther
bank, they could also see that a large body of the
Swedes were already there and being formed into a line
by their officers. How she longed for a glass to be able
to identify someone, but they were no more than blue
and yellow dots, every now and then sinking to their

knees and collapsing upon the sodden earth, just as every now and then one fell away from the line and drifted down the river. And all the while not a shot was fired in reply.

"They will be crushed," she moaned. "They cannot survive."

"They do not even cheer," Kathleen muttered. "But look, Mama."

Lorna raised her head, saw the Swedish line moving forward behind fixed bayonets, still in utter silence. But the Russians made enough noise for all. Screams and shouts accompanied the wild volleys, and smoke clouded into the drizzling morning. Then the shots died, and the screams became louder.

"They have been put to flight," Kathleen shouted, scrambling to her feet.

"But look," Lorna begged. "Oh, my God."

They clutched each other's hands. Trotting up from the right was an enormous cloud of horsemen, dispatched clearly from the Russian centre to go to the aid of the right wing, indeed, to close the trap, as the Swedish infantry was still engaged and the cavalry, deputed to cross last because of the noise the horses might make, were still in midstream. Only some four hundred of them were actually on the east bank, but even at this distance Lorna could make out the splendid uniform of Field Marshal Rehnskold. Four hundred, against not less than ten thousand, she estimated.

"They are going to charge," Kathleen said. "They are going to charge," she shrieked.

Rehnskold was out in front, his sword drawn and pointing at the enemy. And now at last a cheer came, a long howl of joy which quite obliterated the "oora" of the Russians. But four hundred charging ten thousand? Lorna found herself clutching her throat, as the blue and yellow smashed into the green and white, disappeared into the midst of the trembling banners, the waving swords and lances. *I will crush him, like a nut,* Peter had said. How could he do otherwise, with such a superiority of numbers?

She crossed herself and stared, in incredulous amazement as the blue and yellow phalanx, diminished, but still a force, emerged from the rear of the Russians, and immediately drew rein to turn their horses for another charge. If they could catch their enemies. The Russians fled in every direction. Some hurtled into the bog, to become encumbered and be bayoneted by the next regiment of Swedish infantry to arrive. Others hurled their horses into the river itself, to be carried downstream amidst the crack of muskets, for having gained the day the Swedes were now being allowed to use their pieces. But the most were fleeing east, following the clouds of unhappy infantry who could now also be seen, flooding up the slopes beyond the river.

"Holy Mother," Kathleen said. "What will they say of such a victory, Mama?"

Lorna hugged her. "Why, they will say very little of Holovzin, my darling. Charles gains victories like this every time he fights."

# Chapter 14

Yet she asked the same question of Lennart, when he finally returned, to give the orders for the baggage train to cross the river. "Lennart," she whispered. Although she had never doubted, once the battle was over, that he would have survived.

"Princess."

She glanced from right to left. They stood in the shade of her wagon. "Lennart." And was in his arms, feeling his fingers tracing her ribs in search of her breasts.

Before separating again, to stand decorously at attention. "You will see my master is a man of his word."

"Oh, yes," she cried. "What now—Moscow?"

He sighed. "Alas, Princess, our scouts report that the country is even more devastated beyond this river. And we are down to a week's supply of food."

She gasped, remembering her own situation in February. "What is to be done?"

He smiled. "You have naught to fear, Princess. Our King has campaigned too long to be disturbed by so minor a matter. No doubt we could charge for Moscow. But that would be dangerous, with our commissariat low, and with this unceasing rain slowing our footsteps. His Majesty would not wish to be caught before the city by a sudden frost, with empty saddlebags. Besides, we have suffered considerable casualties during this march. No, no, we have been ordered to turn aside and march south."

"South?" she cried.

"For the Ukraine," he explained. "The Ukraine is a vast granary. There we will rest the winter, restoring our healths and our saddlebags, in preparation for the decisive conflict next summer. And there, too, we will await reinforcements. General Lewenhaupt is on his way now to join us, with twelve thousand men, and a wagon train of arms and ammunition."

"Next summer," she whispered. "Another year? Lennart . . ."

"This is possibly the most decisive campaign in the history of Europe, my love," he said, forgetting caution at her obvious distress. "It can be no easy, no speedy matter. And having waited so long, my darling, can we not wait another year?"

A year. She had supposed Holovzin the end of the matter. But as she had said so confidently to Kathleen, it was no more than an episode, to these people, to their King.

"Besides," Lennart said. "There is another reason, most secret. My King does not fight with his sword alone. All this year he has been carrying on negotiations with Mazeppa. You have heard of him?"

She nodded. Who had not heard of the fabulous Ivan Stephanovitch Mazeppa, the page boy who had seduced a queen of Poland, and for his crime been bound naked to the back of a horse and cast loose on the steppe, to be rescued by the Cossacks and rise to the position of Hetman, or King, of those tremendous savage horsemen.

"Well, now they are come to fruition," Lennart said. "Mazeppa has long been antagonistic to the Tsar, who claims suzerainty over the Cossacks. Now he has determined to break with him, and invites us to make our winter headquarters his own capital city, Baturin. Next year, my love, we shall match the Russians in numbers, with the Cossacks in our Army. And as we already beat them at odds of ten to one, why, that will surely be the end of the matter."

*The end of the matter. Mazeppa, Lewenhaupt, Charles. And the rain.*

"Don't you believe me?" he asked.

"I wish I could. Lennart, this rain, this endless, unceasing rain. I have lived ten years in Russia, and I have not known a summer like this."

"You'll not pretend to be superstitious?" He smiled.

"Oh, I am. I cannot help but suppose the very elements fight against us. That fortune has in some way deserted our side."

He laughed. "Then we shall defeat the elements as well, Princess. You may depend upon it. As for fortune, His Majesty does not recognise the word. His fortune is his own right arm."

No sooner had the Swedish army turned south than Mazeppa rode into camp, taking everyone by surprise, for he had been supposed to await them in Baturin. There was a hasty blowing of bugles and calling out of a guard of honour, and Lorna and Kathleen and Michael peered from the back of their wagon, the women in dismay as they discovered less than four thousand men instead of the thirty thousand who were supposed to accompany the Hetman everywhere. But it was unimportant, he assured them at dinner. He had merely come to ask the Swedes to make haste, as he had received news that his treachery had become known to the Tsar, and Prince Menshikov himself was hurrying on Baturin with an army, intent on keeping Charles from so valuable a base. Lorna could only gaze at the old man in disappointment. Because he *was* an old man, wizened, ancient, and timorous, in unbelievable contrast to the epic figure of legend. He trembled all the while, and wine ran down his chin.

Even Charles took this news seriously and commanded double marches. The Swedish army scarcely stopped at all, observing now that they were overseen by a screen of Russian horsemen, clinging to their flanks like the wolves who had followed her own journey from Moscow, Lorna thought. Her depression grew. Something was going wrong, and Charles knew it, despite his confidence, his certainty that he would win, only supposing he could see his enemies before him.

And on a September morning she was awakened by the stench of decaying flesh, brought to them by the dawn breeze.

"My God, Mama," Kathleen said. "Whatever can that be?"

But she knew, and dressed herself with tight lips, and sat behind the horses as the soldiers drove them onwards, and watched that shattered, burning ruin rising out of the plain. Baturin had been razed to the ground as effectually as that village south of Smolensk, how many centuries ago. But here the destruction had been extended to every man, every woman, and every child, saving only that there was an absence of male corpses between the ages of fourteen and twenty; these had been carried off for recruitment into the Russian army.

Charles rode slowly round the ruin, accompanied by his staff and by Lorna. And sighed. "This place would have been impregnable, properly defended," he remarked.

"My lord King," Mazeppa protested. "I did what I thought best."

"I have no doubt you did, Hetman," Charles agreed. "And no man can do more than that." He turned his horse back for the Swedish camp without another word, but surely his heart must be filled with despair and disgust, Lorna thought, for here was his most valued ally now nothing more than a fugitive in his army, and a worthless fugitive as well, for clearly his desertion of Baturin, his desertion of his people to a horrible fate, had been a result of his own terror of the very name of Peter the Tsar.

"Your Majesty," Lorna asked at dinner. "What will you do?"

"Do, madam? You are the most confounded pessimist I have ever encountered, far worse than my own sister. Believe me, Princess, I grieve the loss of so many brave men. But they can have no effect upon our plans. I have here more than sufficient to shatter the Russians, whenever they choose to stand. And besides, there is always Lewenhaupt."

And in October Lewenhaupt caught up with them. But with not more than six thousand men left out of the twelve with whom he had started, and not a baggage wagon left. He had been ambushed by the main Russian army under the command of Peter himself, and had only fought his way through at the cost of tremendous casualties.

"Well, well," the King remarked, having made not

the slightest criticism of his stricken general, but rather invited him to meet the Princess Bogoljubov at dinner. "It seems that the madman is contriving to learn something about the art of warfare after all. And about time, too. I would not have him run from the field at the first shot, when finally we meet. He has done so before, and how may I kill or capture a man who behaves like that?" He beamed at them.

His officers stared gloomily at their wine, and Lorna drank some of hers. But if they dared not speak, surely it was her duty. "Your Majesty," she said. "May a mere woman offer an opinion?"

"Of course, Princess."

"It is that you abandon this campaign and return to Poland, Sire." She bit her lip, as he frowned. "I have other information, Your Majesty, which I did not previously offer. I fled the Tsar, I fled my husband, I fled my home, not merely because of a fall from favour, but because I had become involved in a plot, inspired by the Tsarvitch, to dispose of his father."

"You admit that to me, madam?" His voice was cold. "No man, and no woman, should betray his or her rightful king. You *should* have been executed."

She refused to lower her gaze. "Nonetheless, Sire, I escaped, and I tell you now, the people of Russia grow daily more opposed to the Tsar's madness, to the unending misery he inflicts upon them."

"Then you but support my reasons for continuing to inflict that misery."

"But, Sire, it will be inflicted whether you remain or not. The Tsar will fall, whether you remain or not. And your people will surely die if you remain. While, God forbid, but should you ever be defeated . . ."

"I? Defeated?"

"If it should happen, Sire," she insisted, "can you

not see that at a stroke all opposition to Peter must be wiped away? He will be a hero, instead of a tyrant."

"I? Defeated?" he repeated. "Come, come, Princess. Admit the truth. You fled your husband in search of some more congenial life, and you are disgusted with continual campaigning, continual discomfort. Women are ever so, a source of weakness. But even you, Princess, must enjoy wintering in the Ukraine. There is grain for ourselves, fodder for our horses, trees and birds and blue sky for all. Even you will be happy there, Princess."

*Even I,* she thought, sitting on the ground behind her wagon, stitching industriously, as they all had to, for their clothes were threadbare. But it was a glorious December afternoon. The rain had been left behind, and the sun descended into an expanse of empty steppe. This was how Russia should be. This reminded her of the Bogoljubov estates, way to the east, almost in the shadow of the Urals. In surroundings like these she had obtained what happiness had been found in Russia.

The army was relaxed, spread over a considerable distance, the horses contentedly grazing, the men lounging on the grass, talking, smoking their pipes, and, as ever, polishing their steel. They were rejuvenated, by only a month of comfortable living. They would be more than a match for the Russians when next they met, for all their dwindling numbers. As their enemies no doubt knew. Menshikov's horsemen clung to their perimeter, overlooked them in their cantonments, and departed at speed whenever the Swedes would challenge their presence.

And Peter? Did he rant and rave, scream and shout, strangle those forced to share his bed? What of Martha and Vassily, back in Moscow? What of the pie seller himself, licking his wounds after his defeat at Holovzin? They seemed so far away, here in this endless pasture. She was realising that for the first time since James Butler had ridden into her life, eighteen years ago, now, she was knowing absolute peace, surrounded by her children, surrounded by her friends, surrounded by her lover. And today she was thirty-four years of age.

"So they were defeated," Michael insisted, still arguing Swedish tactics.

"They were not," Kathleen argued. "It was a strategic withdrawal."

Her marriage had been a problem in Moscow. What sort of a problem had it become here, Lorna worried. For she was seventeen, older than *she* had been when the girl had been born. And happily innocent, as perhaps a girl should be.

But would she have changed a moment of her life? Her immediate answer was yes, when she thought of herself lying beneath Butler, trembling before the Tsar in his Smolensk hut, chained to the floor of his torture chamber, or wallowing in the snow while two men had made at her at the same time. But would she? Would she be herself, without a single one of those experiences? Would she have this serenity of spirit, this confidence that whatever needed to be done, she would do it without hesitation? Papa had told her to do that, years ago. And while doing it, be happy.

"Oh, you," Michael declared. "They were defeated, weren't they, Mama?"

Lorna ruffled his hair. "It was a draw," she said, smiling at them both, then getting to her feet as she saw the officers approaching. She had expected them earlier. Now she smoothed her skirt and ran her hands over her hair. *What would Mistress Bracknell say, she wondered, or Mistress Smiley. Or even more, Queen Anne, or Sarah Churchill.* What had happened to the girl they had groomed and dressed and preened to elegance? Who was this simple grey-clad figure, with the mane of undressed titian hair drifting down her back; it had not been trimmed in over a year, and she could envisage it stretching to the ground, should this campaign last much longer.

"Your Majesty." She sank into a curtsey.

"Princess. I am informed that today is your birthday."

She straightened. "That is so, Majesty."

"My congratulations. You shall spend your next one in Moscow, I do promise you. And I am afraid I must ask you to wait for your gift until that happy day, when I shall make it up to you, that is also a promise." He looked away from her, flushing as he always did when forced to speak with her on anything but military matters. "What a pretty domestic scene. Your children are well?"

"Indeed, Sire. The open air suits them."

He nodded, peered at Michael, and frowned, while Lorna's heart pounded. "That lad reminds me of someone."

"Of Prince Bogoljubov, perhaps, Sire," she suggested.

"Ah. I have never met the fellow. But you have a puzzling family, Highness. Your daughter reminds me of someone also, but someone quite different. Ah, well, 'tis of no great matter. You'll dine with me, madam. Perhaps the young lady would also grace our table."

"Your Majesty?" Lorna gazed past him at Lennart in surprise.

"Why not? Two beautiful women? I have neglected

you, Princess. And you, Lady Kathleen. Christmas will soon be upon us. We will show you how we celebrate Christmas in the Swedish army."

As darkness fell, the clouds drew lower, and the evening became still colder. The evenings had, indeed, steadily been growing more chilly over the past month. But then, winter approached. This army had survived winter far to the north, on the road to Moscow. They would find little to cause them discomfort down here in the Ukraine.

But Lorna and Kathleen drew the shawls the more tightly about their shoulders as they made their way through the camp to the royal tent, although once within, all was cheer, with an enormous log fire blazing, around which the tables had been arranged to form a square. Kathleen was invited to sit on the King's left, and Lorna on his right, with Lennart on her right. "For I have eyes in my head," Charles said and gave a brief laugh. "As I can see your eyes fill with pleasure whenever you look upon this Scot of mine."

Lorna flushed and glanced at Lennart.

"So now," Charles said, himself filling her glass with wine, and to her surprise, adding a little to his own. "When you claim you knew the fellow before, what you really meant was that he was your lover, eh?"

"Sire?" she asked, feeling her cheeks burn, and once again glancing at Lennart. "Sire, as you are so discerning . . ." She felt the presure of Lennart's hand on her knee, under the table, warning her. Surely he was wrong. No doubt he knew his monarch better than she, but her instincts told her now was the time.

Now had been the time; Charles had made his sally for the evening. "You are a beautiful woman, Princess Bogoljubov," he said. "But when you blush, you are superb. I feel sorry for the Prince, indeed I do, at having lost you, if only temporarily." He rose to his feet. "Gentlemen and mademoiselle," as he turned to Kathleen. "I give you Lorna of Morne, Princess Bogoljubov."

They rose to drink her health, and she smiled at them all, her eyes filling with tears, as it was the first time there had been such a celebration since she had left England, and perhaps not since she had left Maryland.

"And now," said the King. "Let us eat." For the Swedes were very nearly as hearty trenchermen as the Russians. This night, the King's chief interest, for all his compliments, lay in Kathleen, who was certainly more his own age. *How amazing,* Lorna thought, *that my daughter could possibly be made Queen of Sweden, after having been invited to share the throne of Russia. But why not? She is at once beautiful and well born. And more than that. She is Kathleen MacMahon.*

Again the pressure on her knee, and she glanced at Lennart. "We have been indiscreet," he said in English.

"Indiscreet?" she demanded, saw his frown. "I think we are too cautious, Lennart. I think, were we boldly to assail this obstacle . . ."

"We would fail, and very likely never see each other again."

"And suppose," she said quietly, "I say that I can wait no longer, my love. They say the weather never turns really cold down here. What is to stop us taking a few horses and riding west? Having escaped from the Kremlin, I do not doubt my ability to escape your King."

"I have no doubt you could," he said. "But what of my oath?"

"Men and their oaths," she sighed.

"I swore," he said. "By everything I hold dear, saving yourself, my love, to serve and obey this king for as long as he should need me. And can you doubt, in the midst of a campaign being waged in a hostile country, that he needs his Drabants more than ever, and their commander more than anyone else." He smiled. "Do you know, I thought we would quarrel. And we have never yet done that."

"I shall not quarrel with you, Lennart. I understand your duty to your King, as I understand my duty to my children. I but feel . . . oh, Lennart, I am so lonely for your love." She discovered she was the only one speaking, and looked around her with a flush. "Your Majesty?"

"I wish I knew something of that barbarous tongue you speak," Charles said. "Perhaps you will teach me?"

"We . . . we remembered old friends, Sire," she said. And observed that the meal was at an end, with only fresh bottles of wine being placed on the shattered table. She stood up. "And I see that you gentlemen are now preparing really to enjoy yourselves. If you will excuse us, Sire . . ."

"Ah, madam," said Prince Emmanuel. "May not your charming daughter stay?"

"Oh, let her stay, madam," said another officer. "I do assure you she will come to no harm."

"Let me stay, Mama. Please," Kathleen said. Her cheeks were flushed, and she had drunk a great deal of wine. But she was two years older than Lorna had been when she had met Lennart, after having known Butler.

She looked at the King. "Sire?"

"Oh, please let her stay, Princess. I would you also would do so. It is your birthday."

"I am tired, Your Majesty, I wish to retire." She gazed full into his eyes. "But perhaps you would permit General Munro to walk me back to my wagon."

The faintest of frowns appeared between the King's eyes and then suddenly cleared again. "It is your birthday, Princess. In my camp, you have but to ask, and it shall be given you. General Munro, you are commanded." He sat down again. "Be sure the lady has no cause to complain of you."

Lorna awoke with a start, into utter blackness. For a moment she was not even sure where she was, then the feel of Lennart's body against her reassured her, and in the same moment gave her heart a throb of alarm. He usually left the wagon well before dawn, and all around her was sound, men shouting, and she could not see.

Then she realised that although she was awake, her eyes were still shut. Frantically she rubbed them, dissolved the frozen mucus, blinked in the sudden daylight at Lennart, also awakening, at Kathleen sitting up in her blanket—she must have crawled past them last night without being aware of it—and at the icicles hanging from the back of the wagon.

"My God." She thrust aside the flap, stared at the camp, at the sudden whiteness which had obliterated everything else, in horror at the sentry, who having completed his march, had leaned against a tree, perhaps to rest, and had fallen asleep, and now remained sitting there, face blue, hands rigidly attached to the butt of his musket.

Lennart was reaching for his clothes, glancing at Kathleen.

"Be careful, I beg of you," Lorna whispered. "It must be far below freezing."

He buckled his belt, continued to stare at Kathleen.

"General Munro is your father, Kathleen."

"My . . ." Kathleen frowned, and then her forehead cleared.

"But . . ."

"I should not be here, at this moment, to be sure," Lennart agreed. He reached across, squeezed her hands.

"Perhaps it will be possible for us to be togther, soon." He dropped from the back of the wagon, his feet crunching on the frost. Kathleen crawled to kneel beside her mother.

"Mama," she said, throwing her arms round her neck. "I am so happy for you. So very happy." She kissed her on the nose. "For me too. He is such a lovely man. But . . ." She was looking outside for the first time, at men of whom Lennart had taken immediate command, hurrying forward to remove the dead sentry. "What has happened?"

"Winter has arrived," Lorna said quietly. "Even in the Ukraine."

A winter which had no parallel in all recorded history, in which the wine froze so solid in its casks it burst the iron hoops, and birds fell dead as they flew through the air. While men, like the sentry, died at their posts, their saliva freezing as they opened their mouths. For the first time in Swedish memory the Christmas services were abandoned, as the army huddled in its cantonments, and prayed for the coming of spring.

So then, Lorna realised, as she dressed Michael and Kathleen in every last garment, forbade them even to risk relieving themselves save in the bucket inside the wagon for fear of frostbite, that endless rain was indeed a portent of disaster. And yet, the calamity which seemed to have overtaken them, which seemed to have overtaken the entire world, would pass, and this army would triumph as it had before. She did not doubt this now. Like everyone else, having seen King Charles in battle, having watched him ford the Vabitsch armed with no more than a cane, having listened to him calmly and accurately put his finger on the enemy weaknesses, having heard him outline his plans and carry out these plans to the letter, having seen him shrugging off disappointment and indeed disaster, she had fallen beneath the spell of his invincibility. It required no more than for the King to point, as he had always done, and victory would still be theirs.

So long as the King remained the King. For several weeks Lorna saw little of him; the business of everyone in the Swedish army was to keep warm, to resist frostbite, to stay alive until the thaw. Which came in March. At the first sign that the terrible frost might be over, orders were given to break camp, the Swedes had lost too many people and were down to their very last rations. But not far away was the fortified city of Viprek, where food and shelter could be obtained, and the army given another opportunity to recuperate.

Viprek was commanded by an Englishman in Russian service, but he had a very small force under him, and so Charles summoned him to surrender under threat of hoisting the black flag. He refused, and there was nothing for it but to carry the place. Now there was nothing unusual in this, and the King, who had stormed many a fortress in the past, as Lennart assured Lorna, and far stronger than this, was a master at reducing such obstacles with as little loss of life as possible, calling off his assault and switching his tactics the very moment a quick success was not to be had. On this occasion, to the amazement of his officers, he let the assault continue, so that the women and children in the camp were forced to watch a bloody battle in which not all the Swedish elan could stand them in any stead, as they swarmed up the fascines only to be repulsed time and again by the Russians, fighting like very devils under the eye of their foreign leader. When finally Charles called a halt, the Swedes had suffered more casualties than in any battle under his command, and for no reward at all, as by this time the town was so battered and burning it could no longer be used for any purpose whatsoever. This being so, the garrison now offered to surrender.

Lorna was terrified that the King, angered by his losses, both in men and material, might seek to implement his hideous threat of no quarter, but he merely bowed and accepted the offered swords.

Yet that he had changed was obvious to all.

"Perhaps it was the cold," Lennart said. "Perhaps it is the endless campaigning. I do not know. He never smiles. Not even in action. Why, you remember that hullabaloo the other day? We were out in reconnaissance, King Charles at our head, and some Russian horsemen approached too close. At least a regiment, and we were no more than the staff with a score of Drabants. And do you know, they had got between us and the camp, so I gave the order to charge, and cut our way through them. Which we did, easily enough. And Charles was there in our midst. And never a smile. Why, a year ago he would have been laughing like a madman."

Lorna sighed. "He is going through a period of depression, that is all. For God's sake, are we not all depressed at this interminable war, this interminable country? But you . . ." She rested her hand on his arm. "You should not expose yourself to such danger."

"It is my duty."

"And to us?" But she smiled and would not press the matter. "The King will be well, like us all, once the weather improves."

Supposing it ever would. For now came the real thaw, which she found worse even than the frost, as not a day passed without a thunderstorm to churn the ground into a quagmire and leave them all continually damp where before they had been continually frozen.

The sodden state of the ground was the more unfortunate as once again it seemed there was a Russian army close by. The skirmish with the cavalry in which Lennart had covered himself with glory had been but a pointer to the presence of increasing numbers of troops, and Charles, indeed recovering his spirits at the prospect of at last bringing an end to the war, called out his army in battle array and marched away from Viprek. But just as the Russians were sighted, also drawn up for battle, down came the rain for a whole week, at the end of which time the enemy had melted away.

For the first time in several months Lorna and Kathleen were that night invited to the King's tent for dinner, but in total contrast to previous occasions this was a solemn affair in which the King throughout the meal did no more than sip a glass of water.

His officers and guests ate little and conversed in whispers, afraid to break in on whatever thoughts were chasing each other through that remarkable mind. Lorna, seated as usual on his right, was afraid to eat at all, but drank a deal of wine to settle her nerves. Then suddenly the King sat up straight and set down his goblet with a crash.

"Gentlemen," he said.

There was instant silence.

"And ladies." He smiled at Lorna and Kathleen; it was the first time anyone had seen him smile since Lorna's birthday. "This war goes on too long. The very elements continue to oppose us too resolutely. And why? It seems to me that I have been fighting this campaign as Peter might have outlined it for me, had he been sitting at this table. I chase, and he runs. But he runs to his own hearth. I run from camp to camp, and scarce a day passes but a man or a horse dies. We number no more than twenty thousand men. Twenty thousand days, and the last one of us will perish. That is no way to win."

He paused, sipped some water, and beamed at them. "So it occurs to me that I must oppose Peter with his own weapons. I must bring him to me. And how shall I do that?" He did not wait for an answer. "I had supposed it must be in defence of his holy city of Moscow. But in this climate I find it impossible to get there. So let us look elsewhere. I have done that, gentlemen. What, after Moscow, would Peter find it impossible to let us possess? A place, gentlemen, where he has created a military arsenal, a fortress which, if I possessed, I could use as an impregnable base, filled with every possible weapon of war, with food and munitions to last a lifetime. Gentlemen, my scouts have located such a place."

"But, Your Majesty," Count Piper protested. "If it is so impregnable, so armed, how may we take it?"

"I doubt we can," Charles said. "Yet will the threat, the possibility, bring Peter to its relief. It must."

Field Marshal Rehnskold cleared his throat, clearly annoyed at not having been taken into the King's confidence before now. "And may we inquire the name of this fabulous city, Sire?"

Charles grinned at him, at them all, and then stood up. "We march tomorrow. On Poltava."

Poltava was situated on the western bank of a river known as the Vorskla, and here the Swedish army arrived in the first week of May. For all its reputation as a magazine, it did not look a terribly strong place, and Lennart's first doubt, as he confided to Lorna, was that the King's plans must necessarily go astray right at the beginning, as the experienced Swedish engineers would very rapidly breach the walls.

But once having made a decision, Charles never

lacked the will to carry it out. He entrusted the task to his siegemaster, General Gyllenbrook, clearly so that such word as reached Peter would suggest that he was in deadly earnest about taking the place, but instead of allowing him to use Swedes in his trenches, he allotted him a force of Zaporagian Cossacks whom Mazeppa had managed to enlist. Presumably these wild horsemen were the bravest of the brave when charging an enemy; they were the most arrant cowards when forced to dig and cart under fire, and constantly broke and fled, all of which would have driven Gyllenbrook mad with despair had he not been a party to the royal plan.

As for the King, he had totally regained his humour, and his dinner parties became nightly affairs. "After all, my dear Princess," he said to Lorna, "could you be better placed? Here we have a warm sun, green fields, all the fruit and grain we can eat, all the meat too, and just a distant rumble of gunfire to keep my men happy. Truly, I would suppose that should Peter not come, my army will have quite dissipated in luxury by the autumn."

Lorna smiled and drank some wine. His enthusiasm was infectious, as his genius was infectious, as his dedication was infectious. She had met not a man like him in her entire life and was only sorry that his interest in Kathleen was clearly no more than common politeness. Yet she could not shake off the sense of looming disaster which seemed to have taken hold of her. Or perhaps it was just the certainty that the Russians were indeed coming. Every day revealed more and more of their horsemen on the east bank of the river, watching the Swedes through their glasses and soon bringing up cannon to hurl shot at the Swedish camp. To which the Swedes did not reply; although it was certainly part of Charles's plan to convince Peter that he was low on munitions and thus *had* to take Poltava or perish, the fact was that the Swedes did *not* possess sufficient powder to fight more than one battle.

But still there was no sign that Peter himself had joined the army, and the Swedish command thought it unlikely that the Russians would risk a general engagement without the presence of the Tsar. "Detestable fellow," Charles proclaimed at luncheon on the 17th June, a very special day, for it was the King's own twenty-seventh birthday, and the Swedish camp was in gala dress.

"He will come, Your Majesty," Lennart said and rose to propose the loyal toast, to which the generals responded with tears in their eyes, and even Lorna felt her knees a trifle weak. This time last year they had been ploughing through the mud and rain on their way to Holovzin. Since then they seemed to have made no progress, save southwards, farther and farther away from either their homes or their goal. She supposed they might develop into a nomad host, like that of Genghis Khan, marching forever, fighting forever.

"Let us hope he does so soon," Charles said and smiled at them. "Gentlemen, shall we make our parade?" For it was his custom, every afternoon, to inspect the river, just, he said, to annoy the Russians. "Princess, will you not accompany me, as it is my birthday?"

"It will be my pleasure, Sire," Lorna agreed, although she insisted Kathleen return to their wagon. The Russians were apt to fire at them, and although their aim was invariably bad, there was always the risk of a ricochet.

The staff mounted, Lorna riding sidesaddle next to the King, and made their way down to the river, where indeed a brisk musketry duel was in progress, some of the Russian videttes having actually crossed the water to engage the Swedish patrols.

"Hello," the King said. "These fellows seem to be braver than their comrades." He turned his horse and trotted towards the scene of the fighting. Lorna hesitated, glancing at Lennart, for she could see spurts of dust where stray bullets were flicking the ground close to the King. He raised his eyebrows and followed his master, but she decided to wait where she was, remaining with two orderlies while the King advanced almost to the river itself, then abruptly swung his horse and rode back to her. "Hot work," he said, giving a brief smile. "But futile on both sides."

He seemed, with alarming suddenness, to have lost his humour, and Lorna debated begging leave to return to the camp, but already he was riding towards the siege works to inspect them, and his staff was following. She was not going to return to the camp alone, just in case she encountered a Russian patrol. The only thing in life she still feared was the prospect of in any way being forced to face Peter again.

The staff was gathered in a group, every man with his telescope out, peering at the distant city, no one concerned with Lorna as she walked her horse towards them. They made a strange picture, she thought, for the splendour of their uniforms had long faded, their braid had tarnished, while their swords were even showing signs of rust. But no doubt they were still sharp, as their horses remained full of energy, as . . . She gaped at them in horror. A pool of blood was gathering beneath the King's mount.

She kicked her horse forward. "Your Majesty," she screamed. "You are hit."

He turned towards her, his face suddenly pale and drawn. "Hush, Princess. Would you alarm the men?"

But the general officers had also looked down.

"Sire," Lennart protested.

"Oh, not you as well," Charles grumbled. " 'Tis no more than a flick."

"None the less, Sire," Lennart protested. "It must be dressed. Even a flesh wound can fester in this climate."

"Oh, bah." But he turned his horse. "Women," he grumbled, as he passed Lorna, kicked his horse into a canter, and suddenly tumbled to the ground.

*Just like Father Simeon,* Lorna thought. *Just like Father Simeon.*

She leapt from her saddle, joined the men round the King. But he was not dead, although he had lost a great deal of blood. The ball had entered the front of his left foot and passed right through, smashing several small bones before lodging in the heel. It was easily removed, and there was every prospect that the King would be able to sit a horse, and perhaps even walk within a few more weeks. Unfortunately the weather had by now grown extremely warm; by morning infection had set in, and rumour swept the encampment that the King was dying.

Lorna was horrified at the effect the disaster had on the Swedes. These men were veterans, but only of Charles. They had followed him as a boy of sixteen into Denmark, and then to Narva, where he had gained that remarkable victory in a snowstorm. From that moment they had counted him invincible, and more, immortal, for although ever leading his men from the very forefront of battle he had never suffered so much as a scratch. Without question they had followed him thousands of miles away from their homes, through weather of unimaginable cruelty, until they were almost exactly in the centre of the largest land mass in the world, surrounded on every side by enemies, and yet never doubting that they would conquer in the end.

But only so long as Charles was at their head. Men who had always scoffed at danger and imminent disaster now could think of nothing better than a lifetime of Russian imprisonment. The Cossacks, indeed, deserted without further hesitation, and some undoubtedly went to the enemy commanders with their tremendous information, for the very next day the whole Russian army began to cross the Vorskla. The moment for which the Swedes had worked and waited for so long had arrived. But twenty-four hours too late.

"Mama," Kathleen whispered. "What is to become of us?"

For Michael was quite delighted.

"We have triumphed over greater odds," Lorna declared. But that night she primed five pistols and placed them beside her bed. It was, at the end, come to that.

However, the King did not die. Only two days after his collapse, to the relief of the entire army, he was carried through their ranks in a litter, looking terribly pale and weak, but still alive, and able to think, and to plan, although not to command in the field. This honour was passed to Field Marshal Rehnskold, to achieve the victory for which Charles had dreamed for so many years. For although some forty thousand Russians had by now forded the river, they obviously had no intention of attacking the twenty thousand Swedes, but instead went into a fortified camp. Yet they were there, with the fast-running Vorskla at their backs, and therefore with no option but to accept battle should it be forced upon them.

"Their position is stronger than it looks, however, gentlemen," Charles said at dinner, ten days after his wound, and after his scouts had carried out a detailed investigation of the Russian fortifications. Lennart spread the map on the table, pinning the edges with half-empty wine bottles; as this was a private council of war, only Rehnskold, Gyllenbrook, and Lorna were present, apart from the King and the commander of his bodyguard. "You'll see that the defensive is really forced upon them, because of this marsh here, caused by this stream flowing into the river itself, which prevents them from mounting an assault to the relief of Poltava, but at the same time prevents us crossing to assail them in any force. I doubt they will permit us another Holovzin, gentlemen." He gave a brief smile. "Only on the western flank is the ground firm enough to reach them in force, and here, I am informed, they have constructed redoubts, six in a line extending west from the head of the marsh . . ." He marked them with little crosses on the map. ". . . and four at right angles to the first, extending towards our position." He made another little line of crosses.

"But, Sire," protested Rehnskold. "Then it is impossible to surprise them."

"Ah," Charles said. "There is more to surprise than the place. Gyllenbrook?"

The engineer scratched his head.

"Munro?"

"Ah . . ." Lennart looked at Lorna.

"You'll not put my generals to shame, Princess?"

Lorna wished she too could scratch her head. "By time, Sire?"

"Sometimes. But you may be sure these redoubts are ever manned, ever alert. But gentlemen, Princess, what about method?"

"Sire?" they asked together.

"Think about it," he said. "The Russians know where we must come. They also know, or think they know, that these redoubts, engaging our forces, will give them ample warning of our assault. But, gentlemen, suppose we attack the redoubts, as they intend, but do not waste time in taking them and simply march between them and fall upon the main Russian body."

They stared at him. *How simple,* Lorna thought, *is the reasoning of genius.*

"You cannot, Sire," Gyllenbrook protested. " 'Tis against . . ." He glanced at Rehnskold.

"All the rules of war, to leave fortified posts in one's rear when carrying out a frontal assault?" Charles asked very quietly.

"The redoubts are not two hundred yards apart, Sire," Rehnskold said. "We shall suffer terrible losses."

"More than if we remain here through another winter?" Charles inquired. "I would have you think logically, gentlemen. Think of our advantages. We know the Russians are the worst marksmen in the world. We also know that a Russian merely has to *feel* he is not winning, and he will run. But there is another point, which modesty forbids me to mention. Princess?" He smiled at her.

Lorna knew what he meant. "The Russians know you are wounded, Sire," she said. "Therefore they suppose that the battle will be fought with more caution, more orthodoxy, than the Swedes have shown in the past. Whereas, if the assault is carried out more impetuously than *ever* before, they will assume your wound is indeed slight, that you are at the head of your men, and that they must be defeated."

Charles's smile widened into a grin, and to her consternation he threw his arm round her shoulder to hug her against him. "Princess, had you not proved it before, I would now proclaim to the world, you are an unusual woman, in every way."

"And I will command, Sire?" Rehnskold asked.

"Of course."

"I am a cavalryman."

"Unsurpassed," Charles agreed. "You will command the cavalry and the army. Lewenhaupt will command the infantry, under your general orders."

Lorna saw Lennart and Rehnskold exchange glances; everyone knew that Rehnskold and Lewenhaupt loathed each other.

But Charles was too pleased with himself to consider that point. "Gentlemen, you have my plan. You have but to carry it out."

Midnight, on Sunday, 27th June, 1709. Remarkably, Lorna realized she had slept, and behind her were the faint snufflings of Michael, the steady deep breathing of Kathleen. Like every noncombatant in the Swedish army, they were unaware that anything would happen this day. The King had commanded total secrecy.

But only the noncombatants. For all around her Lorna could hear the gigantic stealthy rustle of the soldiers being roused from their slumbers, and told to prepare their weapons. They too had no idea what was about to happen, that many of them must die.

She heard the clip clop of hooves, moving towards the wagon. She raised the flap, looked out. Her heart no longer pounded wildly, but rather seemed to slow. They were together now, almost as man and wife, and he was riding off to battle.

He leaned from the saddle to take her hand, raise it to his lips. "You'll take care, Lorna. And stay close. There may be stragglers."

"And will you take care, Lennart?"

He smiled; she saw the flash of his teeth in the darkness. "The best safety for a soldier lies in not thinking about safety. This will not take long. I will be with you for breakfast."

He squeezed her hand, rode away.

"Mama?" Kathleen whispered. "What is happening?"

"I had thought you asleep."

"On such a night? Is there to be a battle?"

"*The* battle, sweetheart." And now her heart was starting to pound.

"Mama . . ." Kathleen's voice trembled.

"Aye," Lorna agreed. They had overseen Holovzin. Perhaps they had brought the Swedes fortune. And how could they not oversee this battle. *The* battle. "Quiet, though."

The night was warm. There was no need for even a shawl; Lorna merely dropped her gown over her nightdress and climbed down from the rear of the wagon, feet bare. Already the immediate vicinity was deserted, save for anxious women, calling from tent to tent. How good the grass felt, under her bare feet.

She went round to the front of the wagon, where the cart horse was tethered, grazing, as he had been awakened by the noise. Kathleen was at her elbow. "This? We have no saddle."

"We do not need a saddle." Lorna held the reins, swung her legs across, sat astride. She was back on MacMahon's again, and the animal was named Paleface. She gripped his sides tightly with her legs, reached down, held Kathleen's arm. "Jump."

The girl obeyed, nearly fell over the other side, settled herself behind her mother, arms round Lorna's waist.

Once away from the encampment the night was brighter than she had supposed, and she did not wish to anger the King by being challenged and discovered. It was impossible to identify colours or commanders, but she could see the infantry forming up, away to the right, and taking, she thought, an unreasonably long while over doing so, and the cavalry in a body more to the left. And then she saw what was clearly the King's party, because of the horse litter, moving close to the cavalry. Lennart was there.

She drew rein, and they waited, half a mile from the troops, watched them slowly march off. "There is a rise," Kathleen whispered, pointing, "where we may oversee."

"And where we shall also be silhouetted," Lorna pointed out. "Best to wait, until they are engaged."

She estimated it would take about an hour, and, indeed, it could take no longer, for it would be daylight soon after three.

The last of the infantry disappeared, and the cavalry fell into column, with the King's party following behind them. Presumably this was the first time in his life Charles had followed his men into battle. The lump of lead in her stomach seemed to grow. But now they could advance as well. She touched the horse with her bare heels, and he walked forward slowly, checking at the sudden outburst of firing which came from away to the right.

"They are at the redoubts," Lorna said.

"Redoubts, Mama?"

"The first Russian line. But . . ." She frowned. The firing seemed to grow, and she thought she could hear the shouts of men, in Swedish. That was not the plan; the King's intention had been that his men should infiltrate in silence, as they had crossed the Vabitsch in silence, no matter how they were fired on.

She urged the horse on, topped the rise where she had last seen the King, and nearly exclaimed with pleasure, for as she did so the sun rose out of the steppe to the east to bathe a most tremendous scene in warm light. She thought it was something she would never forget to her dying day, and from the way Kathleen's fingers dug into her shoulders she realised that the girl too was awestruck.

In the distance was the steppe, with the river wandering through in brown serenity. Away to the right were the battered walls of Poltava, already crowded with people; she did not need her telescope to tell her that. Before the walls lay the almost deserted Swedish trenches, and then the swamp of which King Charles had spoken. Beside the swamp, and directly before her as she looked, was the Russian camp, a vast accumulation of men and horses and guns, in a state of total disorder, she thought. Levelling her glass she saw men running in every direction, and even at this distance she thought she could hear their screams. But her heart constricted as she looked at the centre hut, at the royal standard flying there. Peter had at last joined his men. He was there, not three miles away from her, losing his last battle.

For as she focussed the glass nearer, she saw that while large numbers of the Swedes had become bogged down amidst the redoubts, where smoke and screams rose into the air, beyond the fortresses, and between them and the Russian camp, a body of men in blue and yellow coats had debouched and deployed and was at this very moment driving a much larger Russian formation from the field.

"They are beaten," Kathleen screamed, clapping her hands. "They are beaten."

"Not yet," Lorna muttered. The Russians were indeed defeated at this moment. But to complete their rout a cavalry charge was needed, the sort of charge which had won the Battle of Holovzin. And the Swedish cavalry remained motionless, in line, merely steaming into the still air, hooves pawing the ground, swords gleaming in the morning sunlight.

But if Rehnskold hesitated, Charles had also seen what was needed to crown his victory, and as she levelled her glass on the royal party, she saw a horseman spurring from the group towards the cavalry. "Lennart," she whispered, following him with her glass. She could not see his face, but he wore the uniform of the Drabants, and only Lennart rode in that manner. Her throat was dry as she watched him gallop up to the Field Marshal, arm waving. "Now," she said. "Now we will see it, Kathleen." For how long had she waited for this moment, to see the Russians shattered, to see Peter destroyed, once and for all.

She had lowered the glass. Now she raised it again. For the cavalry were still not moving, and Lennart was making his way back towards the King, while smoke exploded around him. "Oh, God," she whispered. "Oh, God," she shouted. The horse emerged into the sunlight, riderless. "Oh, God," she muttered, and kicked her own mount in the ribs, sending him surging forward, while Kathleen gave a cry of alarm and hung on for dear life.

Down the slope they charged, while King Charles sat up in his litter to stare at them. "Princess Bogoljubov," he shouted. "You have no place here."

She was past them in a moment, Kathleen's hands tight on her waist.

"Arrest that woman," the King shouted, but she was already throwing her leg over the horse's head to drop to the ground and kneel beside Lennart.

He frowned at her, trying to focus. "He would not," he muttered. "He would not."

"Lennart," she moaned, attempting to lift him, and becoming aware that she was surrounded by hooves and by men, dismounting.

"Madam," the King remonstrated. "You must return to the camp."

"But Lennart . . . General Munro . . ."

Lennart was trying to rise, while men were stripping off his coat and tearing his shirt to make a bandage. He was, in fact, not wounded at all, but had broken his arm in the fall; the cannon ball had struck the ground next to his horse and thrown him. "He would not, Sire. He said he must wait, for the rest of the infantry to deploy. 'Twas only Lewenhaupt's corps which got through. He would not, Sire."

Charles's brows drew together. "You gave him my express command?"

"I did, Sire. But he replied that you had placed *him* in command, and the responsibility was his. He said Lewenhaupt would certainly be overwhelmed, unless more infantry came to his support. Had you been there, Sire . . ."

"Had I been there," Charles said half to himself, and sat up to peer through his telescope. "The moment is past, in any event. The Russians are reforming." He sighed. "Had I been there. Take your general back to camp, Princess. He can do no more here."

Lennart had been swathed in bandages and set again on his horse. This time Lorna mounted behind him, to hold him up. Kathleen sat the cart horse, nervously.

"He would not," Lennart muttered. "He would not. I have failed the King."

"No," she said. "You have . . ." She bit her lip. She had almost said, died for the King. "No man could have done more."

The camp was before them, the sounds of the battle were fading. And willing hands were surrounding them, to lift Lennart down, lay him in the shade of the wagon. By now a considerable number of Swedish wounded had been returned, and the entire encampment was a scene of tortured activity. The surgeons removed Lennart's bandages and examined him, set the bone while he moaned with pain, placed his arm in a splint. "You will be well, General. Although you may not hold a sword again."

"How do you feel, dearest?" Lorna said, kneeling beside him.

"Tired," Lennart said. "Thirsty."

Kathleen waited with a pitcher of water, and he drank greedily. And now there came the sound of hooves. Lorna stood up, Kathleen and Michael beside her, watched the cavalry surge up to the camp. The King was in the lead, still in his litter. She estimated there were perhaps fifteen hundred men, horses breathing foam and sweat, men themselves sweating with fear and dismay.

The King surveyed the camp, spoke in Swedish. Then raised his hand, and the litter advanced, to halt again immediately before them.

"Sire," Lennart said, attempting to rise.

"Sit, General," Charles said. "We are lost. The infantry is surrounded." He paused and wiped a tear from his eye. "I must leave. My duty demands it."

"And us, Sire?" Lorna asked.

"I have a horse for you, Princess. And for your children. If you wish it. We shall ride for the Turkish border."

"And the general?"

"We can take no wounded." His face twisted. "Unless he be King."

"You would have him surrender?" she gasped. "To the Russians?"

" 'Tis a soldier's lot, Princess. Come, you must make haste."

She hesitated, gazing at him and beyond, at the empty hillside up which she had galloped, so confidently, only two hours earlier. Beyond that hill was Peter. And Menshikov. And the dwarfs. And the chamber beneath the Kremlin.

"I will remain with the general, Sire."

"Lorna," Lennart cried. "You cannot."

"I will not leave you, Lennart. But, Sire, if you will take my children . . ."

"No," Kathleen said. "I will stay."

"I am not fleeing," Michael said. "The Russians are my people."

"Sire," Lennart begged. "She cannot stay. The Russians . . ."

"Are men," Charles observed and almost smiled. "I doubt not your wound is too grievous for you ever to bear sword again under my command, General Munro. I therefore absolve you of your allegiance to me and to Sweden. As of this moment you are on the retired list. Lorna, I do not know if you will survive the Russians, but I do know, if anyone can accomplish that, it will be you. Take care of my Drabant. You may believe that I would rather stay with you, than resume the rule of so shattered a nation as my own." He raised himself straight, saluted them, and the other wounded. "Had I been there," he muttered. "Had I been there."

The cavalcade moved off.

For a few minutes the Swedish camp was quiet, save for the cries of the wounded, the moans of the dying, the terrified whispers of the women; the noise of battle had ended.

"Lorna," Lennart muttered. "You cannot stay here. Should the Russians take you . . ."

"Hush," she cried. "I did not come all this way, campaign for over a year, to find you, in order to desert you at the first obstacle."

"But . . ."

"Mama," Kathleen said, her voice quiet, with only the merest suspicion of a tremor.

Lorna stood up, listened to the rumbling. She turned, looked at the hillside, sucked air into her lungs. Well, then, here is your destiny. What had she once thought? That it rushed at her like a runaway coach, with her bound to the road in front of it? She could not have been more accurate. Well, then, why did she not anticipate it? There were sufficient pistols, waiting to be used. No one should blame her.

But she had considered suicide before, eighteen years ago. And rejected it, in favour of surviving and experiencing. And had never regretted that.

A horseman stood on the hill above the camp. For a moment he stared down, then he rose in his stirrups, waved his sword around his head, and gave a tremendous shout. And was immediately joined by others, ranging the hill, hundreds of them, thousands, but not actually advancing. They were waiting. For the Tsar?

Lorna dug her fingers into her skirts, walked away from the wagon, from the trees. She looked up the hill, felt the sunlight on her face. It was still only midmorning. And saw the Tsar.

He reined his horse on the crest of the hill, then came forward, scarce touching rein or using spur, as usual. Menshikov rode at his side, and then a cluster of other officers. The rest of the cavalry spread wide to either side. They approached slowly, while Lorna waited. Strangely, she thought, she felt no fear. She felt no emotion at all. It was impossible to anticipate, the horror of what might soon be happening to her, happening to them all. But she gazed, not at a twitching madman, but at a beaming, triumphant general.

"Like a nut," he shouted. "I have crushed him like a nut." His horse stopped.

"See, Majesty," Menshikov said. "What that Cossack said was true."

"The Princess Bogoljubov," Peter said. His gaze went past her, and she knew he was looking at Michael and Kathleen. "You wait here, for me?"

Even now, she would not lie to him. "I wait here with my lover, Sire."

"Your lover? You are become a Swedish whore, as well as a Saxon whore, having been both an English and a Russian whore?"

Her chin came up. "You made me a Russian whore, Sire. This man was my betrothed before I was forced to marry Bogoljubov."

Peter stared at her for a moment. His voice remained quiet, his face relaxed. "And where is Charles? Where is that blood-crazed boy?"

"He has ridden, Sire. For Turkey."

"Turkey," Peter mused. And gave a great shout of laughter. "Then we shall follow him to Turkey. He can no longer stand before me. He has no army. Lewenhaupt has surrendered. I have crushed him like a nut. Poltava. There will be a monument. Oh, aye. Do you know what they will say of Poltava, Princess? Here Sweden was shattered, forever."

"No, Your Majesty," she said, seizing her opportunity.

"Eh? Eh?"

"They will say of Poltava, Sire, that here Russia became a great military power."

His brows drew together, and he glanced at Menshikov, almost nervously. Then gave another bellow. "Haha. Ha-ha-ha-ha. She is right, Pieman. She is right. Russia. Peter's Russia. They will not forget us, Pieman."

"We will not let them, Sire," Menshikov said.

Peter dismounted. "As for you, Princess . . ."

"Let me take her, Sire," Menshikov said. "Let me have her. I swear you will hear her scream from here to Moscow."

But Peter merely smiled. "He is right," he said. "I should have you whipped, from here to Moscow, and then I should have you skinned, and then . . ."

Amazingly, her voice remained even, even bantering. "In that order, Sire, there would be no skin left to take, surely."

"Why did you run?"

Once again, boldness she told herself. Only boldness. "I had heard the Swedes were coming, Sire. My lover was with the Swedes. I could wait no longer."

He stared at her for several seconds, the longest of her life. "You ran, from the bed of the Tsar," he said at last. "To that of a common soldier?"

"Not a common soldier, Sire."

He walked past her, stood above Lennart, who attempted to rise, and then fell back against the tree. "Your name?"

"General Lennart Munro, Your Majesty, commander of the Drabant guards."

"The Drabants. I have heard of them." He gave a shout of laughter. "I have fled from them. Ha-ha." And turned again, to face Lorna. "No common soldier, to be sure, Princess. Yet should you be punished. For your subterfuge."

"Sub . . . subterfuge?" she whispered, her knees knocking; the Tsar was looking at Michael, who had been restrained from approaching him by Kathleen.

"For attempting to foist that weakling off on me as my son. That is treason."

She inhaled slowly. "It saved my life, Sire."

"Writing me letters," Peter grumbled. "As if I were

some common clerk." He wagged his finger. "I did not believe that letter. I swore I would have you hanged by your toes."

Lorna's teeth clamped together. She dared not ask.

"Had it not been for Bogoljubov," the Tsar said.

"Prince Bogoljubov, Sire?"

"That ratbag. He did not send after you. The scoundrel. After you had hit him on the head, he still did not send after you. I hung *him* by his toes."

"Oh, my God." Her knees gave way, and she sank to the ground.

"Bah," Peter said. "I would have done so, anyway. He was conspiring and with Alexis. Oh, aye, that was true enough. I received proof of it, within a day of rejoining the army. And he confessed everything. Even the subterfuge."

"The . . . the subterfuge?" she said again.

"Which you practised, Princess. Which makes you as guilty as he. But he confirmed your letter, claimed to have taken you the moment I left Hurd House." He stood immediately above her. "He died screaming your name, Princess."

"Oh, God," she whispered. "Oh, God."

"Aye," Peter said. "You have a way, Princess, of making men fall in love with you. Bogoljubov, this man, I do not know how many others."

*Now,* she thought. *Now, it has to be now. Your life, all of your lives, depend upon it.* "And you, Sire?" Her voice was quiet.

He frowned at her for a moment, turned away, thrust his fingers into Kathleen's hair. The girl trembled, but kept her face impassive. Kathleen MacMahon.

"And this one? Does she have that power?"

"She is my daughter, Sire."

"Oh, aye," Peter agreed. "Martha says I am well rid

of you. Of you all. She says you would bring me nothing but unhappiness. She says, even were I to kill you slowly, your screams would haunt me to my dying day."

*Oh, Martha,* Lorna thought. *Oh, dear, sweet Martha.*

"And I have enough screams to haunt me," Peter said, half to himself. He released Kathleen. "Will your general die?"

"No, Sire," Lorna said.

"Ah. Then care for him. Menshikov. Write the Princess Bogoljubov, General Munro, and their family a passport to leave Russia, and go where they choose." He walked back to his horse, swung into the saddle. Lorna could only stare at him. "Princess," he said. "On two or three occasions in my life you made me happy. I am rewarding you for those, now. Besides, I am the victor. I can afford to be generous." He rose in the stirrups. "I have crushed him like a nut," he screamed and galloped past the camp, his horsemen at his back.

Menshikov alone remained. "You are fortunate, Princess."

Lorna wanted to lie down. Only to lie down, on the warm grass. "I was due some fortune, Prince."

He nodded. "No doubt. You shall have your pass and your horses. But take some advice, Princess. Your fortune lies in meeting the Tsar again in the hour of victory. Do not even presume to remain within his reach this time tomorrow."

"And our people here, Prince Menshikov?"

Menshikov glanced at the wounded Swedes. "They fought well. Their own surgeons may care for them, and they will be returned to Sweden, whenever it can be arranged." He grinned at her. "My master is determined that Russia will no longer be thought of as a barbaric power, but as a part of Europe. He can afford such generosity, having gained such a victory. Besides, they will tell their people how difficult, how impossible, it is to conquer Russia. That is good, eh?" He snapped his fingers, and one of his secretaries rode forward. "Tell this fellow what you wish." He cantered out of the camp.

Lorna sank to her knees, found Michael beside her. "Mama?" he asked in bewilderment. "Why did my father not take me?"

She put her arm round his waist. "Because the Tsar is not your father, Michael. It was a mistake."

"But then, Mama, who is my father?"

"Your father . . ." She hesitated. ". . . was a very brave man, called Vassily Bogoljubov. Do not ever forget that." She regained her feet. "We must make haste. I have no doubt that Prince Menshikov is right, and the Tsar will soon change his mood."

"Lorna." Lennart held her hand as she knelt beside him. "I am broken and helpless."

She kissed him on the forehead. "They have provided a horse litter, and mounts for us all, and food. I still have the money I brought from Moscow. You must depend upon me, until your arm mends."

"But . . . all the way to Sweden?"

She frowned at him. "You wish to return to Sweden? You have family there?"

"No, but I am a Swedish soldier."

"Who has just been retired," she reminded him.

"My God, so I have. We could return to England."

To Mrs. Morley and Mrs. Freeman? "You have relatives there?"

"Why, no. But . . ." His turn to frown. "Ireland? Morne?"

"I have never been there. I have been forced to tread

a long and most rocky road, Lennart, these eighteen years. Now I would go home."

"Home? Do we have a home?"

"We have," she said. "Where we first met. Where I have a house and a farm. Where there are no mad Tsars and no scheming Kings. We will make our way to Hamburg and take ship for Maryland." She stood up, slowly worked the ring free of her finger, dropped it on the grass. Then she hugged her children. "You will be happy, in Maryland."

Peter the Great never did catch up with Charles the Twelfth. The Swedish king remained in Turkey for four years, involving Constantinople in an indecisive war with Russia. Then he was expelled, and returned to Sweden and to campaigning. He was finally killed on the 11th December 1718 when besieging an obscure Norwegian fortress.

By then Peter was moving from strength to strength, and on 22nd October 1721 the Russian Empire was officially pronounced, Peter being given the title "Father of the Fatherland, Peter the Great, and Emperor of all Russia."

Yet had he also been going increasingly mad, and in 1718, in the dungeons beneath the Kremlin, he knouted his son the Tsarevitch Alexis to death. Only in the person of Martha Skavronskaya did he find peace, and in 1712 he divorced the Tsarina Eudoxia to marry her, Martha assuming the name of Catherine. To the consternation of the Russian people, he eventually, on 7th May 1724 had her crowned Tsarina, and designated her his successor, despite the fact that a son of Alexis was living.

Peter's fits grew increasingly worse, and he died, in great pain, on 28th January 1725, in Martha's arms.

The Empress Catherine the First then ruled, ably, with the aid of her friend Prince Menshikov, until her death in 1727. By then, Peter's dream and Charles's fear had become a reality; Russia was a European power.

But these events meant little to the Munros of Maryland.

# Historical Romance

| | | |
|---|---|---|
| ☐ THE ADMIRAL'S LADY—Gibbs | P2658 | 1.25 |
| ☐ AFTER THE STORM—Williams | 23081-3 | 1.50 |
| ☐ AN AFFAIR OF THE HEART—Smith | 23092-9 | 1.50 |
| ☐ AS THE SPARKS FLY—Eastvale | P2569 | 1.25 |
| ☐ A BANBURY TALE—MacKeever | 23174-7 | 1.50 |
| ☐ CLARISSA—Arnett | 22893-2 | 1.50 |
| ☐ DEVIL'S BRIDE—Edwards | 23176-3 | 1.50 |
| ☐ A FAMILY AFFAIR—Mellows | 22967-X | 1.50 |
| ☐ FIRE OPALS—Danton | 23112-7 | 1.50 |
| ☐ THE FORTUNATE MARRIAGE—Trevor | 23137-2 | 1.50 |
| ☐ FRIENDS AT KNOLL HOUSE—Mellows | P2530 | 1.25 |
| ☐ THE GLASS PALACE—Gibbs | 23063-5 | 1.50 |
| ☐ GRANBOROUGH'S FILLY—Blanshard | 23210-7 | 1.50 |
| ☐ HARRIET—Mellows | 23209-3 | 1.50 |
| ☐ HORATIA—Gibbs | 23175-5 | 1.50 |
| ☐ LEONORA—Fellows | 22897-5 | 1.50 |
| ☐ LORD FAIRCHILD'S DAUGHTER—<br>MacKeever | P2695 | 1.25 |
| ☐ MARRIAGE ALLIANCE—Stables | 23142-9 | 1.50 |
| ☐ MELINDA—Arnett | P2547 | 1.25 |
| ☐ THE PHANTOM GARDEN—Bishop | 23113-5 | 1.50 |
| ☐ THE PRICE OF VENGEANCE—<br>Michel | 23211-5 | 1.50 |
| ☐ THE RADIANT DOVE—Jones | P2753 | 1.25 |
| ☐ THE ROMANTIC FRENCHMAN—Gibbs | P2869 | 1.25 |
| ☐ SPRING GAMBIT—Williams | 23025-2 | 1.50 |

**Buy them at your local bookstore or use this handy coupon for ordering:**

---

**FAWCETT PUBLICATIONS, P.O. Box 1014, Greenwich Conn. 06830**

Please send me the books I have checked above. Orders for less than 5 books must include 60c for the first book and 25c for each additional book to cover mailing and handling. Orders of 5 or more books postage is Free. I enclose $_____ in check or money order.

Mr/Mrs/Miss_____

Address_____

City_____ State/Zip_____

Please allow 4 to 5 weeks for delivery. This offer expires 6/78.

A-23